CRYSTAL CLEAR, by Miriam

Crystal Traynor has constructed her world to fit her chronic OCD episodes and need for isolation and security. When her twin sister, Brystal, is murdered in Ireland, Crystal must leave her carefully insulated world to go and identify her sister's remains, and bring her twin home.

When Inspector Ethan MacEnery sees the dead woman in the county morgue walk through his door, he almost loses his mind. Expecting the victim's sister, he is totally unprepared for the identical version of the victim herself. Already captivated by what little he knows of Miss Brystal Traynor's life , Ethan is shocked to meet Crystal, the identical, but totally different sister of the flamboyant, artistic Brystal. Drawn to this brilliant, yet peculiar woman, Ethan quickly volunteers to help Crystal deal with her sister's personal possessions.

Crystal finds this new world of ancient beliefs and unique people is changing her. She is astounded by the acceptance and support she feels... especially from one particular Inspector.

As it becomes clear that Brystal's murder was more than an American gal in the wrong place at the wrong time, Crystal must overcome her personal challenges to help Ethan uncover the secrets in her sister's beautifully cut crystal goblets.

Ethan quickly realizes Brystal's work may hold the key to a diabolical plot that could destroy everything he holds dear... including Crystal.

CRYSTAL CLEAR

MIRIAM MATTHEWS

Janet,
Hope you enjoy
the story!
Miriam Matthews

MIRIAM MATTHEWS, LLC

By Miriam Matthews

Published by Miriam Matthews

Edition 1.2020. v1HC/DIG

www.miriammatthews.com

Cover Design: Miriam Matthews

Hard Copy Production: 1.2020. v1HC

Digital Production: 1.2020. v1DIG

Published in both paperback and digital format by Miriam Matthews, and available at most mail-order or digital providers.

ISBN: 978-1-954384-80-4 (Print)

ISBN: 978-1-954384-82-8 (Digital)

To all of the people who live with a disability that impacts their life every day, in unusual and confounding ways. Remember: there is no normal! We are all individuals, and special in our own ways!

To Sean Daly who sparked my imagination and showed me the amazing world of cutting crystal. I could have stayed in your workshop forever! My short visit with you gave birth to this book, almost ten years ago.

Lastly, to my mother who joined the angels this year. Arguing over words and sharing memories of my Ireland visit will forever be locked in my heart.

CHAPTER 1

One is the loneliest number that there ever was.

Being awarded the biggest bonus of the year should have been a celebration. It should have been the highlight of her week, her month, heck, her year! It should have been a defining moment in her life. It didn't matter that the bonus for this case topped five hundred-thousand dollars, Crystal's stomach rolled, and her eyes darted over the crowd like a frightened finch ready to flit away at the first flicker of danger, the first inkling of a threat. She stood there in abject terror hating the superfluous event, feeling like the newest, most sought after toy in Macy's department store on Black Friday.

Tiny grasping hands reached for her. Screams and pushing crowds inched toward her, all fighting for their place as close to her as they could get. Greedy avaricious hands…

Director Davidson patted her lightly on the shoulder as the audience clapped politely. Their claps were always polite when she scored, however, their looks were pure envy.

Crystal tried not to wince at his touch. She resisted snatching the fake cardboard check from his hand and running for her life. Instead Crystal Traynor grasped the four-foot award check with a gracious nod, paused as she smiled for the appropriate forty-five seconds, and then strode purposefully toward the door.

Outside the conference room she took the real thing from the back of the cardboard mock-up and clenched the crumpled check with white knuckles. It wasn't the money she held on to so tightly. It was her sanity. For her the money was simply a tool which allowed her to exist comfortably, to supply things in her life she needed to survive in a world that hated those who were different. She never worked for the money. It was the freedom it provided she cherished most.

Crystal worked for the joy of the hunt, the pain of deception and the satisfaction of success. She lived for the chase, the puzzle, the triumph of good over evil. She did not do what she did just for the money. She really did it for the numbers - they were her friends. Of course, the insulation the money provided. That was certainly a significant perk.

Calm down.

Breathe.

Crystal counted the tiles from the exit to the elevator. *If that man touched her one more time...* the bile rose in her throat sending her trotting for the lady's room.

Freedom.

Free of the room.

Free of the people.

And free of her thoughts.

Pushing quickly through the swinging door of the restroom, Crystal bent over the sink and took a deep breath, holding it for as long as she could. Her lungs burned but she held it in like she always did.

Exhale.

It was unavoidable.

"Do not lose it. You will not hurl, damn it!" Taking another deep breath Crystal visualized her own nervous system, calming the excessive firing of the neurons, squelching the fight or flight response crowds and attention always evoked.

She chanced a glance in the mirror. Her cheeks burned with heat as bright pink blotches flared where most women had soft cheeks made up to look sophisticated and sensual. Her long velvet auburn hair remained strictly in place, pulled back in a thick braid that hung over her shoulder, dangling just above the water in the sink. The deep auburn highlights and wavy curls were contained by the severe style she always wore; the better to blend into the wall, the better to be ignored, the better to hide from searching eyes.

Crystal did not want to be a wallflower, she wanted to be the wall.

A beige wall.

She focused on her pulse and suppressed the rapid beat with a strong dose of mental Xanax. "Calm down. Go back to your office and everything will be fine." Her long practiced self-talk took effect immediately. Crystal gulped one more deep breath and let it out in a measured cadence. She did not dare count with the beat. It was too risky when she was this close to the edge.

"Crystal, are you alright?" Sandra's soft voice spoke from the door. "Anything I can do, Boss?"

"I'm fine. Just a little...you know."

Sandra remained at the door speaking low and soft. "Coast is clear if you want to sneak back to the office. Davidson has two more awards before he'll let anyone escape his quarterly exercise in torture." Sandra was the closest thing Crystal had to a gatekeeper at work, and the capable assistant knew her boss' Achilles' heel well.

"Good idea. I'm not sure if I can take any more awards. I know that sounds crazy and unappreciative, but I..." Crystal was at a loss for words. It happened often. Numbers were her friends, not words.

"Not to worry. I'll clear the way and make sure no one chases you down. You're the golden goose now." Sandra gave a soft, slightly envious sigh. "What are you going to do with the reward bonus?"

The muscles in her back clenched, forcing Crystal to straighten in an awkward jerky motion. She smoothed her black slacks, pulled her plain black suit coat closed, and turned to her assistant. "Put it in the bank where I put them all." She faced her friend with a blank look, a look that reflected Crystal's mental attitude toward all her awards.

Sandra swung the door wide and motioned Crystal toward the hall. "Get going before the needy masses pour out of that room begging for a piece of your goose. You can worry over being a bazillionaire in your tiny office at your tinier desk. God only knows why you don't bail and live a little." Sandra stepped back to let Crystal move through the doorway without the risk of physical contact.

"God only knows why I am the way I am." Crystal hugged the wall as she passed her assistant holding the door.

Sandra let the door go behind Crystal. "And he's not telling. But I thank Him every day for the talent He did give you. Because if Malikaya Balidefi Abadaff had been successful in transferring that twenty-five billion into his offshore account to pay for those nuclear warheads, the free world would be a free world of hurt." She pushed the up button on the elevator and the doors slid open with a soft chime. "You'll be okay getting back to your office?" Sandra reached inside after Crystal and punched the button for the eighteenth floor.

"Thanks, yeah." Any other time, any other place and any other woman, Crystal knew Sandra would have hugged her.

But not here.

Not now.

And not Crystal.

"I've got a line on a new account Director Davidson wants traced." She tried to smile but her lips were numb. A pathetic wave had to do, as the doors closed. She knew Sandra stood on the other side of the doors looking at the elevator shaking her head. But there was nothing Crystal could do about her awkward social interactions with people. She knew Sandra understood that as well, and it made for a less stressful working relationship, but she still derided herself for her shortcomings in the personality department.

Crystal pressed her back to the far wall of the elevator and stood concentrating on calm thoughts, trying not to look at the brightly lit numbers.

Fifteen was such a cad. He always glowed brighter than the others trying his damnedest to suck her in, make her notice him, make her lose her train of thought.

Eighteen was home. She was as warm and welcoming as the smell of baking bread on Sunday morning. She was Crystal's haven and happiness. Eighteen was where Crystal could be herself and let her special relationship with numbers take over. A chime sounded and the doors slid open.

Eighteen.

Home.

Crystal took a deep breath.

Thirty-seven tiles and one right turn. Twelve tiles and a nebulous stretch of carpet section, then one more left turn. She slid her card against the electronic security lock and slipped into her office.

Safe.

The knots in her stomach untangled, and crept to their respective corners to await the next round. Those knots were the bane of her existence, and she hated them with a passion borne of way too many fights.

Sensing a moving presence, the office lights came on automatically. Crystal removed her jacket and hung it on the peg on the back of her door. Above her desk sat a wooden nameplate that said *Crystal Traynor, #1 Forensic Auditor* in red block letters carved deep into an oak background encased in brass. She was the number one forensic auditor in the US of A, and she didn't just love her job, she lived her job.

What she didn't love was being singled out as the number one forensic auditor in front of a bunch of people… being looked at with prying eyes, being touched without her permission.

The thin Venetian blinds on her small interior window that looked out on the pool of researchists and administrative assistants, separated her from the rest of her peers on the floor who didn't have their own offices and assistants. She reached up and twisted the rod.

Shielded.

Sandra, Crystal's assistant sat right in front of her door like the guard she was. No one came into Crystal's haven without a pass from

Sandra. But there were those days when the blinds were open a crack and Crystal caught people staring as they passed, whispering, motioning. It was aggravating. Why couldn't people just let her do her job without all the fuss?

Sandra understood. She got it. Why couldn't they?

At one point, a long time ago, one of the many doctors she'd seen as a child, explained it to her parents. Synesthesia was what that man in the white coat had called her relationship with numbers. But even he, with all of his degrees and his big office on floor five, didn't get it. Not really…

Sinking into her chair, Crystal checked the bank of monitors for recent alerts then opened the new file. Somewhere, six million dollars had gone missing from an escrow account tied to a government contract. It was her job to find out where it went and how. The file was already two inches thick and no one had been able to decipher the books let alone all the circular bank transfers and alleged pay offs. The file finally ended up on her desk, like all the toughest cases eventually did. In the seven years she had worked for LDE better known as Larson, Davidson, and Evans or *Last-Ditch Effort,* Crystal took on the most difficult and intricate cases. In those years she had only failed to solve one single case. That case still haunted her. Those numbers still mocked her.

"Did it again, huh?" Chance Evans poked his head through the doorway but knew better than to enter Crystal's cave without permission. He modulated his voice and spoke softly, but still couldn't help noticing how Crystal jumped. He waited, his head just barely between the door and the wall. "Sorry. Want me to come back later?" Seven years had taught him a lot about obsessive-compulsive disorders and Crystal's unique personality.

"Nah. I'll be okay. Chance, can't you get them to stop with these awards? I really don't like being singled out. It's embarrassing, ya know?" Crystal remained facing the bank of monitors knowing Chance would not take offense at the lack of eye contact. She couldn't look at anyone just yet. It was too painful.

"Nope. At least you don't burst into tears and run away anymore."

He chuckled remembering her first disastrous award. "One of the best things I ever did, was steal you away from Horshack the Horrible and that dingy little back office. And *you* even have to admit you *don't* run away anymore, right?"

Crystal had to chuckle to herself. "I do inside."

When she'd found two errors in his taxes saving him almost two thousand dollars, Chance had hired her away from Horshack's little CPA firm in New Jersey. A little different himself, Chance immediately recognized not only her talent and speed, but her quirky personality. He created a safe place for her to work her magic with his company. It, or rather she, earned him a partnership. Crystal's incredible work boosted LDE into the top five competing companies for government contracts in forensic auditing. Finding lost or hidden money and assets was big business and Chance loved big business, big assets, and big money.

"Right, but it's what shows on the outside that counts with most people, kiddo. And on the outside, you accepted the award, and even stood there for more than three seconds."

"You were watching? Oh my God!" Now she turned and looked at him, trying to analyze his communication on an intellectual level – the only way she could. She tried to hear the tonal quality in his voice and match it with his body language, like she'd been taught by her sister. Was he teasing her?

Possibly.

Possibly not.

His grin said *possibly*. "I was in the back of the room. I'm always there for you, kid. You should know that by now. And I always will be." He slowly eased into the chair by the door.

Ah… he was teasing… then reassuring. Her hard-won social filter was firmly in place.

Crystal put her hands over her face for a second, then relaxed into her chair shaking her head. "I should know that, but when I have to stand up there in front of people I freeze. I can't see anything but the door. I can't think of anything except where I want to be as soon as I can get away. It has gotten a little easier. What would I do at this company without you, Chance?" She smiled warmly at him, finally, with fleeting eye contact.

Her sister had made her practice *warm* and *eye contact* when they were in college. No matter how many times she had practiced, it still only worked with those she considered close friends. With the rest of the world it was too painful.

"Make a lot more money and probably be a partner." Chance sat very still. His heart quaked. She had no idea how beautiful she was when she smiled like that. He knew what it cost her. "I truly love the fact that what you do earn, makes you one hell of a good living. It also makes me incredibly rich. And I am sure Alana appreciates you no end, even though she doesn't understand you like I do."

Crystal watched him snicker at the statement. His perfect, eye-candy wife had a habit of spending his money like it grew in a private family orchard and the fruit was there for her personal picking.

"Alana… what I wouldn't give to be like her." Crystal sighed wistfully. "Glamorous, articulate, happily married to a great guy, two beautiful kids, and freedom."

"Don't forget shop-a-holic, self-centered, and happily married to a large bank account which is kept filled by a guy she acknowledges when she has to." Chance frowned and changed the subject. "So, you know you'll have to testify in this case, right?"

"Yeah, but I'll be talking strictly numbers and transactions. I'll be fine and the District Attorney knows me." A fidget escaped her calmly clasped hands. "My accreditation will be on file and the validity of my work will not be questioned." Crystal was in her world now and she could maintain direct eye contact. "The case is open and shut. We nailed Abadaff to the wall in so many ways he can't possibly wiggle out of this. Numbers don't lie, like people. That's why I like them so much." She was back on familiar ground and the envious image of Alana was nowhere to be found in her safe little office.

For either of them.

"You're the Mo, kiddo." Crystal glanced above his head and laughed at the picture of Larry, Mo and Curly Joe hanging over her doorway.

"Yes I am. Today anyway." Crystal relaxed a little more and laughed at the personal joke.

Memorabilia from the Three Stooges decorated her office. A few years back, Chance had asked her about her love of the comedic team. She explained how when she was growing up her family watched the reruns together on Friday evenings with some specially created dessert. Her father always joked about Mo being the smart one. The joke morphed into a kind of family tradition and anytime someone in the family did something good, they got to be Mo for the day.

After that, Chance always called her "The Mo" when she broke a tough case. Not even Sandra understood the insider comment, but everyone knew Chance could get away with things others could not. It was apparent to everyone except Crystal that he was her knight in shining armor. He was her guardian angel, her personal savior, and the handsome prince who never got the princess.

He already had the Ice Queen at home.

"Mo for the week, kid. This one was a hell of a payola. My VISA card and Alana thank you." He stood to take his leave. "Say, have you heard from your sister this week?" Chance was one of the few people who'd met Crystal's sister, Brystal. Her twin sister, to be exact. He knew Brystal was Crystal's only sibling and the only one left in her immediate family. He was also privy to their love/hate relationship.

"Nope. She probably has her head in some big project. She can be so obsessive at times." Crystal shook her head with a mild amount of disgust. "She forgets to email for a couple weeks, then I get a book in one rambling text. Usually about some guy, or a tree or a joke the Master Cutter told her which makes no sense to an American bean counter anyway."

Chance had measured the time during their little chat, and it was time to go. He glanced back from the doorway. "Runs in the family, huh?" He grinned and trotted away before Crystal could respond with a quick-witted retort.

Crystal enjoyed her safe and amicable relationship with Chance, and didn't mind his gentle teasing when she could figure it out. He had little obsessions of his own. She was fairly sure he understood her obsessive compulsive disorder on an intuitive level that afforded her social comfort in his presence. It was as close as she'd come to real friendship in her twenty-nine years.

If she didn't count Brystal.

And there were days she didn't.

Turning back to her thick file, she noticed people returning to their desks and reached over to close the blinds completely and shut her door. She had work to do. There was a puzzle that needed to be solved and somewhere deep in this two-inch stack of data was a group of numbers that called to her. Sandra would pop her head in when it was time to leave for the evening and make sure Crystal quit working, and actually left. Crystal built those kinds of external stopgap measures around herself for good reason.

She clicked on the ACCESS icon and transformed into the huntress; a techno-feline on the prowl, tracking, sniffing, ferreting out each single minute clue, meeting and greeting her suspects with schooled determination. Catching a single whiff of the trail, she swooped in for the kill, missing by a hair's breadth. The numbers flew by and swirled around her mind in patterns with illicit surges of value and denomination. Engulfed in torturous winds that ripped at her brain and hid from her eyes, the numbers ran, attempting escape, dancing just beyond her reach. Closer, she struggled against the gale, grasping at their cunningly concealed meaning, clawing at fragments and traces. The answers were just within reach.

Almost…

"Crystal? Crystal!" Soft at first, Sandra's voice tore her from the elation, the hunt. "It's almost five o'clock. Time to have a life, Boss." Her assistant spoke from the doorway.

"Crap! Sandra!"

"What? Crystal, snap out of it. You've been sitting staring at those spreadsheets for almost four hours without moving anything but your mouse. It's time to go home."

"I was so close. I could feel it." Crystal flexed her shoulders and rubbed her dry eyes. "I want to work just a little longer. You go." Those knots in the corners of her stomach inched forward for the fight. Mr. OCD reared his head and screamed for her return to the hunt. Like an automaton, she turned back to the monitors filled with lines and lines of numbers flying by.

"Oh no you don't, Boss. We have an agreement. I don't leave you alone with your work, and I don't leave till you do. From your mouth to my rule book." Her admin assistant took Crystal's coat from the hook and tossed it to her. "I don't want to come into work tomorrow and find you glued to those screens in a coma. I like my primo job and taking care of you keeps me in that job, so scoot." Sandra stood in the doorway pointing toward the elevators.

Physically catching her coat broke the cycle, like a magic spell dissolving in the bright sunshine. "I surrender." The disappointment clearly played across her features.

Crystal hit the save button on each of the open files she created. Overpowered by a flying coat, the knots retreated. OCD slunk back into the recesses of the universal void to await its next opportunity. "Okay. But I was…"

"Scoot, lady. Do something for yourself for a change. Spend some of that lovely reward bonus on a pedicure or a new rubber band for your braid." Sandra stood her ground, not budging. Like the keystone of the castle, she remained immobile and strong. That was exactly why Crystal had hired her.

"You're kidding, right? What's wrong with this rubber band?" Crystal pulled her braid out from inside her coat and let it flop over one shoulder as she slung her purse over the other.

Sandra shook her head. "How did you ever survive puberty, Boss?" She pulled the door closed ushering Crystal out then twisted the handle to make sure the lock engaged behind her boss.

"Not well. I don't like pedicures." It was no news to Sandra who did not understand Crystal's aversion to being touched, but accepted it as just one more odd quirk in her boss' odd personality. After all, geniuses often walked a fine line between insanity and…genius, and Crystal was a true genius.

"I know. At least go home and celebrate a little. Heat up a Lean Cuisine and watch a sitcom. Fill a Sudoku book, or whatever it is you do for fun. Take your hair down and run around your apartment with scissors. Eat dessert first. Water your plants with a wine glass for heaven's sake. I don't know, but do something!" Sandra had talked Crystal all the way to the elevators and pushed the button for her. "Go." It was a gentle command, but a command, nonetheless.

"Thank you, Sandra. I know I don't say that enough, but I do appreciate you following the rules." Crystal stepped into the elevator. "...And I don't go into a coma. It's just a way I concentrate..." The doors began to slide shut.

Sandra peeked through at the last-minute cocking her head in a cute kind of Terrier way. "I'm just saying..."

Crystal stood alone in the elevator contemplating what she might want to do for fun. Nothing came to mind immediately. Fun? Did she even know what that meant?

Her stomach growled. When was the last time she'd eaten? She made a mental note to transfer some of her bonus award into Sandra's account in the morning. Her assistant was worth much more than money, but money was the only way Crystal could show her appreciation. Numbers worked so much better than words.

The corner bistro in her building was one of her favorite spots for dinner. They always had a table near the back with just one chair, especially for her. She stopped there to eat at least three times a week. As a frequent customer, she had come to know the owner and her daughter. Crystal no longer had to order. If she was in her seat at her table, Tasha, the owner's teenage daughter, ordered seafood fettuccini for her, then served it with garlic bread. Magically a full glass of Gewurztraminer, Crystal's favorite sweet white wine, appeared from the quiet hand of the bartender. After dinner, a chocolate volcano with whipped cream automatically materialized beneath her fork, with a glass of Chateau Ste. Michelle Late Harvest Riesling dessert wine placed just to the right of her dish.

Life was easy at Manheim's Bistro. It was predictable and consistent – just how Crystal liked it. No one bothered her with needless social conversation.

They fed her.

She ate.

She paid.

She left.

Reliable, predictable, consistent – painstakingly constructed, Manheim's Bistro was her kind of welcome cuddly blanket at the end of the day.

Without planning or thinking, Crystal pushed through the front door of Manheim's and took *her* place at *her* table. A newspaper lay opposite her plate. On the cover the picture of a scowling Malikaya Balidefi Abadaff in handcuffs being led away by two men in black suits with dark glasses, stared at her with thinly cloaked cynicism. Crystal nodded her thanks to Tasha across the room with what she hoped was a grateful smile. Her fingers stalled at the edge not wanting to pick it up, but not wanting to *not* pick it up either.

She had to know.

Was her name there for the entire world to see? A single bead of sweat broke out near her brow.

Crystal held her breath and picked up the newspaper.

Those hiding knots crept forward bumping knuckles for the first round. Her stomach flipped, tightened, accepted the clench of the fight. At this rate there would be no dinner amid the brawling nerves and tissue.

She took another deep breath and prepared herself for the worst.

The bell rang in her tummy, and the first round was in full swing.

Crystal placed a hand across her abdomen and pressed, in an attempt to contain the nausea. Scanning as quickly as she could, she finished the article with intense relief that washed across her body, like a reviving hot shower after an intense work-out. Having found no mention of the major party responsible for Mr. Abadaff's arrest, she was ready for food just as her dinner appeared with a quiet "Here you are, Ms. Traynor."

Crystal murmured her usual, "Thank you, Tasha," and purposefully relaxed the last remaining tense muscles in her gut. She dug in as she leafed through the rest of the paper. Not much of the world interested her, but she kept up on the financials and politics because it helped her do her job. She never knew when a simple little article on a chain store purchase in Ozark, Nowhere would spark some idea in her mind. That would lead to a conspiracy. Which would then lead her to a terrorist plot, that ended up with the arrest of a multi-billionaire dealing in nuclear weapons in New Jersey.

It could happen.

It did happen.

To Malikaya Balidefi Abadaff.

And all because of Crystal Traynor, the Greer County Gazette, and an outstanding bowl of seafood fettuccini.

Her chocolate volcano appeared with a small glass of Riesling next to it. Crystal was in total control and life was… right.

CHAPTER 2

Two can be as bad as one, it's the loneliest number since the number one.
Yeah...

Ethan MacEnery pulled the crisp white sheet over the girl's face. The coroner slid the table back into the cold storage vault. The rails screeched before the door locked with a loud click.

It was done. All except for the lingering smell of formaldehyde and methanol. Ethan's nose twitched. He hated the smell of the dead. Especially this dead - American girl in the wrong place at the wrong time, and now her body lay in a superbly wrong place.

"Any family?" Carryls Logner asked softly. The coroner never spoke above a loud whisper when in the company of his clients. The hush in the room was an overpowering presence that squelched normal conversation.

Ethan motioned his retreat with a slight wave of his hand and Carryls followed. Even the coroner's footsteps made no sound on the spotless white tile floor. Or maybe they were drowned out by the constant popping in Ethan's left knee, the remnants of one case gone to dunkers.

In the outer office Ethan shook his head. "Just a sister in New York somewhere. The American Embassy's representative was here this morning. They'll take care of notifying the sister and gettin' her here to identify the body. 'Tis not a duty I envy Car. Not I." Ethan closed the file that lay open on Carryls' desk with a flourish. "A crime of opportunity, I suspect. And here lies a life... and the paperwork that goes with it." Ethan tapped the thin file on the edge of the coroner's desk. "Our guest will be here for a while I'm thinkin'." He grabbed the file and headed for the door.

"Will her sister have to come all the way here, to Ireland, to identify the... victim? Were I from the colonies, 't'would not be how I'd like to be seein' the Emerald Isle." It was a sad statement that went well with his contemplative frown, an appropriate fashion statement on the day's business. "Alright then. I'll date, tag and store. Have a topper of a day, Inspector MacEnery."

"And you'd be doin' the same, Car. I'll keep you on the lists." Ethan pushed through the swinging doors and left Dingle's little morgue that was currently storing its only resident in seven years. Well, that was if you didn't count the bull that got into Mrs. Flagerty's Lusitania and ate some of the blooms covered in pesticide last summer. Died right where it munched. Car did the autopsy and was instrumental in avoiding a neighborhood vendetta when he determined the bull had a terminal reaction to Mrs. Flagerty's prize and pesticide protected Lusitania.

The only word for life in Dingle was mundane.

Nothing much went on to raise an eyebrow except for the occasional dead animal, and of course, now, one dead American lass. Ethan sat behind his desk looking at the pictures scattered through the case file. She was gorgeous, this Brystal Traynor. She must have been the most beautiful, most unlucky lass he'd ever laid eyes on. He reviewed the pictures of the crime scene. Ethan was an excellent detective and absolutely nothing jumped out at him. Nothing hid beneath a step or lay concealed waiting to be found.

The few live pictures he'd collected showed quite a different picture. Everything about Brystal jumped out at him, everything but the reason for her death.

A twinge of desire shot through his mind at the spark in the young lass' eyes half veiled by a mass of riotous hair. It was a feeling he'd not recognized in years. In one picture her long tresses hung in a wild mess to her waist, the wispy ends tangled by the wind at the Cliffs of Moher. She stood atop O'Brien's Tower reaching toward the gulls that rode on the heavy winds just out of reach. Her wide glistening smile drew him in and he was there with her, laughing, happy, feeling the wind on his face. The lass in the picture captured a tiny piece of his dead heart, initiating a glimmer of life, a shadow of what he used to feel.

Ethan placed a tight lock on the bubble of emotion that tempted escape and returned to the case file. Brystal Traynor was dead. Her smile was dead. His heart was just as dead and he wanted to keep it that way. It hurt less.

He returned to studying the photos of the crime scene. Nothing looked different in back of the An Droichead Beag than it had in the past hundred years. Except for the bloodstains. The quaint pub known throughout Europe as The Little Bridge was famous for its worldly clientele and bawdy music. It was a popular hangout for locals and tourists alike. Now it would be known for the murder of an American woman right outside its back door. Probably double the pub's take for a wee bit. And that was a trottin' shame, Ethan thought.

His Dingle should be known for its crystal-clear bay, its rolling green hills, some of the best Irish food in the country, and its friendly folk.

Not murder.

Brystal's face returned to haunt him, no longer covered by a sterile white sheet on a slab in the morgue. So young and vital. Even in death there was something so alive about the lass. Somehow, the Grim Reaper took her, but couldn't quell the life in her.

Ethan re-read the Garda's initial report. It was short. Miss Traynor had lived on the peninsula for almost two years, but he'd never seen her. He'd not yet conquered the mental anguish of really looking at women since the death of his wife and daughter. He kept to himself, did his job and spent as much time with his sister and her family as he could. Brystal was an apprentice crystal cutter, talented everyone said. No serious boyfriend had come forward, but a close group of young people seemed to be her constant companions. One picture showed five of them at the beach holding Brystal across their laps like a log. Everyone was laughing and eating pizza.

A twinge cramped his heart. The last time he ate pizza he was laughing, with his entire family; wife, daughter, sister, brother-in-law, their kids... was it really three years ago? The pain felt like yesterday.

Becky's children, especially his niece Daria, helped fill the aching hole purposefully and carefully placed there by the cartel's hit man. The stinkin' murderer had been well-paid to teach Ethan to mind his own, and leave the Irish drug business to the one who'd grabbed the crown and anointed himself Lord. He'd brought the bastards down, but his family paid the price.

And for the rest of his life, he'd pay the price.

It was wrong.

But it was a fact.

Some things in life were simply wrong and there was no help for it. Like his highland lass and his three-year-old daughter lying in their own blood. And an American woman behind a pub with her head bashed in.

And the pain.

He slammed the file closed and hung his own head in his hands for a few minutes. This case had no clues, no evidence, and no motive he could find. Everyone he interviewed seemed to love the lass. Even her employer, Sean MacDougal spoke highly of her talent and commitment to learning the art of producing magnificent crystal in his workshop. The Master Crystal Cutter could not hide his emotions during the interview and Ethan felt for his loss. Apparently, she was not only quite the looker, but possessed a rare talent as well. The only reasonable answer was a crime of convenience. It was clear Brystal Traynor had simply been in the wrong place at the wrong time. Naiveté was a killer, most likely Brystal's killer.

It was past time to be on the road. He promised Becky he would stop by for dinner. In the last few months Ethan had dropped a few pounds and his sister fretted at him over his eating habits. Truth be told, he just worked too much and forgot about regularly scheduled meals now that he had no family to share them with. He set the Traynor case file in his drawer, locked his gun in the filing cabinet and headed for Becky's house and some fine home-cooked food. Corn beef and cabbage, it was tonight, and he could already smell the fond memories of their mother's cooking and the peat fire that heated their stone house on the bay. Things had been simple when he was a child. How he longed for those days.

Before the blood.

Before the deaths.

The sun was setting over the Atlantic as he drove along the bay road and out toward the peninsula. His sister lived in a village a few kilometers away, in a beautiful farmhouse full of love, light, and joy. When he was there, he could taste the love and it wrapped him in a warmth that existed nowhere else in his life. He could spend time with his niece and pretend that his little Kathleen would have been just like Daria, full of unconditional love with just a touch of mischief thrown in to keep him off balance. At least for a while his heart would not be cold and dead in his chest. His mind would not torture him with guilt. At least for a time.

He pushed the redial button on his cell phone and heard his nephew's familiar voice.

"Uncle Ethan, mum's waitin' biscuits on ya. Where are ye now?" Quinn's voice cracked. He was eleven and the voice change thing was beginning. Ethan could never quite understand how his twin niece and nephew, who were born just yesterday, could be eleven going on twelve in a couple months. It was another thing in life that just wasn't right. Children should never have to grow up and face a world where there was convenient death outside a wooden door.

"I'll be turnin' off in a few minutes, Jacko. Tell yer mum for me, would ya?" Ethan relaxed a little and steered his silver Land Rover along the narrow road that wound around the hills and into the village of Murreagh. "Make sure I get my share of soda drops, you scoundrel." Evan heard only a maniacal laugh from his nephew before the line clicked off.

A warmth bubbled up inside and he laughed at the sheer joy of the feeling within. Quinn had developed a unique sense of humor in the last couple years, along with some muscles and another three inches of lanky leg. The boy was a rugby fanatic and never missed a game on the telly. He could be found glued to the game with his father at every opportunity. Daria was exactly the opposite. Slight and petite, she was addicted to books or surfing on her computer, soaking up every bit of loose knowledge that floated free through the universe. She was a smart one, and as precocious as they came, much to her mother's chagrin. Ethan feared Quinn would grow up to dig and dry peat bricks, while Daria would change the world. Her life would not be mundane, it would be a constant string of challenges.

Turning the car off onto the gravel road that led to Becky's house, he could feel a sweet calm settle over his tense muscles. The tightness he had fought all day seemed to melt like warm butter and drizzle from his body, just like the butter on his sister's hot cross buns.

The farm was a wonderful place full of growing things. Big animals wandered behind cement fencing, and two dogs played in the front yard. His brother-in-law sat on the porch smoking a pipe, awaiting Ethan and his dinner.

Rory Kilkerry was a lorry driver and loved his job. It took him all over Ireland and he always brought little gifts home to his children and bride. Becky kept the home fires burning and raised animals and children. Ethan's heart did a little twist in his chest. This was what he'd had, once upon a time. But not now. Now he could only borrow it for short periods. He'd come to learn even a short time was better than nothing despite the lingering pain after each visit. Visiting was like an old trunk of comfortable clothing. You could open it, take something out and wear it for a while, then place it back when you needed to put on the togs of the day, and go about your business. But the clothing and the feeling was always there if you needed it.

Rory raised his pipe to Ethan as he pulled to a stop in front of the house and got out. The rich aroma of Irish oak pipe tobacco tickled his nose and his memories. It had been his father's brand as well.

"Hi ya. Dinner's awaitin' there Ethan. Yer sister's in a tizzy so step lively." Rory's good-natured kidding kept his marriage solid and his mind sound. Ethan had grown up close with Becky and knew his sister's impatience well enough. Somehow Rory tolerated her demanding ways and their love continued to grow. It was such a palatable thing that Ethan often found himself looking away when the couple stood too close, or touched too intimately.

"I'll be right along, Rory." Ethan grabbed a large box from behind the seat as he stepped as lively as he could with his burden toward the porch.

"Ah, Ethan, not another gadget! You spoil the lass such that we can't keep her head about her shoulders." Rory clapped his brother-in-law on the back with a heavy hand.

"Yeah well, she's the only niece I have." Ethan raised a questioning eyebrow to Rory. Becky and Rory had been trying for more children for a while now and he knew Rory understood the teasing query.

"You'll have to speak to yer sister about that one!" Ethan carefully placed the box just inside the front door and watched Rory blush as both men headed for the dining room and the substantial meal that covered the big old oak table.

Becky loved her hand-hewn dining room table. It had belonged to their parents and everyone, family, and visitor alike, gathered there for evening meals and talk, often into the wee hours of the morning. It was scratched and scarred from years of use. Like his life.

A quick peck on the cheek for his sister and a round of hugs ended with the oven chime announcing the biscuits were done. Like the bells of St. Mary's Church in town, the chime called everyone to their seats, Rory to his place at the head of the table and Ethan to his at the foot. Becky sat with her back to the kitchen and the children shared the fourth side of the table with plenty of elbowroom to separate the eleven-year-olds. Different sexes and vastly different personalities, the only time the twins seem to engage in sibling rivalry was at the dinner table.

"Uncle Ethan will do the honors." Becky commanded. Her domain was home and family. No one with any wits objected.

Ethan said a quick prayer being mindful to thank God for his sister's cooking and the joy of family, then crossed himself reverently. Squinting through one half-closed eyelid, he snuck a peek at Becky and was rewarded with the radiant smile on her face. She squinted back at his grin through thick eyelashes that hid deep green eyes. Ethan himself grinned back, suspecting God would not mind their slight irreverence at the dinner table.

"Serve yer uncle first, Quinn." Becky passed a platter of the coveted biscuits to her son.

"Yes, Mum." Quinn palmed a biscuit as he passed the plate on.

"The Lord blesses those who are humble and serve." Becky did not even have to look at her son. Her words floated across the table and slapped the biscuit from his hand. Ethan roared and ruffled Quinn's curly auburn hair.

Daria flashed him the *I told you so look* and giggled which earned her a punch in the arm.

Rory heaped his plate ignoring the misbehavior in favor of adult conversation. "So, I hear there was some excitement at the Station today."

"Right-o. We had a bit of a mythle to deal with." He glanced suggestively at the children who had turned to devouring their meal. Homicide was not family fare.

"Uncle Ethan, everyone knows about the murder and we're not babies anymore." Daria always spoke in the plural. Quinn never did. "It's no secret. Just everyone at class knows. She was an American lass, right? Murdered in back of the An Droichead Beag. That pub's an audacious place." Daria twirled her fork and stabbed a piece of cabbage, her long dark hair only half covering a mischievous smile.

"And just how would you be knownin' about a pub, young lady?" Ethan asked as Becky raised an eyebrow at her daughter across the table. Ethan wasn't in the habit of eyebrow raising but his sister, like their mother, had taken it to new heights. Halfway up was speculation, a little higher was sarcasm, but all the way up was critical disapproval.

"We're going to be twelve. That's almost adult, Uncle Ethan. Twelve! Not two." Exasperated, Daria speared a hunk of corn beef and shoved it into her mouth whole.

"I'd better not catch either of you hangin' about that so-called audacious place until you're much older." Ethan punctuated his statement with his own fork, pointing at both children.

Quinn nodded with his mouth full of his second biscuit. Daria glowered at her plate. "It *is* audacious."

Rory interrupted what promised to be a test of wills between his daughter and her uncle. "So, any clues? Any ideas about the crime?"

"That's the odd thing. Not a clue. Nothing adds up and there was literally no evidence at the scene. In this day and age that is almost impossible. I can only postulate that this American was pure unlucky, came on something or someone she shouldn't have, and paid the ultimate price. No one had a bad thing to say of her. MacDougal practically had a weepin' river over the few questions I asked him."

"There is always evidence," Daria murmured under her breath gaining a stern look from her mother who ate sedately across the table.

"Well then, Dingle's a mystery at last." Rory filled his plate again and set to conquering the mass of boiled cabbage and corn beef.

"What will ya be doin' with the body if she's nay from here?" Daria was always interested in grisly details and eternally curious. She could be a bit of a pill, but Ethan loved her unbridled intelligence and desire to understand all things mysterious. "What did the autopsy say? How was she killed? Everybody at the market was saying someone slit her throat." The young girl's eyes glittered as she spoke with pointed purpose. Daria drew her fork across her own neck making a grisly choking sound with the motion. Her brother's face had begun to turn a unique shade of yellowish-green. "They say that's why there was so much blood. They said puddles of blood."

Ethan bit his tongue to keep from laughing. Daria had not so much as glanced at her twin but, Ethan was sure his niece was aware and gauging Quinn's vomit meter. Ethan'd seen this little game before.

"Daria!" Becky chastised her daughter as Quinn got up abruptly from the table, his hand tightly clasped over his mouth. "'Tis not appropriate conversation for the table. Now look what you've caused."

Daria smiled sweetly at her mother and popped the remaining biscuit from her brother's plate into her mouth. Ethan bit his tongue to keep from laughing and Rory simply shook his head at his daughter's antics. Obviously, there was something special for dessert and there would be extra to go around without Quinn at the table.

"Sorry to disappoint but no slicing and no puddles. Just a knock in the head which is another reason I'd appreciate it if you stayed away from crime scenes and pubs, Daria." Ethan was deadly serious and could tell by Daria's solemn nod she recognized her uncle's tone immediately.

"Yes, Uncle Ethan. Of course." She picked up her brother's plate and her own. "Who's for a bit of dessert? We've apple and barley pudding." She flounced off to the kitchen in a way that left Ethan thinking the girl was quite happy with herself.

"Ah, hence the puddles." Rory commented out of Daria's hearing as he waved toward the kitchen with a full fork of cabbage. "The little mouse loves her puddin'."

"Your daughter is a little duggar, Rory Kilkerry." Becky picked up the remaining dishes and followed Daria.

"Don't I be knowin' it." Rory was shaking his head, but smiling still.

"Don't we both." Ethan added with a chuckle.

"So, this murder, you don't think it's a local? There's naught to be worried about, ya think?" Rory had finally gotten to his point in the entire discussion now that they sat alone at the table.

"Nothin' to be worried about here, Rory. Nothin' to fret about if yer thinkin' you should stay around the farm for a few days. Maybe pass up a few jobs?" Ethan did not want to see Rory give up income in fear for his family when there was no foundation. Unfortunately, history had taught them both a lesson about family safety.

"I was just wonderin' what you thought. You bein' the detective in the family." Rory studied his brother-in-law's face.

"Nah, I'd not be worryin' after Sean's hysterics. I'm quite sure this was not related to any previous happenin' around here." Ethan knew Rory understood the implied message. This new murder was not drug related, and no one was out to target Ethan and what was left of his family. "I've labeled it an official *murder of coincidence*. This lass was a coincidental victim and I believe not intended to be a victim at all. Probably a drunken accident. There is no evidence to support anything more or less." He watched Rory visibly relax as Daria and her mother returned with heaping bowls of hot pudding topped with rich vanilla ice cream.

Their conversation was done for the moment.

Daria plopped a bowl in front of her uncle. "So now, what have you filed as evidence, Uncle Ethan?" Daria ignored the dark scowl from her father as she passed him his bowl.

"Nothin' to be loggin', Mouse. Really." Ethan mumbled around a mouth full of pudding. "Becky, 'tis lovely, sis. It's been a while since I've tasted a wee bit of mum and home."

Becky remained silent but smiled her motherly "indulgent" smile and continued to eat. She had become more and more like their mother as the days, months and years passed. She certainly had surpassed their mother in the kitchen, but often prepared their childhood favorites when Ethan was present for a meal.

She and Ethan had vastly different memories with respect to their parents. Becky had remained at home and nursed their father through his final days. She'd been witness to the months of decline, the drunken tirades, and the inevitable Irish demise resulting in a well-pickled corpse. She had also been the one to find their mother years later, lying quietly amongst her precious flowers with a serene smile on her dead face. Ethan, on the other hand, had been at university or involved in building his career during those years. He'd not seen their father's tortured end, or their mother's peaceful departure. He'd not built a nest or put down root in the thin Irish soil with grazing goats, barking dogs and wrestling children until much later. He could never have cooked apple and barley pudding and remembered to add vanilla ice cream.

"She's a right fit mother with the blessings of the Lord on her shoulders." It was a high compliment from her man, even though everyone knew he adored his wife. Rory patted Becky's hand and a bright pink color welled in her cheeks. The love between the two was a palatable essence that welled up from within, to encircle everyone in their family.

"And for that I give thanks every day." Ethan was full of pudding and feeling the overwhelming love between his sister and her husband. All of a sudden, his gut wrenched threatening to eject some of that same love that was so recently lost to him. He swallowed hard and cleared his throat.

"Da, you're embarrassing Uncle Ethan." Daria grabbed her uncle's empty bowl and waved the rest of the family into the living room. "It's my turn to clear the table. Quinn's game should be on the telly soon. You might be havin' to give him a holler." She snickered over the last few words, knowing her brother was most likely in the loo bathing his forehead and gulping air.

"'Tis easy to be generous when you've had two helpings of pudding, lass." Her father swatted Daria's rump as she danced past, arms loaded with dishes and soiled linens.

"I surely haven't a clue of what you say, da." Daria twirled in the doorway and disappeared into the kitchen.

"You'd best be getting' a larger rifle there, Rory. In a year or so, me thinks you'll be fendin' off half the village." Ethan commented quietly across the table with a sly smile.

"She's a fair lookin' lass but, Ethan, she's still a bit young for that." Rory frowned like all fathers do when contemplating their only daughter's first beau.

"Nah, Rory, I'd be talkin' about the angry mobs stormin' the castle to hang that sprite. She'll be a danger to society someday." Ethan had to chuckle at the look on Rory's face. It was akin to a calm pond in the early morning whose placid waters had just been violently interrupted by a flailing flock of drunken geese attempting a semi-aborted landing. For a split-second Ethan thought Rory might join his son in the loo.

"Rory do call Quinn and set the telly. He'll be loath to miss the team introductions." Becky's calm voice interrupted her husband's mental panic. As she brushed by her brother she muttered under her breath. "...and you'd be wonderin' where she gets it."

Ethan looked up innocently with a smile as brilliant as his niece's. "I've not a fig of an idea what you'd be referrin' to, Rebecca."

The infamous MacEnery eyebrow twitched and Ethan could not keep from feeling a tug on his brittle heartstrings. This was the kind of home he had dreamed of. It was the kind of home he'd had. It was the kind of home that disappeared in flames and a flurry of bullets.

It was time to join his brother-in-law and nephew to immerse his mind in sports. It was time to immerse his mind in anything but the emotions that threatened to consume him. Unfortunately, his damn legs would not cooperate.

"It's okay, Uncle Ethan." Slim warm arms encircled his neck from behind and a whiff of barley and vanilla brushed his cheek. "I understand." The softly whispered words were followed by a masterfully sloppy kiss that wet half his face.

"Daria!" Ethan twisted to capture his niece in a kind of half wrestle, half bear hug.

The young girl let herself be drawn onto her uncle's lap giggling. "Ummmm... Irish Green Tweed." Daria smacked her lips as if she had just tasted her favorite butterscotch candy. "My favorite."

After a fierce hug Ethan stood her on her feet. "You, young lady, be trouble. And how is it you'd be knowin' the taste of aftershave?" It was Ethan's turn to use his version of the MacEnery eyebrow.

Daria pulled Ethan from his chair and dragged him towards the living room where her father and brother now sat in their favorite places, ready for the game to begin. "Oh la, Uncle Ethan. I *am* almost twelve." She gently pushed her uncle down into the refinished rocking chair near the fireplace and covered him with an afghan. "And a lass'd be keepin' those secrets close now, wouldn't she?" Daria winked and patted the afghan as if she were settling an old man in his place for the evening.

"Daria, you are not that old, and neither am I." Ethan grabbed for her and another round of wrestled hugs, but she darted away as his attempt only served to tangle him in the handmade fisherman knit blanket she had strategically tucked around him. He could hear her giggles from the dining room as she finished clearing the table.

Rory drew the channel changer from a pocket on the side of his seat and selected ESPN and the current rugby tournament. "Ethan, you may be right about that rifle." Rory drawled as he settled into his comfortable, well patched recliner.

At the mention of a firearm Quinn perked up on the couch. "Rifle? What rifle?"

Both men roared with laughter and Ethan said a silent prayer for the *old- almost twelve year-old* who had saved him once again with her unique ability to understand exactly what he was feeling and offer exactly what he needed, exactly when he needed it. Her innate empathy was a gift from the Lord himself, for sure.

And the game was on.

CHAPTER 3

Once there were three little pigs,
Who thought to build a house of twigs.
So they did and lived happily in their home of sticks,
Until along came a wolf adding fear in the mix.
You can build a great life but always keep an eye out for that wolf!

"Ms. Burnstein?"

Sandra looked up from the list of hospitals on her computer screen with furrowed brows. She was worried. "Yes, Director Davidson?"

"Where is Ms. Traynor? She missed my eight AM meeting. That is not like her." He stood over Crystal's assistant, his beefy arms tucked behind his back, forcing his sizeable stomach forward.

Sandra's eyes came level with the last straining button on his vest. It was in danger of giving up the ghost. "Sir, I am concerned. I have never known Ms. Traynor to be a second late, let alone two hours. She is not answering her home or cell phone. I am..."

"You are correct. Ms. Traynor is nothing if not punctual. Please find her immediately." It was the typical Davidson Directive.

"I was just reviewing the list of hospitals in the local area - here and her apartment. I have called the local police station and there is no report connected to her name...yet."

"Sandra, what are you talking about?" She had not heard him come up behind her and jumped at Chance's voice.

"Mr. Evans, I can't find Crystal. I've called both her numbers and you know she is never late. She is not on leave and if she had decided to take a day off, she would have emailed me and followed up with a call. Nothing, sir. Something has to be wrong."

"Well, let's not panic right away. She could have had car trouble or a flat or something." Chance was making up excuses to calm Sandra and she knew it.

"She does not have a car, Mr. Evans."

"Alright, stay calm until it's time to panic. Davidson, I'll hop over to her place and see if she is there. If she's ill or something has happened, Crystal may need help. She has no family in the city." He scribbled a number on the bright yellow sticky pad next to Sandra's mouse pad. "This is my personal cell. If you hear from her, call me right away." Without a second thought for the Director, he spun and walked rapidly for the elevators.

Sandra looked up at Director Davidson who still stood over her. "Sir?"

"Right. Evans has it under control. Keep me apprised of the situation, Ms. Burnstein." The portly man nodded and strode purposefully for the same elevators.

At least it seemed to Sandra as if he were purposeful, only she knew from the idle gossip at LDE the Director had little purpose, and actually accomplished even less. His grandiose office took up the entire south side of the top floor of the building and contained a twenty-foot long conference table cut from one single slab of redwood. She'd been there once, with Crystal, and thought the ostentatious table an ecological travesty. Somewhere a great ancient tree had given its life for LDE's flamboyant Director and his boy's club of secret squirrels.

Crystal... where was she and what travesty had overcome her? Nothing short of the end of the universe would keep Crystal from her job, her love of numbers. In fact, if Sandra didn't pry Crystal from the office most evenings, she knew she would find her in the same chair in the same clothes the next morning. She was well aware of Crystal's OCD and ... uniqueness. They had talked rather frankly when Crystal hired Sandra. There were rules set in the beginning and Sandra quickly came to understand why. Her boss was one of those people who existed in a world defined by some distinct challenges. Crystal was successful at life because she counted on others to control access in social or professional situations. Sandra thought it a strange way to exist, but Crystal paid her well to follow the rules and hold the keys to the domain. Over the years, Sandra had come to respect and admire Crystal's skill, despite the quirkiness of her boss. Truth be told, she had come to like Crystal and eventually joined the tiny confidential fan club that protected and celebrated Crystal's many incredible accomplishments. Her boss was truly a genius on the edge. The genius part she loved, the on-the-edge part she protected and kept confidential, not only as Crystal's admin assistant, but as her friend as well.

Sandra stood.

Then sat.

Then stood again wanting to do something but feeling totally helpless, inept... incompetent. Incompetent was never allowed.

Fear crawled across her skin leaving goose bumps behind.

How long would it take Mr. Evans to get to Crystal's apartment? She knew the address but didn't even know where it was. For that matter, Sandra knew very little about Crystal's personal habits, home, hobbies, family, or lack thereof according to Evans. In a moment of guilty revelation, Sandra realized she knew virtually nothing about Crystal's life outside the office. She made a silent promise to herself to rectify that in the future.

Glancing through the doorway into the neat office, Sandra half expected to see Crystal hunched over a spreadsheet or glued to her computer screens. It was hard to pace in the tiny area between her desk and the door, but Sandra was a bit of an over achiever herself.

Finally on the street, Chance hit the sidewalk at a run. Why hadn't Sandra contacted him earlier? She was as familiar with Crystal's OCD as he was. Nothing less than some catastrophe would keep his Crystal from her job, especially with a new case just waiting to be cracked. He picked up the pace, fear and adrenaline pushing his muscles to new lengths. He ignored the pain and his heaving chest. He didn't have occasion to run often. Finding Crystal was all that consumed his mind and body.

Crystal's building was thirteen blocks from LDE. Her apartment was on seven. He knew because she had taken the lease sight unseen. When he questioned her action, her only comment was that it had to be perfect because seven was a prime number. A prime number, for heaven's sake!

Crystal needed a keeper.

Chance ran faster.

He hit the lobby out of breath and gasping for air, didn't even try to answer the bellhop's polite question, and jabbed the elevator up-button four times. Pacing back and forth, Chance gasped in relief when the chime signaled the doors about to open.

Seven.

He pounded the lit button as the doors slowly closed and he felt the car's upward lurch.

"Come on, come on damn it." An overwhelming sense of doom skittered across the steel floor and crawled up his skin, twisting his lips into a grim frown. "How slow can this thing move?" He punched the wall as a chime sounded and the elevator slowed to a stop on the third floor. "Shit."

As the doors opened an elderly lady with fuzzy blue hair and some sort of tiny fuzzy white animal moved toward the entrance. Closer, tedious step by tedious step they came.

"Ma'am, may I..." Chance extended his sweaty hand, still puffing from the run.

"Watch it sonny. I have pepper spray." The woman screeched and stepped back reaching into the bag behind the fuzzy barking thing.

Chance held up his hands as if to surrender to the four-foot tall, eighty-something Q-tip and her animal. "Right. Right, sorry." He punched the door-close button waving the woman off. "Come on."

Though it seemed to take forever, Chance made it to the seventh floor without further assault on the doors. He found number 735, fifteen paces to the right just as Crystal had told him once upon a time.

How long ago?

Why did he remember that minuscule fact now?

Her door was ajar. Panic constricted his throat and he fought to breathe.

In apartment 735, the young woman he sought, huddled in a corner on the floor of the kitchen, her tear stained face pressed tightly against the oak cupboard, her thin cotton nightgown stretched over her folded knees, encapsulating her legs. Her body rocked slightly but her glassy eyed stare focused on nothing. Her cracked lips moved slightly with the whispered words in a personal litany of repeated numbers. Crystal clutched a letter in her hand as if her life depended on the half-sheet of crumpled white paper.

Chance stood in the doorway at a loss as to what to do first. He'd seen Crystal's strange coma-like behavior only once before and touching her had been a disaster. He flipped his phone out and hit the office number for Sandra.

"Mr. Evans?" A frantic Sandra answered in the middle of the first ring. "Did you find her?"

"Sandra, she's here at her apartment rolled up in a ball chanting numbers. What should I do? You probably have more experience with this than I do."

A rush of relief-laden words flew at him through the phone. "Don't hug her. Approach slowly. Don't flap your arms or anything like that. Squeeze her right shoulder and say her name quietly. Don't get close to her face, just speak softly and keep saying her name until she shuts her eyes. Then let go and back off. That's what works for me. Call me when she can talk." Chance could hear the long breath that Sandra had obviously been holding through the carefully modulated instructions. "And Mr. Evans, thank you. She's my Boss, but she's also my friend." A sharp click ended the conversation.

Chance took a deep breath himself, held it for a second then exhaled slowly adopting a calm, centered demeanor he no more felt than a pack of lions on the hunt with prey in sight.

He tested the room with one step and paused. Scrutinizing Crystal for a reaction to his presence, he took another tentative step.

No change.

Another.

Then another.

He stood over Crystal, but she took absolutely no notice. She was completely submerged in her mantra. He knelt slowly, his aching muscles screaming for relaxation instead of more tension. Reaching for Crystal's shoulder, his hand froze as he glanced at the paper so tightly clutched in her hand.

An ornate green and gold crest topped the paper with the words Republic of Ireland and Department of Foreign Affairs in flowers script just below. There was an address and a date, but the first sentence caught Chance's eye immediately. He cocked his head and read;

We regret to inform you of the death of your sister, Brystal Blythe Traynor, and respectfully request you contact our Office of Justice and Equity as soon as possible.

The rest of the text was covered by pale, lifeless fingers clutching what was left of the letter.

"Oh my God." Chance bowed his head and crossed himself out of habit. He'd only met Brystal once, but knew a goodly amount about Crystal's flamboyant sister. He could not imagine being an identical twin, seeing someone every day that wore the same face as you did but was so totally different...and always being compared. He had a pretty clear picture of the two distinctly individual women who shared their exact same DNA; Crazy Crystal who needed structure and control above all else just to function, and, Brazen Brystal who needed nothing more than a latte and a place to go. "I am so very sorry, Crystal."

Chance stared at the woman before him who rocked slightly and whispered strings of numbers, her face never leaving the side of the cupboard. He saw the tear stains on her flannel nightgown. He noticed her bluish lips. He was cognizant of the white knuckles of her right hand that held fast the last connection to the other half of herself.

With excruciating slowness, he raised his hand and lightly squeezed Crystal's right shoulder. "Crystal? It's Chance."

There was no response.

She did not pull away.

She did not stop rocking.

She did not even blink.

"Crystal?" He squeezed a little harder and spoke louder this time. Still there was no evidence of any response from his rocking genius.

"Crystal, come on. Listen to my voice. Come out of it." This time Chance gave her shoulder a fairly strong squeeze and was rewarded with a blink. "Crystal? Crystal."

She stopped rocking and Chance watched her pale fingers relaxed their grip on the letter.

"Come on girl, you can do it. Listen to my voice. Listen Crystal." He continued speaking as he gently squeezed her shoulder again and again.

It was working. She closed her eyes and tried to move her legs. It didn't seem to work. Chance wondered how long she'd been rolled up in a ball like this on the cold floor.

Finally, she looked up in surprise, right into his eyes and her entire body bolted as if she'd been viciously slapped.

He immediately looked away, let go of her shoulder and moved back a few inches. He was well aware that Crystal did not like to be in close proximity to another person, or be touched.

"You there?" Chance tried to affect what he thought was a warm, encouraging smile. Just enough lip movement to invite, not enough teeth to scare the fragile child inches away.

Crystal cleared her throat and croaked, "Where am I? How long..."

"In your kitchen and, I don't know." He watched Crystal try her legs again noticing the painful cringe as she straightened the stiff joints. "Want help?" He took a chance and stood holding out a hand. He kept it light and non-threatening.

"Ah... I don't think I have a choice." She put her icy hand in his and let him pull her to her feet. "What are you doing here?" She tucked the letter behind her.

"You didn't come to work and didn't call in. Sandra was concerned and I was coming this way, so I thought I'd stop in and see if you needed something." He tried the unconvincing lie on for size and found it lacking. His face was still covered with sweat from the run and his usually tanned handsome face sported bright red cheeks.

"Right. But thanks for the attempt, Chance. And the hand." Crystal rubbed her limbs and tried a step. Stumbling, Crystal caught herself on the edge of the counter. The letter slipped off the counter and floated to the floor landing face up. Before she could motivate her limbs to stoop, Chance bent and retrieved the paper.

"Brystal?" He did not look at Crystal ,but scanned the text as if it had been the first time he'd seen the contents. "What? Who? I mean, this didn't come in the mail I hope." Chance casually leaned against the same counter, close enough to catch Crystal if she collapsed or fainted, but far enough to give her the comfort of distance considering her exaggerated concept of personal space.

"No, a guy from the State Department brought it." Chance watched closely out of the corner of his eye as he pretended to continue reading. He was pretty sure Crystal was not given to fainting, but he was prepared to play catcher just in case.

"Just like that? So early in the morning?"

"No. Last night. I think. It's fuzzy, you know, my ah..." Tears appeared hanging off her long dark lashes. Crystal placed both hands flat on the marble countertop and rocked silently trying to ignore the wet rivulets that ended on the creamy marble in tiny drops.

"Ah hon, I'm so sorry. What can I do?" The implications of her sister's death, even more so, her twin's end, were incalculable. Chance's heart twisted in his chest. His checkbook twisted in his pocket and he could see his department twisting in ruin. He mentally slapped himself for even considering the last two.

Crystal was the backbone of his 06 Department. Hell, she was the backbone, muscles, and brains of 06, the last-ditch effort of any investigation. There was a reason 06 carried the nickname of VD. It'd meant *very difficult* in the beginning anyway. The implication of the nickname was that every unsolved and extremely difficult case was like a communicable disease, infecting the finances of the innocent. However, until he'd stolen Crystal away from her dead-boring job, 06 had a cure rate of less than thirty-five percent. His Crystal was pure genius at finding the offending viruses they sought, and targeting them with the full extent of the legal treatment. In the last year alone, she had diagnosed and *treated* ninety-eight percent of the VD cases that came into his 06 forensic *clinic*. VD now represented *vehemently determined,* mostly because of Crystal.

"I don't..." she turned to him beseechingly, "half of me is gone. And I didn't even know it." She moved a step closer. Standing side-by-side now, Crystal leaned her head against his shoulder and wept silently.

Chance wanted to take her in his arms and comfort her like some small wounded animal, but he was afraid to move. Instead, he stood there strong and tall, his hands and arms hanging by his sides letting his star employee literally cry on his shoulder. At some point, he tipped his head laying a cheek against the top of Crystal's tangled hair. Amazingly she tolerated the contact for a few seconds before moving away. It was a kind of head to head hug that would have to suffice for emotional support. At least he'd been able to offer some kind of human contact, some form of physical comfort. Still he felt inept and ineffectual.

"So, what now? What do you have to do? What can I *help* you do?"

Ineffectual was a horrible way to start his day. Usually eloquently poised, Chance couldn't keep his hands from fluttering with his questions. Something had to move, or he would explode just trying to keep his own emotions suppressed.

He saw the blank look and heard the garbled mumble. His heart twisted a little more, but thoughts of his pocketbook had crawled away, appropriately chastised for the moment. He was Crystal's boss, but he was also so much more, her mentor, her confidant, her fashion consultant! Really? He was definitely her keeper and now, what? Her surrogate family in the absence of any family left? The mere thought *of no family left* was appalling to him, a family man.

That peacenik sixties song struck a chord in his mind: *He ain't heavy, he's my brother. So, on we'll go. His welfare is my concern. No burden is he...*

Crystal's welfare was his concern whether she was a burden or not, because her welfare was his department's welfare. And, somehow in a weird way, they were truly friends, together without judgment, without competition, without defined boundaries. He could tell her anything knowing she would respect his confidence, and she could tell him...what she could. And they both had at various times over the years.

"May I?" He pointed to the forms on the counter with the same crest as the letter.

"Of course. I'm going to go wash my face." Her hair hung in crimped strands blocking his view of her tear-stained face. It was the first time he'd ever seen Crystal's hair unbraided. It was thick with rich chestnut hues and hung almost to her waist. How had he missed that all of these years? He wanted to reach out and freely run his fingers through it, just to feel the luxury of it. Alana's hair was plastered into place and glued to her head. He wanted to feel the freedom in each strand but kept his hands to himself and clamped a lid on thoughts about hair. He clamped a bigger lid on his somewhat surprising and wandering libido. The Ice Queen... remember the Ice Queen.

When did he start thinking anything about Crystal *that way*? On the other hand, how had he not thought about Crystal that w, in all the years they had worked together? That arms-length closeness had spawned a warmth in him over the years, but he always considered it friendship, a collegiality of shared anticipation and exhilaration. Occasionally there had been a few stray thoughts, but his job actually excited him and working with Crystal was the top of the pinnacle when it came to finding huge amounts of hidden money. Crystal loved the hunt like he loved the win… and the money. The hunt was sexy, but the win was sex itself.

He mentally shook himself again. It was the fear and stress. It had to be. He picked up the two forms and scanned them. One was a request to release and ship a body. The other was an official identification form that required the next of kin to physically identify her sister's body in person.

Chance froze.

In person?

Crystal?

Ireland?

She didn't go anywhere but work, home and three select restaurants. She hadn't even been to his home on Long Island for dinner, despite numerous invitations from him, Alana, and their kids. And Crystal liked his kids a lot.

Ireland? Holy Mother of God!

"So, what do you think?" Crystal stood leaning against the arching entrance to the kitchen, a washcloth held to her eyes and forehead.

"I think you have some planning to do." He phrased his words carefully with measured tone and watched Crystal's response. He saw little. "Have you read the forms?"

Behind the washcloth came a semi-muffled groan. She'd read the forms.

"What can I do to help?" Ineffectual settled in his gut again.

"Get a sex change operation, grow your hair long, and dye it auburn in the next twenty-four hours."

Chance had to chuckle at the picture in his mind her words created.

"No good. The twin thing, remember?" Oops. Damn his mouth.

Crystal threw the wet cloth on the counter. "You think I could forget?" Her eyes studied the patterns on the floor tiles. "How can I ever forget?" She leaned on the counter with both hands again and Chance took a step closer just in case. Minutes ago, she'd been rolled up in a ball on the floor and that picture was fresh in his mind.

"You don't ever forget, Crystal, you just make peace with yourself. No matter how bad or good the relationship." His voice softened and Crystal looked up with a nod.

"You would know, wouldn't you?" For a few moments they stood in companionable silence, each remembering very different things.

Chance saw the neck flex and knew his Crystal was back for good. "So then, I guess I have some planning to do." She took the papers from his hand and read through the first one. "Forms. I so love forms."

The second one under her belt, Crystal seemed surprised. "Ireland? I have to go to Ireland? That's just crazy. Surely someone in that village place knew her and can identify her…her remains." The last two words came out a little wobbly.

"The letter from the embassy stated that by the law of the Republic of Ireland, all remains must be identified by a competent relation of the first or second degree." Chance pointed to the letter on the counter.

"A competent relation of the first or second degree? Well that lets me out then, doesn't it?" Crystal tapped her head with one finger. "Not competent."

"Somehow, I don't think anyone will view you that way, kiddo. You head up the most successful forensic auditing department in the most successful federal contracting company in the US. I don't think incompetent will fly." Chance grinned, then thought the better of it and frowned. He just wasn't sure how to behave ,or what emotion to allow to show. After all, he was standing in Crystal's apartment having just lusted after his most prized employee's hair talking to her about going to a foreign country to identify her dead twin. Her nightgown covered most of her body, but did little to disguise a fit and well-endowed figure in the late morning light.

He was becoming distracted. Damn, when was that bitch he married ever going to give him some? He forced his eyes back to the letter and the task at hand. "Foreign countries have their own laws. I don't see a choice." He tried to soften the message.

"But I can't..." Crystal looked like a frightened kitten about to bolt.

Chance pointed to the dining room on the other side of the arch. "Let's take a moment to consider things. This has been a shock for you. Take it slow." Any other woman he would have taken by the elbow and guided her to a chair. With Crystal, he simply stood rooted to the tile pointing and hoping she would go sit down. "Can I fix tea?" He knew she liked Earl Grey Tea. A clear container on the counter held a wealth of teabags. It would be easy to keep an eye on her and a kettle at the same time. He didn't wait for her response, but turned away and set to work.

From behind him he heard her sad voice. "Cups are in the cupboard on the right side of the sink. Sugar's over here." Apparently, the offer had been accepted. Chance made himself busy to allow Crystal some time at the table alone with the forms and letter. Out of the corner of his eye he could see her studying the papers. Well... at least he thought she was looking at them.

He took the tray from behind the cookie jar and placed the cups, spoons, napkins, etc. in a definite pattern then carried the tray to the dining room table.

For the first time he actually looked around at her apartment. The place was not small, but not so large as to be considered New York grand. Everything was in its place. There was no idle newspaper, no shirt draped over a doorknob, no glasses, or cups on the coffee table, not even a stain ring on the glass top. Even the books in her bookshelf were lined up perfectly despite their size. The dining room table was a polished glistening surface of granite with glittering veins of silver that shot through the darker shades of gray and blue. He set the tray between them and handed Crystal her cup with a napkin beneath the bottom.

"Thanks, Chance. I appreciate your coming over here. I know it wasn't on your way to anywhere... but here." Her first tenuous smile was out of place and a little strained. She peeked at him from beneath a jumble of gorgeous, crimped hair.

"You'd do the same if things were reversed. As a matter of fact, I recall you did. In this case, contrary to popular belief, paybacks aren't a bitch." He sipped the hot beverage even though he detested tea and would have loved to be having a double latte cinnamon skinny with whipped cream and chocolate sprinkles rolling across his tongue at that very minute.

She was coming around quickly, back to her old in-control self. "Why are you drinking that? You hate tea." He was surprised she knew that. Alana didn't know it. His wife served him tea all the time. And he drank it rather than argue, which would just end up in some blow-out costing him about a grand in shopping *therapy* later. Alana was big on shopping therapy. Drinking therapy. Mani-pedi therapy. Just about any kind of expensive therapy that kept her away from home and kept her out spending money.

But when she walked into the office, he was the envy of every man in the universe. There were times when it was worth it. The rest of the time he tried to remember that simple truism and live for the next time it was worth it. And of course, there were his children…

"Tea? Something to do. I want to make sure you're okay before I dash off. The staff is bound to be wondering where I am." His phone chirped as if it had been pre-arranged. "That is probably Sandra." He glanced at the caller ID. "Yep. You want to take it? She's just gonna call you afterwards anyway." He slid the chirping phone across.

Crystal flinched like the sleek black phone was a coiled Bushmaster about to strike, took a deep breath and picked up the chirping gadget. "Hello Sandra. I am alive."

"Crystal! Thank God. I was worried. It's not like you to not show up for work. I thought something had happened." Chance could hear the flurry of words from the breathless admin assistant. "I'm glad you're all right. You are all right. Right?"

"Something has happened and I will explain later. I'll be in the office later this afternoon. I'm sending Mr. Evans back there right now. Goodbye." Crystal touched the disconnect icon. "You'd think I was a three-year-old without a babysitter." She slid the phone back to him. "Don't say it! I know."

They sat in the silent sunshine for a few minutes, Crystal enjoying her tea and Chance drinking his in tiny sips. Finally, with a heavy sigh Crystal asked, "Do you think I really have to go to Ireland? Can't I send a proxy or something?"

Chance sat back added another spoon of sugar to his tea and vigorously swirled the mixture. "I think it would be good for you to go. Get away from the office. Spread your wings a little and see something besides the insides of your apartment and the office." He licked his spoon and used it to emphasize his point. "You just earned a huge bonus. It's not like you couldn't rent a private jet and travel in whatever style makes you comfortable. I hear Ireland is beautiful and green. Very green. Like all that money you keep socking away. Spend some, Crystal. Live a little." The reason for the trip came back to him in a flash. "I mean, all things considered." He tried to school his face back to subdued and serious, but the thought of going to Ireland with Crystal made his insides want to smile and jump on the next plane with her in tow. Heck, he'd rent the plane if she'd just ask. He tried to convince himself the feelings tightening his slacks were born out of protective instinct, but the evidence was completely contrary.

"This is something I guess I have to do." The resignation in her tone was a pathetic statement on Crystal's part. He couldn't conceive of what she must be going through behind her placid, sad expression. Losing a sister was bad but losing a twin sister must be worse than horrible. He wanted to kick himself for the "live a little" statement. And... the thoughts about jumping on a plane with her.

"I'll figure this out, Chance. I will." She set her cup down and stared into the amber liquid as if she could find the answers at the bottom. "Brystal was all I had left. Now it's just me." Tears welled up but she just sat there.

"You are not alone, kiddo. If you need something, anything, all you have to do is ask."

She didn't.

"Really." Chance took another sip of the sickly-sweet tea. Crystal's tears made him uncomfortable in the typical man-hating-tears way. Tears always upped the ante when it came to feeling ineffective and incompetent.

"You know I owe you one anyway." To his surprise Crystal got up, walked to him, and actually placed her hand on his shoulder.

"No owing between friends, Chance. Just friendship. I appreciate that more than I can ever tell you with words." She gave his shoulder a little squeeze. A squeeze? Crystal had never initiated physical contact with him before.

"I'm going to shower and head over to the office. I'll be all right by myself now. You might as well go back and head off the worry wart who guards my door." Crystal wandered down the hall apparently not giving a thought to leaving her boss sitting at her dining room table. After all, they were friends.

Friends? It hit him like a ton of cupcakes, all sweet and messy and light, but leaving behind a kind of sick stomachache. For the first time he had to admit to himself he wanted more than friendship from this fragile woman who had no one left in the world. He wanted more than to be the most envied man in the universe a couple times a year. And there was absolutely nothing he could do about it, but go back to the office and focus on work. The Ice Queen, he told himself. Remember the Ice Queen.

CHAPTER 4

Four little bugs went out to play,
On a spider's web one day.
Soon they made quite a bunch,
Until a long came a spider,
In time for lunch.

Be careful who you invite to eat...

Ethan spent the next two days desperately searching for anything he might have missed in the Traynor case. Word had come down from the Garda Síochána High Commissioner to tackle the situation with a fine-tooth comb, serious scrutiny. There would be no international incident in Dingle. However, like he originally reported, there was nothing to find. If he hadn't known better, he might have thought this a professional job. But who would want to kill a twenty-eight-year-old apprentice crystal cutter in Dingle, Ireland? He hadn't even found anyone who came close to saying a negative word about the woman. Everyone in the village who'd known her, loved her without reservation. There wasn't a boyfriend. No excuse for a crime of passion when there was no passion.

Ethan sat at his desk scrutinizing the last picture of the crime scene with a magnifying glass. He could find nothing suspicious about Brystal, other than her death. Perhaps it truly was some kind of weird, once-in-the-world kind of accident? But...

Nothing.

Daria's words taunted him, "There is always evidence Uncle Ethan."

Not this time.

Ethan slammed the magnifying glass into his drawer and gathered the pictures strewn across his desk into a pile. The top picture gave him pause. Brystal Traynor hunched over a vertical grinding wheel, a fragile wine glass in her red tainted hands.

Blood? He studied the picture. Felt marker. She had sketched a wild pattern in red marker to follow on the wheel. Her smile was brilliant and the sparkle in her eyes nearly set him to hyperventilating. Talented? Almighty God! She was talented, and gorgeous... and so alive in her element with crystal in her stained hands.

Alive?

Ethan swallowed hard.

No, not alive.

The desk phone buzzed. It was his district superintendent. "Well, this ought to be fun." Ethan answered, "Inspector MacEnery."

"Ethan? Glen. Tell me you have something."

"As a matter of fact, I do, sir. I have a headache, blurry eyes, and I've had nothing to drink in days."

"The American woman's case, Ethan. And don't be callin' me sir. I didn't want this damn job and I've to tell you I'm not cut out for the politicin'. You're the best investigator I know. Please tell me you found something, anything." Glen O'Grady and Ethan had come through the academy together and their friendship went far beyond the job.

"God's own truth, Glen, nothin'. No weapon, no prints to identify other than locals who are all accounted for. No forensic evidence at all. Not even a rumor and knowin' my village, that's a hard one to be wrappin' me arms about." Ethan rubbed his eyes.

"Well, I got word the sister will be comin' on Thursday, from the states she is. She'll be in Dingle by the afternoon so be ready for her. She has your contact information, but for the life of me, I don't know what you'll be tellin' the lass." Ethan could hear Glen sigh on the line. "I don't envy you this one, Ethan. Call me if you've need."

"Right-o. Bye-ya." Ethan hung up and sat staring at the picture of Brystal and her creation. "The sister, huh? Thursday? This week just keeps getting better, doesn't it ol' boyo." Why did he have to meet the sister?

He thought about calling Glen back and getting him to meet the woman when she landed, but then thought the better of it. Glen's wife had four kids at home and a new baby in the basket. That's all Ethan needed was a weepin' woman and a tired new father. Hopefully, the sister wasn't given to bouts of fainting or hysteria. He'd not much personal experience with American women. His quiet Dingle wasn't on the hit parade for American tourists.

He closed the file and headed out for lunch. There wasn't much food at his house and he'd forgotten breakfast. Maybe if he sat for a spell at the An Droichead Beag, had a bite to eat, something would come to him. Maybe not. At least he'd have a meal under his belt. The infamous restaurant was down by the bay and a right nice little place to get a hefty meal and a pint in neighborly surroundings.

Pulling up to the turn off at the pub, he almost gasped out loud. A bright blue tour bus was unloading what seemed like a million visitors. Strung across the windows was a huge banner that read Murder on the Dingle Express - the An Droichead Beag Homicide and Lunch – EU 49.50. In small letters below the title was the website address, *http://www.murderindingle.com.*

"Jesus, Mary and Joseph!!! This is unbelievable." He drove past and around back to the parking lot which was no longer a parking lot at all. A rope cordoned off the area and tables and chairs surrounded the back door where yellow and red tape outlined the crime scene. A band played on the west side of the lot and patrons sat eating lunch while wait staff scurried around the building, dishing out food and gossip.

Murder was definitely big business at the An Droichead Beag.

A big sign in the shape of a pointing finger was nailed to the side of the pub, with the word *blood* painted in red capital letters for everyone's edification. The sister will be here on Thursday? Ethan had to do something. This was a circus, not something a next of kin would want to see.

He parked the squad car in the street with the caution lights blinking and walked around to the front since the back had become restricted ground. Heaven forbid anyone should step on the red paint that had been splashed all over the back steps and blacktop near the door. A human didn't have enough blood to cover the area that now gleamed reddish-brown in the noon sun. Ethan automatically thought about Daria's calculating little mind and what her comment would be. *Uncle Ethan, it's not the right color. The splash marks and spatter pattern are all wrong, and there is way too much for a real head bashing. Scalp wounds bleed, but really? These people didn't do their homework and have no taste.*

The no taste part was definite.

"Barney!" Ethan strode to the bar and yelled for the owner. "What the hell is goin' on a 'here?"

Barney materialized next to Ethan, grabbed him by the arm and dragged him into the manager's tiny office off the bar. "Shhhh! Sorry about this Ethan but me boys got a right smart business goin'. He's got him a plan to make some big money fast! We're on the Internet! We've gone viral, whatever that means. Ain't that hot shit!"

"Viral? Barney, what are ye doin' man? 'Tis a fair crazy circus out there. Who'd be paintin' the steps? Are ya knowin' how bad this looks? You gotta shut it down, Barney." Ethan tapped Barney's chest with his index finger. "I got the dead woman's sister comin' to the village Thursday to identify the body. She's an American. What's she gonna think of us with this zoo outside and a tour bus chargin' for a ride and lunch at a murder scene? 'Tis grisly, I tell ya." Ethan shook his head. What had happened to his sleepy little village in five short days? Had everyone gone berserk?

"It's me own property there, Inspector. This here is still Ireland, and we gots a right to use our property the way we wants to." Barney puffed out his chest and glared at Ethan.

"Yeah, ya do Barney. But whatever happened to right and wrong? This is wrong, Barney." Ethan glared right back. "You got a daughter. How would you feel if the dead lass was yours and you had to see this..."? he waved at the frolic going on. There was no word in his vocabulary to describe it.

All of a sudden the wind seemed to leave Barney's sails and his face fell a might. "But we be needin' the money, Ethan. Things been bad this past year."

"I'm just asking ye to take it inside and get the banner off the bus. Clean up the paint. Holy Christ Barney, there's enough paint on the steps for a village massacre, not a single homicide." Ethan pointed out the dingy little window that overlooked the back parking lot /outdoor dining area. "And that finger has to go. Really. This is not some footbol game."

"Gimme a day and I'll get it cleaned up, but we're still doin' the tours." The barkeep shook his finger at the Inspector. "I'll make the bus park in the back if it makes ya happy." Barney hung his head. "The woman's sister is comin' here? What fer?"

"It's the law. The lass has to positively identify her...the remains. I'll not be likin' it either but 'tis nothin' I can do. I guess there was only the two sisters. Folks are deceased, so says the paperwork."

"The good Lord give her strength then. It's not the way I'd like to be seein' Ireland." Barney was shaking his head and Ethan suspected his comment about Barney's daughter had hit home. "I'll get this cleaned up, Ethan, a 'fore Thursday."

"I'd be appreciatin' it. Thanks for understanding." Ethan took Barney's hand and shook it like two gentlemen agreeing on a wager. "I think I'll get a bite while I'm here."

"Right-o. I'll set you up with a table right away, knowin' how busy you are at the station and all." Barney rushed out to the bar and signaled to a waitress pointing back at Ethan.

There was no wait despite another tour bus at the front door and

Ethan was served within minutes. He suspected the preferential treatment wasn't due to the handshake, but the desire to get rid of him as soon as possible.

Halfway through his beef and cheese, Ethan noticed Dharág Hadley take a table near the door with two other men. He'd not yet interviewed Dharág, an apprentice crystal cutter who worked in the same shop as Brystal Traynor. There was really no need since Dharág had been on the continent when Brystal was killed. He nodded to Dharág, but the man seemed to ignore the Inspector. The three men lowered their heads and continued to talk privately despite the pressing crowd and escalating noise. Ethan attributed Dharág's behavior to a local boy in a local watering hole surrounded by imported strangers. Ethan finished his sandwich as quickly as he could. So, it seems did Dharág. Even he wanted to get out of the restaurant with its crazy atmosphere.

CRYSTAL STOOD under the hot water and let her emotions go with the flow. Her salty tears mixed with the water trickling down her body to end in a puddle at her feet before running down the drain. Like her sister's life – gone, down some nebulous drain… in a foreign country.

Crystal sobbed letting her anguish go with the water. Why did Brystal have to go to Ireland? What happened there that took her beautiful, irresponsible life?

It was not right. Everyone who met Brystal loved her. She was the rainbow on a stormy day. She was a carefree spirit that rode on the wind and touched everything with a light caress, as she drifted in and out of lives. There wasn't a mean bone, no not even a mean molecule, in her body.

Why?

The *Question* slid from her mind to perch itself on the edge of the sink and point its ugly finger at her.

There was no answer in the shower.

There was no answer in the universe.

As Crystal toweled her long thick hair it dawned on her, maybe there was an answer…but it had to be hiding in Ireland. The idea sent shivers of terror up her spine, across her shoulders and down her arms. She hugged the fluffy towel around her and stood staring at her reflection in the half-fogged mirror. Like looking at some stranger through a veil of secrecy, she tried to identify a glimmer, a hint of strength in that person in the mirror. Crystal's very nature kept her rooted to her home and job, everything that had controlled her life since childhood. Where would she find the strength to battle her own self? Her…inability? Or worse yet, her dis-ability.

Question sat on the sink mocking her, bouncing up and down in glee. It stuck its tongue out and blew a raspberry at her. The knots in her stomach that hid in all the corners and crevices, joined hands, and crept toward her throat. She could feel their stealthy footsteps just below her sternum. The whispered thump of each step made her morning tea churn in foamy waves. Paralyzing fear reared its head, peaking above the foam.

"Breathe, Crystal. Just breathe and focus." Her self-talk became a mace that hammered the knots back and forced them into submission. It pulled rising fear back beneath the waves. "Breathe."

Success in the endless battle. She took a hair pick and separated her long tresses as she continued to reassure her reflection. "You can do this. All you need to do is focus and… let's just stay with focus for now."

Damp but straight, Crystal separated the strands into three sections then braided them together in a tight pattern. She worked automatically, counting the braided patterns. At eighteen she stopped, grabbed a plain tan rubber band off the counter and wound it three times on the end. *Question* sat patiently waiting for her attention. No more sneering or laughing, just patient waiting, biding its time. Pensive.

Noticing the hour for the first time since surfacing from her OCD episode, Crystal flew into her bedroom, yanked on black slacks, pulled on her ice blue camisole, and grabbed her black suit jacket.

Slipping into a pair of black pumps on the way out the door, she almost ran for the elevator.

Question slid through the door behind her at the last minute and snuck into the black shoulder bag that dangled from her arm. It wasn't going to be left home.

It was after noon by the time Crystal entered the elevator in her office building. As usual, she pressed her back to the far wall of the elevator and stood concentrating on calm thoughts, trying not to look at the lit numbers. There were three other riders and one almost blocked the lit panel. "Eighteen, please."

Eighteen was home.

A chime sounded and the doors opened.

Thirty-seven tiles and one right turn. Twelve tiles and a nebulous stretch of carpet section, then one more left turn.

Sandra sat at her desk frowning at her computer screen. "Morning, Boss."

Crystal was thankful she did not look up. Right now, any emotional display was trouble.

"Good morning, Sandra. Thanks for the call." Crystal managed the thank you with some trepidation hoping Sandra understood.

"No problema, Boss. Reports are on your desk. I'm tracking some interesting account movement connected with the new FI. An AA rundown will be ready by close of banking hours. If you need anything, just buzz me."

Crystal took a deep breath in relief. Her admin assistant understood and would wait until Crystal was ready to talk. And... she had already begun work on the new forensic investigation with account activity following.

Crystal hung her jacket on the peg behind her door. "Note to self, thank Chance Evans for allowing me to hire Sandra. Big thanks."

She sat in her chair and stared at the generic blue wave on the computer screens. *Question* crept from her purse and sat its fat little body right on the edge of her desk. It smiled showing vicious jagged teeth behind slimy red lips. Crystal tried her best not to look it in the eye. She opened a drawer and unceremoniously dumped it in, and quickly slammed the drawer ridding herself of the pesky *Question* for the time being.

"To work, girl." And so, began a new day and continued the new hunt. Crystal smiled to herself and dug in. *Question* pounded on the metal drawer, but she ignored it and focused on the new FI with vigor.

By five PM most of the staff was gone. Crystal heard Sandra rustling about and felt the soft knock on her door. "Boss?"

"Come on in. Hang on for just a sec." Crystal hit the save key committing the information on her screen to the computer's memory. "Yes?"

Sandra handed her a ream of papers in a folder. "The AA tracking. Interesting stuff. Virginia's Attorney General commented on CNN about an on-going investigation that has been handed to a contract source for follow-up, this morning around ten AM. Ever since account numbers and money have been moving all over the world." Sandra took her we'll-get-'em-stance, arms crossed over her chest, feet slightly farther apart than normal. "One hundred and sixty-two transfers by three PM. Ten major banks and five offshore accounts. And those are only the ones we know about."

"Good work, Sandra. I guess the jig is up. I wonder if the conglomerate knows LDE has the contract?"

"I would assume so. There is something dirty and political going on. Why would Dick Torensen make a public announcement, if not to warn the conglomerate and send them into a flurry of funds manipulation otherwise? Makes a gal wonder if the incredibly good-looking-fair-haired-son of Virginia is somehow connected. Maybe his blonde locks hide some dark roots."

Crystal listened as she flipped through the AA spreadsheets then paused at a dossier on Torensen. "Interesting. You did a workup on Torensen. Good call."

"Take a look at the financials on that guy."

"Pay dirt. Literally. Unless this guy has a sugar momma stashed somewhere, he should be in debt up to those dark roots. We have to find his lines of cash."

"Already on it, Boss." Sandra took the file from Crystal's hands. "Tomorrow. It's quitting time. Traynor's Rules."

"Right but I have some personal issues to attend to tonight before I leave."

Question thumped at the drawer and dragged its nails along the metal. It was time to face the little gremlin.

"Is this a good time to offer condolences or should I wait a while?" Sandra's eyes locked on the rug. There was little emotion in her schooled tone.

"Evans?" It was hardly a question.

"That would be confidential." Sandra wrung her hands for theatric effect. "But it wasn't his fault. I pried it out of him. I was so worried."

"Okay, but please keep it quiet. I don't need a lot of sappy cards and people assaulting me in the hall so they can tell me how bad *they* feel." Crystal shook her head in disbelief. "Tonight, I need to make some arrangements. I'm not even sure what I want to do yet."

"Well, I probably don't have to say this but I feel like I should. If there is anything I can help with, day or night, please don't hesitate to call." Sandra was still looking at the rug and Crystal was grateful.

"If I go home, I'll probably just get lost in… things. So, I'm going to stay here and work the issue. Like it was a new FI."

"Then I stay too." Sandra turned to go back to her desk. "Shout if you need anything. I'll be working on Wonder-boy with the gorgeous tan and mystery money."

"Wait, Sandra, you don't have to stay. This is personal stuff." Crystal jumped up and followed her admin assistant back to her desk.

"Traynor's Rules, Boss. Besides," She smiled sweetly at Crystal from her chair, "I love overtime. Mama has her eye on a little company that is about to go public with a stock split in its near future. If I invest carefully with a little overtime pay, it may just be a big payday when I want to be old and free."

Retreating in the face of overwhelming logic, Crystal watched her assistant from the doorway as Sandra swiveled her chair around and did a little wave over her shoulder. "Buzz if you have need."

"Right." It was a mumbled surrender.

Question had escaped his prison and now paced back and forth across her desk. It was time to deal with him and Crystal hesitated to sit down so close to the source of her agitation.

Where to start? She drew the letter and forms from her bag. In her office, sitting in her chair in front of her computer she could be detached, professional. It was simply one more formal Forensic Investigation to sort out, information from which she could derive an answer.

Crystal opened a database on her screen and set up an action record; contact, date, issue, comments, resolved, critical info. Control and organization were soothing.

Populating the data fields was a little more difficult. The only contacts in all of the paperwork were the Republic of Ireland, Office of the Minister of Justice and Equity, Mr. C.V. Kosshi from the Department of State, and one Inspector Ethan MacEnery. The Inspector's signature was on the form that requested Brystal's identification certification from the Office of the Minister of Justice and Equity.

If the Irish officials knew who she was, why in the heck did Crystal have to go there and identify her sister's… her sister? Crystal pounded the wireless mouse on the tabletop. *Question* did a little happy dance across her keyboard. It was deriving way too much pleasure from its own existence.

"Tisk, tisk. Break mouse, no cookie after dinner." Chance leaned against the door jamb; his hands casually tucked in his pockets.

"I am one of the country's top forensic accountants and I am at a loss as to where to begin." Crystal waved her mouse at him.

"Where you don't begin is by breaking your computer. I can help if you want." He took his usual chair by the window and purposefully affected a casual slouch.

"I thought I could handle this but… now, I… I just don't know." Crystal picked up the documents on her desk and shuffled through them again.

"Well, I checked online, and you don't need a visa so why don't we book you a ticket and a rental…"

Crystal interrupted Chance, "No. I mean yes. Not no to the ticket, but I mean... Oh for heaven's sake, Chance, I don't know what I mean. This is not like me at all." She put her head in her hands and leaned her elbows on the desktop.

Question snuck between her elbows and tapped on her heart. "I have to know what happened, ergo; I have to go. Don't I?" She looked across at Chance.

"That would be the way I see it, kiddo. Tell ya what, I'll take care of the arrangements on this side of the pond, and you can let me know what you need from the other side." He stood to leave. "Actually, Alana will love helping. She likes to travel and rallies for a good cause. She'll find the best accommodations to be sure."

Crystal closed her eyes and sat back in her chair trying to find a socially acceptable way to refuse Chance's help. Her brain was spinning, and nothing came to mind. Opening her eyes Crystal found herself sitting alone in her office.

Uh oh...

Too late.

Now she was really committed and there was no turning back. If Alana was on track, there would be no choice. The woman lived to shop. And she was as good at shopping as Crystal was at chasing down money.

Quickly Crystal opened a Word doc and began making a list of things she would need to take with her and possible contacts she would need to make. After fifteen minutes, the page contained three items: clothing, money, passport. Her passport had been opened once when Crystal received the small blue book in the mail. It was a pathetic place to begin but it was a beginning. She added driver's license as an afterthought.

When was the last time she had used that?

Crystal clicked SAVE and pulled her security card shutting the system down for the night. "Time to go, Sandra. I've had enough for one day." She grabbed her jacket and briefcase and headed for the door. "I've had enough for a lifetime."

Question tried to catch a handhold before the door slammed in its face, but it was left behind, banging on the office door.

By the purse, briefcase and tennis shoes on her feet, Sandra was ready to leave at the slightest notice. "You'll get through this, Crystal. Everyone does. Just take it one step at a time and remember... you have people who can help if you need it.'

They walked in companionable silence to the elevator and then down to the lobby. At the front door, Sandra paused. "You *will* be okay, right?"

Much to her own amazement and to Sandra's as well, Crystal impulsively hugged her assistant. It was a quick hug. Not warm and cozy, or anything like that. It was a quick clench and release.

"I will. Not to worry." With an apologetic smile Crystal spun and walked away leaving Sandra standing in front of the building with her mouth open. Crystal didn't look back but walked as fast as would seem polite, her mind pummeled with emotions she was just beginning to evaluate.

Why did she do that? She'd never hugged anyone outside her family.

Her family.

What was that now?

Tears unexpectedly dribbled down her cheeks and her steps slowed. At the corner of the block Crystal leaned against the light pole and watched people cross in front of her. Everyone was going home to their families, to their friends or significant others.

The light changed and cars raced by headed home, or to rendezvous with children, or join the hyperactive mêlée at any of a hundred clubs or parties. She could smell the exhaust and hear the noise, but somehow she stood in a world apart. She had none of that, no children, no family, no rendezvous. How had her life become unacceptable since just last night when everything was under control and carefully constructed the way she liked it?

She liked it.

She liked her life.

It was under control and planned.

She liked that.

A man carrying a huge bag from a bedding store bumped past her.

"Sorry, ma'am." He hurried on by, going home with new linens. Something special. Maybe a surprise for his girlfriend or wife? Or possibly a new cover for his child?

Crystal stepped into the street and put one foot in front of the other. Like a robot, she followed the same route to her building that she did every day. Like a robot she unlocked her apartment, placed her briefcase on the small bench near the door, hung her coat on the hook in the hall and set her purse on the counter in the kitchen.

Outside of her job she was a robot, an automaton without new bedding, without rendezvous at clubs... and now without family. But wasn't that what she had always wanted? Felt comfortable with?

The concept of isolation, both social and physical, crashed over her like a giant tidal wave, a tsunami of historic proportions drowning her in an emotional wave of despair.

Crystal stood in the middle of her kitchen and burst into tears. Unrestrained, she cried as much for her sister as for herself. She cried until she could cry no more and sank to the floor in exhaustion. She lay on the cold tile feeling the aching chill fill her soul and let her desperation flow in place of tears.

What was there left in the world for her? The only answer she could come up with was "a job". Was that enough to live for?

It was yesterday. But today...

Would it make her want to get out of bed every morning, go to her office and face endless searches for the greed that fueled some of the most despicable elements in society?

It did yesterday.

The doorbell rang interrupting her downward mental spiral, but she ignored the sound. No one ever came to her place. She was not expecting a delivery.

It rang again.

Twice.

Crystal covered her face and curled into a ball.

"Crystal?" A recognizable, but muffled voice crept through the door and pulled her fingers from her face. "Crystal, it's me, Chance."

Crystal groaned and clawed her way up a cupboard to stand

wobbly against the counter. She knew he would not go away until he saw she was okay, especially after this morning's little episode.

"Just a minute, Chance." She ran for the bathroom and cold water. The face she saw in the mirror would not be fixed by a few splashes of cold water that was for sure.

Giving up she returned to the living room and unbolted the door. "Come in. Sorry, I'm not really ready for company."

"That's good because I'm not company. I'm the delivery boy this evening." He laid a folder of tickets and papers on the dining room table, pulled out a chair and promptly sat down. "Courtesy of Alana." He used his index finger to push the pile toward Crystal.

"Oh God. Tickets?" She visibly paled and tucked her hands behind her back.

"Yep. But not just any tickets, first class tickets from New York's LaGuardia to Shannon, Ireland, rental car reservations, a hotel reservation for your first night and detailed maps of the entire country, with the best of shopping opportunities marked in hot pink, if I know my wife." Chance tapped the pile. "Alana is efficient at traveling if she is anything. And fast."

"Oh Chance, I don't know..." Crystal stuttered.

"Uh, Uh, Uh. If I have to send her with you, I will. In fact, that might be a... nah, not even you deserve that! And it won't be a pretty sight unless there is shopping and Internet on board the plane." Chance chuckled then shook his head.

"But I haven't decided..."

Chance chuckled again, this time it sounded more like a half-strangled gasp for air. "Ah honey, Alana never gives me a choice either."

"Yes but..."

"She doesn't take buts, or no's, or even questioning looks. Trust me on that." Crystal had met Alana many times and knew of what Chance spoke. She had to laugh.

Sinking into a chair across the table, Crystal slowly walked her fingers across the marble and drew the documents to her with care. "I guess I go to Ireland then."

Opening the folder, her itinerary lay folded on top of the e-tickets. Immediately Crystal gasped. "Tomorrow? I can't..."

"Sure you can. Pack a few things then buy whatever you need there. I'm sure they have stores in Ireland. In fact, if you need anything, text Alana. She was there about two years ago. She still gushes about the tartans she found and the wool sweaters."

"But I don't..."

"Crystal, you just deposited a half of a million dollars to your personal account in the form of one hell-of-a bonus. You can afford whatever it is you can't pack between tonight and eight-thirty AM when a town car will pick you up and transport you to the airport."

"She really does think of everything, doesn't she?" Crystal thumbed through the documents, all in her name.

"Oh, you have no idea! Now what can I do to help?"

Crystal immediately took offense at Chance's outright laugh.

"I've never seen a more blank look on anyone in all my years." His chuckle followed him right out the door, leaving Crystal rushing into the bedroom to find the key to her storage unit in the basement. She couldn't go to Ireland without a suitcase. A tan, plaid box of a suitcase her mother had gone off to college with, in 1964.

CHAPTER 5

Five little speckled frogs,
Sitting on a hollow log,
Eating some most delicious bugs.
Yum, Yum!
One jumped in the pool,
Where it was nice and cool.
It is never smart to jump without looking...

Her seat pressed too tightly around her body and she squirmed for the hundred thousandth time.

"Not fond of flying, miss?" In the seat next to her, one of the tallest men she'd ever seen in person tried to move his legs. "I can feel your pain." He winced as one knee crunched against the seat in front.

"No, it's not the flying, it's the seat. I hate feeling closed in." Crystal had been in the air for forty minutes and wanted to crawl out of her skin and ride on the wing in the open air.

The man sneered. "You could always change with someone in the back. Maybe you'd like one of those seats better."

Crystal inched closer to the window... away from the man, his long legs, and his nasty attitude. "Sorry." She turned her face to the glass and closed her eyes, thinking about the little blue pill in her purse, a gift from Alana who, amazingly enough, had accompanied her to the airport in the back of the luxurious black town car.

No. She did not need drugs.

She fidgeted again and re-crossed her legs bumping the over-sized man next to her.

"Miss, please. It's a long flight and I need to work." His face wore a permanent frown.

Crystal mumbled her apology and tried to melt into the curved plastic wall of the plane.

She did not need drugs... but at the moment she wanted them.

"Ma'am, could I get a bottle of water?" Crystal motioned to the flight attendant.

"Of course, just a moment." The perky blonde flight attendant returned with a miniature bottle of Evian. "Anything else I can help you with?"

"Please make sure I wake up in Shannon, okay?" Crystal opened her palm to show the pill she had taken from her purse.

"Of course. Enjoy your nap. We still have six and a half hours to go." The flight attendant smiled sweetly and handed Crystal a red fleece blanket wrapped in plastic.

"Thank you so much." Crystal tore into the plastic and wrapped the blanket around her.

"My pleasure. Enjoy. Don't worry, I'll wake you when we start our descent."

The big man snorted and mumbled under his breath. "Finally."

Crystal popped the pill into her mouth and drained the small water bottle in three gulps. "Finally," she said out loud, and settled against the window as far from the man as she could get.

She felt the coolness of the wall against her cheek and tried to think about being anywhere else but where she was. Her mind melted into the wind outside the plane and fluttered off into some secret billowing cloud. She was enveloped in the soft white nothingness and floated between moist molecules of pure oxygen. They surrounded her and massaged her skin with their soothing droplets. Her head lolled and found a substantial cloud and leaned against it in total relaxation, safe, secure. Crystal thought she would stay there forever, just existing with no worries or cares.

"Miss? Miss Traynor? We're descending near Shannon. Time to wake up and prepare for landing. Could you put your seat up for me, please?" It was the perky blonde, but she was way too early. Crystal had just fallen asleep.

"I just put my head down. We can't be here already." Crystal stretched from under the blanket and looked out the window.

"Yes, ma'am. You had a nice nap." The flight attendant smiled sweetly just like she had moments ago and handed Crystal a damp rolled washcloth. It was hot. "Careful, they're very warm. A nice end to a long flight."

"Long? More like a drugged flight." Crystal had forgotten the nasty man next to her. "Quite a way to fly, literally and figuratively." He shifted and the sneer returned to his ugly face.

"Mr. Carson, if you need to use the facilities, I suggest you do so now. We will be locking the door for landing soon." The flight attendant's perkiness and smile were gone. Apparently, Crystal's short flight had been a little longer for Mr. Carson and the flight attendant.

"Yeah. Right. I better take a piss. Changing altitudes always makes me want to pee like a racehorse." He seemed quite at home announcing his biological needs to the entire first-class section of the place as he struggled to stand and bashed his head against the luggage compartment. "Damn! Why can't airplanes be a decent size."

As Mr. Carson limped to the toilet, ducking the exit sign, the flight attendant winked at Crystal and whispered, "Knock yourself out, sir."

The young couple sitting in front of Crystal chuckled. The lady cracked, "And there goes one heck of a nice ogre. He's just not green and sweet like Shrek."

Everyone within hearing range either chuckled or grinned. Crystal wondered what she had slept through, just as the plane's intercom chimed signaling the ten-thousand-foot mark.

"Gotta go do the "close up shop" announcement. Will you be alright?" The perkiness was back, along with the woman's sweet smile.

"I'm awake now. Thanks. And thanks for reminding the racehorse to check out the facilities." Crystal placed her used washcloth on the flight attendant's tray. "That felt wonderful."

The flight attendant returned to her station near the door and began her announcement as Mr. Carson exited the restroom. One step into the isle and everyone in the plane heard his foul expletive as his forehead impacted the hanging exit sign with a resounding crunch. Half of the first-class passengers murmured, "knock yourself out" and Crystal had to cover her mouth to hide her grin.

Carson crumpled himself into the seat, rubbing his head where a red welt was rapidly appearing. "I suppose you think that was funny." He growled at Crystal.

"Hey buddy," a voice from a couple seats back was easily heard by all, "does Trans Atlantic charge you for breaking their planes?"

"Funny guy." Carson responded blackly. He was still rubbing his head.

The exit sign was hanging by a couple stretched screws and no longer glowing orange.

Crystal thought the better of the situation and felt for the guy who was, like she herself, obviously living in a world where he didn't fit. "Are you okay?"

"Why the hell do you care?" The cross question struck her like a slap in the face.

"You have a point, Mr. Carson." Crystal turned her face to the window and watched the lights of Shannon draw nearer.

Shannon, Ireland.

A strange city in a strange country.

Strange.

Uncomfortable.

Different.

All of the descriptors she hated. Goose bumps rose on her arms and those pesky knots that always hid near the edges of her stomach did a little do-see-do and danced to the center.

No! She suppressed the nausea and held her breath as the lights of the runway appeared and she felt the wheels jerk on the tarmac.

Down.

The plane taxied for what seemed to be several miles and finally pulled to a stop at the gate.

Shannon, Ireland.

She was in Shannon, Ireland.

"Miss Traynor, your jacket?" The flight attendant was handing her the light jacket that had been hung up at the beginning of the flight. First class had its perks.

"Thank you. Do you know where I claim my luggage?"

The flight attendant handed her an immigration form. "You were asleep when everyone filled this out. It's easy. Just follow the signs to Immigration to check in, then to baggage to claim your luggage, through the security check and then out the door. It's pretty much a cattle shoot, so just follow the herd. Have your passport handy. They'll scan it and stamp the form. Keep the stamped form in your passport and use it when you leave. Have a great trip and enjoy the beauty of Ireland, whether it's vacation or business."

With the form was a coupon for one hundred dollars off Crystal's next flight and a small tourist coupon book for Shannon and the surrounding counties. "What?"

"Just our little way of saying thanks." The blonde smiled and nodded after Carson as he deplaned. "For putting up with Mr. Personality."

"Wow. Nice but I slept through it all."

"We like to keep our first-class passengers happy and returning. That's all. Have a great visit and we hope to see you again soon." The flight attendant handed Crystal her bag and blocked traffic so she could depart.

"Thanks again. And you will... see me again soon. My business won't take long." Crystal waved her passport and form in goodbye, but the flight attendant had already turned to help an elderly man get his luggage from the compartment overhead. Always with a cheerful smile and a helping hand.

Halfway down the jet-way it hit her. No, her business wouldn't take much time. How difficult was it to identify her sister and make arrangements for the bod… remains to be shipped home? How long did that take?

She paused and leaned against the railing for a moment hanging her head.

"Miss, are you okay?" The man who had yelled at Carson was behind her.

"Yes. Yes, I am fine, just a little nausea. I'll be alright in a moment." Crystal kept her eyes on the rug but straightened and walked up the jet-way to the terminal.

Where was Immigration?

Where was the baggage area?

She stared at the illuminated signs as if she could not read plain English. Behind her she heard the same voice.

"Immigration is this way. Just follow the rest of us." The gentleman laughed and motioned with his briefcase down the corridor. "The yellow line leads to Immigration and the red line leads Baggage Claim and then to freedom. Yellow then red." He walked beside her companionably. "Never been to Shannon before?"

"No. This is my first trip. To anywhere actually. Thanks for the directions." She tried to smile but couldn't quite form the emotion.

"Business or pleasure?" He smiled looking hopeful.

Hopeful? Was he trying to pick her up? She studied his expression and body language. A pickup? Just friendly chit-chat? Her social filter was back in the States. Crystal had no idea so she answered his question honestly.

"Neither. I'm here to identify my sister's body. She was murdered in a village called Dingle." It was too much information, but her mouth just tore off its duct tape and rambled on.

"Oh my God. I'm so sorry. I didn't mean to pry into your personal business."

Obviously, honesty was a bad choice.

That was something Crystal never understood about people and communication.

All of a sudden the man was pointing to the carousel. "Here we are, and I believe I see my kiosk. So sorry about your sister. Have a, have a..." He looked totally at a loss as to how to end the conversation quickly, without letting Crystal feel like he was doing a break-and-run. "Have a successful trip." He winced at his own dry comment. Making a motion that passed for a quick wave goodbye, he trotted for the Citizens line as quickly as looked appropriate.

Crystal shook her head at her unrestrained comment and scanned the directing signs. All of the Non-citizen lines were long with all kinds of people waiting to be processed. Crystal chose the line that seemed to contain single individuals instead of those with families and traveling groups. It still seemed to take forever to pass through Immigration. When it was her turn she stood at the end of the yellow line and wasn't quite sure of the protocol for approaching the stern Garda in the kiosk. Standing there completely lost, the Garda finally called out "Next." in an impatient voice and Crystal move to the desk.

"Passport?" He frowned like she should know what to do. "Business or pleasure, Miss Traynor?" Her name came out more like Try-na. Crystal opted for a little less honesty this time.

"Pleasure."

"How long will you be staying with us, Miss?"

Crystal said the first thing that came to her mind. "A week."

The officer swiped her passport under the scanner, glanced up and stamped her immigration form. "Have a nice holiday, Miss Try-na." He pointed toward the exit as he waved at the next in line.

Emotionless, efficient, and just fine with Crystal.

The red line took her to a crowded baggage area and the next long line. She scanned the carousel for her suitcase trying to remain free of the bumping and milling crowd. After several minutes of passing luggage she spied her battered old case taped together and sitting on the carpet near the open door, with a pair of skis wrapped in plastic and a kennel that contained two tiny barking Chihuahuas.

Taped together?

The plaid covering was intact but one rusty hinge had given away and one of the locks was completely missing. A good dozen wraps of strapping tape encircled the case and a part of one blouse hung out the side.

Hand to her mouth, Crystal approached her suitcase with care.

"This piece of shit yours?" Carson stood a few feet away laughing. "Hey, maybe you can get a replacement out of the airline, but if I were you, by the looks of that thing, I wouldn't bother to ask."

She gave him what she thought was a scathing look and grabbed the leather handle which promptly gave way.

"Holy shit lady, where'd you come up with that antique? The Goodwill?" He sauntered off, rolling his shiny silver hard side alongside him.

"What a jerk." The young couple who'd sat in front of Crystal on the plane stood close. "Mark, help her. I'll get our stuff."

"Of course, I'm Mark Johnson. That's my wife of three days. We're newlyweds." His huge grin was a dead give-away as he motioned toward the beautiful young woman who winked back. "Let me help you." He grabbed her suitcase, hoisted it onto his shoulder, hanging blouse and all, and hefted it over to where rolling carts stood waiting for bags.

"Here ya go." He set it gently on the cart for her. "I don't think the airline will do anything about fixing or replacing your suitcase, but you could try asking. It's awfully old but a great color." He smiled sheepishly then trotted off after his bride with a wave.

Yellow line to red line, red line to freedom. This day was going downhill rapidly. Crystal piled her jacket, bag, and purse on top of the abused suitcase and pushed the cart down the red line. Red line to freedom. The words echoed in her mind.

Freedom?

What was freedom?

Crystal had never known freedom, only control.

Brystal knew freedom and she was dead.

She entered the immigration security line that said *FOREIGNERS* in big red letters. She was a foreigner? Of course, this was Ireland, the country that killed her sister. She was not only a foreigner, but an alone and afraid foreigner.

With a broken suitcase.

"Passport please." The officer watched her with beady eyes. She quickly handed her passport and form to the man.

"Business or pleasure?" He scanned her form but did not look up as he spoke.

Crystal locked her social filter in place. "Pleasure, sir."

"Anything to declare?" He glanced at her form looking for... what? She had no idea; she'd never been out of her own country. Then she caught the look on his face when he saw her case. It was enough for him.

"No, sir." Her tone was flat, and she kept her eyes down.

"Welcome to Ireland. Next." The officer shoved her form back at her and looked at the next person in line.

"Thanks." Crystal mumbled as she shoved her passport into her bag and pushed her cart through the exit to freedom.

Freedom?

Really?

Crystal glanced around looking for the rental car agency. Alana had indicated the company office was at the airport and all she would have to do is find the agent and pick up the car. Her reservation was paid for.

She looked up the terminal... then down. Nothing. What she did see was an information booth and a kiosk for the Bureau of Change. Information was what she needed. Pushing her cart to the booth, she pulled the folder Alana had organized and given her before she left from her bag and ruffled through the papers.

"What can I be helpin' ya with, my dear?" Startled, Crystal dropped her folder scattering papers for several feet around her.

"Oh no," she wailed quietly scouring the terminal exit to see if she had drawn unwanted attention to herself. A few people meandered around the doors and some stood at a green counter. Above the counter a lit sign advertised Alamo and Europcar.

Son of a gun! She gathered her papers, apologized to the kiosk attendant, and scurried toward the counter dragging the cart which now boasted a loose stack of papers and an open folder. How could she have missed the sign?

"Next reservation." A tall man with flaming red hair called out. He looked directly at Crystal and waved her towards his position at the counter.

Fishing her reservation confirmation from beneath a MapQuest printout, she handed the paper to the man whose nametag read *Ollie*. "I have a reservation. I'm not sure what I need to give you for this." Crystal nearly threw the paper at the man. "Sorry, I just got off a plane." She fanned herself with a hand "I don't think I like flying."

Ollie chuckled. "Well, I hope ya like drivin' because we have a right top car for ya." From the wall behind him he pulled a key attached to an enormous key chain with a rubber tag that outlined the word ALAMO in hot orange.

"That's certainly inconspicuous." Crystal took the key, holding up the tag.

"We don't like our clients to lose their key, so we make it easily identifiable." He chuckled again. "May I see your license? You're from the States?"

Crystal handed her license to the man. "Yes, why?"

"Well now, mum, you may find drivin' here in our country a bit twitchy." Ollie waved to a young man who looked to be in his teens. "William, would ya take Mrs...." He glanced at the receipt, "Miss Trina out to the lot and show her where her car be stowed?"

Why couldn't they get her name right?

William jumped to and grabbed the cart handle. "Not a problem. I'll take your bags, ma'am."

Crystal caught the sliding papers before they hit the ground and trotted after William.

"If ya don't mind me askin', where ya from in the States?" William swerved around a blue car just missing the bumper by an inch with the loaded cart. Crystal prayed for her poor suitcase. She was sure it would not survive another bump or crunch.

"New York. The city."

William shoved the cart over a curb and continued on toward a line of what looked like toy cars. "You drive there? What kind of car would ya be havin' then?"

"Oh, I don't have a car. I live in the city and work a few blocks from my building."

William stopped abruptly and Crystal stumbled to avoid running into the young man. "You don't drive? You kin drive, right?" He looked at her skeptically.

"Of course. I have a license and I used to drive before I moved to New York." She looked at the number hand-written on the back of the tag. "This is my *car?*"

Crystal pointed to the immensely tiny car behind which they stood. The bumper was at ankle level and she could see over the top to the next row of cars.

William opened the hatch and stared at the trunk area scratching his head. "This little beauty' d be a Twingo Elf. Great car. Easy parkin'." He gingerly picked up her suitcase and set it in the empty well.

Then he removed it and repositioned the thing.

Removing it again and rotating the case, he set it in the trunk on its side.

"No good. Ma'am, I don't think this will fit. I'll have to put the seat down." He reached forward, pulled a strap, and watched as the seat back fell forward to lay flat against the front seat. With a stout shove, the suitcase slid into the back. William slammed the hatch. "There ya go. Snug as a kitten curled in a basket of pansies." He peered through the back window. "Ya might consider shoppin' for a new bag, ma'am. I've me doubts about that one."

"It'll be fine. Thanks for your help. It sure is a small car." Crystal considered fishing in her purse for a tip.

"You'll be glad for that right soon. So ya know, ma'am, we don't drive in Ireland like ya do in the States, right?"

"What do you mean? Are drivers here crazy, like lane hogs or something? Are the rules the same?" Crystal's stomach began to tighten. She had heard Chance talk about the berserk drivers in Asia from his last trip.

"Well now, we drive on the opposite side as the States. Watch out for the round-abouts, we call them roundies. And," he walked off a bit then paused, "watch for the finger."

"What? People here flip off Americans or something?" Crystal was beginning to dislike Ireland and she'd only been on Irish soil for about an hour.

The young man saluted with his index finger, shook his head, and mumbled something about having bought insurance as he strolled toward the office.

"Well Crystal Traynor, here we go." She tossed her light bag on the passenger seat, slid her purse on the floor and attempted to get into the car, soundly bashing both knees before she ever got close to the seat. Standing on the pavement once more, she bent to slide the seat backwards and found the steering wheel... gone!

Gone?

Nope.

Just on the wrong side of the car.

Holy shit! It took several minutes to process the fact that not only did citizens of Ireland drive on the wrong side of the road, but their cars had steering wheels on the wrong side as well. She felt her brain seize in a painful spasm of disbelief that set sparks to flying behind her eyes. She held on to the car door and took deep breaths until the sensation passed.

Now what? Her small bag was neatly tucked behind the wheel and her purse lay on the brake pedal. Removing them was the first step.

That accomplished, Crystal slid the driver's seat backward as far as it would go until it could move no further and pressed on her suitcase with a crunching noise. She would definitely have to get a new bag before leaving Ireland.

The second attempt at cramming herself into the space allotted for a midget, correction, leprechaun, was successful and she sat studying the dash and steering wheel. And the stick shift...

Stick shift?

Crystal had never driven a car with a manual transmission. She had no clue they were even still made.

"Okay, Crystal Traynor, you can do this. There have to be directions somewhere. I am the leading forensic auditor in the most powerful country in the world. I will not be defeated by a Tingle Elf."

"That's Twingo Elf, mum. William said you might be needin' a spot of help." Ollie smiled benevolently and proceeded to explain everything to Crystal with a soft lilt that had an incredible calming effect on her tattered nerves.

An hour later and completely behind schedule, she was practicing shifting while driving around the parking lot of Shannon's Alamo car rental service with a map of the area and her route drawn in heavy felt marker. On the fourth circle of the lot, the agent waved her toward the exit and crossed himself… twice.

It was just before noon and her white knuckles gleamed on the wheel in the sunshine. She was on her way.

God help her.

God help the people on the road with her.

The folder of directions lay open in the left seat and the rental agent had taped his scrawled map to the dash behind the steering wheel. She could see it without taking her eyes off the road. Thank God because up ahead was her first round-about, roundie, whatever.

"Holy crap! Which way do I…"? Crystal stopped as cars whizzed by her beeping their silly little horns. Looking to the right she tentatively pulled out and immediately slammed on the breaks stalling the engine as a bus flew by from the left.

"Oh God, oh God, oh God! I can't do this." She pushed her forehead to the wheel shaking from head to toe. Horns behind her began to sound as cars pulled around. She didn't need to look up to know the kinds of signals she was getting.

Taking a very deep breath, she depressed the left pedal and turned the key. The engine roared to life as she wiggled the stick shift trying to find first gear with her left hand. As it fell into place, she let the clutch out very slowly with one foot and added gas with the other. The roaring engine engaged, and she was moving forward with less than a smooth motion, but she was going forward, right into the roundie and traffic.

On the fourth trip around the circle she found the correct exit, cut off a yellow Saab, then sped down the road in second gear. Sweat trickled down her back and Crystal finally began to breathe again. Her fingers were welded to the wheel and her left foot was poised for a gear change. She couldn't stay in second forever.

Second was straight back but the car jerked as if it would self-destruct for a few seconds. Third was much easier but she was headed for another roundie. Her map showed a straight line, so Crystal made a command decision, said a prayer, and sped right through looking straight ahead.

"American behind the wheel, watch out!" she yelled out the window. It did no good at all, but she felt better and shifted into fourth gear as horns beeped in all directions. How had her sister managed driving in this crazy place? Crystal laughed at her own mental question. Brystal was as wild and crazy as this land and its roads. They probably got along just fine.

An hour down the road Crystal passed a sign that indicated Galway was ahead.

Galway?

Oh for Pete's sake! She was going north, not south toward Limerick and the Dingle Peninsula.

CHAPTER 6

Six marbles rolling down a hill,
Let's follow them,
It will be a thrill.
... and just where will they lead to, and what kind of thrill?

After several minutes studying the directions stuck to her dash, Crystal pulled back onto the road and headed in the correct direction... back to Shannon and more roundies. Her plane had landed at ten forty-five in the morning and now it was almost eleven at night and dark as the inside of a leprechaun's cave with no gold. She'd stopped for lunch somewhere and gotten lost a total of five times.

Her reservation was for a house only ten or eleven miles south of Shannon, and on the way to this place called Dingle, via the town of Limerick. The Irish names floated around in her head as she drove and played with their pronunciation.

"I certainly know what a limerick is, but what the heck could a dingle be?" She spoke to her rearview mirror and nervously laughed at herself. This travel thing was all new to her and she was on shaky ground. Her reflection looked weary and well worn. Her eyes showed puffy red rims and she had chewed the skin from the left side of her lower lip. "I should of..."

Horns blasted and a set of on-coming headlights reminded her to keep on the left side of the road. "Holy..." Crystal took a deep breath and focused on the road; the right side which was really the left side... which was... "Oh, crap."

Crystal pulled over to the side of the road again and consulted her scribbled directions. She'd turned onto E20 but the sign in front of her said N18. On her rent-a-car map it said both numbers equidistant apart. What? The country couldn't decide so they gave the road two different numbers.

"That figures. After all, Ireland is the home of Guinness and something called black pudding which is really a kind of sausage." Talking to herself always made things better in her book, so on the conversation went in a somewhat affected British accent, even though she was an American in Ireland. "E20 to N18 to M20 to Patrickswell and on to Adare where me lady may lay her head for the night, or maybe the week." A quick lane shift avoided the on-coming headlights once again as she drove into the night, second gear whining away in her miniature vehicle.

About ten miles from downtown Limerick, the village of Patrickswell slept as a lone American driver crawled through the tight main street and on toward Adare and her waiting hotel room. She still thought in miles even though the sign clearly showed km for kilometers. Her mind simply converted automatically multiplying each kilometer by zero point six two one three seven one nine two.

Simple.

For a genius.

Remarkably simple for Crystal.

A softly lit sign ahead read, *Welcome to Adare, Wedding Capital of Ireland. Established 1202 AD.* Crystal snorted, "Thank heavens they added the AD, or I never would have known." She checked her directions again. "Take a left on first road after crossing the River Maigue.

Follow it around to the Manor House. Easy to find." The *easy to find* was underlined twice.

So, it was easy to find, huh? What kind of house was this? An address would have helped. Maybe a color, or left-right side of the road? Crystal began to sweat. What if she missed the house? What if...

"Holy crap!" Lit up like a Christmas tree loomed an amazing structure the size of Sleeping Beauty's Castle at Disneyland, only more beautiful and even more spectacular. Although it was almost midnight and she was tired enough to sleep right there at her wheel, Crystal stopped in the middle of the road to gawk.

The gardens were lit with soft subtle green light casting a fairy tale glow to the sculpted trees and bushes in the massive garden that led to the castle entrance. The manicured lawns looked like emerald velvet. "A house? Really Alana? You booked me a castle? Wait till I tell Chance." She tested first gear and crept forward. "Wait until his credit card company tells him."

At that gleeful thought she found second gear, whined up to the front entrance and dumped the clutch. The car died with a loud crunch and a screechy lurch. The doorman winced but stepped forward to open Crystal's door, moving just in time to avoid being struck by that same flying door. Obviously, Crystal was not used to having car doors opened for her.

"Oh, sorry." She kept her eyes on the man's expertly shined boots.

"Mum, please to be welcomed to the Adare Manor House. The clerk can be found awaitin' your check-in. Your company called to alert us to your late arrival." He stepped to the back of the car. "May I?"

"May you what?" Crystal was confused for a moment. No one had ever carried her luggage before. She'd never been anywhere to have her luggage carried before. "Oh, of course." Her brain turned on, then her skin turned a lovely shade of red. "Um, it broke at the airport." She turned the key in the trunk lid and pointed to her destroyed bag. "I can get it."

"That will not be necessary, mum. I'll be most careful with your handsome trunk." He rolled a brass luggage rack up to the car. "I'll deliver it to your room as well. Please be assured we here at the Manor House take extra special care of our guests." He winked at the befuddled American woman. "And our guests take extremely good care of us."

"Thanks then." Crystal grabbed her purse from the front seat and turned toward the ornate doors.

"Ah, mum?" The doorman stood with his hand out.

"Yes, of course." Crystal hiked her knee up and balanced her purse attempting to unzip the large bag in search of a tip. She only had American money and hoped it would do. How much a tip should be in Ireland she had no idea.

"Ah... no mum. Your keys, please. I'll park the car for you."

Completely embarrassed and feeling like the village idiot, she blushed even more fumbling with her keys. Much to her horror, she clumsily dropped the keys at his feet. "Ah jeeze. Sorry. I..." She bent to retrieve the keys at the exact same time the doorman did. With the expected result. The keys remained on the stones as their heads met with a resounding thud.

"I am so sorry. I..." Crystal stood and rubbed her head. She couldn't think of anything more to say so she stood there... rubbing her head and praying she would turn to stone. They could place her in that beautiful garden, and she would never have to embarrass herself again.

"My fault entirely, mum. May I suggest you check in and get a good night's rest. Things will look better in the morn." He motioned toward the entry before bending to pick up the keys. However not before looking twice at the woman to clear the way.

"I am exhausted and so sorry. Please accept my apology..." Crystal was rooted to the spot.

Somehow the doorman knew exactly what to do. He motioned toward the door. Circled her to open it before she could make another ungainly mistake and ushered her inside. "Thank you." She whispered and concentrated on making it the twenty feet to the counter without destroying any of the exquisite furnishings and antique décor.

A young woman in a starched white blouse and a gold name tag stood behind an ornately carved counter. A diamond pattern carved deep into the grain circled small intricately designed bouquets of wildflowers and clover.

Five, ten, fifteen…

No! Her mind screamed within itself. No numbers. It was too dangerous, and she was too tired to fight her way back.

"Mum?" Sabine murmured softly. It was enough.

"Crystal Traynor. I have a room here for the night. I think." Crystal pulled a confirmation record from Alana's previously organized folder. "She told me it was in a house. A manor house." Crystal gazed around the room in awe of the lobby.

The young woman gently took the paper from Crystal's hand. "Yes, mum. 'Tis the Adare Manor House. And this would be yer reservation. Welcome." Her soft lilt washed over Crystal's frayed nerves like a soothing balm. For the first time since she had stepped out of her apartment in faraway New York, Crystal took a deep cleansing breath and began to relax. "If you would, mum, sign here."

It was a short-lived relaxation.

Crystal took the form and almost choked. Her reservation was for the Caroline Room for one night. For a total of…five hundred and eighty Euros! "Holy…" She just barely resisted using the crap word in front of such a young and clearly composed woman. Her mind clicked and she began to breathe again. What was Alana thinking?

Seven hundred forty-four dollars and seventeen cents?

For one night?

"Ah… I think there has been a mistake. I wanted one room, not the entire castle." Crystal stared at the paper like it was a snake ready to strike.

The sweet Sabine took the form from Crystal's hand. "No, mum. No mistake. A Mrs. Alana Evans has booked and paid for yer reservation. She meant for this to be a wee surprise. I assume she was successful?" Sabine's serene smile held an impish flavor. She leaned across the counter. "And she was quite insistent on the room choice. Your friend has also included a morning facial and sea salt scrub for tomorrow in yer package. It is the most exquisite treatment after a long flight."

"I've never..." Crystal was at a loss for words. Alana paid for her room and some kind of beauty treatment?

"You'll be loving it five seconds through the door. Will there be anythin' else I can help you with, mum?" Sabine handed the form back to Crystal pointing to the signature line.

"No. Ah... thanks." Crystal scrawled her initials and handed the paper across the counter in a daze.

A scrub of some sort?

With salt?

Someone.... touching her?

With salt?

Crystal's mind spun out of control. Her knees locked. Her heart hammered inside her chest as if to beat its way out. Blood rushed past her ears and lights began to sparkle behind her eyes, and a black hole beckoned from somewhere near, drawing her away from the counter.

"Madame, you be exhausted. Please allow me." A kindly gray-haired woman appeared at her elbow speaking in low calm tones. "I'll take you to your room. Mrs. Evans is a dear friend of mine and she has asked me to see after you in this difficult time."

Crystal heard but did not comprehend. Nor did she have the ability to do anything but be led to her room by the old woman in deep burgundy velvet and antique lace. The woman's touch was soft and directing and Crystal let herself be directed. She was so close to the edge...

"Now I'll be helpin' you into bed, dear. When you wake in the morn, all will be well and bright. 'Tis the promise and blessin' of the Lady Caroline and her lovely chamber." The woman cooed as she undressed Crystal and slipped a voluminous nightdress over her head and shoulders. "And 'twill be God's only truth in the light of day. Just you wait and see."

Crystal heard the voice and felt the gentle touch, but could only sit while the world turned around her. The numbers were gone. Her fear was fading into the shadows of the night. She was bone tired and her eyelids felt like lead weights.

As her head hit the downy pillows, the woman began to hum a quaint Irish lullaby. Crystal's eyes closed. Didn't her mother used to sing that very song when she and her sister couldn't sleep?

Her sister?

Brystal.

She would see Brystal tomorrow and be sure to tell her of this woman and Lady Caroline's room.

Tomorrow.

Outside the massive doors that closed Lady Caroline's room from the rest of the manor, stood Sabine and Geoffrey, the doorman. "'Tis a looney, that one."

"Hush now, Geoffery O'Haillin. 'Tis a dead sister she's come to claim. Would that yer sorry soul be haulin' better straits if you'd be doin' the same."

"But did ya see her bags? Me da had one just the like. I'd be thinkin' we buried him with it."

Sabine punched Geoffery's arm and the two chuckled their way quietly back to the lobby. "She's me prayers on this night, to be sure. The sister was her twin. Her very likeness, if I'm to be believin' Mrs. Evans."

Geoffery sobered at her soft statement. He paused a moment and crossed himself before the stately portrait of the Lady Caroline Adare, wife of Windham Henry Quin, the 2nd Earl of Dunraven. The Adare Manor House was originally designed and constructed by Lord and Lady Dunraven back in the early eighteen hundreds. Her hand was evident in every corner of the colossal Tudor mansion. Even though the family no longer owned the property, Lady Caroline served as the de facto patron saint of the manor and the tutelary spirit of newly hired employees.

"Aye, Geoff." Sabine stood before the painting. "May the Lady intercede this night. But I'll be addin' me prayers along with yers."

"How did ya be knowin' all this about the lass?" The poignant moment dutifully met with prayers and homage to the Lady Caroline, Geoffrey's curiosity rose to the forefront.

"Mrs. Evans stayed a month with us last year. She fell in love with the stables... and I believe, the stableman. Very nice woman who wore her habit with pride."

"She was a nun?" The young man cocked his head like a Spaniel puppy attempting to understand his master.

"Nah, silly." She playfully punched Geoffery again. "A wee bit of a shopping habit. Come now, there's work to be done. Mrs. Gilcrest will take fine care of the lass. And Mrs. Evans will be back to see us come spring." She winked at the doorman and dragged him by the arm to the closetry to tidy up the night's bills. No one else was expected for the rest of the night and the security cameras would alert the staff if a car approached.

Mrs. Gilcrest sat in a wingback chair sipping a bottle of tonic water. Her charge lay still, sleeping peacefully in the mammoth four-poster bed beneath the watchful smiles of the angels above her. Alana Evans had contacted Binne Gilcrest early in the day to beg a favor. That favor now slept beneath the thick down comforter. In the month that Alana had stayed at the manor, she and Binne had formed a friendship. The resort manager was only too happy to keep a watchful eye on Alana's *quirky* friend. The fact that Alana planned another month-long visit in the spring had little to do with Binne's aid. One look at the American lass about to faint dead away and Binne's motherly instincts surfaced immediately. And to think the child was in Ireland to identify her dead twin. Such a shame. And so young.

Binne studied Crystal's face. The lass would be pretty enough if she'd smile and add a touch to her cheeks. Maybe unwind the massive braid that lay across her chest. Her thick chestnut could use some attention but all in all, the gel was a sweet picture against the white Battenburg lace pillow slips.

"Rest tired eyes a while. Sweet is thy baby's smile. Angels are guarding and they watch o'er thee. Sleep, sleep, grah mo chree. Here on your mamma's knee. Angels are guardin', and they watch o'er thee." Binne's lilting voice floated past the angels above and settled into Crystal's dreamy world.

A hint of a smile played across Crystal's lips as she murmured softly in her sleep.

"The birdeens sing a fluting song. They sing to thee the whole day long. Wee fairies dance o'er hill and dale. For very love of thee." Binne rose silently, placed a feather light kiss on Crystal's brow, then departed on fairy feet, her tonic water bottle in hand.

Tomorrow was another day, and she would be there to ease Crystal's way. Quirky or no, Binne took the lass to heart and prayed long into the night.

Crystal slept on, sweet dreams dancing through her mind, chasing away the cares and fears of the day.

CHAPTER 7

Facts are the basis for all science. Did you know...
• There are seven rows in the Periodic Table?
• Lady bugs usually have seven spots?
• There are seven basic musical notes?
• There are seven bones in the neck of most mammals...
...and they break oh so easily.

Crystal woke to sunshine streaming through the windows. It was bright and warm and inviting. She snuggled deeper beneath the down coverlet, cocooning in the enormous bed. She felt amazingly refreshed and awake...in Ireland!

Last night was a faraway memory slowly drowning in the black waters of oblivion. The weariness in her limbs was gone, leaving behind no deleterious effects. A sweet song played on and on incessantly in her brain and soon she began to hum along. Its hypnotic effect drawing joy deep into her soul.

Was there magic in this place? Or had she finally reached the end of her rope and...what... jumped?

Held on for dear life?

Let go of everything?

Everything let go of her?

There was no answer. Only a sweet melody, the sunshine, and a loud growling stomach.

"Up girl! It's time to eat and move on." Her heart wasn't in the moving on part, but her stomach was up for the eating part.

Crystal crawled out from under her luxurious coverings and sat delicately on the edge of the bed. The floor was covered in thick area rugs, and for the first time, she gazed about the room. "Holy crap!"

The Lady Caroline Room must have been the master bedroom in another era. The era of sumptuous grace and elegance. Beneath a leaded glass window lay a carved window seat covered with a padded tapestry woven in rich flowery patterns. In the stream of sunshine, split into rainbow colors by the beveled glass panes, a marble tea table with a wrought iron base shone bright and clean. Upon it gleamed a silver tea set, complete with tiny, crested sugar spoons and Royal Albert cups. A lace doily covered what looked to be some kind of fruity scone, and next to the plate was a butter crock.

"Score!" Crystal rubbed her noisy tummy and stood on the thick carpet. It was warm and soft on her feet. Crystal wiggled her toes, feeling the silky fur. Apparently, the castle floor still boasted its original stone floor, and the area rugs mitigated the cold. Like a small child playing the crack-in-the-sidewalk game, Crystal hopped from one rug to another, picking her way to the table in leaps and bounds. As she sat and prepared to break her first fast in Ireland, a soft knock preceded the entry of a quaint maid in a crisp blue and white uniform.

"Mum, I be Rachel MacAllister, yer handmaid fer the day." The woman popped a curtsey.

Crystal giggled, which was probably against appropriate protocol, but the maid was so cute and had such a charming accent. Then it struck her; what is a handmaid supposed to do in the year twenty-nineteen? "Ah, what is it you do for me?" Crystal was perplexed.

"I'll be helpin' ya to dress, bringing yer mornin' tea, doin' the laundry, and takin' ya where ye'd like to go about." Rachel popped another curtsey.

Crystal looked at her scone and tea. "This is a great breakfast, Miss...ah..."

"Ach nah, mistress. Breakin' yer fast be in the hall at ten. There be all manner of meats, white and black puddin', eggs, vegetables and potatoes, soda and brown bread for the soakage, tea, and juice. Aye, and we've coffee for the guests from the States, if you prefer." Another bob-curtsey punctuated the last of the menu.

Crystal's mouth dropped open and she thought she could detect a bit of a giggle from her hand-made-for-the-day. "Okay then... what do I call you?"

"Rachel'd be fine, mum." Another bob.

"Okay Rachel, I think I'll just sit here for a bit and wake up. I surely don't need help dressing." No one had dressed Crystal since she'd been about two. "But I do need to find a new suitcase. Mine got trashed on the flight over. Can you recommend a store nearby?"

"Me lady, Mrs. Gilchrest has taken the liberty..." Rachel opened the door a little wider and rolled a shiny navy-blue suitcase into the room by its chrome handle. "This should do. I can dispose of the damaged trunk, if ye be wantin'."

"Mrs. Gilchrest?" Crystal hadn't quite got to the remembering part of the previous night. She'd been so tired and confused...

"If'n its not to yer likin', I'll be happy to arrange for a..."

"No. No! It's wonderful. At least I won't have to drive around a lot looking for a luggage store or a Walmart." Crystal's stomach was done with procrastinating and she took a bite of the scone on her plate. "Oh my God! This is divine."

"I'll be leavin' ya to it then, mum. Just push the button on the bed table to summon me." Rachel curtsied again and left, closing the door with a resounding click this time.

Crystal sat there, gazing out the window and munching on her delicious scone. It was eight thirty AM and official breakfast wasn't until ten? What would she do until then? Somewhere in the back of her mind, she really wanted to try black pudding. Then, as miscellaneous bits of trivia floated across her over worked brain, she wondered why anyone would call sausage a pudding. It was an intriguing dichotomy she would hang around to see.

Next to the Royal Albert Country Roses teacup was a small pamphlet that included a welcome ticket and a schedule of services the resort provided. Didn't that front desk woman say something about a spa treatment? A facial? Salt scrub... oh God no!

Crystal had always had an aversion to being touched, even as a child. Whereas Brystal hugged everyone and cuddled up with complete strangers... who always ended up good friends in the end. Her smile was as bright and engaging as her arms and available to anyone. Crystal envied her sister's ability to meet people and make friends quickly and easily. Crystal was the cold, unattached one who kept her distance and saw lies behind every turn. She wasn't open and trusting like her identical twin, who grabbed life with enthusiasm and invited the entire world in. She was the reticent twin who planned everything and led a structured life. She hadn't led the exciting kind of life her sister had.

But then again, Crystal was alive and eating scones in a magnificent hotel room with a handmaid outside the door.

Brystal was alone on a morgue slab somewhere... She was the alone and dead twin.

Crystal wondered how much Alana had paid for the spa treatment that would never get used. It'd most assuredly come up when Chase checked his credit card bill. She cringed. She would have to pay him back, of course. Her mind focused on the recent addition to her bank account. Money wasn't the issue...

She rose and strolled to the bedside table, like the princess Chase had paid for. A slight touch of the buzzer and Rachel came through the door, bobbing as she approached. "Mum, what can I be doin' fer ye?"

"Rachel, how much is..." Crystal peered at the small type on the ticket, "an oatmeal and honey facial, and an Atlantic Sea Salt Body Scrub?" What was Alana thinking?

"Mum, spa costs are listed in the Caroline Adare World Class Spa and Salon at Dunraven Guide." She reached into the bookcase and drew forth a leather-bound album, placing it on the marble table next to the tea pot. "Will there be anything else? Can I show you to the spa, mum?"

"No, no! I was just wondering..." Crystal sat at the table and poured her second cup of tea, adding one cube of sugar to the deep red liquid.

"Alright then mum. I'll be helpin' with the breakfast now, so if ya be needin' a thin', just call the front desk with a zero on the phone pad." With another cute little bob, she was gone.

Crystal finished her scone, deep in thought. There would be sadness ahead, but she could spread a little joy along the way. She took a Dunraven envelope from the small drawer in the writing desk near the door, and wrote *Rachel* on the front in concise, even letters. Inserting the spa ticket, she placed the envelope on the tea tray and set to packing. She would need to be on the road right after breakfast and black pudding.

~

INSPECTOR MACENERY SAT at his desk watching the drizzle through his office window. He was dreading the coming arrival of the sister and formal identification of the murder victim in the county morgue. He hated tears. He detested histrionics and emotional outbursts. He'd had enough tears to last a lifetime when he'd buried his own wife and daughter. Mary Mae's mother had fainted and her sister, Tarrys, carried on so that Ethan thought she would collapse as well. Instead the woman accused him of being the reason behind her sister's death. She came at him with vengeance and a doubled fist, laying a punch to his chest.

It didn't hurt.

Nothing hurt after the first shovel of dirt dashed across the polished coffin that contained his heart and soul. And nothing could hurt more than the fact that Tarrys was right. The lives of his wife and daughter lay squarely on his shoulders. Tarrys just advertised the fact to everyone at the graveside service. Father O'Shea took the woman in hand, but the damage was done. Every man, woman and child in their village knew it was true.

Ethan rubbed a hand across his face finding it damp. Tears were just a sign of weakness. He wiped them away and grabbed his teacup. Some strong black tea would buoy up his spirits. "Damn rain!" He growled as he made his way to the break room, three doors down.

Standing next to the Garda at the front desk was his murder victim.

He dropped his cup and missed the shattering noise as it hit the tile.

"Ah, sir?" The desk Garda tried to grab the cup as it fell but missed. "Ah… I'll get this mess cleaned up." He looked from the Inspector to the wet, bedraggled woman by the counter. "This is Miss Traynor. Says she's got business with ye, Ethan." Garda Leroy disappeared around the corner in search of a broom and dustbin.

Ethan was frozen in place. He tried to move a foot, but it wouldn't obey his command. He tried to say something, but no words would come from between his lips. He tried to look away from the face he'd learned so intimately in the sterile morgue. The same face that glowed with life and beauty, stood looking back at him with a bit of a smirk.

Leroy was quick and returned with a hand broom and dustbin. He stooped to wrangle the broken china on the floor just as Crystal spoke. "I understand my sister's bo… remains must be identified. I am here to do just that." She exuded calm, matter-a-fact-ness as she tried to quell the knots in her stomach. It was a practiced response she'd perfected long ago.

The word sister hit Ethan like a bolt of lightning out of nowhere. He coughed to cover his awkward response, then smiled sheepishly. "Of course, lass. Of course." He coughed again.

Leroy ducked from under the Inspector and disappeared back around the corner from which he'd come, carrying the full dustbin.

"There is some paperwork that must be completed before…"

Ethan strangled on the last part of the sentence. He was in surreal land without a map or compass. The dead body in his morgue was alive and well and looking at his tie with an unreadable expression.

He checked his tie.

There was nothing amiss.

Crystal snorted uncharacteristically. "We are... were twins. You're not seeing a ghost, or a doppelganger, or whatever you want to call me."

Her voice cut through Ethan's thick skull and lodged in his language center.

Twins?

Identical twins?

It wasn't even a question, just a shock.

"Right-oh. This way Miss Traynor. Let's talk in my office." He led the way and Crystal followed. "I had no idea you and the... your sister are... were twins. I have to admit it was a bit of a shock... seeing you standing there after all of the pictures I've been going over in the past..." Ethan waved her into his office and pulled out a chair for her to sit down. He closed the open file on his desk a little too quickly. "I collected a lot of pictures of Brystal during my investigation and you are the spittin' image of your sister."

"That is the definition of identical twins, Mr.... what is your name?" Crystal kept her eyes on the little logo on his tie. Eye contact was too dangerous, and her emotions were too high. She swallowed.

"Oh, I am sorry." He stood and extended a hand across his desk. "Inspector Ethan MacEnery, at your service.

Crystal steeled herself for contact and reached out tentatively.

An astute student of body language, Ethan immediately recognized the girl wanted no physical contact with him, so he dropped his hand and sat back down before she decided to bolt and run from his office. He couldn't imagine how hard this must be for the lass. "Things are a bit different here in my country, so you'll have to bear with me. The republic requires..." Ethan looked up from his file. "My condolences on the loss... I mean..." He rubbed a hand across his tired features.

Without taking her eyes off of his tie, Crystal schooled her features and replied in a flat voice. "I understand, Inspector. I will do whatever needs to be done. I just want to take care of this business and go home."

Ethan studied the woman who sat across from him. The only real reference he had for any inkling of understanding was the pictures and interviews with Brystal's small tight group of friends in Dingle. According to everything he'd learned, the woman was overflowing with life. Extremely talented as a crystal cutter and well above the average pattern designer, each person he'd interviewed had commented on what a beautiful soul she was and how loving. Across his desk sat a shell of that person who could not even bring her eyes to meet his. He knew death of a loved one and grieving. This was not it.

Crystal clasped her hands in her lap and worked a hangnail. "What happened to my sister, Inspector?" Her blunt query caught Ethan off guard.

And there it was the question of the century.

How was he supposed to tell that same face he'd photographed in a pool of blood behind the An Droichead Beag, that someone had stolen her life in the most violent and disgusting manner? Then abandoned that beautiful soul on the stone steps next to a dumpster. How could he tell the victim what he didn't know? Ethan was walking on shaky ground with unsteady feet. He looked past Crystal at the rain pelting the window.

"I know this is difficult for you, Inspector." Crystal recognized the Inspector's reaction. She'd seen it many times when she and Brystal were kids. Someone would meet Brystal and fall under her magical spell... then meet Crystal and the confusion would begin... followed by the uncomfortable and embarrassing questions whispered behind her back.

What's wrong with your sister?

How are you two so different and yet identical?

Does she have to be so...weird?

"Excuse me? Difficult for me? No Madam. I can't imagine what you are going through or thinking right now." He tried not to stutter.

"I am thinking I'd like to know what happened to my sister." Crystal crossed her legs and re-crossed her hands in her lap. She finally raised her eyes to his lips. A dangerous move on her part, but necessary to get the full meaning of what he would say.

Either the still waters ran very deep with this woman, or she was the best actress Ethan had ever met. "There is no good way to say this, so forgive me if I am a bit blunt." He took a deep breath. "Unfortunately, your sister, Brystal, was..." Killed? Murdered? Died of blunt trauma? What would be the best way to tell Crystal? "...died... killed behind the An Droichead Beag one evening." Once he started recounting the event as he knew, it came out like a report. "Her body was found early the next morning. Blunt force trauma was the coroner's reported cause of death. We've an on-going investigation, but I have to report, there wasn't any evidence and this... murder is quite the mystery."

Ethan had not realized he'd leaned forward, pressing against the desk as he spoke. He sat back and looked at the rain again. "It was a glorious morn, not like today." He sighed. "I am very sorry, lass."

Crystal watched the Inspector wrestle with the tale, like recounting some horror movie where everyone yells to stay out of the basement. Yet the unsuspecting innocent, heads down the stairs anyway. She knew the proper response yet couldn't quite bring herself to let the words out.

Crystal studied the bloody hangnail, took a tissue from her handbag, and dabbed the leakage. How many times had Brystal coached her on appropriate behavior? The correct and acceptable thing to say? The right response, despite the lack of feeling behind it.

"How can there be a crime with no evidence? Isn't there always something? Some little shred of DNA?" Crystal licked the hangnail, then daubed it again.

"My niece said the same thing!" Ethan shook his head, "Yet... here we are. One body and no evidence."

Crystal shifted uneasily.

"Ah, again my apologies. I was not thinkin', mum." Now Ethan was shifting about. "May I get you a cup of tea, mum. I'm sure you've been drivin' a bit." He had to escape. The walls were closing in on him and the dead woman sitting in his office chair.

"Please. That would be nice." Crystal was on the verge of losing it and needed a minute to compose herself. How could there be no evidence? There was always evidence. Didn't they get NCIS in Ireland? Or Law and Order - Special Victim's Unit? Olivia Benson would have found evidence! Gibbs would have solved the case in ten minutes.

Ethan tried to depart with a certain amount of professional aplomb and failed as his size twelve feet caught the side of his desk. He stumbled against the wall, apologized once again, and trotted for the break room. He needed a touch of respite from this bizarre case and the perfectly live copy of his dead woman... sitting in a chair at his desk. He needed to give himself a few minutes to mentally shift his thoughts and deal with this insane situation. Why hadn't someone mentioned Brystal had a twin? Why hadn't he looked at the birth dates in his file? Why hadn't Brystal stayed out of a bar in a foreign country? And... why was she dead?

Crystal sat alone in the Inspector's office contemplating the information... or lack of information she'd just received. There was always evidence. Brystal would not become one of those cold cases, unsolved for decades. She would not be allowed to die all alone behind some filthy bar in the dark of night, without explanation. Crystal was a forensic auditor. She found leads and followed them with extraordinary success. Solving a murder, her sister's murder, would be one more case she would solve! She had the financial resources to stay in Ireland for as long as it would take. As the steaming tea appeared on the desk in front of her, Crystal made a promise to herself. If the clumsy Inspector could not solve this case, she would. "Thank you, Inspector." She steeled herself and looked into his eyes.

She saw a very tired man.

She saw a very frustrated man.

She also saw a touch of fear.

“If you are ready, we can get started on the paperwork.” Ethan took his seat across from Crystal. Finally, she was looking at him. The exact same eyes studied him, as the ones he’d studied for days. It was disconcerting. Hopefully, this thing would be over quickly, and the dead woman’s doppelganger would go back to wherever she’d come from… and take this unsolved murder off his desk.

CHAPTER 8

Everything has a pattern, a relationship in life. If you look hard enough...

9 x 9 + 7 = 88

98 x 9 + 6 = 888

987 x 9 + 5 = 8888

9876 x 9 + 4 = 88888

98765 x 9 + 3 = 888888

987654 x 9 + 2 = 8888888

You do the math!

As they worked through the many forms, Crystal's nerves began to slowly fray. The knots in her stomach crept forward and her resolve stood on the brink of suicide. It was after noon and her knots growled at each other.

"My, will ye look at the time. I've kept ye a bit too long." Ethan stretched, flexing his muscles and tension. "Would ye care to sample the local cuisine?" His own stomach growled back at Crystal's.

"I'd like that. Where should I go?" Though Dingle was a small village, Crystal hadn't any idea where she would find something her picky stomach would accept. "Do you know of a place that is quiet? I'm not ready for noise and people staring." Crystal grimaced. "If people here knew my sister..." She let the idea sink into Ethan's starved brain.

"Ah, yes. It may cause a stir, what with no warning and such..." Ethan smiled. I know just the right place. If I may?" He couldn't wait to see Carryls' face when they appeared in his morgue to conclude their business later that afternoon.

Crystal hesitated. Was he asking her to lunch or to the door? She wasn't sure.

"Not to worry lass, I'll not be leavin' ya drivin' around to find a meal. Dingle is small, but we've our traffic and unique drivers. If ye don't mind, I'll take ya." Ethan remembered not to hold out his hand, rather he waved toward the door. He spent enough time in the company of his niece to recognize a 'unique' person when he met one, and he already figured out Brystal's sister was some form of unique.

"I guess that would be fine." Crystal was relieved. She'd faced death on the Irish roads no less than a dozen times just getting to Dingle. Having to watch for a restaurant and the road would be next to impossible. She picked up her copies of the paperwork, stuffed them in her oversized handbag and followed the Inspector. "You probably know the best places to eat." Then she thought the better of her statement. "I like plain food. I'm not much of a big eater."

Ethan chuckled. "Right then. I know an American restaurant down by the pier. It serves burgers and chips, I mean fries. That's what you call them, right? Fried potatoes?"

"Fries, yes that is correct." Her response was professional and clipped. Crystal winced. Why couldn't she just act normal with this man? She bit her tongue and thought about the numerous times their mother... her mother, she corrected herself. It would never be 'us' again, only me, I, and my. Her mother had always reminded Crystal to be polite and soften her pattern of speech, even if she felt the need to recite lists of facts and statistics – *always be polite!*

And just how did a youth of twelve figure out *polite* when her brain was anything but? How could the world understand that she sought patterns and solutions, not sweet nothings, and polite recitations? Her focus was critical and speculative, not nail polish and giggly boy stuff. While she excelled at algebra, physics, and statistical analysis, Brystal slopped globs of greasy paint on huge canvases and called it art. The Inspector's gentle cough brought her back to the here and now. "I am sorry, Inspector, I am not myself. You understand." It was all Crystal could think of to say after standing in the doorway for almost a minute, like an idiot who couldn't even make a decision about lunch.

"To lunch or not to lunch. That is the question..." Crystal muttered to herself.

Ethan stood close enough to hear the whispered comment. "Whether 'tis nobler in the stomach to suffer the pangs of hunger, or go with the Inspector to lunch and by eating end them?"

Crystal felt a chuckle well within her troubled mind and batter at her skull to exit through her mouth. Was it acceptable to laugh, considering the purpose of her visit and the office in which she stood? Too late! A half gurgle, half snort with a quarter something she'd never produced before, whooshed from between her lips. She couldn't hold it in, even if she'd tried. Crystal shook her head with a silly grin.

"Now that was almost a smile. Come, lass, off to fight the dragons of hunger." A loud growl from his stomach punctuated the statement. He touched her elbow, issuing her forth to her waiting chariot... his car.

Crystal jumped at Ethan's touch but, for once in her life, found his physical urging tolerable and a bit comforting. Like the way Chance had structured her job life, he actually had her figured out and took pains to make her as comfortable as possible, considering her uniqueness. This Inspector seemed to understand Crystal... and he knew Shakespeare!

As they wound their way toward the dock and the bay front. With the Inspector driving, Crystal could take in the sights without risking life and limb. The small town was a tight mass of brightly painted shops and homes. It was amazingly clean and well-marked for a village. Crystal had yet to figure out the strange markings on the roads and wondered if her sister had driven in Ireland or just taken public transportation, as was her preference. Crystal cringed at the thought. Crammed into a public bus? Everyone touching each other, bouncing along the country roads? She shivered in revulsion.

As his passenger sat silently watching his quaint town pass by, Ethan wondered if she'd ever been to Ireland. He wondered a lot of things... why didn't he know she was the twin of his murdered girl? That was a stupid mistake, and he wasn't used to makin' those things, at least not before... "Have ye been to Ireland afore?" He needed to know more about this woman.

"No." Crystal caught sight of a huge intrusive billboard that advertised an aquarium as he drove toward the Boatyard Restaurant and Bar near the harbor. "This place has an aquarium?"

"Aye." At least she was speaking. "And a grand one it 'tis. The largest in Ireland." He ventured a glance at Crystal. Despite the fact that his brain understood the concept of twins, it was still a bit of a shock to see the live version of the gal in the morgue. "We've six thousand years of history and culture here in Corca Dhuibhne, our words for the peninsula, then tourism came to the town." He made a snorting sound. "Now we've people from all over the world come to watch our dolphins, eat our plain Irish food and litter our pristine beaches. My Daingean Ui Chuis is not what it used to be."

Crystal sighed and clasped her hands in her lap. "Nothing is ever what it used to be." Tears threatened but she would die before she cried in front of a perfect stranger... an Inspector, to boot.

"Truer words were never said, lass." He pulled into a tiny parking spot in front of the restaurant. "Mind the door, 'tis a tight space. Used to be..." He let the sentence trail off. No sense recounting the past. It only held demons and heartache. What was he thinking, coming here with Crystal? He used to bring his wife and daughter to this very same restaurant on Sunday mornings for brunch. They'd sit by the window and watch the fishing boats unload their overnight catch. Villagers would flock to the wharf to buy the week's fish and clams. Memories threatened to engulf him in a net of sorrow and grief. Why had he come to this particular place? And, for heaven's sake, why had he brought the lass here?

"They serve American cuisine?" Crystal was back in control of her emotions and spoke easily.

"Aye, they do. And hand made. Everything." Ethan cleared his throat.

"I don't eat a lot. Especially in strange places." The sentence struck Crystal's ears a little odd. "Not that this place is strange. It's just strange to me... I mean it's not strange, just..." She was searching for the right word and stuttered along.

"I understand, Miss Traynor. No need to explain." Ethan smiled at the sun playing off the water. "Trust me, I understand." His niece, Daria, often spouted curious statements... anything that crossed her mind usually. She was a lot like this lass he was about to have lunch with. "Shall we?" He motioned toward the door. But unlike Daria, Crystal seemed to shrink from physical contact. It could be the circumstances of her visit... or she could just be a bit shy. Her sister certainly wasn't. Every picture he had of Brystal showed her in someone's arms or scrunched in the middle of a group. Her smile was brilliant, and the true passion of life showed clearly in every still.

"I've only got American money. Do they take it here?" Crystal was appalled at the thought of being so unprepared... and unknowledgeable. Of course, this trip was not planned or even executed by herself.

He opened the huge oak door of the old boathouse turned restaurant. "Aye, they take all kinds of money. Dingle's become a Mecca for surfers and ocean lovers from all o'er the planet."

As the waitress seated them by the windows facing the harbor, Crystal surveyed the menu. It was very plain and rather International American. It was a gastric relief to know what everything actually was, and what would come on her plate.

The waitress took their orders and Ethan decided to jump right in. It was dicey territory, but his flighty lunch companion was corralled for the moment. "Would ye mind tellin' me a bit about yerself? If n' ye feel up to it, that is."

Crystal watched the boats and people engaging in their daily business on the docks. "There is not much to tell. Brystal is the exciting one. I'm a forensic auditor in New York City." Without really looking, she noticed Ethan's puzzled expression. "I look for illegal money for prosecution. Larson, Davidson and Evans, Inc. is one of the top forensic accounting firms in the world." This was safe territory for Crystal. Her job was her life and about as impersonal as it could get. "I work on the eighteenth floor of a high rise. I live in the city close to my job."

"Married? Kids?" Ethan knew Brystal was twenty-eight so, so was Crystal, young for a family, but she seemed to be educated and well established. Living in New York City was not cheap.

"No. My job takes up a lot of my time. I like numbers." She absently lined up her silverware and napkin. "I like patterns. It's easy for me." She moved her teacup a quarter of an inch to the left and turned the handle, so it pointed to the nine o'clock position. "You?" Crystal remembered the social grace of returning a question as if she were interested in the person's life as well.

"Had me a family… once." Ethan's quiet response made Crystal look at the man for the first time. The pain in his voice was unmistakable as she watched him study the pattern on the china plate in front of him. "Now… I just work." He had an interesting face, not unhandsome, with wild wavy hair that hadn't decided which way to go on this day. She wondered if he owned a comb. While his jacket and shirt were pressed, there was a rumpled nature about his appearance, as if he didn't really care what he wore. That struck a familiar chord with her. There were days she couldn't care less about what she wore either, or how she did her hair. A braid was good enough. Her life was about the chase… the catch.

"Hum… I've never met a policeman. Only detectives who need LDE's services. Met a lot of judges though." Crystal snorted. "Not especially fond of them."

Her comment surprised Ethan. "Why's that?"

"Because they don't think logically. I mean," Crystal leaned forward. She was completely comfortable and immersed in the subject in a second. "I can put an air-tight case together with a ream of supportive evidence and some holier-than-thou judge comes along in a long black dress and throws it all out on a whim." She made a disgusting face and waved a hand across her empty plate. "Whoosh, just like that. Five months of painstaking research, tons of hard-copy back-up, and just like that, inadmissible. The perp goes free and the defense congratulates themselves on a case well done." Crystal plopped two sugar cubes into her cup and stirred with vigor. "Lady law is blind, deaf and the judges are dumb, a lot of the time." She tapped her spoon on the edge of her cup and placed it neatly next to the butter knife. "But most of the time, now anyway, when I go to court on a case, there is little question about my evidence, research or credentials."

The waitress appeared with their plates, replacing the empty ones with those containing their hamburgers and chips. Crystal was on a roll and continued. "I actually had one attorney ask me for my high school and college transcripts. Can you believe that? What an idiot. Did she really think LDE would hire an accountant that did not have a degree and was only passably good at what she did? Really? Of course not." Crystal opened her sandwich and removed the onions, lettuce, pickle, and tomato. She proceeded to scrape the cheese off onto the plate before replacing the bun. "I just finished my last case when…" She took a bite of her burger to cover the awkward moment.

"Aye, I've the same experience with some of our magistrates. It's the sign of the times. Politics before… anything, I'm thinkin'." Ethan took a huge bite of his sloppy hamburger. Ketchup and mustard mixed with hamburger juice dripped from the sandwich, landing square on his white shirt. "Ah, bugger." He took a napkin and proceeded to smear it down the front.

Crystal giggled. How many times had she done the same thing? In a high-pressure meeting? In a classy restaurant? In her office? "Oh, sorry. It's just that I do that so often…" She took another bite of her own hamburger, careful not to repeat Ethan's move.

He set his sandwich back on his plate and peered down his chest at the streaked stain, holding the shirt a bit away from his skin. "This will not be received well. Me sister gets a bit ruffled about me laundry. She does it for me now that…" Again, Ethan paused before finishing his sentence.

"Your sister does your laundry? Is that an Irish thing? Men don't do laundry?" It wasn't meant to sound like a sexist challenge, but it came out a little incredulous and confrontational. Damn her lack of social filter anyway.

Ethan didn't take offense at the statement and chuckled. This lass was a puzzle to be sure. "Nah. Since I lost me wife, Becky helps me out with the home chores."

Without even thinking past the blunder it would cause, Crystal said, "And where'd you lose her?" Then she took a big bite of her burger and licked the mustard off her finger as it dripped from the bottom.

The look on Ethan's face should have explained it all, except Crystal had a lot of trouble interpreting body language and gleaning meaning from what Chase always called *the look*. But the look was there, and Crystal's brain wasn't.

Ethan was stunned. Did this lass really not get what he was referring to? Was she really a block of granite in fleece and flats? His image and imaginary picture of Brystal, built from endless hours of detective work was so far from what sat before him, he couldn't quite consolidate his thoughts. He blurted out, "She was killed three years ago, along with me wee daughter."

Crystal dropped her hamburger and stared. "Oh My God! I am so sorry. Sometimes I..." She didn't know what to say... or do to get past her serious faux pas. "I've never been good with... people. That was Brystal. I'm just some sort of serious nincompoop." Now it was her turn to study the little green pattern of intertwined vines on her plate. "Sorry," she mumbled with her head down.

Well, there it was, Ethan thought. His Daria all grown up, but with a touch of the sprite in her. Someone had chased the sprite out of this lass, he corrected himself. "No reason to apologize. You couldn't have known." His attempt wasn't lost on Crystal who looked up with huge watery eyes. He was struck by how identical the two sisters were.

For the first time since she'd arrived Crystal looked at Ethan's face, his eyes, and found a glimmer of understanding. Usually it was painful to look into someone's eyes and see her own reflection in the judgment of her. Ethan was different. All she saw was a welcoming warmth that spread throughout her body landing just short of... some place no one had ever been. She smiled as a tear slid down her cheek and said the first thing that came to her mind. "At least you've got a sister left." She picked up her hamburger and pretended to take a bite.

Ethan swallowed hard and did the same.

The two diners sat at a window table, in a lovely old boathouse-turned-restaurant, watching the sunshine on the water, and the busy activity of the villagers on the quaint docks.

Silently pretending to eat.

CHAPTER 9

First you make a circle,
Then you add a line.
That's how you make,
The number nine.

Nine has always been a roly-poly jolly fellow with a family of three. Number families are a constant. They never change... never are lost... never leave you... and never, ever die.

"You ready?" They stood outside two stainless steel doors with the huge letters proclaiming MORGUE in blood red.

"I don't have a choice, do I?" Crystal kept her head down, her hands in her pockets.

Ethan just nodded. He didn't trust himself to speak. Lunch had been a dismal process and he wasn't ready for more tears. Especially in this cold, inhumane place. He'd texted Carryls Logner on their way back from lunch with a warning. It would be just like the fellow to take one look and stroke out on him, right there on the floor. Carryls'd been the county Medical Examiner for many years in their little town. He didn't deserve such a shock. He would be hard to replace. "Carryls Logner is our ME, here in Dingle. He'll help you through the…identification and proper paperwork, Miss Traynor."

The walls began to close in on Crystal. "You're not coming with me?" She dared a look at his face. It was stone cold.

"Nah. I've spent me time in there. I've no need…" He really didn't mind the morgue, when it didn't involve his own family, but he didn't know if he'd stand up under Crystal's tears. Especially after the lunch… thing.

"I… I don't know if I can." She leaned against the wall and took a deep breath. Her knees were shaking and those pesky knots in her stomach began their happy dance. Her stomach was threatening to expel its lunch with vigor.

While his face may have been stone cold, his heart was breaking. This lass stood in front of him, ready to identify the body of the last member of her family, worse yet, her twin… her mirror image. He'd asked Carryls to clean up the remains after the autopsy and make sure any visible damage to the gel's head was disguised by her long flowing locks, but dead was still dead. There would be no life in the face, no color to the woman who'd been vivacious and fun-loving just days before. The law was the law, but they were twins. It was clear who the woman in the morgue was. Why require this formality when the answer was clear. Crystal clear.

"I guess this is it then." Crystal let out a deep breath and straightened. She steeled herself for the next step in extinguishing her sister's life. As long as she had not actually seen her sister's dead body, she could pretend it was all some malicious mistake. That Brystal was still off on some crazy, last minute adventure somewhere in some exotic location being… Brystal. She pushed the swinging door open with a little more force than was necessary and jumped when it hit the wall with a bang.

Carryls sat behind his desk, a manila folder lay in front of him, bland and unassuming. He jumped when the door banged open, then sat stunned as he looked at the woman in the doorway. Ethan had told him the sister, coming to identify his guest was a twin, but he didn't say identical twin! Jesus, Mary, and Joseph! She was beautiful and... alive. Just like the woman on his table in the next room... only she was beautiful and dead.

Ethan remained in the doorway. He cleared his throat. "This is Doctor Logner. He'll be helpin' ye now."

Three steps and one chair. Crystal counted as she walked. Numbers are your friend. Numbers are safe. Concentrate on the numbers. Crystal repeated the mantra in her head as she fell into the chair across the desk from Doctor Logner. "What do I need to do?" She kept her eyes on the folder.

Now it was Carryls turn to clear his throat, but the words still came out squeaky and barely audible. He opened the folder and slid three pages toward Crystal. There were little pink flags where she would need to put her initials. The signature line was highlighted in neon yellow. "Initial these places. They indicate you were here..." he pointed to the first little flag. "...and this one says you understand you are here to identify a member of your immediate family..." Carryls almost choked. "... and this one indicates you understand that it is a provincial offense to falsely identify..." He left it at that. "Then sign the bottom." He added, "Please," as an afterthought.

Crystal scribbled her famous initials on the tiny lines, then signed at the bottom. Three initials and one signature. Concentrate on the numbers. Three... one... She'd initialed and signed countless formal court documents in her past, but this one was different. This one was personal... This one was an end to a very short life that was genetically tied to her own. Crystal didn't feel the tear that slipped down her cheek and dropped right next to her signature, blurring the neon yellow and the first letter of her name. She laid the pen exactly parallel to the papers and...waited. She could wait like this forever... as long as Brystal wasn't really dead.

Carryls closed the folder and stood. "Alright then. If you are ready..."

Crystal sat perfectly still, staring at the folder. She had to do this. Her mind focused on a cascading algorithm that defined astrological time and distance. It was intricately complicated and calming. She rose and followed the man in the white coat through another set of swinging doors that read, Authorized Personnel Only. As her mind rode the elements and flow of the calculations, a part of her thought process wondered if the dead needed authorization to enter. It was silly and she almost smiled… but not quite.

Carryls was not comfortable leading this woman into the cooler. He should have taken her arm, or at least walked beside her. But Ethan warned him in their short conversation that, unlike Miss Traynor the dead, Miss Traynor the live, did not like physical contact. So, he proceeded to vault number seven and opened the latch. As the table automatically rolled out, he prepared to catch his visitor if she fainted.

Crystal watched from some place other than her own body. Number seven was a good number, a prime… the beginning or the end in any numerical calculation. In this case it was the end… but it was still a good number. She stood immobile as the doctor pulled a pristine white sheet away from the body's face. Brystal's face was white as the sheet that had covered it a second ago. So, it was final. The fleeting thought crossed Crystal's mind that at some point Brystal would jump up and shout "Gottcha!" Then they would hug and go for coffee. That was Brystal, always the prankster.

But not anymore.

Crystal nodded in the affirmative. That was what she was supposed to do, right?

Carryls gently replaced the sheet and pushed the button on the stainless-steel panel. The table rolled back into the refrigerated vault and he placed his hand on the closed door and bowed his head. "Into your hands, O Lord, we humbly entrust this beautiful soul. In this life you embraced her with your tender love. Deliver her now from all evil and bid her eternal rest." The *Catholic Prayer for the Dead* was his own way of sending a person off, even if he'd no idea what religion they did, or did not practice. "The old order has passed away: welcome her into paradise, where there will be no sorrow, no weeping, or pain, but fullness of peace and joy with your Son and the Holy Spirit forever and ever. Amen."

Crystal whispered, "Amen."

Simply because she didn't know what else to do.

She and Brystal did not grow up with religion. In her mind it was a ritual to teach behavior. To Brystal it was a social event and a reason to hug each and everyone around her. But a God? A Holy Spirit? That was an alien concept to Crystal. And if there truly was a God somewhere up wherever, why did he let Brystal die like she did?

"Thank you, Doctor..." She couldn't remember his name.

"Ye be most welcome, lass. I'll be takin' care of the rest." He motioned toward the door and moved in that direction, hoping Crystal got the clue.

She did and followed the coroner back into his outer office.

"We can make transport arrangements at the conclusion of the case." Carryls shook his head. "Yer sister will need to remain with me for a time. I am deeply sorry, but she..."

Crystal interrupted "I understand. We have no family. Since our folks died it was only me and Brystal." Crystal paused. Now it was only Crystal, no me and Brystal anymore. "I mean... when will the case be closed?" It was better to talk about *the case*, instead of her sister's body... or Brystal's remains.

Carryls escorted Crystal to the outside doors where Ethan waited. "That is a good question and one more for Ethan here, rather than me." He stuck out his hand as if to shake, then thought the better of it. "But you can rest assured, yer sister will be well taken care of in the mean while."

"Thank you. I appreciate your... sensitivity." She said the words even though she had no idea what sensitivity she was talking about. Her sister was dead. That was it. Dead and gone. Who cared what happened after that? People were just weird about that sort of thing. That's why she preferred numbers. They never died and left you alone.

Ethan noticed the tear stains on Crystal's cheeks and pulled a tissue from the box on the wall next to the doors. Someone had aptly attached a shelf to the wall for just that purpose. How apropos for the hallway off the morgue. He was sure it got a lot of use.

Ethan held the tissue out to Crystal.

Crystal took the tissue and stuffed it in her pocket. "Now what?"

As they headed for the elevator, Ethan tried to reconcile his thoughts. His mind kept flashing back to his own experience in that room with Carryls. Then, of course, he'd been identifying his wife and daughter. He was a mess for weeks. Crystal seemed all business and professionalism. Maybe that was her way of handling things, but he knew it would hit her at some point and she would need to let the emotions out. "I guess, if ye be up to it, ye should take a look at yer sister's flat." Ethan watched for a reaction. He got none.

"Alright." Crystal looked startled. "I've no idea where she lived. Or if she had a roommate, or boyfriend, or… did she have a car here? What about her job? Do they know?" As the elevator doors closed, Crystal ventured a look at Ethan. There was so much she did not know about her sister's life, yet they were sisters… twins.

Ethan almost chuckled, but reconsidered, considering their location and what Crystal had just done. "Dingle's a small village… well it used to be anyway. Everybody knows everybody's business here." Then he thought about the An Droichead Beag and the murder tour. God help Barney if he'd not cleaned the place up. Brystal's flat was a block away. He'd been there several times during the short investigation and had placed the security lock on her door himself. "I'll need to release the lock on her flat. It was put there to secure the contents when the case first opened."

Crystal nodded.

"I'll take ye there. Dingle is small, but it can be tricky gettin' around our village for someone from the States. Her flat is in the old part of town." He rambled on to fill the silence. "She lived in a small apartment above the Sweeney Bakery. 'Tis a lovely little store. Makes fresh scones every day. You drove and there is very little parking on Maivey Street."

The Inspector's constant dialog began to rub against the one nerve Crystal depended on. Her mind was a tangle of constant calculations and warring emotions. He was describing scones and she'd just closed the last chapter of her sister's life.

"The locals may find yer appearance a bit disturbing, being an identical twin and all." Ethan was careful to school his words.

"We're mirror twins, not identical." Crystal blurted out. "She was right, and I am left. Her dimple was on the right side of her mouth. Mine is on the left... if I smile."

Ethan did not know how to respond so he just carried on. "If we take my auto, it will be easier." He pointed to the crest on his jacket pocket. "There's always a spot for a copper."

Ethan led the way to his compact car and opened the door for Crystal. It struck her that the Inspector was old school. No one in New York opened doors for women anymore. In fact, it was common to rush through a doorway and not even look back to see if there was another person following, let alone hold a door.

She got in.

Ethan pulled onto the main road and concentrated on driving slowly and safely. His purpose was two-fold. This woman would be driving in his town and she was from the States. Not only would she have to drive on the opposite side of the road than she was used to, but many of the old village streets didn't have signs. "So, if ye turn by the hardware store here," He pointed to the building on his left, "ye may be able to find a decent spot to park round back of Sweeney's."

He was right. Crystal saw two very small places by the large dumpster near the back door to the bakery. One was marked Deliveries Only. The other was empty. The Inspector parked his car and set the brake. "Places are tight since the tourist trade has invaded our sleepy town. What kind of car ye be drivin'?"

"It's not like yours. I think it's a Fairy, or Sprit... or Elf. Something like that." Crystal began to get out and found the Inspector had already gone round and opened the door. He presented his hand to help her get up from the very low vehicle. "I'm good." She mumbled as she struggled with one leg caught on the inside. The car was only inches off the pavement and Crystal felt like she was getting up off a short stool, only more ungainly and awkward.

Ethan stood back and let Crystal have her way. He'd met a good deal of women from the States and found them very independent and self-sufficient. He watched his passenger bend her leg in an odd fashioned manner and then pull her foot around the door. She should have put the seat back, but he didn't think his assistance would be appreciated, so he kept still.

Up on two legs with only one scrape to show for the effort, Crystal followed the Inspector into the bakery through the back door. "Since ye be goin' above, ye can enter this door and take the back stairs. Colleen Sweeney is proprietress of this fair establishment. She'd be the one rentin' the place to yer sister." He took the high, skinny steps on his toes.

Crystal watched her footing as she followed. Eight steps up, a landing and one turn, then six steps to the top floor. Eight was not a good sign, but six was a happy home. A small hallway led to the front of the building and two doors. One was marked with an A and the opposite doorway was marked with a B. Yellow tape crossed the entire door and a shiny new padlock hung next to a strange combination handle/key lock.

"I'll get the padlock off tomorrow." The Inspector apologized. "I'll need to bring a tool for the screws." He tore the tape from the door and inserted a key into the regular door lock, then handed the key to Crystal. "No need to keep the place locked tight now."

He held the door open for Crystal.

Crystal was anchored in place. Why wouldn't her feet move? This was the last threshold, the last bastion of her sister's life, and Crystal was paralyzed with... what? Fear? Apprehension? Emotion? Definitely not! She took an awkward step across the stoop, then walked into what was left of Brystal's life.

Ethan waited in silence as he watched Crystal fight off her own demons and come through the door. He'd not gone home for days after Mary Mae and Ciara's burial. Lord bless his sweet sister for puttin' up with his sorry carcass all that time. And the drinkin'... she'd been a right solid gel. He thanked God every day for his sister and her family. At least he had them. Crystal had no one. And every day she looked in the mirror, she would be reminded of that.

Crystal looked around what the Inspector had said was a small flat. Small? That was a complete misnomer. This was a closet! An overstuffed chair occupied the living room and butted up against a counter that separated the kitchen area from the... chair space. The kitchen consisted of a counter with a hot plate, a microwave and toaster. Food stuffs were stored on a shelf that extended from the counter to the ceiling in a disarray of un-arrangement. A plastic box held utensils on the first shelf and a frying pan hung from a hook on the side of the shelf. One small pot sat atop the hot plate and a dormitory-sized refrigerator was built into the wall below the counter. An undersized doorway that led the way into a bedroom, aptly named since all that would fit was a bed. What served for the door was an old, accordion sliding screen, and a bathroom could be seen off one side of the bed. A flowered sheet hung from a metal pipe across the entryway and was pulled halfway across the entrance of the bath. Crystal peeked through the doorway. On a variety of hooks haphazardly stuck in one wall, sported the extent of Brystal's colorful wardrobe. "Holy mackerel, this is where my sister lived?"

Ethan had remained in the outer room, all of five feet away. "I'd be believin' this is where she slept. Livin' she did all over the place, according to my investigation." As soon as the words were out, Ethan thought the better of what he'd said. He tried for a re-phrase. "She was very social. Lived for her work and a good party." It still didn't sound very good to his ears. "I mean she didn't spend much time sitting around at home. Lots of energy. But I never met the lass..." He figured he'd said plenty and it was time to shut up.

"Well, you're right about her lifestyle, Inspector. My sister was a very social woman." Crystal stepped beside the bed to look out the huge window behind a stack of fluffy pillows in brightly flowered pillowcases. "What a view! This should have been the sitting room!"

The ceilings in the entire flat were maybe twelve or fifteen feet high, and the window extended from about three feet off the floor to within a foot of the ceiling. There were no curtains or blinds. It looked over Maivey Street and the mini bustle of Dingle life.

"Could use a shade or two. I'd not be likin' everyone on the street to see my backside." He stood on his toes and looked over Crystal into the street and at the tall building across the way.

Crystal had to laugh. Her face broke into a smile that almost hurt. It'd been so long since she even grinned. "Your investigation should have told you Brystal had no inhibitions about much of anything. She was the wild child incarnate." She was beginning to use the past tense and it felt so wrong. Crystal sobered. "She was always right, and I was always… wrong."

"Not wrong, just left. You look like you've done fine in your life. And Brystal did… a lot of drawings." Ethan surveyed the small sitting room. The walls were covered with large sheets of newsprint paper containing any number of patterns and dimensional formulas. Her sketches showed outlines of goblets, vases, plates, and other glass figures. A large square of plywood sat on the floor next to the lounge chair, a paper neatly taped to the wooden surface. He pulled the board from its slot between the chair and the wall. It was covered with an intricate pattern of lines that made a cutting pattern. At the bottom was a string of measurements that must have been increments for cutting into crystal. "I'd no idea cut crystal was so… mathematical."

Crystal tried not to look at the numbers. It wasn't time to see into her sister's soul so soon after… "She definitely loved cutting. That's what her emails to me were mostly about. She loved her boss and apparently, he thought she was talented. Crystal cutting and the food… and her group of pals… and the countryside. She seemed to travel a lot with a select group of friends." Crystal wandered through the tiny dwelling.

"Aye. I spoke with several of those folks. They were all shocked. Seems everyone liked your sister. Some I'd even say loved…" He moved a foot toward the only other window in the place. It was positioned near the foot of the recliner and extended, like the one in the bedroom, from knees to the ceiling. Not as wide, it looked over the alleyway between the bakery building and the clothing store next door. If one looked directly across the alley, a matching window in the other building seemed within arm's reach. It wasn't, of course, but the streets were narrow and the buildings high, a sign of older times.

Ethan glanced across the way and noticed movement in the other window. Someone had been there a second ago, watching. The hair on his neck stood and danced around his collar. Was there really someone surveilling Brystal's place, or was it his overactive imagination so soon after a visit to the morgue? He watched for more movement before turning away. "Where will ye be staying the night? Miss Traynor?" He'd not thought to make arrangements for the lass and had no idea if she had.

Crystal let out a sigh. "I guess right here, if it's permissible." She joined Ethan in the sitting room, but took a step back into the bedroom doorway. He was too close for comfort in such a small space.

"Of course it is permissible. We have concluded our search of this place, but wouldn't you rather stay in a hotel with a few more... amenities?" He glanced at the bedroom and kitchen spot.

"This is fine. I can figure out what to do with all of this... stuff. My sister and I have very different tastes in decorating, but at some point, the landlady will want to rent this closet to someone else." Crystal snorted. She just wanted to be alone and sort out her thoughts. She wanted to be alone with the numbers. And she needed to check in with her company to see if there were any fires she had to put out. "I'll be fine. This place has Internet access and I need to check in." She pointed to Brystal's computer plugged, old style, into an Ethernet port in the wall.

"In fact," Ethan lifted the top of Brystal's laptop, "The password is right here." He pointed to a yellow stickie with the scribbled code. "Not very secure, but I doubt yer sister entertained much here. Unless it was the wee people."

Crystal giggled just a smidge. Wee people? Now that would be right up Brystal's alley. "Got it. Thanks. Should I go get my car now?" Crystal looked at her watch. It was almost four o'clock. How late did the police in Ireland work?

"Tell ya what, I'll call me Admin and have him fetch the keys, then retrieve yer car while I block the parking spot. No tellin' but if I move, it'll be filled in a second." Ethan pulled out his cell phone and called the Garda Síochána. "Leroy, can ya come over to the Traynor flat for a quick transport?" He listened for a second, "Aye, the sister's car. Sure enough. I'll meet ya on the back street." He closed the phone. "He'll come over and fetch ye keys then bring yer car back here. It's a short walk and he's already closed the station fer the day."

"Thanks. I think I can find my way around. I've a couple maps. It's really nice of you to be so accommodating." Crystal still stood in the bedroom doorway. There was no other place to go with Ethan filling the sitting room space just with his presence.

"No problem at all. Are ye sure ye be wantin' to stay here tonight?" Ethan was concerned by how calm and disconnected this gel seemed. There was no weeping, no hysterics, no emotion at all. He was beginning to think the two women were not close at all. There seemed to be no connection, or at least no outward connection. Was Crystal one of those American women who cared only for her job and money, or was she just very private and would fall apart after he left? He'd have a word with Colleen before he returned to the Garda Síochána. Just in case...

"I'll be fine." Crystal's voice brought Ethan back into the here and now. She was bent over surveying the contents of the fridge. "I'm tired and sure I can find something to eat in here." She took a green slimy package from the crisper and tossed it in the trash bin next to the counter. "Or maybe I'll just go downstairs and get something at the bakery." She wrinkled her nose at the smell. "And empty the garbage."

"Aye." Ethan could smell the rotten vegetation. "If ye'll be givin' me the keys to yer car, I'll be back in a pint. Colleen should be open for a bit yet. Ye might want to pop down and scare the livin' daylights outta her, then get some dinner." Ethan shook his head with a smile. "I'd love to see the look on her wrinkled ol' face. She's an old believer, don't ye know."

Crystal handed her keys to the Inspector. "Old believer?"

"Aye. The old ways, ye know. She still believes in the fairy folk and bullaun stones. She'll close the shop if a magpie lights on her bench. Colleen'll love ye though, red hair and all." Ethan took the keys. "My country is a curious mix of ancient and modern, but there be one thing sure, a belief is a belief and there's no tryin' to change the mind of an Irishman once it be set." He ducked through the doorway with a quick wave. "Be back in a...."

"Pint? What does that actually mean?" Crystal's brow wrinkled. This was such a strange place.

"A few minutes, in American. The time it takes to down a pint..." He watched Crystal struggle with the saying. "...of beer."

"Ah. Alright... I'll just be here." Already the drawings that covered the little wall spaces were calling to her. Their patterns and graceful lines held a magic thrall. Crystal could feel herself falling into the addictive pull of her need. She peered at the sketch closest to the small sitting room window, completely missing the shadowy movement in the matching window across the alleyway. The drawing was so... complex, yet simple. The intersecting lines formed small square and diamond patterns of threes and sixes. The swirls connecting each sequence sat at a forty-five degree angle to the... Crystal wrenched her mind away from the black hole that threatened to suck her out of reality. "No." she muttered to herself. "Not now. I can't..." She turned toward the kitchen spot and took a deep breath. "Eew, what is that smell?" Back in the moment, she remembered the garbage and the dumpster behind the building.

Crystal steeled herself and began filling the garbage bin with old bread, the coffee filter, still full of grounds from some cup brewed who-knows-when, and more unidentifiable things from the tiny fridge. Brystal had been gone for nearly two weeks, yet her fridge looked like it hadn't been touched in months. Crystal grabbed a tissue and removed something lumpy and bluish-green, attempting to drop the thing into the bin. Halfway there, it crumbled, falling half in, and half out of its destination. "Crap!"

More tissue and the floor was nearly clear of what Crystal thought may have been some form of cheese. The last crumble had gone behind the bright blue trashcan. As she pulled the can away from the wall beneath the counter, she noticed several folded sheets of papers. "Couldn't even hit the can, Brystal." Crystal smiled to herself. There'd been days when they were children, sharing a room at home, that

Crystal would attempt to organize her sister's completely erratic side of their bedroom. While Crystal's clothes were always neatly folded in her drawers and hung by color and type in her side of the closet, Brystal believed in the *heap* style of organization. Heaps of stuff everywhere there was space, or not. Piles didn't bother her sister at all. They covered every inch of her half of their space. It drove Crystal mad.

She dumped the folded papers in the trash and began to pull the plastic bag from the container when she noticed the fold had come open a fraction. She could almost make out a calculation in red pen. Retrieving the papers from the trash and cleaning them off with the last tissue, Crystal unfolded the sheets and stared.

They had her.

The numbers chuckled and sang as her mind spun out of control, willingly following the flow and ebb of the structure and arrangement. Her sister's flowery script was like a fleece comforter on a stormy night. Crystal relaxed into the sequences and drew comfort from the cozy unemotional blanket they offered. Around and around, the numbers wound down, like a whirlpool, sucking her into a void that promised complete oblivion, complete respite from the harshness of her immediate reality. In Brystal's chaotic way, the calculations followed the edge of the pages, moving in a square. In the center of the square was a delicate, graceful drawing of a goblet. The four sheets were alike with the only difference being a slight alteration of the calculating stream around the edges. Each goblet was more magnificent than the last with amazing detail and form.

Crystal couldn't breathe. The beauty in the numbers was literally breath-taking. She stood entranced by what her sister had created on the stained newsprint. While her hands shook and her knees threatened to give way, she could not pull herself from the designs. What her admin assistant called the *weird switch,* had turned on in her brain and she was at a loss as to how to turn it off. The calculations kept spinning and working, condensing, and expanding. The numbers and letters developed into stories without end and caressed her neurons like a rich shot of heroine. She needed it. She wanted it. There was no reason she couldn't just..."

"Miss Traynor? Crystal?" Ethan stood a foot away. The lass hadn't even noticed his presence. He tried again. "Crystal!"

He touched her elbow.

Crystal was gathering her favorites to her like a mother duck gathered her ducklings before bedding down. Their soft furry bodies cuddled into her aching soul, adding salve to the open wounds Crystal didn't even know existed. They chased the knots in her stomach right out of existence and tickled her heart with their success. Nine was especially fat and happy, settling just next to her ear, blocking out anything she didn't want to hear. Seven gave her strength and four supported her with its structure and strength. She reveled in the incredible pleasure of their company...

"Ach!" A hot poker touched her elbow. "Ouch!" Crystal dropped the papers and jumped away, tripping over the recliner an inch away. She half fell, half slid into the overstuffed seat. Like the needle of a turntable scratching across a vinyl record, she was screeched back to reality. Every muscle in her body rejected, but it was too late.

"Sorry, lass. I didn't mean... how long were you standing there?" Ethan noticed a slight bluish tint to her lips and the awkward way her legs had tried to work. He picked the designs off the floor and placed them on the counter.

Her voice was rough and cracked as she spoke. "Face down... put them face down."

He did as was directed then took a bottle of water from the fridge, cracked the top and handed it to Crystal. "Have a sip."

Crystal downed half the bottle before replacing the cap. "You gave me a fright." She tried a simple excuse in lieu of what she knew had happened... again.

"I'd be guessin' so." He stood an arm's length away, afraid to move. "I see you've been cleanin' the place a bit." He looked at the walls, now devoid of sketches.

Crystal jumped from the chair and wavered on her feet. "What? No!" She stepped around the Inspector and placed a hand on the empty wall that had been covered with pinned sketches moments ago. "Where'd they go?"

Ethan stared at the lass. Was she crazy? He'd been gone, possibly twenty minutes. "Well..." He wasn't quite sure how he should proceed. "You didn't take the papers down?" Who else would have?

"No. And I was here the entire time." Crystal spun in circles looking at the walls. She rushed into the bedroom. The walls showed nothing but small pinholes where sheets had previously been tacked up haphazardly.

"You didn't go down to the bakery for a bite?" Ethan was puzzled. She'd been in a trancelike state when he returned. She'd not even heard his steps let alone his voice.

Crystal returned to the sitting room. "No. I was here the entire time. It was just a minute. Did you get my car?" The confusion was apparent on Crystal's face and Ethan was beginning to worry. This woman hadn't been aware of his approach. Who else could have come and gone while she was...there, but not there?

Ethan tried for the soothing card. "Well, it's been a very trying day for you. Maybe you just...started the clean up on autopilot. People do things they don't always remember when they've been under a great deal of stress." He held his hands out questioningly and shrugged. The lass was bonkers.

"No Inspector. I was here. The only one here. And I didn't take anything off the walls." Crystal was very much aware of how this must look to the cop. "You are a detective. Where would I have put the drawings if I did take them down?" She put her hands on her hips and glared at the Inspector.

Ethan had the good grace to glance at the garbage that held all manner of colorful gooey substances, but definitely no crumpled papers. "Did ye latch the door after I left?"

"What? No. Why?"

"I left ye in the recliner. You were tired. You could have fallen asleep..." He was reaching. "Maybe someone came in and removed them, not wanting to disturb ye asleep in the chair."

"And who would do that?" The idea creeped her out. Something had happened to the sketches while she was caught in her OCD mind meld, but what was it? "Who would want a bunch of crystal sketches? And why wouldn't they make themselves known? Wake me up? Say hi, or something?"

Again, Ethan shrugged. "I'll have a word with Sean and Dharág."

"Who are they?" The hairs stood on the back of Crystal's neck at the names.

"Sean MacDougal is the master cutter yer sister worked for. Dharág Hadley is his apprentice. They all worked very closely together. Maybe Dharág came to retrieve yer sister's work and thought he saw a ghost. I don't know. A wink is as good as a nod to a blind horse." Immediately he recognized his mistake. This gel didn't understand their colloquial talk at all. "Meaning, I won't know until I ask. Ya know, a blind horse can't see…" He was sounding stupid, even to himself.

"Right. That would be the definition of blindness. Got it." She snagged the last remaining papers from the counter and folded them in neat squares, sliding the packet into her rather large pocketbook. These weren't going to disappear.

CHAPTER 10

The Commandments came in ten and I think I've broken thirteen.
Charlton Heston on the making of his famous movie.

"She's a queer one, that gel." Ethan sat with his sandwich and a cup of strong black tea. "She didn't even know I was there. Anyone could have come and gone, and she wouldn't have noticed. She just stared at this one drawing like she was on the tod." Ethan shook his head for the tenth time. "I don't know what gives with her. Not anything what I expected."

"I've seen it before. The Tallyards. They be a group of mystics on the rocks that do a Druid trance. They become so deeply attached to the spiritual essence they are impervious to the world around them. They are impervious to pain, go all rigid about their limbs and fall unconscious. It's a mystic thing where they say they depart the earthly level of being." Carryls smiled at the Inspector. "Course, me being a man of science be belivin' it's all a heap of hogwash." He stuffed a cookie into his mouth and talked around the crumbles. "Tourists throw money at their prostrate bodies."

Ethan guffawed. "I'd be lyin' down on the job if'n people'd throw money at me body too. Be my luck, they'd throw sod and dung."

Both men had to laugh at that thought, then sobered in respect to the place they sat. After all, lunch in a morgue wasn't exactly a picnic, but it was quiet and less bothersome than the offices above.

"I left her at her sister's apartment for the night. Told her I'd come 'round after me lunch hour." Ethan finished the last part of his sandwich and snagged the last cookie. "Me sis makes the best butter cookies in these parts." He bit the center dollop of chocolate out of the middle. "Our mom used to make this same recipe for church." He popped the rest of the small cookie into his mouth and closed his eyes as he chewed... remembering.

"Aye. And I be rememberin' some skinny scoundrel used to hide in the kitchen and steal the pecans right outta the middles." Carryls and Ethan had grown up together and knew more about each other than any two men should have.

"And just why do ye be thinkin' I became a copper?" Attending university in England was just about the only time Ethan had been off the peninsula for an extended period of time. He'd hated the pompous British with their exclusionary cliques and prejudicial attitudes. Course, those were the days the Brits thought the Irish to be dogs from the wilds, a group to be shunned and put down. Everyone in Great Britain thought all Irishmen were dyed in the wool IRA agents out to blow up Parliament.

"I know there'd be an excellent reason behind a nob turned copper." Their good-natured ribbing was one of the things that kept Ethan above the waters after Mary Mae and his daughter were laid to rest. Too many times he'd stood on the edge of the cliffs and listened to a Siren's call, only to drag himself away from the one action that would damn his soul to the lowest level of Hell forever. Suicide was a mortal sin.

"Alright then. 'Tis after me lunch so I best be getting' on me way." Ethan crumpled up his lunch remains and dumped them in the garbage bin next to Carryls' desk. "I stood outside the door last night until I heard the lock engage. The lass is from New York City, for

God's sake. Ye'd think she'd better sense... or at least the sense to latch the door."

Carryls took a small hard-bound book from the shelf behind his desk and handed it to Ethan. The title was simple; Aberrant and Debilitating Neurological Disorders. "Check out the chapter on psycho-motor epilepsy. Knew a gel once, in Africa. She'd have a kind of seizure that kept her in thrall. Whatever she was doin' at the time, she just kept doin'. Sounds like yer gel." He stood and slipped into his white coat. "But then I only treat the dead, not the livin'."

Ethan took the book and departed with a thanks. He had some thinkin' to do before he met Crystal again. She was such an enigma. During his investigation of Brystal's murder, he'd formed this picture of a fun-loving, wild child from the States. Every picture he'd collected showed a woman that embodied life and adventure. Her passport was full of stamps from countries, some of which he'd never heard of, yet here was her sister. He tapped the title of the book. Maybe something between the covers would provide understanding. At the moment, he was prone to believe the live twin was mad as a box of frogs.

"Inspector? I've a call for ye from the States." The desk Garda made a phone hand signal as she spoke. Bridget O'Hanrahan's son was deaf as a twig and she often made hand gestures as she spoke.

"I'll take it in me office, Bridget." Ethan trotted down the hallway. Now what? Who'd be callin' from the States. Crystal was the only family member left to his victim. He picked up the handset and sat in his chair behind his desk... in his office... in Ireland. "Inspector MacEnery, here."

"Ah, hi. This is Chance Evans...ah, from New York, sir" Chance added the sir as an afterthought. He had no idea how formal the police were in Ireland.

"Aye. How can I help ye, Mr. Evans?" Ethan thumbed through the book Carryls had given him as he held the receiver to his ear with one shoulder.

"I'm Crystal Traynor's Boss... I mean friend. And I wanted to check and see... if she is. I mean," Words came rushing out in a haphazard manner. "If she's okay. Did she make it to your town? Is she still alive? I mean... I don't know what I mean...Actually I do know what I mean, but maybe you don't. I mean Crystal is a unique kind of person. She hasn't been out of the United States before and I was very worried. Well... we all were..."

Ethan kept the chuckle out of his voice. "Of course, Mr. Evans. Miss Traynor arrived unscathed. She has completed the required documentation and spent the night at her sister's flat."

"Oh God no! She stayed at Brystal's? And that was a good idea?" Ethan detected a bit of an accusatorial note in the man's tone, but obviously he knew Crystal well. Otherwise why would a supervisor check up on an employee's personal condition in a foreign country. And who was the *we* in his comment?

"Actually, it was her idea. She seemed...alright with it when I left her there." Ethan tried to remain professional and concise. "Is there something I should know?"

Silence ensued on the other end of the line.

"Mr. Evans? Are you still there?" Ethan closed the book and sat up. This might be an opportunity to figure out what was wrong with the lass. This man was calling from the States to check up on her. Maybe he knew something that would help Ethan.

"Yeah. Yeah, I'm still here. Look..." There was another long pause. "Crystal's more than just an employee at LDE. And I am more than her Boss, kind of. See, Crystal..."

Another long pause.

Ethan decided to wait it out. This fellow was struggling with something and maybe...

"Crystal is a very unique person. If you've spent more than three seconds with her, you probably know what I am talking about."

"I believe I do. Are you and Miss Traynor... mates?" Ethan hoped his question opened the door. If they were friends...

"Oh God no! I'm married. Crystal is my friend as well as my employee. A fantastic employee at that."

"Of course, I did not mean to infer you and she were involved in a relationship." He was back to interpreting normal Irish speech into American. "We use mates for friends, sir."

"Of course. Then I guess we are mates. You see, Crystal is special. The total opposite of her sister."

"You've met her sister then?" Now Ethan was taking notes.

"A couple times. Complete and total opposites." The man on the other end of the line laughed. "The only thing Crystal and Brystal had in common was their face. You see, Crystal is a genius...." Another long pause gave Ethan time to scribble a big G on his note pad. "But with genius comes certain quirks... with Crystal, it comes with a lot of quirks... and some really challenging... ah, behaviors."

"I'm believin' I get the point, Mr. Evans. May I call you Chance?" He could mine this source for more information if he was careful.

"Of course. I was fortunate to hire Crystal several years ago, and I am kind of, her keeper. No that's not right. I help her get along. She's an incredible forensic accountant, all numbers. Frankly, between me and you, she's made me a millionaire, and herself as well. She has solved eighty-nine percent of the most difficult accounting cases in the last two years. She's single-handedly made LDE the top forensic accounting and financial investigation company in the United States." This Mr. Evans was full of information and it was spilling out over the phone lines.

"I see. So how can I help you?" Ethan let the question dangle like bait.

"Well, that being said, Crystal needs... help with... life." An exhausted sigh floated across the pond. Obviously, this man was incredibly worried... possibly with good reason. Ethan remembered the trance-like state he'd found Crystal in the night before.

"Without crossin' the lines here, can you tell me what I should do to help the lass? She's had a rough time of it, and I'll be admittin' I've seen some... awkward moments." Ethan was treading softly but wanted to get the point across. Now, he too was worried about Crystal. What was wrong with her? Was she truly mental?

"Crystal walks the fine line between genius and...awkwardness with people. I mean... she's not mentally ill or anything, just different in some really important ways." The flood gates were open, and the information began to flow. "She has this crazy thing called synesthesia, in a big way. Numbers are her food, friends, and comfort. She does this thing in her mind with numbers and patterns and after a while, voila! Whatever she is concentrating on unwinds on paper and... there it is. Another whopping case solved." He paused again. "But in the meantime, while she's obsessed with the numbers..." Another telling pause, "she won't remember to eat, take a break, look out the window, go home at night. That's why I said she needs help with life. It wasn't a mean comment, but reality. Crystal's reality." The fellow was almost panting over the phone when he stopped talking.

Who was this guy?

Why did he care so much?

He'd said he was married, but could he be having an affair with Crystal?

"I understand. Last evening, I found Miss Traynor staring at one of her sister's sketches that had mathematical equations around the edges. She was not even aware of my presence until I touched her elbow."

A huffing laugh came across the wires. "Did she hit the roof and climb the wall?"

"Just about. You seem to know this woman well. How about some ideas of what I can do to help her. She has said she wants to pack up her sister's effects and ship them home. We are done with the investigation. There wasn't much to investigate."

Chance interrupted. "Done? What kind of murder investigation is over in a matter of days? Did you catch the perp?"

Ethan sighed. How did he address the issue of no evidence and a murder of convenience from thousands of miles away? "Unfortunately, seems to be a crime of convenience. There be little evidence, if any and our Chief Superintendent for the Garda Síochána has determined the case closed unless something else comes to notice."

There was silence on the other end of the line.

"Please understand, Mr. Evans, Miss Traynor, er... the former, Brystal, was well loved here in Dingle. By her employer, her friends, her neighbors. We've no reason to expect anyone would want to harm the lass. The location of her death indicated she must have come on someone or something she shouldn't have, to end up the way she did. I'll not be comfortable with the closing either, but I'm just the local Inspector."

Now it was Ethan's turn to pause. After a long moment, Crystal's employer/friend spoke quietly. "Crystal can't be around numbers, Ethan. Don't let her see a calculation, she'll... have one of her spells. We're used to it because we've been around her for a long time. We've built an insulated life for her, complete with a handler she calls her admin assistant. We all get it and help make her life a little easier. But others won't understand. Google OCD and synesthesia." The word was spelled for the Inspector. "Just read up on it, then multiply by a hundred. That's Crystal." The man sounded tired. "You've got my number on your caller ID. Call if Crystal needs... anything. I'll come."

"Right-o. Ring if we need ye. And thanks for the information. I was a bit stymied, but I'll figure this out and see how I can help." Ethan rang off and sat for a moment looking at his notes. OCD? Synesthesia? He couldn't pronounce it, let alone know what it was.

He had homework to do, but first he'd need to go round to Brystal's... correct that, Crystal's flat and check up on the lass, genius or not.

~

CRYSTAL'S HEAD throbbed and her eyes burned by the time her head hit one of the many pillows covering Brystal's calico coverlet. She had slept the night with a towel across her face. Brystal's window on the Dingle world had been intriguing... at first. When the sky finally cleared and the stars appeared, she found herself searching for constellations, one after the other. Even though they were in the wrong places, her brain would not let go until she'd found and named each one. It was an exhausting process for an already exhausted woman.

Close to the dinner hour the previous night, a soft knock preceded the entry of a tiny adult woman holding a wooden platter of bread and cheese. She had a bottle of wine tucked beneath one arm and a cloth napkin under the other. Introducing herself as the Proprietress of the Sweeny Bakery shop below, she set her items on the counter and brushed her hands on the ruffled apron she wore. She did not seem surprised at all to see someone standing in the apartment that was the exact picture of a dead woman. "You must be Crystal. Brystal, may she rest in peace, told me all about you." The *may she rest in peace* came with the typical Catholic sign of the cross. "And here ye are, in the identical flesh and blood." A sad smile played with the woman's wrinkles before she brightened. "I brought ye some sup. If ye be needin' anythin', just give a holler. I open right sharp at seven and close at the same. But mostly," She banged on the wall next to the cupboard, "Me and Nialls be right next door." Again, the sad smile appeared. "'Tis a fair mess, this one, but I be glad to meet ye in any gale." Then the tiny excuse for a grown woman breezed out the door. As she crossed the threshold, she muttered something quite unintelligible and dropped a few grains of something white from the pocket of her apron.

At the last second, Crystal remembered her social training. "Nice to meet you..."

Colleen was gone, but the food remained, and Crystal realized she was very hungry. In Brystal's tiny apartment, the counter doubled for a drawing table, dining room table and just about any other table, since it was the only flat surface in the place. Crystal pulled a stool up and sat before the feast.

A small loaf of fresh, hot bread lay next to a bowl of what Crystal thought to be butter. She tested it with the tip of her finger. Creamy whipped honey butter! Slices of three kinds of cheese formed an arc on a shiny plate with some sort of writing around the edge. One slice was white. The other two were shades of yellowish orange. A bread knife and a two-pronged fork lay next to the plate, wrapped in an embroidered linen cloth. A beautifully detailed porcelain cup contained a tea infuser ball. Crystal picked up the round metal container and smelled it. Earl Gray! How had Colleen known Earl

Gray was her favorite? Maybe she was in touch with the fairy folk after all.

Crystal laughed at her own thought. This place was having a strange effect on her, and she'd only been in country for two days! Fairy folk indeed! They were the thing of wild tales and legends, not reality. Like all fables, they were invented by some adult to teach a child right from wrong, good from bad, and consequences for behavior.

Her stomach growled. It sounded like a freight train in the small room. The consequences of not eating for several hours... Crystal cut a generous slice of bread and slathered it with honey-butter. One enormous bite in her mouth, she filled the hot pot with water and plugged it into the outlet. Chewing the hearty bread, Crystal shook her head. Even the hot pot was the simplest it could be. Just like Brystal... the easiest possible life. Plugged in, it was on. Unplugged, it was off. When Brystal was plugged into life, she was on... full force, in any direction, she boiled fast and high. Unplugged... Brystal was never unplugged. She was first born and thrust screaming into a world where she wanted to know and experience everything. Crystal, second, was dragged forth, resisting all the way. She even refused to take a dangerous, risky breath at first... until Brystal, a version of her identical self, raised the roof screaming to the heavens. All through their childhood, Crystal followed Brystal's tutelage, always watching until it was safe. Later, as they grew, Brystal was Crystal's social filter. She knew Crystal was a very different kind of person but never made it apparent to anyone. She would just remind Crystal in their quiet twin-speak, how she should behave, speak, walk, look... what was *normal* and what was...Crystal.

The pot whistled dragging Crystal from her memories. Even Brystal's pot was telling her what to do.

What *would* she do?

Now that she was all alone in the world?

She filled her cup with hot water and added two sugar cubes. The caffeine and sugar would help her mind sort things out.

Sort?

What was there to sort?

Brystal was dead. She didn't have many personal possessions. Just enough to fit in her backpack. That way, if the wind blew from another direction, she could be off in a heartbeat. Following her dreams, she'd called it. But there was more to life than chasing pipe dreams.

Brystal pursued her version of life... until someone stole her dream... her life.

Crystal sunk into the old beaten up recliner with her cup of tea. For the first time, she studied the room. A faint outline on the walls showed where Brystal's drawings had hung. There were pinholes everywhere, but two places were outlined as if the sun had faded the paint everywhere but the two spaces. Crystal usually had complete and total recall, but for some inexplicable reason, she could not pull the sketches from her mind.

The folded sheets rattled in her pocketbook on the floor. They wanted out. They wanted her.

Crystal kicked the pocketbook away.

Not now.

Not tonight.

A small, two-shelf bookcase crowded the far corner of the room. Crystal could read the titles from where she sat. Most were pattern books or about crystal recipes and the science behind cutting and processing crystal, except one large blue spine. She set her cup on the windowsill and took the book from the case. It was an album. The first page contained two birth certificates under the plastic covering! The official embossed stamp of the State of Ohio was smashed flat. They were originals.

How?

She traced the signatures of Callista Caroline Traynor and Randall James Traynor.

Their parents.

Now only *her* parents.

CC's flowery script was familiar to Crystal. She'd practiced it until she could produce the ornate letters exactly as if her mother had written it. It was a handy talent for all kinds of official things, like suspensions and grade reports. She'd only seen her father's signature twice in her life. His handwriting never changed. All caps, strong and vivid. There was nothing soft and flowery about their father.

The next page was a bit of a shock. There sat CC, in a fur edged robe holding two bundles. As usual, Brystal's face held a grin, even as a newborn, looking directly at the photographer. Crystal's face was turned away, hiding from the camera... from the world. The next page held two black and white photographs. Each picture showed the typical photo of the times, a naked child on her stomach on a fuzzy rug. They could have been pictures of the same child, but Crystal knew the one trying to lift her head was Brystal. The other, her face down and away, was Crystal.

She turned the heavy page.

It was the same story, over and over again. Brystal and Crystal holding hands on their first day of nursery school. Brystal smiling as if she won the lottery and Crystal pulling back, fear all over her face. Brystal at six in her ballet costume, twirling for the camera. Crystal sitting on the porch working a Rubik's Cube. Brystal on a starting block in her bright green Speedo, ready for the gun to start the race. Crystal in the science wing of their school, weighing rat poop for a research project on obesity. Brystal on the winner's stand receiving a gold medal for running the hurdles. Crystal's scholarship certificate for the State Mathematics' Competition Award. There wasn't even a picture because Crystal skipped the banquet, afraid to stand up in front of so many people just to get a piece of paper, when she'd won by almost a hundred points. The last page was a full-size picture of their family at high school graduation, in their robes and silly flat-topped hats. Brystal stood next to their mom, arms around each other, laughing. Crystal in front of their father, head down, clutching her diploma in front of her, like a shield.

A tear fell on the plastic covering. Crystal wiped it away, closed the album, and replaced it in the bookcase.

That was then.

This was now.

CC was gone. Taken, like her daughter, way before her time.

RJ was gone too. Taken by his own hand, way before his time.

Brystal was gone. Taken by... some unknown person, way before her time.

Crystal finished her tea, glancing out the window at nothing in particular. A movement caught her eye in the window across the way.

She focused and watched.

It was twilight, maybe the light was playing tricks...

There it was again.

A shadowy movement.

A face appeared in the window for a split second.

A split second was long enough for Crystal to freeze-frame the face and burn it into her memory. The hairs stood on the back of her neck and arms.

Then the face was gone.

She locked the flat door and pushed the stool under the handle.

This weird place was getting to her, for sure. Intuition had never been an element in her thinking. Now it screamed at her. Great! Another voice in her head that wouldn't leave her alone.

Just for safety's sake, she piled two large garbage bags of clothing against the door as well. Her actions may not have kept someone intent on entering, out of the tiny apartment, but it would cause a ruckus and alert her to the fact that someone was breaking in. She shook herself. New York City paranoia...

The papers in her pocketbook rustled louder. They wanted her attention. They begged...

"Not tonight." She reminded herself out loud for emphasis.

The papers shut up and lay quiet.

"Good boys." Why were most numbers boys? Misbehaving boys to boot?

The sun had set, and Crystal sat in darkness contemplating her next move and drinking her tea. She'd taken care of the most important items and now where was she?

Her eyes drooped and the empty cup slipped from her fingers. Landing in her lap, the tea infuser ball rolled to the floor. Immediately

Crystal set the cup on the counter and knelt on the floor looking for the round strainer. It wouldn't do to stain the wood floor before turning the apartment back to the owner.

The floor wasn't big enough to hide a little metal ball, but it was doing a fine job of making Crystal crawl around anyway. Near the wide baseboard that covered the end of the counter, she spied it!

"Ah hah! There you are you little rascal." She crawled to the end and grabbed the ball. Her knuckles hit the wooden wall and it moved. Just a smidge.

"What the heck..." Crystal rolled to a sitting position and felt the panel that covered the end of the counter. Pushing slightly where she'd retrieved the infuser, the panel clicked and fell open just a crack. "Will ya look at that." She pried the door open. It was a hidden cupboard that extended at least three feet into the space below the counter. To Crystal's surprise the shelves were covered with all kinds of crystal goblets, plates, bowls, and vases, all cut in intricate patterns. As she withdrew each one, she studied the cuts. In the dim light she could tell which ones had been Brystal's first tries. But as she got to the back of the lot, the skill level increased. It was apparent that Brystal had developed quite a talent for cutting crystal. At the very back, almost hidden by the four-by-four that extended up through the counter to the roof, sat four magnificent goblets. Each one an intricate pattern of crisscrosses and diamonds. Crystal held them up to the minimal light that came through the window from the lamplight outside. The cuts virtually glowed with rainbow colors and patterns. It was so entirely beautiful; it was hard to look at. Crystal returned it to the cabinet quickly, recognizing the mouth-watering draw of the patterns. So, this was what had drawn her sister to this place and kept her for so long.

How long?

How long did it take to master such beauty? To learn to make a treasure like the goblet?

Was it Brystal's work at all?

And why was it hidden in a secret cabinet?

Those simple questions plagued Crystal as she lay in bed, trying to sleep and counting constellations instead of sheep.

Now in the bright sunlight of the Irish morning, Crystal was even more tired than when she'd finally gone to bed. Dragging herself around the flat, stacking Brystal's belongings into two categories; keep and ship, or donate to... who? The Salvation Army? Was that even a thing in Ireland?

At some point in her morning wanderings, Crystal had found a carpenter's box under a corner of the bed. It was a polished oak box with gleaming brass hinges. The little latch on the front was held closed with a very small padlock, like the TSA locks one would put on a suitcase when traveling. It was broken and hung by its hoop, dangling lopsided. Crystal opened the lid and found what must have been Brystal's tools. The top tray held a bunch of child sized basic tools; two different screw drivers, a couple pairs of pliers with different ends, something that looked like an ice pick, pencils and markers, rulers of varying sizes and units, a small hammer, and several files. Beneath the tray were rags, gloves, a small can of some kind of powder and an old-fashioned oil can, like the kind their mother used on her sewing machine. There was a stack of pictures at one end. Crystal removed the stack and thumbed through the lot. There was Brystal, her wide smile and bright eyes jumped off the paper. Every picture showed the stages of learning to cut crystal. There she was, drawing a pattern with a balding man standing over her. His thick glasses and muscular arms were a testament to the hard and detailed work he'd done all his life. He could have been a father to the woman who sat on a stool sketching a wild pattern on the newsprint. The warmth and care between the two was apparent. The next picture showed the man behind Brystal, his hands guiding hers as she held a glass to the grinding wheel. In another picture, a second man sat across from Brystal at the drawing table, a pencil in his hand pointing to a line she'd drawn. His frown clearly showed his displeasure with Brystal's work. There was nothing warm or accepting about this second fellow. The last picture she viewed showed that first man on a massive glistening Harley motorcycle with Brystal on the back.

They were on a road near a bay and Brystal's long curly hair flew behind her. Obviously, someone following had taken the picture. Brystal's hand was raised in a wave, the other tucked around the driver. More than smiling, Brystal was exuding joy and passion as she rode with the man.

Who were these two important people in her sister's life? Obviously Brystal's teachers, but how did they relate to Brystal and her life… and death?

Crystal had just poured herself a fifth cup of tea when a knock drew her from her thoughts. She dragged the bags away from the door and went to open it, but thought again. She'd no idea who was on the other side. Friend or foe?

"Who is it?" She asked before turning the lock.

"Inspector MacEnery, Miss Traynor."

Crystal unlocked the door and stepped back to allow the Inspector to enter.

"Good morn on ye. Looks like you've been busy." Ethan glanced around the room. Small piles dotted the floor and two large bags sat in the middle. He studied Crystal for a moment. She looked haggard and worn. He recognized the look. He'd worn it for months.

"Yes, I've been trying to figure out what I should ship home and what I should just… donate…?" The last word came out more as a question. "Brystal wasn't much of a material girl. She didn't like things that tied her down."

She handed the stack of pictures from Brystal's toolbox to Ethan. "Can you tell me who these men are?"

Ethan took the pictures. "The bald one is Sean. Sean MacDougal. He was Brystal's employer and teacher. The other is Dharág Hadley, his apprentice. Sean owns the Dingle Crystal Shop. Came home some years back after Waterford sold out to the Finns and production moved to Slovenia. He's the master's master, that boy-o. Now Dharág, he's a bit of a newcomer. Been with Sean about five years. Used to be a fisherman. He lost his boat to a storm and couldn't keep it on the up. Lost his entire crew and a cousin to the briny. 'Twas a sad day for Dingle." Ethan paused, looking out the window. "Dharág used to be the number one fisherman in this village, and a right straight fellow. Sean tells me he is a passable cutter."

"That's a horrible story." Suspicion was building in Crystal's mind, more so fueled by this Dharág's expression in the photograph. "Could he have been..." She stopped herself. She'd been in Dingle for two days and the Inspector might take offense if she intonated one of his citizens may have been a murderer.

"Involved in yer sister's death?" Crystal was relieved that the Inspector said it for her. "Nah. He's a local bloke. Never had a lick of trouble with the boy. He downs a tankard or two when he's got a euro to waste, but usually sleeps it off in his lorry."

"I didn't mean to..." Crystal felt like an apology was in order.

"No problem, Miss Traynor. Ye be from the States and ye don't know our little village. I understand." He looked around the place again. "Ye'll be wantin' to dispose of some of this?"

"Yes." Crystal jumped at the chance to change the subject. "Do they have a Goodwill around here? Maybe I can donate some stuff. Brystal's... you know... clothing? She and I have very dissimilar taste in clothing."

They always had.

Brystal was wild, colorful, and eccentric in her style and life. Crystal liked to match the walls and carpet. Less of a chance of being noticed. Her wardrobe contained three colors: gray, blue and black. That was her style and life.

"We've no religious army here, but the Widows and Orphans of the Sea is a fine charity. They've an establishment to gift and sell items." He peered into one bag. "They'd be sore grateful for anythin' you'd be wantin' to shed."

"Great." Crystal took a deep breath. "There are only a few things I want to take home." She pulled the blue spined album from the bookcase and placed it gently on the counter with a soft pat. "Will they pick-up? My rental is about the size of that recliner."

"Nah, but me brother-in-law has a truck. I'll be happy to borrow it and help ye out. 'Tis the least I can do." Rory and Becky had done the same for him after he'd lost Mary Mae and Ciara. Family was a Godsend and now Crystal had none to lend a hand.

"Do you think those books should go back to the shop?" Crystal pointed at the technical books on crystal that were left in the shelves.

"Dunn know, Miss Traynor. I'd be inclined to call Sean and see." Ethan took a book and thumbed through the pages. Some had notes in the margins in a tight flowing script.

"Please, could we dispense with the Miss Traynor. Call me Crystal. Miss Traynor works on the eighteenth floor of the Amberford building on Tenth and Main. Here, I'm just Crystal." She managed a lip curl she hoped looked like a smile.

"Right-o. Then 'Tis Ethan, and Just Crystal." Ethan grinned.

"I saw that movie. Just Joann, right? The Jewel of the Nile. Nineteen eighty-five. Douglas, Turner, and DeVito. Made ninety-six million dollars on opening." Crystal winced. Her awkwardness was showing.

Ethan couldn't help the chin drop, just a tad. Crystal's employer said she was a bit odd and had a mind for numbers, a genius he'd said. Apparently, her memory was infallible as well. "That be the one." He closed his mouth.

"Sorry." Now Crystal's smile was real and apologetic. "I do that. It's facts and numbers. I love them. That's what makes me good at what I do."

"Speakin'of what ye do, yer employer rang me up this mornin'. Wanted to check on ye. Seems ye don't have a cell."

Crystal winced again. "Checking up on me, huh? Well, I don't doubt it. He's actually a good friend. One of the few who tolerate me." She sighed and pulled a few mismatched dishes from the shelf that doubled as a dish cupboard. "And I make him a great deal of money which his wife loves to spend."

"Ah." What could Ethan say. He didn't know her boss, but he could tell from the call, the man was concerned. And he'd given Ethan a shade of a picture of Crystal. His mind centered on Daria and her quirky thing with facts and research. His niece and Crystal had something in common.

Daria too, would often blurt out some disassociated fact during dinner conversation. Her family was used to it, but he couldn't imagine what her school chums thought... all three of them. Was Daria destined to end up like Crystal Traynor? The thought was disturbing on several levels.

"He hired me away from this guy I used to do taxes for. I don't think he was a very good employer, but he left me alone and I was fine with that. I met Chance when I did his personal taxes. Next thing you know, I'm in an office with a view of the city, making huge amounts of money I can't seem to spend." Crystal dropped a plate on the floor and jumped as it shattered. "Crap..."

"Allow me." Ethan took off his jacket and grabbed a brush and dustpan that hung from under the counter. "Have a care for yer toes. Stay where ye are 'til I get it in the bin."

Crystal was barefoot. Porcelain shards surrounded her feet along with bigger pieces that had shot across the floor. "Will do. I don't need puddles of blood on the floor."

Puddles of blood? Where had he heard that before?

Daria!

Of course.

CHAPTER 11

The number eleven is a master number which signifies intuition, insight, and enlightenment. If you see this number, it means that you are spiritually awakening.
Pay attention to guidance from the universe! It can be very important.
Numerology and Sign, 1968 Revolution of the Mind

They worked amicably throughout the afternoon. Ethan bagging or boxing what Crystal wanted to donate, carefully packing those items to be shipped. They made a run to the market and purchased wrapping paper, shipping boxes, as well as drinks and sandwiches. By four o'clock, Crystal was dragging, and Ethan's hands were dry and cracked.

"Should we not take a break? I'm bushed and ye look to be whipped." Ethan sat on the floor as Crystal dropped into the recliner.

She rubbed the arms on the old, soft chair. "I could sleep for a year. If I could sleep at all." She laid her head back and took a deep breath, letting it out slowly, then sat up straight. "How will we get this chair outta here?"

Ethan had to laugh. Her mind never stopped. "I'll get Rory to help me tug it down if Colleen doesn't want it left." He leaned back against the door as the afore mentioned Colleen stuck her head in.

"I've a nice cup of tea and a basket of scones fer the hard-working mob." She edged through the door and tiptoed around the mess of stacks, boxes, and bags. I'd be hearin' ya all day and thought ye might enjoy a bit 'o tea and a snack."

"Ye be an angel from heaven." Ethan was off the floor in a second and grabbing for a warm scone.

Colleen poured a cup, handing it to Crystal along with a scone on a napkin. "I'd not be thinkin' Brys had so much to consider." Colleen eyed the boxes and bags.

"Brys?" Crystal had never heard her sister called anything but Brystal.

"Aye. Me little pet name fer yer sis. A right pleasant gel, she was." Colleen poured a cup for Ethan and handed it to him. He was already on his second scone. Crumbles littered the front of his shirt.

"Yum..." Crystal bit into the scone and groaned. "This is amazing."

"I'd be thankin' ye there. I've been doin' the baking since me mum passed some twenty years ago. I must admit, I do love the job." Colleen's smile was reward enough for the compliment.

Ethan had paused in demolishing his third scone. "Colleen, would ya be wantin' the stuffed chair there? I sincerely doubt Crystal here will be shippin' it home."

Colleen giggled and crossed herself. "That monster be followin' me like a shadow. I put it out on the stoop for charity and Brys took it right up. Now seems it's come back home." She moved toward the door. "Leave it and I'll see if it'll be wantin' to go on its own, or if I be sendin' it on its way." With a half-hearted wave, Colleen moved to leave. "What will ye be doin' with yer sister's motorbike?"

Both Ethan and Crystal were stunned. Ethan spoke first. "Brystal had a motorbike?"

"She sure as you and I sittin' here, did." Again, Colleen crossed herself. "Rode like a windstorm, she did. I kept bandages and salve in the kitchen just for her scrapes and burns. She loved that bike but wasn't especially good at stayin' on the seat. Her gettin' it was that Sean MacDougal's idea, I'm sure. They'd go out on the Ring and watch the sea, at times." She shook her head. "Me boy has the key. Brystal let him make deliveries on it. I'll see ye get it straight away."

Ethan could tell Crystal was amazed that her sister had an entire secret life here in Ireland she'd known nothing about. Brystal on a motorcycle? Not surprising to him.

"I've got a rental car so he can keep using the bike. It'll take me some time to get this place cleared out. How long was Brystal's lease?"

"Lease? Brys rented by the month. She be paid up until the end of this month so ye've got time. And I'll refund the balance if ye leave early. I'll be down below if ye have need." Colleen breezed out the door. Her bakery was calling.

Ethan turned to Crystal. "So, yer sister was a biker-lady, isn't that what ye call it in the States?" He laughed.

"Biker babe. And no, she wasn't. Brystal was very athletic, but I can't imagine her careening around Ireland on two wheels and a prayer. Actually, I can imagine it. I'm sure she rode like she did everything, like there was no tomorrow. What ring was Colleen talking about?" Crystal paused and took a breath.

"Ach, the Ring of Kerry. 'Tis N-seventy." Ethan smiled at Crystal's confusion. "Across the bay. A road goes round the peninsula through Killarney, Molls Gap, and a couple of other small towns. It's called the Ring of Kerry. 'Tis a wonder for the tourists, but a bit dicey to drive. You should see it afore ye be leavin'. If nothin' else, but for a beautiful memory of yer sad trip." He finished the last scone as he looked out the window. Crystal's tears had begun, and Ethan was a tad uncomfortable with the female habit. It was close to the dinner hour and across the alleyway he saw a flash in the window. Someone was in the building next door. That someone was watching Brystal's apartment. The shadow moved again and was gone. Ethan's cell phone chirped, and he withdrew it from his jacket pocket.

"Inspector MacEnery here."

"Ethan, yer sister be makin' coddle and biscuits fer sup. She wanted to know if ye'd be interested." It was his brother-in-law, Rory.

Ethan brushed the crumbles off of his shirt. "Will there be enough fer an extra mouth? I've a friend who needs sup as well." He winked at Crystal who was rubbing her tears away.

She shook her head in the negative with vigor.

Ethan shook his head in the affirmative with the same vigor. It would not do to leave the lass alone to dine on cheese and soda bread another night. Maybe an evening with his sister's family would be a sleep potion. Ethan looked across the alley again. Something bothered him about the shadow in the window and the missing drawings.

"The more the better. I'll have Daria set two places at the table. Who'd be a comin'?" Ethan could tell Rory had already had a few. He was jolly and didn't think to ask his sister about company.

"Crystal Traynor, a gel from the States. We'll be on our way then. Need I bring anythin'?"

"Ye really want to be insultin' yer sis? Dangerous ground boy-o." Rory rang off.

As soon as Ethan stowed his cell, Crystal blurted, "I don't think I should go. I'm not the best company right now. I wouldn't want to impose."

"Trust me, 'tis no imposition. Me sis, Becky, won't mind a bit. In her house 'tis the more the merrier. And I've a notion my niece will be a wee surprise." Ethan immediately had second thoughts. Maybe it wasn't such a good idea. Daria could be rather intrusive and, meddling? Almost to the point of being rude and insensitive.

Ethan could see Crystal was hesitant. "I'm not good with strangers. I have this problem-"

"We've a saying in Ireland. There be no strangers, only friends ye've yet to meet. And me sister is one of the best cooks in the county. It'll be a good break for ye." Ethan was trying his best persuasive copper-self. He glanced across the alley again and saw a hint of movement. The hair stood on the back of his neck. He was not about to leave Crystal alone until he figured a few things out. "I'll take ye out and bring ye back when you want. Are ye tellin' me ye don't like free food there, Miss Traynor?" He tried to give her his most disbelievin' detective look.

Crystal laughed at the attempt. "All right. But what if your family doesn't like me?"

"What's not to like? Besides, me Becky collects strays from everywhere." The statement didn't sound quite the way he'd meant it. "I mean to say, she's a born mother and can't help thinkin' all God's creatures that enter her door need love and attention, and it's her job to be providin' it." Ethan chuckled. Indeed, his sister did mother everything from wanderin' puppies to adult brothers who'd lost their families. She was an endless open well of warmth and concern that seemed to flow around people. Like a tsunami at times. "Ye'll be fine in her house, believe me."

He motioned to the door. "Shall we?" He was very much aware that Crystal needed a little encouragement. Who wouldn't in her place? "It's a bit of a drive. Ye can relax some before we get there."

Crystal nodded in his direction, collected her pocketbook, ran her fingers across her braid and followed Ethan out to his car.

As they drove west toward Becky's house, Ethan filled Crystal in on his family's history. "Me mum and da lived on the farm when Becky and I were kids. When mum passed, Becky kept the place. She's amazing. Raisin' kids, cats, dogs, sheep, chickens, and pigs, anythin' that needs a home. Rory drives a lorry. He's gone for days at a stretch and Becky just keeps keepin' on. They've two wee bairns, well, not so wee now-a-days. Daria and Quinn are twins, but about as different as black and white. Quinn be a jock-o like his da. Daria, I've no idea about that lass. She's brilliant and a touch fey, if ya be askin' me."

"Fey?" Crystal had not spoken a word since they'd left Brystal's flat and Ethan took it as a beginning.

"Fey. Means touched, ya know. Different. Touched by the fairy folk. I guess you Yanks would call it different, eccentric, weird. But in a good way."

"Trust me, I understand that." He glanced at Crystal as she squirmed in her seat. Maybe meetin' his Daria would be good for this gel with so much in, and on her mind.

"The place is na a grand hotel by far stretch, but it's me childhood home. 'Tis," he paused, "comfortable." He set his blinker for a left turn. "The road's a rough way, gravel."

Ahead, at the end of a short gravel road, Ethan's 'childhood home' came into view. The sprawling wooden structure glowed in the twilight. The interior sent enough light through the windows to cast a soft glow on the many baskets and pots of various flowers and vegetables placed about the wide porch. Wooden pole chairs sat about the bright green front door. Ethan knew the scrolling letters round the edges of the door were Gaelic prayers to ward off evil and keep the Aos Si, the mischievous fairies and leprechauns, away. The sight always warmed his heart and sent rivers of love through his body. The memories of his boyhood washed over him and set a soft smile on his lips.

"This place is very cute. I live in a high-rise. On the seventh floor. I have a big window that looks over the city street." Ethan knew people lived that way, but couldn't imagine never sitting on a porch with a Guinness, watchin' the world from a place of comfort and safety, a place where his mother and father had made their home a refuge from the worries and hateful things beyond their control. "It's nothing like this. And your sister takes care of all of it? On her own?"

Ethan didn't mind bragging a bit of his sister, she was so like their mum. "Mostly. The kids help out with chores and what-not. But ye'll just have to meet her to understand. There isn't another like me sis." He parked the car in front of a huge flower box that didn't contain flowers. Instead a profusion of vines and latticework held a variety of ripening tomatoes. In front of the entrance stood a quaint couple, arms around each other, silhouetted by the light from the house. "Speaking of me sister."

Ethan got out and came around the car to help Crystal, only to find that the independent American lass had gotten out just fine on her own. He knew Crystal was sensitive to touch, so instead of taking her arm, as any Irish lass would have allowed, he motioned toward his sister and her husband waiting on the porch. "Ah… Rebekkah, Rory, this is Miss Crystal Traynor. A friend, from the States."

Before Ethan could move, a blurring mass sprang from the

shadows and shot in his direction. "Uncle Ethan!" Quinn kicked a soccer ball out into the yard and lunged, arms spread wide for the best catch. Connecting at the first try, Ethan found himself beneath his young nephew, rolling in the grass as the first of many attacks ensued.

Ethan caught sight of Crystal pressed against his car. "Quinn, boy-o, we be scarin' the ladies." He pushed the exuberant young boy off his chest and tried to stand. Apparently, Quinn was having none of it and grabbed him just below the knees. Down he went one more time before Rory came to the rescue, pulling his son away by the collar. Ethan rolled to his back with a hoot. "Ye'll be boxed for sure tonight. No dessert be the penalty, ye rascal." Ethan crawled to a stand rubbing his left knee.

Quinn struggled free of his father and ran to hug his injured uncle. "I'm bein' sorry, Uncle Ethan. Did I hurt ye much?" Ethan could see the beginnings of a tear in the boy's eye. His nephew was such a sensitive child. It had always seemed like Quinn got the lion's share of emotional DNA and Daria got the brains with the sensitivity of a newt.

Ethan bent over like an old man of the woods. "Ye'll needs be a bit more careful with the old man here, boy-o. I'm not a young strapping fella like yer da." He leaned heavily on Quinn to the point that the boy collapsed under his weight, and the match was back on.

"That'll be quite enough! Ye all be scoundrels and heathens." Becky waved them into the house as she approached Crystal, still pressed against the car, watching the melee with a touch of trepidation. "Welcome to our home. Céad míle fáilte!" Ethan caught Crystal's slight wince as his sister leaned in close. "Means a thousand welcomes. Come in and have a sit. Supper is almost on the table."

Pausing in the doorway, Ethan introduced his guest to everyone at once. "This is Miss Crystal Traynor. She's here on business but all alone so I thought to bring her. All ye scoundrels on yer best now." He turned to catch the eye of his niece. "Especially you, gel. No showin' yer fangs."

Daria ducked out of the shadows. "I'll be pleased to meet' ye, Miss

Traynor." Then she executed a perfect curtsey, the likes fit for the Queen herself.

"All right, me Bridget. Into the kitchen with ye and fetch up supper. I'm famished and faintin' away."

Crystal caught up to Ethan and asked quietly, "I thought her name was Daria?"

"'Tis. Bridget's what we call the maid." He laughed an ushered her into the cozy house that was almost a manor. "We've a complex language, we Irish. Made up of the ancients, the conquerors, the Priests, Brits and just about everything else. Then there be football. You Yanks call it soccer."

"Of course." Crystal wasn't shy by a long shot, just uncomfortable in new environments.

Ethan pointed the way through the great room to the dining area. A heavy polished wooden table took up a good deal of the floor space but seemed warm and inviting. Set with decorated china, the green bands of leaf and floral design on the placemats matched the place settings and silver. Twining leaves curled around the stem of each knife in silver relief and matched the other flatware. "I see Becky has used the drive time well. This was our mother's good setting."

Not to be left out of any conversation that required facts and information, Daria pointed to a special plate with strange letters encircling the center of the china. "That be the place of honor for a guest." She picked up the plate and showed it to Crystal. "The plate says, 'May what fills this plate, fill yer heart'. In Gaelic, of course. I think." She studied the letters. "Anyway, 'tis what I was told. Could be anythin' as far as I'd be knowin'. I'm a modern gel." Daria replaced the plate and winked at her uncle.

Everyone took their places. Crystal in the place of honored guest, Ethan next to her and his niece and nephew across the table. Rebekkah sat at the end nearest the kitchen entryway and Rory took his place at the head of the table.

"Ethan, will ye be sayin' grace now?" His sister held out her hands for all to join in the prayer and Ethan hesitantly held his out for Crystal. He was relieved when she actually placed her soft fingers in his and closed her eyes.

"Bless us O Lord, and these Thy gifts, which we are about to receive, from Thy bounty. Through Christ, our Lord. Amen." He crossed himself and was surprised to see Crystal do the same. There had been nothing in her sister's file to indicate the family was Catholic. In fact, he remembered seeing pictures of Brystal celebrating the Winter Solstice with a group of notorious women from Dingle. They were said to be old believers, those who still followed the Druid ways and made no bones about flaunting it to the usually devout villagers. The picture showed a wild haired Brystal dancing, hand in hand with other women, around a bonfire, her flimsy dress made transparent by the light. She had a wondrous figure and...

"Uncle Ethan?" Daria's question dragged him from his wondering thoughts. She held a plate of soda biscuits away from her brother, offering them to Ethan and his guest. "These are Irish biscuits but if ye don't be quick, some jack-o will have them all."

Ethan took the plate and passed it to Crystal. "Becky makes the best soda biscuits in the county. And her coddle is to be eaten' with joy" Ethan took two biscuits and pointed a finger at Quinn. There would be plenty to go around but he loved to tease his nephew.

As the soup tureen was passed around, each person ladled a pleasurable helping of coddle onto their plates. "Coddle is like yer stew, I think. Only I make it with me own vegetables and pork sausage. I grow most everythin'."

"And she bakes from scratch as well. 'Tis why I've grown a bit over the year." Ethan was proud of his sister's cooking and home skills. He tried to find a roll of fat to pinch but was unsuccessful.

"Aye, and if ye remember to eat at all." Becky's retort held a touch of concern that Ethan did not want in the conversation at the moment.

"Crystal is from New York City. She lives in one of those skyscrapers." He tried to change the subject.

"Oh. My. God! Really?" Daria almost jumped out of her seat. "I've always wanted to see New York. They say ye can't be seein' the sky from the street. Is it true, Miss?"

Ethan watched Crystal push the various vegetables into small piles of like color and kind. She carefully separated the meat on one side of her plate. "When the weather is foul, the upper floors of very tall buildings can often not see the ground, so I suppose that is correct. If you were on the ground, you couldn't see the sky. I live on the seventh floor." She forked a piece of meat and put it to her lips, sniffing a little before placing the chunk in her mouth.

Quinn was stuffing coddle and biscuits in his mouth, but Daria hadn't touched her plate. "Can you see the sky at your flat? I mean, is it right in the big part of the city? The part where the big park is? You know, where the horse carriages ride around with rich people in it?"

Crystal smiled as she continued to chew the sausage. "No. That is a very expensive part of the city and I'm not a millionaire. Well, actually I am, but I don't live like that." The words just came out matter-of-factly and Ethan watched his sister choke on a carrot. Crystal was more like Daria than he first suspected. Things just flowed out her mouth without much thought most times.

"Why not? If you are rich, why not live like it?" Daria's words were just as matter of fact.

"I live by my job. It is," Crystal looked at the young girl across the table, "...convenient. Comfortable."

"I have a job, too. I be raisin' sheep fer the table, like me mum. Three are Cheviot and six are Black Faced Mountain devils. Those buggers climb the hills and I be needin' to fetch 'em often. That be me job." Daria sighed as if she bore the weight of the world on her shoulders. "But I really prefer me studies. What do you do?"

Crystal had just put a piece of biscuit in her mouth, and a piece stuck to her lip. "I'm a forensic accountant." Ethan watched as the flavor finally hit and Crystal smiled. "These are incredible. I've never had anything like this before."

"'Tis an Irish thing." Daria pointed to the honey pot in the middle of the table with her fork. "They are simply excellent with real butter and honey."

Ethan guffawed. "When did you learn to speak American?" Daria had used an accent that made her sound exactly like a teen from the state of California, complete with a Valley Gal inflection.

Daria giggled. "YouTube, Uncle Ethan. I was looking up murder stuff and found this hilarious clip of a woman who fights with a sword. She kills all of these people and cuts off their arms." Daria demonstrated with her butter knife. "Whack! The blood sprays all over the place. It's funny and kind of stupid. Blood doesn't really spray like that. Not like the real murder here in the village. Our murder had puddles, didn't it?"

The silence that followed had Ethan swallowing hard. Obviously, his niece didn't know Brystal was Crystal's sister. How had he missed that?

"That be enough, young gel. Eat yer sup." Becky covered the silence as Ethan watched Crystal's reaction. She seemed fine. How could that be? Daria's prattling was very close to home.

"So, are you here helping Uncle Ethan with the investigation?" Daria had not gotten the point. "He said there's no evidence in the woman's murder, but..."

"Daria! Stop. Now." Ethan had to put an end to the line of conversation before it sent Crystal into some kind of coma, or whatever it was that she did. "Leave us to this wonderful dinner yer mum fixed. Let the adults talk."

Suitably chastised, Daria buttered her biscuit and shoved half of it in her mouth, smiling sweetly at her Uncle, mashed goo covering her teeth.

"I do apologize for me little heathen, Miss Traynor. She's usually a bit more ladylike." Becky's dirty look at her daughter was to no avail. Daria simply smiled at her mother, goo, and all.

"Rory, did ye get the breakers fixed on the cooler yet?" Ethan tried for a complete change of venue.

"Nah. It'll be a week afore the parts come in. I've hired out for a long lor, up to New Haven's Sleidle. Be gone some ten days deliverin'. I've not taken a long one since the...." Suddenly, Rory didn't want to finish the sentence, so Ethan finished it for him.

"Cooler went buggers?" It was a bit of a cover and he couldn't even tell if Crystal had caught the segway.

"Yes. The cooler." Now Rory was looking for an out.

"Well, I have to be tellin' ye, New Haven's a haul. As long as me sis is fine with it." He sopped up the last of the coddle juice with his biscuit. "I'll be around if 'n Becky needs a hand."

"Like I can't handle this place on me own." Becky grinned and threw a kiss Ethan's way. "That'll be the day snakes return to this blessed country." Becky stood and collected the dishes. "Dessert is apple crumble with a touch of Bailey's. Who's for it?"

Quinn hadn't said a word since the food was on his plate. It now sat before him sparkling clean. "Aye, the biggest piece, please."

"Ye'll be taller than yer da soon, Jack-o." Ethan chuckled. "I'll be for a piece, but light Bailey's. I be drivin'."

"Thank you, but no. I don't care for sweets." Crystal patted her stomach as if she'd eaten a gallon of coddle. In truth she'd hardly touched her food at all. "I can help with the dishes, if you'd like."

"Nah. Ye be a guest in me home. Ethan can help. He'll be good fer somethin' besides fillin' his maw." Becky got up. "Would ye be carin' fer another cup 'o tea? Daria can pour."

As Ethan followed his sister into the kitchen with a load of dishes, he heard Becky's whispered comment. "She be the sister of the dead gel, yes?"

He nodded in the affirmative. "And a bit fey, that one. "'Twas a shock to see her at first. They be identical. Not like yer brood, sis."

Becky stopped suddenly and faced her brother. "What are ye sayin'? Lord bless that gel." Becky crossed herself. "I can't be thinkin' on how she must be feelin'." She set the tureen and butter on the center counter of the large kitchen. "You did right bringin' her here, Ethan."

"I was hopin', but Daria-" Ethan shook his head. "I should have warned you, but I was standin' in front of the lass when I took Rory's ring."

As soon as the dishes were out of Ethan's hands, Becky hugged him fiercely. "I'll have a word with me brat. Not to worry. Now go sit with the adults. Talk. And send Daria in to me to help serve the crumble." She released her brother with a gentle shove. "Go."

Expelled from his sister's domain with love, Ethan returned to the dining room with orders for his niece. "Daria, yer mum wants help with the dessert."

Somewhat compliant, Daria rose with another Queen's curtsey, sent a wink her uncle's way, and twirled out of the room.

"She be a bit of a handful, that lass. But we love her anyway." Rory chuckled. "Miss Traynor forgive my ignorance, I'm a simple driver. What does a forensic accountant actually do?"

"I look at finances and information." Crystal came to life. "If you want to bring criminals to justice, you follow the money. I work for one of the most successful forensic accounting firms in the country, my country. I have a staff who feed me information through their research, and I figure out who's doing what." She took a sip of tea. "I just finished a case that ended with several arrests and soon they will be convicted in our court of law."

Daria placed a generous portion of apple crumble in front of her uncle and a smaller one in front of her father. "So, you look for evidence? How?" They were back to dicey territory.

"Like I said, I have a staff of people, four to be exact. When we get a case that can't seem to be solved, it comes to me and my people. We are the best. I work for LDE, Larson, Davidson, and Evans CPA firm. The Feds call us Last Ditch Effort because we get the most difficult or stalled cases. I've only ever not solved one case. It still bugs me."

"That sounds so exciting!" Daria spread her arms and twirled. "Livin' in New York City. Catchin' the bad guys. Like that telly program, Law and Order!"

"Nothing like that program. I sit in an office and follow the evidence. It's hours of hunting through thousands of documents. I love it, but most people would think it dull and boring."

When Crystal spoke of her job, she was as relaxed and confident as a starlet on the red carpet. Ethan was seeing a different side of this woman and was blown away. Now if he could just keep Daria away from the Dingle murder.

"I simply love numbers. I'll be doin' accelerated math now. 'Tis all formulas and equations. Grade ten mathematics, they say. I can't leave it sometimes. Next year I can start Statistical Analysis and that will be amazing! Me mum says I be queer that way."

"That was my favorite class in high school. They didn't know what to do with me, so the school let me study on my own. It was university material." Crystal had relaxed and was now looking directly at Daria as she spoke. Ethan had not seen Crystal this animated or emotional about anything since she'd arrived. "When I finally got to university, it was boring and mostly review, but my sister made me stay with it." Crystal studied the liquid in her cup. "Not that Brystal ever stayed with anything very long in her life." She looked up at Daria and Quinn. "We were twins, identical. Not like you two. I'm left and she was right. Handed, not political." Crystal qualified her statement. "We looked exactly the same, but two sisters couldn't have been more different."

Quick to pick up on everything, Daria asked, "Were? Where be she now?"

Ethan sat up. He had to stop this line of conversation. "Daria, let Quinn say something, fer Heaven's sake."

"It's all right, Ethan." Crystal took another sip of tea in the silence that ensued. "She was killed. That's why I'm here." Crystal was back to studying her tea.

CHAPTER 12

The number twelve means completion, the turning of a new leaf in life. A new beginning.
It is comprised of a one and two –
the deeper meaning; one of two, one part of the whole,
one of twins, or crystalized combination linked to a second.
Numerology is an ambiguous science!

Dessert was a quiet event followed by a somber evening. Until Quinn, in his eleven-year-old exuberance, fell over Crystal's pocketbook spilling the contents across the living room floor. Daria, somewhat repentant for her earlier verbal blunder, dashed to the rescue. Brystal's drawings, forgotten in the pocket of Crystal's bag, landed at her feet and fell open.

"Will ye have a look at this." Before anyone could tell the child not to intrude in Crystal's belongings, she had the drawings open and laying on the hard wood floor. "'Tis magnificent. Look at the patterns."

"Daria, give those back to Miss Traynor, right now." Rory ordered before Ethan could say a word.

"Aye, Da. But they are so beautiful. And perfect. And..."

"Daria!" It was a stern warning Ethan had heard before. Apparently so had Daria.

"Straight away, Da." The imp carefully placed each page in a neat stack and picked them up to hand to Crystal.

"No." Crystal turned away in her place on the couch. "I can't look at them."

"Sorry." Daria stood holding the pages. "They were yer sister's, aye."

"No. It's the patterns. They talk to me and I get stuck." Why was she revealing this 'thing' that she suffered from now? Here? Ethan took the pages from his niece and folded them carefully so none of the drawing showed.

Daria perched on the arm of the couch next to Crystal. "I know exactly what ye mean." She placed a light hand on Crystal's shoulder and to Ethan's amazement, Crystal did not pull away. "Sometimes I get lost in my studies. It's like the numbers have lives of their own and they want to come play. 'Tis a queer thing, but I understand."

"You do? You are the only one I've ever met who can actually say what I feel." Tears formed and Crystal sniffed. She placed her hand atop Daria's. "Thank you." She whispered just loud enough for Daria and Ethan to hear.

In the meantime, Quinn had gathered all of Crystal's possessions and placed them carefully in a pile on the couch next to her. "So sorry, mum. Me feet are too big fer me legs."

"Nay, me brother, yer feet be too fast fer ye brain." Daria stood and knocked on the side of Quinn's head. It initiated a game of chase and the twins sped outside to see which one had the fastest and most coordinated feet.

"Aye, those two be the death of me yet. Please accept my apologies fer me boy. He's grown a foot in the last year and doesn't quite know where his arms and legs go anymore." Ethan knew the apology was heartfelt, but he could also see the humor behind the whole thing.

Daria was a little fairy dancing through life with nary a touch to the ground. Quinn was the Incredible Hulk, smashing into anything and everything. He would grow another foot and learn to manage his body, but at eleven, he was lucky to walk and talk at the same time. He was Ethan all over again. "And my prayers fer ye sister's passing. It took me a bit to understand yer connection to yer sister's tragic end. Unfortunately, me gel's been fascinated by the case since the beginning." Becky shifted uneasily in her chair. "That sounds so cold and final. I didn't mean it that way. Sorry. Again" She looked to her brother for help.

"Please, call me Crystal. And you have nothing to apologize for. Your daughter is enchanting. I do believe she and I would get along just fine. In any other circumstance. She's brilliant, isn't she?"

"'Tis a gift from God and a curse of the Devil, that one. She's got double the brains and such passion for whatever the thing be at the moment. Unfortunately, she's also a mouth that roars." Over the awkwardness, Becky relaxed and so did Ethan. "Quinn, on the other hand, me boy be teary-eyed when he steps on a spider. Ye know, he tells his mum, it could have a brother or sister somewhere. Honestly."

Crystal laughed and so did Ethan. "Your children are precious, and you are lucky to have this family. Brystal was all I had left. My parents are dead, and I've never sought out any relatives. It was always Brystal and me."

"Well, not anymore, lass. Ye've been adopted and ye will always have a place here." Becky's warmth seemed to slide across the polished wood floor and encircle everyone in the room with unconditional love. "Those be not just words, Crystal. I mean them with all me heart. If ye've a need, this be the place to come. Any time."

"Thank you, Becky." Crystal seemed to collapse with those words and Ethan remembered the lass had not slept well for days. It was time to go.

"You, me beloved sis, are too good fer words. But I'd be thinkin' this one needs a bed and rest." He stood and extended a hand to Crystal. She was wilting fast and allowed Ethan to pull her from the comfy couch. "Thanks be fer the sup and crumble. I'd say ye out did yerself, but ye do it the same every time." He led Crystal out the door, her restored pocketbook on her arm with a quick farewell kiss for his sister. "Tell the heathens good night fer me."

He helped Crystal into her seat and they were off down the bumpy road. Despite the rough drive, he saw Crystal's eyelids droop then close. The lass was exhausted, and he should have made their good-byes sooner. He wondered how long it'd been since she had a decent night's sleep. Hopefully, tonight would be the beginning of a new lease on life.

As he pulled up behind the bakery, Crystal snorted and woke. "I snore." Her groggy statement was definitely not required.

"Aye. That ye do. But it's cute." He added.

"No. It's a nasal problem. I've had it since I was a child." Crystal got out of the car and swayed, catching herself on the side mirror.

Ethan got out and trotted around to her side of the car. "Ye be beat. Take me arm. The stairs are steep."

As he pulled Crystal up the steps, he felt a kind of contentment wash over him. She let him touch her without protest, or shying away. As they made the landing outside Brystal's flat, he froze.

The door stood halfway open. Through the opening he could see a box smashed open and the contents strewn across the floor. "Stay here, Crystal." He leaned her against the wall and withdrew his pistol.

Carefully opening the door with weapon drawn, he scanned the room for intruders, then tiptoed across to the bedroom entrance, scanning all the while. There was no one.

"Clear... You can come-"

"What?" Crystal stood right behind him. "Happened?" Tears filled her eyes and she stumbled.

Ethan holstered his weapon and caught Crystal as she slid to the floor sobbing. "There now lass." He held her close as she cried in huge, racking sobs. Ethan picked her up and settled her on Brystal's bed, pulled a coverlet over her, and sat on the table next to her. What should he do? Her sobs subsided to be replaced by a light snore and Ethan knew Crystal had finally succumbed to exhaustion and grief. He got up quietly and moved into the living room.

It was a disaster. Every box they'd packed was ripped or torn open; the contents strewn across the room. Several carefully wrapped family treasures were smashed and scattered. The lone picture left on the wall had been torn down, it's back sliced and peeled. All of the cupboards were thrown open, some of the dishes broken on the floor or thrown onto the tiny counter in a stack. The over-stuffed recliner had been pulled away from the wall, it's back and sides slashed open to reveal, what? He stood in the shadows peering out the window, thinking. Again, movement in the other building caught his eye. He wanted to charge over and force whoever was watching to tell him what was going on, but Crystal slept in the other room. Her safety was more important than a momentary chase after a shadow across the way. He checked his watch. It was nine-thirty. Calling in a forensic specialist at this time of night wouldn't be easy, but maybe there were prints, or something that would lead to whoever had done this and why. He pulled out his cell phone and called the An Garda Síochána.

"Aidan? Right-o." He recognized the new intern. The boy must have drawn the short straw to pull the late shift. "I'll be needin' a print team. I got a messed flat. It's got something to do with the Traynor murder. Can ye roust 'em tonight?"

"Sir, yes sir. They won't be liken' it much. I'll do me best, Inspector." The young Garda rang off. Ethan wondered how long it would take to get the boys out of the pub and geared up. Apparently, he'd be here for the long run. In the meantime, he'd check with Colleen to see what she might know.

Before heading downstairs, Ethan quietly checked on Crystal. From the doorway he could hear her soft purr and even breathing. She looked like a small child, curled up clutching her blanket for security. What this lass had gone through in the last weeks was unconscionable. She was at the end of her mental and physical resources. She would sleep. He would investigate.

He checked the window across the alley. There seemed no movement. On silent feet, Ethan left the flat, being sure to lock the door. For good measure, he placed a small piece of cellophane tape at the top of the door. If anyone entered or left before he returned the tape would come off and he would know.

Colleen was in her flat with her son, but it required Ethan to go down the back stairs and come up the front. He could hear her laughter before he knocked. A young man, about sixteen answered, His hand held a splay of playing cards.

"Who be there, Christian?" Colleen called from somewhere inside the flat.

Christian opened the door wide. "Inspector MacEnery, mum. Should I let him in?"

Ethan heard rustling before Colleen pulled the door wide. "Of course, boy." She threw the door open. Come on in, Ethan."

Colleen's flat was a mixture of mixtures. He knew she was an old believer, but she was also an astute businesswoman. Her husband spent his weekdays in Galway and only came home on weekends leaving Colleen and her son to run her beloved bakery. Professor Sweeney was some kind of instructor at the National University of Ireland Galway. NUI Galway was a highly respected member of the Coimbra Group that numbered forty some schools across Europe. Their research department was well venerated, and the education program produced Ireland's finest teachers. Ethan knew Sweeney's specialty was Ireland's ancient history and archeology. He often wondered if Sweeney married their local baker as part of his research, however, their marriage had stood the test of time producing three children and a doctoral thesis on megalithic art of Newgrange. Some of that art now graced the walls of Colleen's flat.

"Is anythin' a miss with Brys' sister?" The worried look on Colleen's face touched Ethan's heart. This woman had a good soul and an outstanding way with baked goods.

"Nah. I was just wonderin' if ye saw anyone in her flat in the last few hours? The place was tossed. We found quite the mess when we returned from me sister's and dinner."

Christian was the first to speak. "Heard some queer rustling sounds when we was fixin' supper. I figured the gel was still packin'

Brys' stuff, ye know. Inspector, would ye be thinkin' the sister be selling the motorbike?"

"Christian!" Colleen was appalled at her son's insensitivity.

"'Tis business, mum. Nothing more. I loved Brys as much as you, but she be gone, and the bike be here." The boy was not to be dissuaded. "Sales be up twenty percent with delivery." He folded his card hand and stuck it in his pocket.

Ethan chuckled. The boy was business through and through. "Some kind of rustling, ye say?" Ethan took a chair near the fireplace. "Can ye describe it fer me, Christian?"

"Like boxes bein' shoved around. I heard a couple crashes, like somethin' was dropped and broke. I didn't think anything of it at the time. Stuff happens, ye know." Christian plunked down on the floor near the coffee table where they'd obviously been playing cards.

"Aye. I herd it as well. I was thinkin' Crystal was still packin'. 'Tis a sorrowful business, that." Colleen offered a plate of butter cookies up for Ethan.

"Don't mind if I do. Me thanks." He took a cookie. "So have ye any idea of the time?"

"Sure do." Christian popped a whole cookie into his mouth and chomped with relish. "Just before da's usual call, mum. About six-thirty."

"Oisin calls every night at six-thirty to check up on this rascal." Colleen pointed to her son across the low table. "Christian here will be goin' to university with his da next year."

"I'll be studyin' business though, not old rocks." Apparently Christian was all about the grand dollar, not glyphs and history.

"So ye be hearin' shufflin' about six-thirty? Any idea how long it lasted?" Ethan brought the focus back to his case at hand.

"Nah. After a while, I sorta tuned it out." Christian commented. "Ye live in a flat with other's around and ye get good at ignorin'."

"Ye mean tuned in, to yer stocks. This young man'll be on that computer checkin' his earnings, and losses, every second, if I be lettin' him." Colleen, like many modern-day parents, did not approve of the technological influence the digital age had on her child. "It wasn't long though. I distinctly remember things quieted on my third sheet of cookies. So about seven thirty, or so."

Ethan took another cookie which produced a wide grin on Colleen's face. "Well, if ye be rememberin' anythin', let me know, will ye?"

Christian got up to let Ethan out of the flat. "Ye could talk to Dharág. Lives across the alley, he does." The scowl on Christian's face spoke volumes. "Always complains I be parked in his spot. Never yet seen the squire's name on the cement."

"Ye got crossways over parkin'?" Ethan knew parking was tight and worse yet since tourism took a jump in their little village.

"Not often. The bodach thinks he be ownin' the world since Sean made him journeyman." Christian leaned on the doorjamb. "If ye be askin' me, there be somethin' bolloxed with that bucko."

"Brystal's gaffer lives across the alley?" Ethan was a little surprised, but then again, Dingle was a tight little town, and finding a flat was not easy these days.

"Sure 'nough. He kept his eye on her. Brys is pure binneas." He bowed his head. "I mean was." This boy was obviously head over heels for Crystal's sister despite their obvious age difference. Ethan could easily see how this young man felt. He'd never known the lass alive, but it didn't take long to fall for the woman through the eyes of those who did. Including Christian.

"Aye. 'Tis a right mess." Ethan took his leave with a thanks to Colleen for the cookies. He'd have to remember to ask Crystal about Christian and Brystal's motorbike. The boy was a go-getter and headed off to university the following year. A bike would be a treasure for a first-year student.

Climbing the back stairs again, Ethan paused. Was someone above? The floorboards creaked and he drew his weapon. The walls in this old building were as thin as paper and every step made its own announcement. Slowly, he took each step with trepidation. He no longer considered Brystal's murder a crime of convenience. There were too many questions now.

At the top of the stairs, the door was still closed. He checked his "poor man's security system". The tape had not been altered. He checked the floor for marks or dirt. Nothing.

~

Crystal woke to chaos and confusion. The stars were not in the right places. She lay in an unfamiliar bed. The place smelled of tamsin and rosemary with a hint of lilac around the edges. Her head throbbed with a pounding that matched her heartbeat, and her stomach threatened to empty itself right then and there. She closed her eyes and fought back the nausea. It wasn't an unfamiliar feeling.

Whenever life lurched to overwhelm her, she focused on some complex calculation. Numbers were safe. Numbers were her friends, and her enemies. She lay in the strange bed with her eyes squeezed tight, going over Brystal's drawings in her mind. The cascading formula was more than just design elements. There was meaning behind the patterns and descending numbers. The patterns taken in sequence would produce an exquisite design, but there was more to Brystal's work. It wound down into a deep dark hole, but what was the end result in the black space? The answer eluded Crystal but working the equation settled her stomach and her nerves. She opened her eyes and focused. Where was she?

Ireland.

Brystal's flat.

She was in Brystal's bed.

Brystal was in the morgue.

Tears began anew as Crystal crawled from the strange bed. It was dark outside, but the town lights shone into the small room, lighting her way to the bathroom. It dawned on Crystal as she banged her knees on the plumbing, this was the true definition of a water closet. Only smaller.

Wandering the three feet to the kitchen spot, Crystal surveyed the mess. How long had she slept? How did she get into Brystal's bed? Why was everything all over the place? Too many questions and too few answers. Her head began to swim, and she caught herself on the edge of the cupboard. Dizzy and leaning heavily, her hand contacted the door of the secret cupboard and the door released.

Crystal had forgotten all about the precious hidden crystal goblets and decanter. Her physical discomfort forgotten, she withdrew one of the delicate glass pieces and held it up to the ray of streetlight shining through the living room window. Immediately her mind engaged, and she studied the patterns with a focus only she could project. It was perfect! Not a single dimension out of line or a tiny misscut anywhere. She gazed at the array of colors against her hand as the ray of light was bent and manipulated by the intricate segments of crystal. She turned the goblet back and forth, watching the patterns form and fade with the onset of a new pattern. Curiously cold and daunting, each pattern gave her a sense of a vile and treacherous omen. The brilliant display clawed at Crystal's mind with endless possibilities.

Her fingers continued to turn the stem, rotating the goblet, producing flash after sinister flash of ultimate gloom and death. What had her sister created? Intellectually Crystal knew this incredibly intricate monster was only a compilation of silica, potash, and red lead combined, annealed and cut, but this thing she held? Did this array of cuts in the crystal portray a potential path to pain and destruction?

Startled by the flat door opening, she released the demon. It fell to the floor with a hideous crashing sound as the crystal piece self-destructed on impact. The evil was gone, broken into a million tiny shards.

"Crystal are you all right?" She could hear Ethan's voice, feel his cold hand on her arm, but her mind was still caught in the web of horrific discovery. What had Brystal done?

Crystal stuttered and took a deep breath. "I–"

"Come over here away from that mess. I'll clean it up." Still overcome by her sister's diabolical creation, Crystal let him steer her to the recliner.

"I'm fine." She breathed out as her legs gave and she sat with a plop.

"Right-o. Fine. Yes, you are. Now." She watched as Ethan gathered the dustpan and small hand broom. Bending to sweep the powdery mess, he spied the secret cupboard. "Hello."

"No, don't take them out! They're dangerous." Crystal was up on her wobbly legs and attempting to stay Ethan's hand. Unfortunately, her body wasn't up to the task and she collapsed after her second step, landing square on Ethan's bent figure. They both went to the floor, Crystal's hand smacking the floorboard right on top of the pile of broken glass shards. "Ow!"

"Buggers. Here, let me help." In a flash Ethan had her up and back on the edge of the recliner.

"Ethan, I'm okay. I can handle this." Blood covered her palm, and one large piece of crystal was embedded in the thick of her right hand.

"No, ye can't, lass. Be still. Are there any medical supplies in the loo?"

"No idea." Crystal peered at the shard. The demon had punished her for accidentally decimating his threat. A trickle of blood seeped down her hand to drip on the floor.

Ethan had disappeared into the bathroom and she could hear him rustling around. His voice came from behind the wall. "I can't find a thing. Yer sis didn't keep a med kit? She was a crystal cutter. Didn't she ever get hurt?"

"Colleen said she kept bandages and salve for when Brystal fell off her motorcycle. Maybe– " She picked at the shard with a wince.

"Back in a flash. Don't ye be messin' with that yet. Just," Ethan was already at the door, "...sit for a bit."

"Okay." Crystal realized she wouldn't be able to remove the shard without help. The piece was slick with her blood and caught on a piece of skin. "I'll just," Ethan was gone, heavy footsteps could be heard as he ran down the stairs. "get a towel."

With the burst of adrenaline, her legs returned. A few feet away, a tea towel hung near the miniature sink. Crystal managed to get to both the sink and towel but thought the better of rinsing her hand under water until Ethan returned. She surveyed the mess in her palm. It wasn't so much painful as it was inconvenient. Damn! That monster, her sister's creation, had done its job well. A tinkling sound interrupted her wound inspection. There were three more goblets in that secret dark place. They were laughing at her. She closed the cabinet door with her foot and pulled a tea towel from its rack. By the time she returned to the recliner, dabbed up the blood on the floor and put the towel beneath her hand, Ethan, Colleen and Christian came bounding through the door. Colleen held a large plastic box with a big red cross on the side.

"Ach, child. What have ye done?" Colleen knelt before Crystal taking her hand gently. "I'll be fixin' this in a minute." She pulled a pair of tweezers from the box and proceeded to remove the stuck shard, then pulled a magnifying glass from its case and surveyed Crystal's palm.

Ethan and Christian paced the one-foot-wide path they had in the small apartment as Colleen removed tiny fragments of glass from Crystal's injured hand. With four people in the room, there was not an inch to spare! Though she'd had little injuries in her past, Crystal found the attention a little overwhelming, but also comforting. These people had cared for her sister and now they seemed to immediately transfer that care to her. Being twins probably made it easier, but they seemed to accept and tend to her as if they'd known her all of their lives.

"All right then, lassie. Let's just wash this in the sink and set a plaster." Collen got up and helped Crystal to the sink. "It may burn a wee bit, but better to have it clean than start an infection."

"Plaster?" Crystal did not understand.

"Ye folks from the States call it a bandage." Colleen chuckled as she held Crystal's hand under the warm flow of water. "Chris, bring a pad from the kit. In a flat blue package next to the salve."

As Colleen finished cleaning and bandaging Crystal's palm, she watched Ethan eye the cabinet suspiciously. She could tell he was itching to dig into the secret cabinet and see exactly what was there. She hoped he held off until Colleen and Christian departed.

"There ye be." Colleen applied tape to the bandaged hand with a flourish. "Try to keep it dry and clean. I can check it on the morrow.

Come on by the bakery." Colleen winked at Crystal with an impish grin. "I've heard a scone or two can help with ye healing process."

"Thank you, Colleen. I'm sorry to get you up this late. I know you'll be in the bakery very early tomorrow." Crystal felt bad to have inconvenienced Brystal's landlady. "It feels better already. Can I pay you for the supplies?"

"Ah lass, what are friends for? Ethan, be takin' care of himself." She picked up her first aid kit and pulled her son out the door. "Night ta ye all."

"Good night!" Crystal called after the retreating pair. "And thanks again." As she closed the door to the flat, she caught sight of Ethan, still standing next to the end of the counter, his foot pressed against the secret cabinet door.

"Will ye be sayin' what this be all about?" His voice was low and held an accusatory note. He pushed with the toe of his shoe and Crystal heard the door click open.

"Ethan, please, don't take those out." Crystal crossed the floor and sat on the torn recliner. "I can't explain it yet, but there is something wrong with," Crystal stalled.

"With a glass yer sister made?" His curiosity peaked.

"Yes. No! I mean…" She couldn't quite get the information out. It was still a swirling mess of calculations and patterns that seemed to be running a marathon in her brain.

"Crystal, what do you mean? I be tryin' to understand this thing that happens with ye, but honestly, I'm havin' a wee bit of trouble." Ethan sat on the edge of the windowsill and hung his head. "When yer supervisor called me, we spoke about yer way with–"

"Oh my God! Chance told you?" Crystal was shocked. Chance had talked about her thing with numbers with Ethan.

"Calm yerself. It was," He looked up at the lass he couldn't quite figure out, "a good thing. He told me ye were a genius with numbers but, ye may need some support with other things, social things."

"Oh, you just wait till I get my hands on that traitor." Crystal was half laughing, half horrified. What did Ethan think of her now?

"Twas a helpful conversation, it was." As comforting as Ethan's statement was, Crystal was still suspicious. She hunted criminals for a living, and that was her living. Her life. Her day. Often her night as well. She knew it was hard for other people, normal people, to understand.

Her chest tightened and she found it hard to breathe. Would he laugh at her now? Would he think her somehow crazy? Weird and nerdy? All of the lovely negative nouns she'd collected in her perfect mind remained forever, like facts listed on a spreadsheet. She gasped for breath.

Ethan lightly patted her knee. "I find ye fascinating, lass. Like me wee Daria, ye can do things I can't even imagine. Only, the mouse's tastes run to the macabre, if ye know what I mean. Ye got a bit of it tonight at supper with me sis' family." Ethan shook his head.

Crystal's chest relaxed at the word fascinating. No one had ever called her fascinating before. Yes, people had said she could do what they couldn't, but never with admiration in their voices. Her world came back into focus and she literally breathed a sigh of relief, and oxygen. "Daria is a special girl. I liked her. We could talk the way I like."

Ethan chuckled. "I noticed. Everyone else was on the edge of their seats and you two were just gabbin' away. I thought Becky would die of embarrassment. Daria can be a tad descriptive. Especially at the supper table. Gets the lass more dessert. Quinn's got a touchy constitution."

Ethan was rambling and it gave Crystal time to collect herself. She suspected he knew more about her than he let on, and he was fine with it? That was a first.

He nodded toward the cabinet. "So?"

"Well, I've figured out that those pieces are very special. Besides being intricate and incredible, and all of the other *I* words that mean fantastic." Her head was back in the reality game. "I think they may have something to do with this mess. Someone was looking for something they didn't find, obviously, or they wouldn't have cut open the chair, or pulled the towels out of the bathroom. But they didn't find *...that...*" She pointed to the cupboard. Her hands ached to start a spreadsheet of clues and outcomes. "What I have concluded, the hard way," She held up her bandaged hand, "is that the drawings in my bag are the designs for the glasses. They correspond to some kind of calculation that must produce something. What, I have no idea. It may just be, I mean, have been Brystal's way of figuring out a pattern. I don't know enough about what she did here to figure it out." She couldn't keep the disappointment out of her voice. As children, the sisters had been closer than close. They'd even had a twin-speak, a language all their own that no one could interpret except themselves. It used to drive their father to distraction. How had they grown so far apart that one didn't even know what the other was doing for over a year. Tears threatened again and Crystal pushed the thought from her mind. "Every time I look at the drawings or the goblets, I end up in a kind of state. The beauty is a threat. I can't really explain it, but I get sort of trapped. In my own head, you know?" She hoped he could figure it out without her explaining a lot. She didn't even understand her own attraction to numbers, let alone how they seemed to ensnare her cognitive process, and twist it up in a mental prison. She hated being out of control.

"Obviously, Brystal was a genius at numbers too. Just in a different application" Ethan's statement caught Crystal by surprise. She'd never considered her sister smart, let alone genius level. Brystal was a social butterfly, flitting through life, finding pretty flowers and sunshine everywhere. She barely made it out of school and wouldn't have graduated if Crystal had not dressed her sister's part and taken some of her exams. The instructors never seemed to notice that Brystal was writing with her left hand! That had been the only identifying difference between the girls as kids. That was how their parents could tell them apart for a while in junior high when they dressed the same and copied each other's behaviors and speech. It was actually Brystal's way of teaching her sister "normal" behavior when it had become evident that Crystal was so different, she'd become a target at school. No matter how hard Crystal had tried, she could never eat or write successfully with her right hand. But the social imitation had worked for a while.

"I never considered my sister anything but frivolous. She was always more interested in fun and boys than anything serious."

"MacDougal told me she was the most talented apprentice he'd ever been teachin'. She loved cuttin' and worked more hours than she got paid for. He'd have to send the lass packing at times, she was so involved in her work."

Crystal laughed at that. "Chance does the same thing for me. My admin assistant, Sandra, is my watchdog with orders to shoo me out at quitting time." She rubbed the tips of her fingers sticking out from the bandage. "This has all got to have something to do with my sister's murder, don't you think?"

"I'll be thinkin' that as well. May I?" Ethan picked Crystal's bag off the floor and indicated the pocket where she'd stowed the drawings.

"Sure. But I don't want to look at them yet." Crystal averted her eyes and looked out the window. "Look!"

Ethan spun fast enough to catch sight of a shadowy movement in the window across the alley. "Aye. That'd be Dharág. I'm told he lives there. Handy, no?" Ethan's suspicious tone only magnified Crystal's feelings about the man. "He's been watchin' this place. Kind o' weird, but then again, if he knew yer sister and now sees you in her flat, it's probably a bit of a shock. Like seein' a ghost, but not." Ethan waved.

The shadow disappeared without response. "Not the friendly type, huh?" Crystal poured water into the hot pot to make tea. "A cup of tea? Or do you need to get home. What time is it anyway?" It was better to do anything to stay away from the drawings.

"Comin' on eleven. I was thinkin' I might camp here for the night. I'm nigh' on leavin' ye alone." He was studying the papers and missed Crystal's surprised squeak. "Our village's been safe and sweet since I can remember, but this case has me worried. Seems times are a changin', like the song says." He continued to study the drawings while Crystal studied the hotpot, waiting for it to boil. He rambled on and she listened. "Last year we had a big drug bust. Very unusual, and deadly." His voice softened. "I got the bastards, but they got even."

"Tea?" She'd not gotten an answer before.

"Aye. Some caffeine will do me good." He neatly folded the drawings and placed them back in Crystal's bag. "I can na make head nor tale of those numbers."

She handed him a cup and perched on the stool next to the counter. "Do you think this Dharág would have hurt Brystal? Maybe jealous over her talent? Or maybe he stole her designs and didn't want anyone to find out?" She stirred a cube of sugar into her tea and offered the box to Ethan.

"Nah thanks. I take mine straight. I've known Dharág most of me life. The only thing he'd kill would be a sloppin' fish. He's not got the guts fer more." Ethan sat back in the recliner, sipping his hot tea.

"Have you talked to him yet? Brystal's boss?"

"We interviewed Sean but he's not a suspect. He was in Galway tendin' his wife when yer sister got–" Ethan took too large of a gulp of hot tea and coughed, sticking out his tongue to cool it quickly. "when yer sis died. Maggie has some kind of cancer and goes there fer the radiation treatment. Sean takes her, stays with her, and then brings her home. She's down fer a couple days after."

"Well, maybe that guy across the alley can't believe I'm Brystal's sister, not her ghost. Maybe he keeps watching out of some superstitious belief in doppelgangers or phantom, or something." Crystal blew on her tea smelling the flowery scent of Lady Earl Grey. She needed to let Ethan know she was not comfortable with him staying in the flat while she slept just a few feet away, but without sounding ungrateful for all he'd done.

Ethan yawned despite the tea.

"You must be tired. I'm sure I'll be fine here, and you'll sleep much better in your own bed." She hoped she sounded casual but thankful.

"If ye've a mind I be sleepin' anywhere but this raggedy chair tonight, ye'd be wrong." He sat up and pointed to the door to the hallway. "That door was locked, and the bugger got in to do this." He motioned to the mess all around them. "I'll not be havin' another murder on my watch." Crystal knew he was looking to see how she would respond to his ultimatum. "Or I can check ye into a cozy hotel fer the night."

"I'll be fine right here." She sipped her tea. "I mean right in there."

Crystal indicated Brystal's bedroom. "By myself." She added in case Ethan had gotten the wrong idea about American girls.

"Of course. I did not mean to indicate anythin' else, lass."

Her blunder was no more awkward than any of the other million or so blunders in her life. Still, she had no idea how to extricate herself for the misunderstanding of her statement, as always.

"The only intentions I have are to keep Brystal's sister safe, alive and well. Nothin' more." He settled back into the torn-up recliner. "And drink her weak American tea."

Crystal saw the hint of a smile cross Ethan's lips just before he took another sip of the hot liquid and gasped. "Weak, but hot American tea." He stuck out his tongue again.

He'd done it for her, despite her mixed-up misinterpretation of the situation, he'd put her at ease with a simple comment. He didn't take offense or laugh at her like some of the men she'd met, or make some salacious crack. Then he finished with a joke too! Or was the tea she made really weak?

"No." Ethan muttered.

"No?" Crystal was confused. "No what?"

"No, the tea isn't really weak. No, I do not plan to leave ye alone. No, I'm not some pervert to take advantage of ye at a time like this."

Crystal caught his eye as he looked up at her. It didn't hurt! What she saw was truth, empathy, and sorrow. Truth: he was here to protect her. Empathy: he felt her confusion and mistrust, but it didn't bother him. Sorrow: he felt her loss as if it were his own. This was a man who saw through her awkwardness and fear. He didn't require perfect communication and easy social niceties. He only asked for her trust.

"All right. Maybe Brystal has an extra blanket." Crystal put her tea down and started to look for some kind of covering.

"Not to worry. This place is warm enough without any linens. I think the bakery heat comes through the floor." Ethan slid the recliner back and accepted the pillow Crystal handed him.

"Then I'll say good night." Crystal took the teacups, set them in the sink and stepped into the bedroom.

"Sleep with the peace of the angels, lass." Ethan murmured and turned on his side, curling his hands beneath his head. He looked like a little boy, curled in his father's chair.

Crystal pulled the accordion door shut and got ready for bed. Ethan was right, the flat was warm and cozy.

Her favorite sleep T-shirt lent a feeling of home and she drifted off as soon as her head hit the pillow.

CHAPTER 13

If you think the number thirteen is unlucky, consider money!
Did you know on the one dollar bill;
There are 13 bars on the shield.
There are 13 leaves on the olive branch.
There are 13 fruits.
There are 13 arrows. There are 13 stars above the eagle.
There are 13 plumes of feathers on each of the eagle's wings.
There are 13 steps on the Pyramid.
There are 13 letters in "E PLURIBUS UNUM" meaning "Out of many, one".
There are 13 letters in "ANNUIT COEPTIS" meaning "God has favored our undertaking".
Maybe thirteen isn't so unlucky after all!

At some point in the middle of the night, Ethan's bladder woke him. Should he go outside to relieve himself, or chance the water closet off the bedroom? He had not missed Crystal's message earlier. She was not comfortable with him being in her space. Was it just him, or all men? She'd never mentioned a boyfriend or family, except Brystal. Crystal was a professional, top earning forensic accountant and twenty-eight years old. Had she never had a man in her life? Or did she have some horrible experience that had completely colored her view of men in general. He'd no idea. She wasn't the easiest woman to get to know. Though they were equally beautiful, by all accounts Brystal had been the exact opposite.

He sat up considering his options. He could hear a soft purring sound emanating from the bedroom. Crystal slept. Finally. She'd been so exhausted and emotionally drained he worried for her health.

Quietly tiptoeing to the door, he opted for nature and taking a piss under the stars. As his hand turned the nob, he heard the distinct creak of the boards on the stairs. Someone was outside coming up to the flat.

Ethan pulled his sidearm and threw the door open. He was in time to see two shadowy figures depart the staircase in the dark. They'd heard his movement and ran. Down the stairs, after the figures he sped, but not in time. The two figures were gone, and he was alone in the parking space. Finishing his business against a bushy rhododendron, he contemplated this new turn of events, congratulating himself for making the decision to spend an uncomfortable night in Crystal's flat. What if he'd gone on home and the two visitors had broken in? Would Crystal be alive come morning, or joining her sister in his morgue?

Returning to the flat, he checked on Crystal. She still slept. It was almost three in the morning and he'd gotten about an hour of sleep so far. That would not do him any good. He stepped back into the hallway and called the night Sergeant. "Biffy could ye ask the patrol unit to swing by Colleen's Bakery and take a look. I just chased off a couple perps that may have been tryin' to burgle the Traynor flat. Again."

"Right-o, Inspector. On it." Biffy had been the night Sergeant for three years and loved his job. There was little to do at night in Dingle, except catch up on paperwork. Biffy was working on his advanced degree in Forensic Sciences and used his free time for homework and research. He was a good copper and a pleasant man to be around. As a fact, Ethan couldn't think of a single bugger in their close unit.

"Thanks." He rang off and pocketed his cell phone. As much as he needed it, there would be no more sleep for him this night.

As quietly as he could, he withdrew a goblet from the secret cabinet and sat to study it. Sure enough, it was an incredible sample of cut crystal art. The cuts and spaces were uniform and symmetrical. Each slice divided the areas into tiny squares and diamonds that sparkled with only starlight shining through the window. The extraordinary piece drew the eye with its intricacy and balance. He turned the stem in his fingers trying to feel or see what Crystal had said when she dropped the first glass. Such a shame to lose a precious piece like this one.

He held the goblet up. Closer to the stream of starlight and watched as the lead crystal split the light into rainbow elements producing a pattern of squares and diamonds on the floor that was truly beautiful and entrancing. As Ethan rotated the goblet again, he watched the stream of squares and diamonds move past his foot. It reminded him of something, but he couldn't quite put his finger on it. Something niggled the back of his brain, but the more he chased the information, the more elusive it became.

Giving up on his tired mind, Ethan replaced the goblet in the secret cupboard and curled up in the recliner. As he pushed back, the sound of tearing material preceded the contact of his posterior with the tip of a metal spring beneath the fabric. His exit from the chair was rapid and rather inelegant as a large hole opened in the back of his pants. "Mary, Mother of God! I've been wounded by a Danforth." He felt for blood and came away with nothing but a touch of grease and a white fluff of seat stuffing. "The station will ner' be believin' it."

The recliner was done for, so he cleared a place on the floor and lay on the dusty braided rag rug. It wasn't soft, but it was something. Closing his eyes, he couldn't get the pattern from the goblet out of his head. Lines of twinkling squares and diamonds raced around like tickertape, mixing, tangling then separating and continuing on their way. What was it supposed to mean? Why was he even trying to put meaning to what he saw? It was just a glass. Cut by a murdered woman. A simple piece of art.

His head settled against the pillow. Twinkling patterns or not, he found sleep.

~

"What be I tellin' ye, ye bastard! The Inspector was spendin' the night. Sheesh, a bunch of jackeens ye be." Dharág spit into the phone. "I told ye before, I'll not be part of killin'. I'll not go to hell fer all ye money or anythin' else." He paced, careful to stay away from his flat's window facing the alley. He wasn't a suspect in his apprentice's murder, yet.

Dharág stood near the far wall of his flat, watching the place across the alley through his matching window. He'd taken up his flat shortly after starting Brystal on his design. He had to admit, she'd more talent in her little finger than most cutters had in their entire teams. She'd taken to the craft like a fish to water, and seemed to gain great joy in difficult patterns and cutting challenges. Not half as fast or competent at the saw, he'd given her his complex design to speed its production. He knew she'd completed the pieces he ordered, but for the life of him, he could not find them. Nor could he find his design drawings. This whole mess was his fault. He shared her blood on his hands as much as the vicious Albanian brothers who did the dirty deed.

He knew something was really bothering Brystal. She discovered something. After finishing the last goblet in his set, she'd been obviously upset and disturbed. He'd seen her studying the drawings late one night as he watched from his flat. She'd sat at her tiny counter puzzling over his drawing, scribbling numbers for hours. The next day she was dead, and he could not find the crystal or his designs. He'd ransacked her place with no success and now his head was on the line. What could the lass have done with the set and his papers? He'd already searched the warehouse and shop in town.

Nothing.

His hands shook as he reached for the half empty Guinness. With a long gulp, it joined the other five empties in the trash bin. Now the cops were involved, and that detestable Inspector was shepherding the gel like he was in heat. Granted she was an American, but did he have to sleep with the chit? Brystal had her way with men, but had kept Dharág at arm's length. She was a tease, that one, but spread her legs for everyone else. It had been a sore spot for him, but he preferred her talent to her cunt. He'd decided to use her to make himself a shilling or two, rather than pay for her delights. Dharág still thought of his country's money in terms of pre-European Nation status. He hated the EU and blamed the Waterford crisis, and all of the financial and social ills in Ireland on joining the union. In his mind, and the minds of most of his countrymen, it was the downfall of Ireland, its hard-working people, and their cultural heritage.

Why had he ever gotten involved with the Illianescu family? He was better than that. He'd been an upright man, founded in the Irish tradition of fishing, faith, and family, until that all went south. He reached for another Guinness and popped the cap off. Now it was just him, with a death warrant hanging over his head. Why the hell were a couple pieces of cut crystal so important to an Albanian crime family? Why such a specific pattern?

Back to the wall, he slowly slid down to sit on the dusty wood planks that served as a floor while he finished the last beer. He'd figure out what to do in the morning.

~

ETHAN WOKE WITH A START. His phone buzzed and chirped in his jacket pocket. Rolling onto his back with a groan, he fished for the phone. His back was stiff, and one leg was asleep. How long had he slept? He was exhausted, sore, and frustrated. His simple murder of convenience had turned into the mystery of the year and now he was sleeping on the floor playing castle guard for his victim's sister. He found his dancing phone. It was four a.m. "Aye?"

"Inspector, this is Biffy. Sorry to be disturbin' ye at this hour, but Squad II reported in a B&E. Sir, it's Sean MacDougal's place. Burglars tossed the shop. Feldig is there now, takin' evidence. The store be a mess, but Sean and Maggie are all fine. They be up in Galway right now."

"Someone broke into Sean's studio and messed it up?" Ethan knew Sean and Maggie lived over their business in a cozy apartment. He'd been there several times. Sean was a Harley fan and he'd stopped by for a look-see when Sean's new bike arrived. It was the talk of the town, all candy apple red and chrome. "Sean's bike all right?"

"Sure enough. Sean doesn't need more stress in his life, what with the wife getting' chemo and all. Though I hear Maggs is doing better these days."

"Does he know about the break in?" Ethan couldn't imagine the mess. Sean's shop was his pride and joy as well as his only income. "When are they expected back?"

"Don't know. I left a message at their commons at the clinic. Hasn't called me back yet." Ethan knew chemo patients at the Finn Cancer Treatment Clinic up in Galway stayed in a commons type hostel set up for long term patients. They and their families could bunk there during treatments, since tourism had made the hotel industry in Ireland's western most city financially out of reach for the common Irishman, hence the name. "They'll probably get it in the morn. Won't do any good to be speedin' back here in the middle of the night anyhow. Damage is done."

"Right-o, Biffy. I'll go over to the shop now. I'd like to see the place and talk to Feldig, see what's up."

"No problem, Inspector. I figured ye'd be wantin' to know. Ye thinkin' this has something to do with the Traynor gel's case?"

"I'd be bettin' me last spud on it." Ethan rang off. During the infamous potato famine, men would gamble with potatoes since that was all they had worth any value. Many a child went hungry in a betting man's family. Ethan leveraged himself to the edge of the recliner and sat, stretched his back, careful to avoid the gaping hole and offending spring. Several popping noises accompanied vertebrae moving back into place in his spine.

"You shouldn't be sleeping on my floor, Inspector, you're going to need some serious chiropractic adjusting." Crystal stood in the doorway to the bedroom. Ethan looked up and saw the woman silhouetted in the streetlight shining through the big bedroom window behind her. She wore a long T-shirt that ended just below her butt and left little to the imagination of a man who loved legs. She leaned against the doorjamb. Her hair was a wild mass of crazy curls and her eyes were only half open.

"Sorry to wake you, Crystal. Go back to bed. I have to check on something a couple blocks away." He scribbled his number on a piece of packing paper. "This is my private number. Call me if you need anything." He stood and stretched again producing a couple more loud pops. "Ah, that was a good one."

Crystal laughed then sobered. "Does this have anything to do with my sister?"

Ethan wasn't sure how much she'd heard of the phone conversation. "Not sure. Possibly. Maybe just a simple burglary. Sean's shop. Won't know till I see fer me self."

"Then I'm going with you." Crystal spun and disappeared into the bedroom.

Ethan followed. "No wait. Ye need to be–" He froze. Crystal had already removed her T-shirt and was slipping on a pair of jeans. His mind tried to tell his eyes to move away from the gel's figure, but it didn't work. He stood just a few feet away from this gorgeous woman in nothing but panties, jeans halfway up her legs. Her well-endowed figure had been hidden by baggy clothing since she'd arrived, but now Ethan could not deny the fact that Crystal Traynor was as beautiful and statuesque as her sister had been. She didn't seem to be the least inhibited as she dropped her jeans and stood straight, staring at him.

"I can get dressed without your supervision, Inspector." Ethan didn't know if Crystal's comment was sarcasm, or a statement of fact. Nudity didn't seem to bother her much. It was a strange juxtaposition considering their previous conversation.

"No. I mean, yes. I mean–" His words stumbled as he tried to explain, which was totally unnecessary since he continued to stare, rooted to the spot, unable to move anything but his stupid lips. "I've no idea what I mean." The sentence came out slow and deep, almost seductive.

"Please don't tell me you've never seen a half-naked woman before." Crystal duck walked around in a circle, the jeans still around her ankles. "Happy?" She bent and pulled up her jeans. All the way.

"No, I mean yes. No." Ethan turned around and stepped into the kitchen one foot away. "I should just be keepin' me trap shut." He spoke from behind a kind of thin clapboard wall. "My sincere apologies, Crystal. I didn't mean..." He was flustered and couldn't quite engage his social protocol.

"Understood." She came out of the bedroom fully clothed and more awake. "No big deal. Brystal and I lived in a kind of communal home after our parents were gone. Until I got out of grad school. I got used to people being around at odd times. Never really cared for it, but Brystal loved the lifestyle. It was necessary at that point in our lives. We weren't born with a silver spoon in either of our mouths. It was financially expedient."

Her comment was odd coming from a woman who needed organization and had a mind that could out calculate a supercomputer. There was more to this gel than Ethan realized he would ever know unless... He wiped the idea from his mind. She didn't like to be touched, but communal life? How did that work?

She breezed by him, finger combing her wild hair. "Sean employed my sister. My place was ransacked. Now this burglary? In the middle of the night? What are the odds?"

Still a bit shaken by his lapse of appropriate behavior, Ethan murmured, "No idea."

"Seven million six-hundred fifty-two to one."

"What?" Ethan turned to see Crystal standing by the door with a jacket on, her pocketbook slung over her shoulder.

"The odds. Seven million six-hundred fifty-two to one." She opened the door waving him to the stairs. "You wanted the odds that this burglary is related to my sister's murder."

Ethan stared at this woman who stood in the doorway, calculating the mathematical odds that some probably random break-in was related to her sister's mysterious death. As he moved past her and took to the stairs, he mumbled, "How do you do that?"

Crystal followed on his heels. "You take the sum population of County Kerry and divide by the average… you don't really want to know, do you?" Crystal got into the car as Ethan held the door for her.

"Nope." He rounded the back of his car and opened his own door. "Damn!" He slammed the door and stood looking at the front tire. Motioning Crystal back out of the car he swore again. "Jesus, Mary and Joseph! Damn it, looks like we walk. It's only a few blocks. Do ye mind?"

"Seventeen to one." Crystal commented, eying the flat.

"And just what is that number?" Ethan was frustrated and stewing.

"The new odds." She looked at him and frowned. "The trend is not looking so good, Inspector."

"Then let's be about it before the trend gets to... What would it get to if there is no doubt anymore? Zero?" He took her arm and steered her down the alley at a fairly quick pace. He wanted them out of the tight space, just in case.

"No. Zero is not applicable to the calculation of odds. It is a numerical digit representing nothing. There is no possibility of nothing to one, so to speak." Crystal rattled on as Ethan watched for any sign of impending danger as they walked. "Curiously enough, it wasn't even widely used until the fifteen hundreds. Ancient Egyptians did not have a zero in their numerical system, even though they used base ten. The previous civilization of Babylonians, um, around two-thousand BC, used a sophisticated sexagesimal positional system that left a blank for the value of nothing. It didn't work well since there was no end position that showed blank, so numbers like one-hundred twenty looked the same as twelve. They just had to use context. Good thing there was no national banking system. What a nightmare." She paused in her lecture on the numerical history of the zero. They were almost at the shop. "I've done it again, haven't I?"

There were two squad cars parked in front of the Dingle Crystal Corner and all of the lights were on inside. Broken glass twinkled in the streetlights and three men could be seen moving inside. "Done what, lass?"

"Brystal used to call it my encyclopedia mouth. I impart information when I'm nervous." She looked up at the Inspector with a kind of apologetic half-smile. "It just comes out like verbal vomit."

"Not to worry. Ye only impart information when ye be nervous. Me mouse does that the entire time she's awake. Ye've no idea how mentally exhaustin' it can be."

Something he said must have tickled Crystal because she giggled. A lot.

"Let's be at it. Odd or even, I'm beginnin' to be of the belief, this be related to yer sister's murder." He was comfortable talking in concrete terms since he'd gotten used to Crystal's way with things. Like his Daria, Crystal could see and organize information without a great deal of emotion, even when the issue at hand was fraught with emotion.

"Yes." Crystal's attention had turned to the mess as they approached the shop. She had yet to let go of Ethan's arm and he was enjoying her tight grip. She may not show it on the outside, but she was afraid and needing security. He could at least provide that small amount of support. "Ethan, the glass is broken outward. That indicates the robbers were already inside when they broke the windows? Why would they do that? Not very subtle." Her grip tightened as they picked their way through the glass and entered the shop.

They both gasped at once.

The many shelves were virtually empty, and the floor was covered with broken crystal pieces and the accumulated dust of a thousand pieces smashed to smithereens. "Not much left of Sean's inventory."

Crystal's mind had already mentally calculated the shelves, number of pieces each could hold and the average price of what she knew the value of the cut crystal to be. "Three million twenty-five." She looked at Ethan. "Give or take seven-hundred."

"The odds?" Was she back to working the odds?

"Value. The destroyed inventory. In American dollars, of course." At her comment, Garda Feldig approached.

"Inspector MacEnery." He shook hands with Ethan. "Bit early in the morn' to be out for a stroll." He nodded at Crystal then took a step back. Feldig had also worked the Traynor case and now Ethan was seeing the shocked look associated with actually meeting a dead woman walking.

He intervened before Feldig ran for the door. "May I introduce *Crystal* Traynor." He emphasized Crystal's first name.

"Holy Mother of Mary!" Garda Feldig crossed himself. "Gave me a bit of a start, lass."

Ethan chuckled. He'd felt the same at first seeing Crystal walk into his office. He'd wanted to rush down to the morgue and check the vault. "Biffy rang me up. Said there was a B&E. Bit of an understatement."

Crystal had let go of Ethan's arm and walked to the cash register. It was open and full of money. "This wasn't a robbery, Ethan." The drawer itself was unhinged and sitting at an odd angle.

"She a detective? From the States?" Feldig thumbed toward Crystal.

"Nah, just smart." He smiled at the Garda and whispered quietly. "Really smart."

Crystal was scrutinizing everything, square foot by square foot.

"We been at it fer an hour now. Not much to find, Ethan." Feldig shoved his gloved hands into his pockets and shifted feet. "Looks like someone wanted to destroy Sean's business. Nothing taken that we can discern." He stared at the floor and shifted feet again. "Not that ye can account fer much, what with all the pieces."

Crystal had knelt behind the counter. "Ethan, did Sean or his wife smoke?" She had taken two pens from the cup on the counter and picked up a half-burned cigarette.

Ethan peered over the counter along with Garda Feldig. They looked at each other and both nodded in the negative. Feldig was the first to comment. "No one would smoke in here. Maggie MacDougal is undergoing treatment for cancer. Sean wouldn't allow it." He held out his gloved hand for the butt and hollered at one of the other Garda's. "Lenny, bag this will ya." He turned to Ethan, "Smart, ye say?"

While the men talked, Crystal moved around the shop, not touching anything, but looking, studying. After a few minutes she called Ethan. "These supposed robbers weren't interested in robbing. They were looking for something." She pointed to the broken locks on the metal cages where more broken crystal ware littered the shelves. "Each cage has been broken into. Whatever they were looking for, they didn't find." She turned and looked up at Ethan with a serious and calculating face. "Remind you of another break-in?"

"Sure enough. Calculatin' the odds now?"

"Definitely one to one. What was someone looking for?" Crystal turned a little too fast and tripped on a large broken half of what used to be a magnificent bowl. As she caught herself, her foot slid under the wrapping table and Ethan heard a distinct clink.

"Have a care, lass." He bent and peered under the table. "Feldig? Will ye bring a pair of gloves?"

"What did ye find Ethan?" Feldig handed Ethan a pair of blue latex gloves.

Properly gloved, Ethan cautiously cleared a place for his knee and knelt, feeling for the object he'd seen. After a few seconds and a couple grunts, he withdrew a small cylindrical object. All three studied the object in Ethan's hand. "Some kind of flashlight?"

"Maybe you can get a print off that thing. I've never seen a flashlight like that before." Ethan held the flashlight with two fingers.

Before Feldig could holler for another bag, Lenny held one out for the Inspector. "Got it, sir."

"It's a laser expander. I once saw a case where a guy kept shooting a laser beam at commercial planes trying to land. He'd hit the pilots and knock out their vision for a few seconds. Was holding the airlines up for ransom. He could adjust the width of the beam by that ring near the lens." Crystal pointed to the part of the flashlight she was describing. "We got him after setting up a sting." She shrugged at the two Garda's who obviously didn't know what she did for a living.

Ethan nudged Crystal. "Followin' the money, right?" He turned to Garda Feldig, "Miss Traynor is a forensic accountant back in the States. Her boss says she's the best at it." He was bragging just a tad.

Ethan's warm praise made Crystal smile. He was sure she didn't hear that very often, or at least realize it very often.

Lenny spoke up as he inspected the object through the plastic bag. "Not English. This is from the continent, Boss."

Crystal was intrigued. "May I?"

"What? Now ye be a polyglot too?" Ethan took the bag and handed it to Crystal. "Hold it by the tab."

Crystal took the bag by its ID tab and looked carefully at the strange letters. "Russian. It's made in Russia according to the writing." She pointed to small letters on the end of the barrel.

Ethan was impressed. "Ye know Russian?"

"Not much, but I can recognize *made in Russia* in Cyrillic. I saw it once on a carton full of counterfeit twenties." She handed the bag back to Lenny and tapped her temple. "I don't forget."

"Anything?"

"Anything." Crystal nodded with a frown.

"I guess not." Ethan shook his head. So, she had this thing about numbers. She suffered from some serious OCD, and, she had a photographic memory.

Crystal turned to the cages, then back at the light, then to the floor full of broken glass. Ethan could tell her mind was working, but what he couldn't tell was where it was going. All of a sudden, Crystal blurted out, "I have to go!" And ran for the door.

"Crystal, wait!" Ethan hollered after the fleeing woman. "Later." He patted Garda Feldig's back as he chased after Crystal. Something had sent her running. He had no idea what it was. "Crystal!" he called as he watched her turn down the alley. She was headed to the flat.

What had set her dashing?

CHAPTER 14

The number 14 alludes to cosmic debt. People born under this number are urged to tread carefully in whatever they choose to do in life, because their actions have far-reaching consequences.

Crystal hit the stairs without thinking. All she wanted was to get back to Brystal's flat and make sure the hidden goblets were safe. They were the key! A theory was building in her mind.

The expandable laser light.

The cut crystal.

The spectrum crystal separated into individual colors.

The patterns of light that played through the cuts.

The squares and diamonds.

Zeros and ones... binary... base two.

Her mind spun so fast she almost missed the top step, falling through the doorway at breakneck speed.

Something was wrong.

Crystal slid across the floor, now clear of rugs.

Someone had been in the flat in the short time they'd been gone.

The rugs were piled against the wall and the boards were scratched and dented as if someone had tried to pry the boards up. She froze as a loud screech came from the bedroom. That someone was still there! She heard the bathroom window slam.

Ethan flew past her into the tiny bedroom with a string of swear words. "He's gone. Damn it to hell."

Shaking like a leaf in a gale, Crystal realized someone had been in the flat when she came in. Immediately she knelt in front of the secret cupboard. Depressing the door latch, she peered into the darkness, expecting the worst.

The goblets remained intact. Whoever had been in the flat had not found the cabinet or the goblets. With a huge sigh of relief, she plunked down on the floor.

"I've had just about enough of this bullshit! What the hell is going on here, lass? Why did ye bolt?" Ethan was catching his breath in between sentences.

"I, I... I don't know yet." Crystal crawled over to her pocketbook lying up against the recliner. She'd tossed the bag as she slid across the floor. "I have this idea in my head but it's still a baby. When I saw the laser light, something clicked. I just knew I had to get back here and make sure Brystal's goblets were safe." She pulled the drawings from her bag and spread them on the floor.

The world faded away leaving only the numbers, swirling around the edge of the papers. Around and around they spun down into a whirlpool of calculations that gripped Crystal's cognitive process in an iron hold. She rocked back and forth as the numbers tore at her mind and ripped at her sanity. Again, and again, they attacked, pummeling and twisting her thoughts.

At one point a feeling struck out at her.

"Pure evil." She mumbled and reached for a pencil, pen, anything to write with.

Ethan watched her but couldn't quite believe what he saw. Into her outstretched hand, he placed a pen. It was the only thing he could think of to do. This woman was crouched on the floor, mumbling some mantra about evil and scratching numbers all over the backside of one drawing as she rocked back and forth. "Crystal?" he whispered.

Crystal was trapped. She couldn't tear away from her numbers. The outside world didn't exist anymore. All she needed was in the calculations that spun crazily, sucking, pulling. Was there an end, or would she spend the rest of her existence running the numbers, seeing the patterns, drowning in the universe they built, destroyed, and rebuilt. She saw the evil and kept her distance, but eventually she was pulled into the sticky web of malevolent and foul outcomes. She rebelled, only to be pulled deeper into the wicked abyss. Her fingers ached from holding the pen in a steely grip. She was running out of space.

"Need more paper." She ground out through gritted teeth and cramping lips.

Ethan still stood. Crystal had been in her numbers trance for almost half an hour. He was afraid to move. His legs were tired, and he couldn't imagine how Crystal could crouch for that long a time, scribbling numbers.

"Need more paper." She sounded possessed, never taking her eyes off the equations in front of her.

He pulled a sheet of wrapping paper from the counter and carefully placed it before Crystal.

Without a single word, she snatched the paper, placed it next to the other one, now filled with all kinds of weird symbols and strings of numbers. Not even pausing, she continued onto the new page.

Ethan watched for another few minutes then figured he should do something. But what? He couldn't let her crouch like that much longer or she wouldn't be able to walk.

"It's not working." She mumbled.

"What, Crystal? What's not working." He tried to get her attention with a question.

"Why won't you devolve? I know you're in there somewhere."

Who was she talking to? "Crystal, who is in there?"

"I know I can find you , if you'd just hold still for a second. That's all I need, a second." Her rocking increased and she bit the pen as she studied the numbers. "No, no, no! Don't you run!" She took her pen and drew lines between some of the numbers and symbols. "You can run, but you can't hide. I will find you before you do harm."

Ethan never got an answer to his question, but after a few hectic minutes, Crystal rolled out of her crouch and lay on her back on the floor. "Aghhhhhhh!" Her eyes focused on the room and Ethan. "It's gone."

"What? What's gone? What are all of those numbers?" He took a stool and watched the woman on the floor. She seemed to have come out of whatever had happened, and now looked angry and a little sad.

"The code." Crystal took a deep breath and let it out slowly. "That's why they are looking for the goblets Brystal made. Look!" She sat up pointing to Brystal's original calculations. "My sister wrote these equations from the angles and shapes in the drawing for the cuts into the crystal. I can decipher the equations, but I can't follow the operations to a conclusion. I don't know what the numbers stand for." She broke the pen in her hand out of sheer frustration. "Sorry." She handed the two pieces back to Ethan.

"My favorite pen?" Ethan looked horrified.

"Really? I'm so sorry."

"No. I was just teasin' ye lass." He looked at Brystal's calculations, then at the two pages of numbers Crystal had just added. "Can you tell me what just happened to ye? Is that what yer sup was tellin' me?"

Crystal hung her head. "I have this thing with numbers. They get to me." She folded up Brystal's pages, so no writing showed. No numbers to laugh at her. "It's weird but I get stuck in calculations. The psychiatrists all told me it was a rare form of obsessive-compulsive disorder, with a high level of synesthesia mixed in for grins and giggles. It's what makes me good at my job." She paused and looked out the window. "And uncomfortable with people. Awkward, Brystal used to say. She tried to teach me how to be normal but gave up a few years back. That's when she started her adventures." Crystal used her fingers to put imaginary quote marks around the word adventures. "It was after Chance hired me and things started to click. LDE is like a home away from home for me and I have an admin who understands me and my craziness. We made up rules." Crystal looked at Ethan still perched on his stool. "This is probably more than you want to know. Awkward, right?"

Ethan could see the tears begin to form. "Nah, lass. Everyone has their way, and the good Lord doesn't make mistakes, so says me sis." The sun was not yet up and Ethan was hungry. He could smell Colleen's handiwork and knew the baker was already at work, making the day's delights. "I wonder if Colleen would be fillin' me empty space this early. Shall we see?"

"Ethan, we have to keep these goblets secure until I can figure out what my sister created and why those, whoever they are, want them so badly. I feel so awful for Mr. MacDougal. All that work destroyed for nothing." She quickly replaced the door and made sure it clicked closed.

"Not ye fault. Besides, he keeps most of his inventory in his–" Ethan tore out his cell phone and used the speed dial feature. "Biffy, send a squad car to Sean's warehouse. See if anythin' is a miss." He ended the call. "Come on, Crystal. I've a bad feelin' about this."

Ethan ushered Crystal into her rental car, and they sped off, for Sean MacDougal's warehouse and a possible disaster in the making.

The squad car beat them there and two Garda's were walking around the building shining lights inside. The tallest Garda recognized Ethan and called to him immediately. "Nothin' to be seein', Ethan. Why'd ye be sendin' us on a rabbit chase?"

"Sean's shop was trashed. I thought maybe they'd hit his warehouse as well." Ethan peered through the front window full of beautifully cut bowls and vases.

"Who?" The Garda looked confused.

"Dunno, Raulph. Dunno."

"Christ on the Cross!" Raulph stumbled before catching himself against the Squad car. "So, it be true! Your murdered gel has a twin."

"Word's gottin' around I see." Ethan smirked as Crystal approached. "Garda Clauson, this is Crystal Traynor."

Crystal put out her hand to shake, but pulled back as the shocked

Garda crossed himself several times. "I'm Crystal. My sister was Brystal." She didn't know what else to say.

"Ma'am. Sure 'nough nice to be meetin' ye." Getting over the visual surprise, Garda Clauson shook hands. "Welcome to Ireland. I mean, well, it's probably not a great welcome, all things considerin'." Garda Clauson was studying the ground at Crystal's feet.

"Thank you, Garda Clauson. Was anything wrong inside?"

"No, nothin' at all. What were ye thinkin'?" The other Garda had joined the conversation.

Ethan interrupted. "Sean's place in town was a complete loss. Everything smashed like there was a personal grudge. Or somebody was lookin' real hard for something they did na find."

"You might want to talk to Dharág Hadley. He was workin' the kiln this morning, but he closed up around happy hour. The man loves his drink." Garda Clauson chuckled. "Sean told me Dharág actually works better a sheet or two to the wind. At least he works. Not like most of the young'uns these days." He took a play punch at his fellow Garda who was clearly younger and new on the force.

"Alright then. If there be no problem here, I'll be after me breakfast." Ethan took Crystal's arm and steered her toward the car they come in. "Will ye keep tabs on this place? Sean doesn't need to lose any more than he already has."

"Sure enough, Inspector." Raulph waved as the Ethan and Crystal sped off.

Inside the car, Ethan chanced a suggestion. "Maybe I should lock up those pretty glasses yer sister created. I've a sneekin' suspicion they be what everyone is lookin' fer. What do ye think, Crystal?"

"I think I'm missing something. Something important." She patted her bag that contained the drawings and her additional figures.

"Like breakfast. It's almost seven and Colleen should be open by now. How about scones and a drop of tea?" Ethan's stomach chose that very moment to growl.

Crystal giggled and turned to his speaking belly. "I think that is a great idea. Scones and tea. With honey?"

"Of course."

CHAPTER 15

"In the future, everyone will be famous for fifteen minutes."
Andy Warhol, 1968

As they sat in Colleen's bakery munching on fresh apricot and cinnamon scones, Crystal wracked her brain, trying to figure out what her sister's string of numbers meant. They checked the cabinet upon returning and the goblets were safe and sound. "Ethan, something is picking at the back of my brain, but I just can't get a hold on it. I'm so tired." She broke off a chunk of scone and popped it in her mouth. "Why aren't scones in New York this good?" She licked her fingers.

Colleen came around the counter with a pot of hot water. "Because they don't have me mum's recipe." She smiled at Ethan with a wink, for the Inspector. "Besides, everythin's better in Érie. We invented scones, don't ye know. And tea, of course."

Crystal knew the legend that told how in the year 2737 BC, a Chinese Emperor watched a green leaf blown into a bowl of boiling water. Coloring the water and giving it taste, he called it tea. He was nowhere near Ireland at the time. She winked at Ethan who grinned right back.

"Would yer son be wanting' to make an extra twenty today? I've got me a flat round back."

"Sure enough. Christian?" Colleen yelled through the kitchen door.

The young man appeared in a second, his ruddy hair under a net and flour on his face and hands. "Somethin' amiss, mum?"

Ethan spoke up. "I've a flat on me left-front. Could ye change it out fer me fer, say, a twenty?"

"Aye! Be me pleasure, fer a twenty!" The young man dusted off his hands on the baker's apron he wore and tore the net from his hair.

Ethan handed him the car keys and the money. "Jack'll be in the back with the spare."

As the sun broke through the clouds and everything in Ireland glowed with the bright green of the countryside, Crystal and Ethan finished their breakfast and returned to Brystal's flat above the bakery. What they had finished packing, now needed re-packing and they still had no answers about the drawings or goblets. At some point, Christian appeared in the doorway with Ethan's keys and a big smile. He asked Crystal to use Brystal's motorbike for some deliveries and went away with keys and a soda pop. Just before noon, Ethan's cell phone chirped, and he answered it.

"Aye, sis. Good to be hearin' yer sweet voice." He pointed to the phone and mouthed *sister*. Wait a minute and I'll ask." He covered the speaker and asked Crystal, "Becky wants to know if ye'd be interested in lunch. Rory be out on a run and the kids are home on holiday. I think she's needin' law enforcement."

"That would be nice, but I'm awful tired." Crystal hedged, then thought the better of staying at the flat alone. "On second thought, I think that's a great idea."

"Sis? What time? Right-oh." He rang off and replaced his phone. "We'll be expected at twelve thirty. Smoked salmon spread on home-made sourdough bread."

"Can we take the goblets with us? Maybe drop them off at the station on the way back?" Crystal didn't want to leave the cut glass in the flat when she wasn't there. Though they'd yet to be found in their hiding place, a simple misstep could open the cabinet and they would be found.

Ethan reached for a small soft-sided ice chest. "They can go in here and no one be known' the difference."

Crystal opened the secret cabinet and withdrew the goblets one, by one. Ethan wrapped them in packing paper and placed them in the carrier with extra padding for safety. These glasses held the answer to some mystery that had already taken one life and practically destroyed the business of another. They would be secure in the vault at the station and maybe they both could sleep better.

Putting the carrier in the back seat of his car, Ethan held the door for Crystal. "Thanks, but I can open the door for myself." Crystal was not used to European men and their manners. People in New York barely looked at each other, let alone open a door for someone.

"Understood." He returned. "However, did ye ever hear the sayin', *when in Rome*?" He closed the door and got in the driver's side.

"Yes, but you really don't have to–"

"Me mum' d be rollin' over in her grave if I acted the Jackeen." Ethan pulled out of the tight parking space and headed for the road to his sister's home on the peninsula.

Crystal laughed. "I keep hearing that word, and for the life of me, I don't know what it means."

"What? Jackeen? Means a contemptuous, worthless fellow. I think ye all from the States say stuck out."

"Ah. You mean stuck up."

"I've no idea what I mean. I'm not adept at speakin' American."

"American isn't a language. It's a country. You should know that." Crystal countered and as they drove, each one took turns debating the roots of different languages. Their banter was easy and comfortable

At the driveway, Ethan was just about to launch into a list of Irish words that had no translation in American when Crystal gave in. "Alright! I give up. You win but at least I know one Irish word. Jackeen, a worthless fellow who is stuck out!" As tired as she was, Crystal was having fun with the verbal repartee. It was a first for her. There was something about Ethan that put her at ease, and she could relax instead of second guessing every word and behavior, evaluating every remark. He'd seen her at her worst, caught in an OCD episode, and he was still taking her to lunch at his sister's house. That was a first! Usually men steered clear of her when they got a glimpse of her personality and disability in action. Until now, Chance was the only man who had ever shown her any form of care or consideration. He'd immediately recognized that her former boss treated her like a blemished mushroom, kept in the back room in the dark and fed shit. She did the tax cases put on her desk and stayed in her little world, working for half what other CPAs would have made. It was safe. It was abuse and Chance pulled her out of there. He saw her talent *and* her disabilities and gave her Sandra. He understood and paved the way for Crystal to become one of the world's best forensic auditors. She paved the way for him to become a multi-millionaire.

"Ah, me thinks ye've made a vast friend." Ethan pointed to his niece who stood on the edge of a flower box, one arm full of tomatoes, the other waving madly.

"More like her favorite uncle has arrived."

"Aye," Ethan laughed and waved from the driver's seat. "Could be. Don't let her put ye off, Crystal. She's a tad different and truly loves anything morbid. Poor Rebekkah is hopin' 'tis a fad she be goin' through."

"Please! If there is one thing I understand, it's obsession with something." Crystal did not wait for Ethan to come around and let her out of the car, she got out and stood at the door waving back, pretending the welcome was all for her. It was a good feeling, even if it was fake.

She watched Daria drop the tomatoes in a basket by her mother's feet and dash over to her uncle. After a hug-tackle, the young girl raced around the car and grabbed Crystal's hand. "Come. Ye have to see me tomato. It be ginormous!"

Crystal let the girl drag her to the flower box. There, beneath a bushy limb sat one. It had to be *the* largest tomato Crystal had ever seen. Around it was a protective framework built of toothpicks, holding the mongrel off the dirt. A thin black hose wound around the base of the plant and ended in the dirt.

"I've been experimentin' with different nutrient base's direct and indirect application." She pointed to the hose. "Solanum Lycopersicon is not indigenous to our area so I've a need to supplement. They are botanically classified as a berry but everyone," She nodded to her brother who held a basket for his mother pulling carrots from the next box over. "Especially the sodden ones, call it a vegetable."

At that comment, Crystal caught a glance of Quinn sticking out his tongue at his sister. "These are determinate, annuals, don't ye know. Tomatoes were the first genetically modified commercial crop. A bunch of scientists got together and sequenced the tomato genome a long time ago. I think the research was made public in 2012." Daria continued her lecture as Ethan stood by, patiently listening as if he hung on every word with incredible interest. Crystal knew the stance. "Did ye know there be even a Germplasm Resource Information Network in the States? They provide regionally adapted breeding lines and hybrid seeds for experimentin'." She pointed to her huge tomato. "I cross-pollinated three varieties they sent me, keeping to the Cartagena Protocol on Biosafety and hybridized this gel."

Finally, Becky came to the rescue of Crystal and Ethan. "Enough, Daria. Everyone on the planet is not enamored with tomato farmin'." She patted her daughter on the head as Quinn followed his mum into the house, carrying his basket of home-grown vegetables.

"Why not? This is our future!" Daria morphed from a university professor lecturing on the most important topic since Galileo's theories of heliocentrism, to a heart-broken eleven-year-old who'd just lost her favorite doll.

Ethan caught her outstretched arms, pulling her toward the door. "There be no future for me if I do not fill me belly soon, Mouse." He emphasized each word then tapped the end of her nose gently.

The entire situation peeked Crystal's interest. "How did you get the GRIN to send you such coveted seeds?"

Daria paused before going through the doorway and stared at the floor. "I wrote a letter." She dashed through and disappeared into the bathroom. "Got to wash me hands."

Crystal heard Quinn laugh from the kitchen. "She wrote a letter and signed it Professor Daria Kilkerry, Dunquin University of Agriculture. I saw it before she posted it!" He came around the corner with a huge smile. "She be a liar."

Liar or not, Crystal thought the girl was amazingly inventive.

"There be no Dunquin University and no Professor Kilkerry. Liar, liar, peat's a pyre!" Again, Quinn stuck his tongue out at his sister.

"Isn't that *pants on fire?*" Crystal queried Ethan and they both laughed.

"Only in the states." He explained the localized saying. "If a peat bog catches here, it'll smoke fer years. The smoke covers yer nefarious deeds." He tussled Daria's hair as she sped past and into the kitchen.

Becky had the table set for five and was placing a platter of smoked salmon in the middle when Crystal heard Quinn yelp. Apparently, the young girl had gotten even with her brother for ratting her out.

"Please, have a seat. I believe we are ready." A heap of sliced bread sat next to the salmon platter and small dishes contained all sorts of condiments. Becky indicated a chair for Crystal and as soon as she sat, Daria slid into the chair next to her.

In a quiet voice, Daria explained, "It doesn't really matter how I got them seeds. Point is, I cross-bred them successfully and be keepin' the appropriate notes for me future report. I can show you the growth chart. It be truly amazing. Me breed is out growin' the lastest, fastest hybrid in the scientific research reports."

Ethan took his seat. "Are ye sure ye be only eleven?"

Daria gave her beloved uncle a scathing look. "Twelve in eighty-four days, Uncle Ethan."

That sparked a new round of debates between the twins and their uncle. Each wanted to make sure their ideal prospective gifts were made clear to Ethan, in a non-materialistic and completely grateful manner, of course. As they ate, Crystal studied Daria's body language and speech patterns. She was something! Sweet and idealistic one second, heartbroken and seriously concerned about famine and world drought patterns in another. Wanting a specific glittery tween nail polish at first, then trading the girly idea for some scientific magazine subscription the next. She finally settled on a microscopic borescope camera that would connect to her new computer to examine her vegetables, inside and out!

Quinn wanted new shin pads and a goalkeeper's helmet.

Crystal found herself relaxing and enjoying the meal as well as the kids' chatter. Becky sat at the head of the table monitoring her daughter's social monopoly and breaking in to give Quinn his share of the limelight with his uncle. Crystal was happy Ethan's sister deftly steered the conversation away from the Dingle Murder case so she could forget, if only for a few minutes, the tragedy that had brought her to this table and this family.

When lunch was over and Ethan's belly was full, the adults retired to the porch and the sunshine for a glass of iced tea while the children went about their activities. Quinn took his soccer ball out into the yard to practice goals in a mini-soccer field his father had built across from the driveway in an open field. Daria went back to measuring her ginormous tomato crop and drawing graphs of growth tables.

"Your daughter will change the world someday." Crystal commented, watching Daria's all-consuming attention to her project. She sat in a comfortable rocking chair, sipping her tea, and chatting amicably. It was a new experience, and she was loving it.

"Aye, if she survives her brother and the teen years. I fear fer her in the grades." Becky sighed. "She be so smart, yet so naïve. How can two children born of the same womb, be so different?"

Crystal giggled and Ethan froze. "You never met my sister, did you?"

"Oh, for heaven's sake, I be apologizin'. I didn't think–" Becky crossed herself hanging her head.

"Not to worry. It's fine. My sister is gone. I made my peace with that, but what I'd like to know is why." They all sat quietly for a moment before Crystal continued. "It's all very mysterious and somehow related to these drawings and calculations Brystal made.

She cut goblets based on the numbers and, well, I can't figure it out. And for me, it's an irritant that keeps hammering at me. I'm supposed to be so good with numbers, yet–"

"There was no evidence at the scene." Ethan mused. "I even called me mate from university. Stephan be a crack detective in Shannon. We used to make fun of his name and fame as the best in our class. Ye can't hide from O'Haide!"

"There's always evidence." A mumbled statement came from behind a leafy tomato bush.

"Sorry?" Crystal peered around the bush at Daria and that was all it took for the girl to jump into the adult conversation.

"There is always evidence." She came around the flower box of very tall and lush tomato plants and sat on a stool near her uncle. "Ye just need to be knowin where to look."

"Come on, Mouse. Two straight up detectives be knowin' where to look, and be findin' nothin', I tell ye." Crystal knew Ethan was more frustrated with the case than with his niece.

"Daria, mind ye manners, gel." Becky scolded her daughter.

"Aye, mum. Sorry Crystal." Appropriately chastised, Daria got up to return to her project.

"Daria, I know there is always evidence of some kind. But it's not always readily visible. Like these darn designs." She pulled the papers from her bag next to the rocker. Unfolding them, she pointed to the strings of numbers circling the edges of the paper. They danced their freedom before her eyes and Crystal squinted to keep their taunting at bay.

Daria leaned in and studied the numbers for a minute. "Mmm. Looks like some kind of equation that combines those numbers, but the combinations don't work together." She pointed to a string and the answer at the end. "That's not the correct answer if you do the process and," She pulled the design closer as Crystal watched her eyebrows wrinkle. "This isn't correct. See." She pointed to the combinations. "I did these kinds of things in calc last year. But it's not right. Didn't ye sister know math?"

"Daria!" Both her mom and uncle gasped at the same time.

To Crystal's enjoyment, their comments passed right over Daria's head, but Quinn heard. "Maybe it's some kind of code that stands for other things. See how that number repeats?"

Now it was Crystal's turn to gasp. "You could be right, young lady. I did not think of that. It could be a number to letter cypher. Mmm..." Crystal was turning the papers as she studied at the numbers in light of this new revelation. "I may not be able to solve this without a computer. It's very complex if it's a cypher."

Daria straightened. "I have one!" She pulled Crystal out of the rocker and dragged her toward the door.

"Daria, wait!" Becky was concerned that her daughter was dragging their guest around for her own interests.

"Might as well save ye spit, Beck. Crystal is as unusual as yer Daria, bless her heart." He chuckled as he sipped his tea. "We may not be seein' them till next week." He set his tea on the small glass table next to him and closed his eyes. Within three rocks, he was snoring lightly.

They'd been at it for almost an hour when Daria sat back and stretched. It reminded Crystal to do the same. Her back was stiff, and her eyes were beginning to blur with exhaustion, but the chase was on and she didn't want to stop. They'd run three algorithms, and nothing seemed to work. That just made Crystal want to search further. Daria's fingers worked the keyboard at lightning speed and Crystal was impressed that the eleven-year-old could develop such sophisticated algorithms in such a short period of time. She was a mathematical wizard and had a mind like a steel trap... like her own!

"Maybe the cypher idea be a miss more than a hit." Daria rubbed her chin like some venerated scientist examining a critical puzzle.

Crystal tore herself away from their latest try. "Or maybe, it's just the pattern for a beautiful goblet." She took a deep breath and let it out all at once. "I can't believe that though. It makes something. I get this feeling of impending doom. Not because I can't figure out the answers, but because I sometimes get feelings from numbers." The only other person she'd ever told about her numbers synesthesia was Brystal.

"I be getting' ye there." Daria pointed to one long number. "Especially that one. He be hideous, screamin' all evil prattle."

The two looked at each other and burst out laughing. Between gasps for air, Crystal blurted out, "You too?"

Daria giggled. "Aye. Me too. But nobody understands." She spontaneously hugged Crystal, "But ye."

For a few minutes, they just sat, studying the numbers until Becky appeared at Daria's bedroom door. "Yer uncle's fallin' to a coma, young lady. It be time to let this gel get back to the real world and what she be needin' to do. Yer uncle's a workin' copper. He needs to be on his way."

"But mum!" Daria pleaded. She didn't want to lose this new friend who was more like her than any other.

"It's okay, Daria. You keep working on these numbers and let me know if you can solve it. Or even if you have a new idea." Crystal scribbled on a scratch paper square. "Here's my email and cell phone. Let me know what you find."

"Perfectious!" Daria had the tween speak down to a tee. She carefully folded Brystal's drawings and tucked them in Crystal's bag with reverence.

Another hug and Crystal was back outside looking at Ethan who still snoozed peacefully in the sunshine. She turned to Becky. "We were up half the night. The Dingle Crystal Corner was broken into and completely trashed. The owner isn't even in town."

"Oh, my Lord. Sean and Mags will be heartbroken. That shop be their baby."

The conversation woke Ethan from his slumber, and he yawned. "I could be happy just sittin' here fer a month." He rose slowly and several loud pops accompanied his movement. "But duty calls. Be ye ready to go, Crystal?"

Her exhaustion had returned. "Yes, before I join you in that chair. Daria has all of the equations on her computer and said she will keep working on it. I gave her my info so if she comes up with anything, she can contact me."

Ethan chuckled and took the car keys out of his pocket. "Ye may never rid yerself of that pest. Me mouse be indomitable when it be involvin' numbers and puzzles. Has been since a babe."

He escorted the two women to his car, hugging his sister goodbye. "Me thanks for the sup, sis." He opened the door for Crystal, hollering and waving at his nephew who was tackling the next goal with his feet.

"Thank you for the beautiful lunch. You have a lovely daughter. And you are right. Someday she will do something to save the world!" Crystal stuck out her hand to shake. Becky ignored the hand and hugged her lightly.

"Thanks to ye, she has a new project to work on. She'll not be terrorizin' her brother for a bit and I'll be appreciatin' the peace." Becky smiled warmly at Crystal. "Be safe. And Ethan, get some sleep before ye drop where ye stand." She kissed him on the cheek.

"Aye, mum." Ethan joked as he rounded the car and got inside.

Daria was nowhere to be seen. Crystal had a sneaking suspicion she was glued to her computer and algorithms.

CHAPTER 16

Abraham Lincoln was the 16th President of the United States.
That didn't end well.

On their way to Brystal's flat, they stopped by the Garda Síochána offices to stow the goblets in the evidence vault. They would be safe and out of sight there.

"Afternoon, Inspector. How's the craic?" The desk Garda had the good graces to not gasp or show shock at Crystal's appearance. The word had gotten round rapidly. The murdered gel's *identical* twin was in town, so no actin' surprised at meeting her.

"Good day ta ye, Randal. We'll be placin' this into evidence." He held up the cold carrier.

"Ye lunch, Inspector?" Randal looked smug at his own joke.

"That'd be it, Randal. Me Becky's corned beef and cabbage. It be needin' protection from the likes of ye all."

"That'd be right-o. Yer sis makes the best in the county." He chuckled and held the countertop up as they passed from the visitor area into the secure station. "Right down the hall. First door on the right, Inspector." He ushered Crystal down the hall trying hard not to stare at her face.

"I know where the evidence vault is Randal. And stop staring at the gel." He laughed at the newest Garda at the station.

"Yes, yes of course, sir. Sorry sir. Sorry ma'am." With one last suspicious look, he returned to his post.

Crystal was beginning to enjoy the effect her appearance had on the folks in Dingle. She'd never considered her resemblance to her sister a shocking experience, until now. To her, their identical-ness was a fact she'd lived with all her life. Their small circle of shared friends could easily tell them apart by their behavior. Brystal was social and comfortable anywhere. Crystal was not. Brystal was openly loving and huggy. Crystal kept her distance. Growing up, their close-knit group accepted them both, for very different reasons. Brystal was the life of the party and up for just about anything, even marginally illegal activities. When one of their friends needed academic help, Crystal was there with the answers.

Brystal was fun.

Crystal was smart.

"He thinks you have cocaine in that ice chest?" Crystal looked after the retreating Garda.

"Cocaine? What be givin' ye that idea?" Ethan opened the outside door to the vault room.

"He asked you about crack." She followed him into the dim room where an enormously thick door stood open. Inside the small walk-in vault, Crystal cold see a series of shelves holding cardboard bank boxes."

Ethan laughed and took up the log from a shelf next to the door. "Nah. He be talkin' Irish, gel. He's a youngster. Crack in American means cocaine. C-r-a-i-c," He spelled the word for her, "in Irish is like," he paused. "Well it doesn't really translate, but *how's the craic* means what's happenin'. Kind of."

"Ah, here we go again." Crystal winked at Ethan.

After completing the log and adding a number from the front of a bank box he took from the vault, Crystal helped Ethan carefully place the goblets into the box. They had wrapped them at the flat so they would be safe and not break if someone jostled the box accidentally. Ethan placed the box back on the shelf and came out of the vault. "That should do it."

"Do they ever lock this door?" Crystal was amazed that they had just walked into the room and the vault was open.

"Sure do. When we've a need to protect somethin'." He swung the heavy door closed and spun the lock. "And I am believin' we do."

On their way back to the flat, Ethan saw Christian buzz by on Brystal's motorbike. Behind the youth sat a stack of pastry boxes that extended over his helmet. Ethan waved. "That boy-o is a goer. Makes his mum proud." Before Crystal could ask, Ethan provided the answer. "Goy-er is a person who goes the extra mile. Wonder how he keeps his balance with those boxes."

Crystal waved, shaking her head. "I have no idea how anyone even stays on those things."

As they pulled into the parking spot behind Sweeney's Bakery, Dharág Hadley came down the alley. As he caught sight of the Inspector and Crystal, he froze. "Isn't that the guy who worked with Brystal?" Crystal trotted toward the man.

"Crystal, wait!" Ethan ran to catch up. In his mind, everyone who'd had anything to do with Brystal was suspect until proven innocent now.

As usual, Crystal was focused on speaking with the apprentice crystal cutter and ignored Ethan's warning. She held out her hand as she got closer to Dharág. "Mr. Hadley, I'm Crystal Traynor, Brystal's sister. I'd like to speak with you.

Dharág's knees shook as he stood there, staring at the image of the woman he'd spent the last year training. The woman he knew to be dead. He took a deep breath but couldn't seem to release it. He couldn't move at all, except his knees that seemed to set up a vibration through his entire body.

Ethan had caught up and now was observing the man's behavior with scrutiny. He was either incredibly shocked at seeing Brystal's twin, or he really didn't want to talk to them. Fear was reflected in every movement, or lack thereof. "Hadley snap out of it, man. This be Brystal's twin sister."

Crystal tried to bridge the gap. "I know my appearance is a bit of a shock, I'm sorry to startle you."

Dharág finally recovered his wits and tentatively extended his hand. "Me apologies, mum. Bit of a shock to see the walkin' dead, if ye know what I mean."

Crystal smiled at the man, hoping her expression was solicitous. She'd never been compared to a zombie. "Yes, I do know. I was wondering if I could talk to you about my sister. If it's not too upsetting.

Dharág hedged. Ethan got the immediate idea that talking to Crystal was the last thing Dharág wanted to do. "I've got to tend to the shop. Sean called me this morn. Someone broke in and robbed the place." Dharág kept his eyes on the pave stones of the alley. "I'm to clean up the mess and evaluate the losses. Sean'll be back on the morrow."

"Just a few minutes? After tomorrow?" Crystal begged.

"Yeah, yeah. That'll be fine, mum." Dharág bobbed his head. "Inspector." He hurried on by. In the opposite direction of the crystal shop.

"That was weird." Crystal headed up the stairs to Brystal's flat and a waiting bed. She was exhausted and her full belly was calling for sleep.

Ethan followed, dragging with each step. He really wanted to go to his own home, but felt uneasy leaving Crystal all alone, considering everything that had happened and their last little interchange with Dharág. "I'm needin' a nap. I love Becky's cookin', but it be like a sedative. I'm bushed."

"Why don't you go home and get some sleep. I'll be fine. I'm going to take a nap and I can put the table in front of the door. That should keep anyone out."

"Ye sure? I don't mind the floor." He really did, but would not admit it if Crystal wanted him to stay.

At the door, Crystal turned around and placed both hands on

Ethan's shoulders. "I do not mind. In fact, I will repeat your sister's orders. Go home and get some sleep before ye drop where ye stand." She tried her hand at Irish.

That was all it took for Ethan to give in. Between the corny accent and her urging, he was ready for his own bed. "Alright. Ye've me number. Ring me if ye need anythin'. Or even if ye get the feelin' somethin' be suspicious." Crystal knew he was serious in his warning because he was staring right into her eyes, looking for some headstrong retort.

"I will. I promise. Now go home and get some rest. I'll be fine." Crystal was beginning to feel something she'd not felt ever before. No man ever had her safety as his main concern. Usually it was the need to get away as soon as possible. "Colleen is downstairs and Christian will be back soon. No one will try anything in the light of day." She let go of his shoulders and he wobbled and leaned against the doorjamb.

"Alright, but–"

"No buts about it. Home, Inspector, or I'll throw you in my rental car and drive you there myself." Crystal laughed at the thought. It must have scared Ethan enough because he crossed himself and stumbled back down the stairway. With a half-hearted wave, he was gone.

Crystal closed her door and turned the lock, then pulled a table in front of the door as promised. The next thing she knew, she was flat out on Brystal's bed, still fully clothed but drifting into sleep.

~

DHARÁG HADLEY WAS MORE distraught than he'd been when they took his boat away. More than when his wife had deserted him and taken their children. Making money selling original design cut crystal was one thing. Murder was another. Then seeing the gel he'd had a hand in killing, was way over the edge of sanity. The woman even brushed her hair aside like the bitch he'd conned into doing his work. Aye, they were twins, but he hadn't been ready to see how *identical* they actually were. The first thought that'd struck him was, Brystal'd come back to avenge her death and he was going to be dragged into the

Seventh Hell for sinners who took an innocent life. Then that damn inspector had yelled his name and Dharág gained a new fear. He was worried he'd been found out.

It was bound to happen. He had yet to find his original designs or the goblets Brystal had cut. She'd insisted on working late that last day and had done something with the stuff she cut, the stuff he needed. He'd no idea why the Albanian's wanted the goblets cut to their tight specifications, but he knew their money was as good as anyone's, so he'd taken the job. Yes, it was an astronomical amount for a single use design cut specifically for one person, but what the heck. He could do it without Sean knowing and make his money on the side. But only if he could find the items. What could Brystal have done with them? The designs were not on her wall like he expected. He knew Brystal kept intricate notes about crystal cutting and cataloged all of her own designs, but his? He couldn't find any information or the sketches anywhere. Maybe whatever had been disturbing about the design made her throw the drawings away. That would be a tragedy, his own personal tragedy.

He racked his mind and still came up with nothing. As he swept and cleaned the shop, he focused on the reason behind Kujtim's threats. His older brother was the one who really scared Dharág. He'd heard the rumors, like everyone who had dealt with the man. He was vicious and without mercy. His word was law, even to his little brother Kujtim, who everyone called Timmy.

Like calling up a specter, Rudaij materialized in front of the shop, peering through the space that used to be a plate glass window. Now it was a gaping hole waiting for a sheet of plywood and a handful of nails.

"Hey, Dharág? What happened here?" Rudaij's smile reminded Dharág of a great white shark, all teeth and implied danger. "Somebody really messed this place up, eh? Too bad." The man had the ill grace to laugh and poke at shards that still clung to the wood frame. "Maybe looking for something they didn't find?"

"What be ye wantin' Illianescu?" Dharág was nursing a mother of a hangover headache.

"Nothing, of course. Just adding my condolences for this… little inconvenience." He clasped his hands in front of his immaculate tan suit and stood there, smiling at Dharág like a cat viewing a rat caught in the corner with no way to escape. The cat wanted to play with the rat for the fun of it all. "Any idea when my special order will be complete?"

Dharág paused and leaned on his broom. The last two ounces of courage flowed out his mouth. "No. Find someone else to threaten, ye piece of shit. Take yer pointy shoes and pretty-boy suit back to yer own filthy country and stuff it." He shook the handle of the broom at the Albanian. "Get outta me face."

The look on Rudaij's face turned to ice. "That would be the wrong answer, Mr. Hadley. We have a contract. I would suggest you uphold your part, and I will do my best to refrain from implementing the breach of contract clause. There is a great deal at stake here and you are in it up to your neck." He stuffed his fists into his pockets. "I will expect delivery of my merchandise on time and in perfect," He pointed to the pile of crystal dust and shards on the floor, "condition." Not waiting for any kind of answer or more conversation on the subject, Rudaij strolled off down the street toward the Sweeney Bakery.

"Piece of cod loving mongrel of a whore house." Dharág mumbled as he set to work on the floors again. He had three days to come up with the goblets. He'd have to find them or he'd be dead, or worse. He remembered the story about one of the fishermen in the next town. He'd taken a loan from the Albanian crew to keep his boat in the fleet. As things went down, he couldn't repay the loan. They took his boat and both his hands.

~

Rudaij Illianescu was livid. No one treated him the way this rotten Irishman did. As soon as he held the goblets, he'd find a special way to kill this asshole. He'd worked hard since he was a teen, to gain the respect of those around him and he'd been successful, for the largest part. The rest he killed. His father finally recognized his worth. Out of the five sons born to Dacic Illianescu, three survived and Rudaij had taken his place as the oldest and strongest. He'd been forced to take his youngest brother along on this little enterprise and it had almost been the end before the beginning. Kujtim was still a child in many ways, even though he was almost twenty-one years old. Their father still called him by his baby name, Timmy. When he begged to come along, their father had relented almost immediately, warning Rudaij to make a man out of his youngest brother by showing him the ropes. The boy couldn't even do a simple hit. Rudaij pushed the door of the bakery open a little too hard, slamming it against the wall.

Colleen sat behind a case of small fruitcakes covered in icing and sprinkles. At the crash, she stood. Christian came rushing out of the kitchen.

Immediately, Rudaij thought the better of his miniature tantrum. "Please forgive me. Your door was lighter than I thought." He smiled endearingly and tenderly closed the door. "Those look and smell wonderful!" Crossing the floor, he stood before the case of sweet treats. "Now what would be a good snack with a cup of tea." He was grooming this woman for later conversation. If Hadley wasn't going to follow through, he needed to find the goblets himself. This baker was the Traynor woman's landlord. Maybe she would know something about her projects and where she kept her designs. His father was expecting results and a successful operation here in Ireland. Dingle was slated to become their next shipping hub, and it was imperative the first big enterprise set the tone and the financial base for the family's outreach in Ireland. He'd spent hours at the pub on the docks, counting boats, making friends, putting out the word that he might be in the market for transportation in and out of the bay. "I think I'll take that one." He pointed to a dinner plate size apple fritter with icing and cinnamon. "And a cup of black tea, please." Rudaij pulled out his wallet and waded through a handful of bills before selecting a twenty Euro note. It was way more than the cost of the fritter and tea, but he was buttering them both up. "Thanks. Keep the change." He handed Christian the bill and took his food to a small table in the sun by the front window. Preparing to savor the snack, Rudaij sat back and watched the traffic and locals walking to and fro.

"Sir?" Christian held Rudaij's change. "Me mum says it be too much. Sorry." He laid the money on the table.

Rudaij nodded between bites. He watched the clock and made sure he spent at least half an hour in the bakery, pretending he liked tea and wanting nothing but a double shot of vodka. Halfway through the time, he heard the mistress tell her son to take Brystal's motorbike and deliver five loaves of bread to an address across town. A young couple came and went with cakes and bread. An old woman stopped by to gossip and bought dry flour and yeast. When the shop was empty, Rudaij took his plate and cup to the counter. "That was truly a delight. I left a little something for your son. He's such a great kid. He could use it for gas." He turned to go then, playing like it was an afterthought, he asked. "Didn't the American gal who was killed, live just above?"

"Ye heard, did ye? Aye. Brystal was her name. I rented her a flat, poor thing." Colleen crossed herself and mumbled a quick prayer. When she said *amen*, Rudaij repeated the word and crossed himself.

He leaned on the counter, "I don't know if this town has ghosts, but I could swear I saw the gal walking around live as can be, just yesterday."

Colleen patted Rudaij's arm. "Nah, it be her sister. Twin she is. Identical. Truth be told, 'Twas a bit of a shock when first I saw her." Colleen crossed herself again, kissing her fingers and extending them to heaven, the way the nuns had taught her at a very young age.

Rudaij did the same, in a manly way.

Colleen was taken a bit aback at the man's reverence, considering he used the wrong hand. She covered it well as something inside began to squirm, and voices told her to beware. "But then I must be about me kitchen. Buns in the oven, ye know." She excused herself and ducked into the kitchen keeping an ear to make sure the strange man left. When the bell over the door tinkled, she peeked out of the kitchen, then finally relaxed.

What had she told the man?

Why was he interested in Brystal's death in the first place? Morbid curiosity, or fear for himself as a countryman?"

She peaked around the corner and saw her son outside, standing next to the man on the sidewalk. Christian was pointing up toward Brystal's flat, the motorbike leaned against her window. The man was clearly asking questions and Christian was answering. She moved to the window and knocked, pointing to the motorbike. Christian got the idea immediately. She'd told him several times not to leave the bike on the sidewalk for someone to take a tumble.

Colleen watched her son nod energetically, shake hands with the man who didn't know the correct hand to use when he pretended to be a Catholic. What else was he pretending to be? As Christian grabbed the bike, the man quickly slipped something into the boy's hand. However not quite quick enough to keep Colleen from seeing.

The man waved amicably to Colleen and ambled on down the street toward the docks.

CHAPTER 17

Did you know you have to use 17 muscles to smile?
It takes 43 to frown.
Conserve energy.
Smile more!

Crystal woke to the buzzing of her cell phone. Only three people had her number in Ireland: Chance, Ethan, and Daria! She rolled over with a groan and looked at the caller ID. Daria!

It was five thirty p.m.

"Hello Daria." Crystal's voice was a touch hoarse.

"Crystal, ye have to come now! Me thinks I've figured it out. 'Tis so diabolical and evil. Ye've been right all along. Hurry! It be stupendously important." It all came out without the girl taking a breath.

"Daria, hold on." Crystal sat up. "Have you spoken to your uncle? He went home to sleep for a while."

"No, Crystal, ye have to come and see this. Make sure I am right. If what I've found out is correct, it's truly horrible. Come quick. Please!"

"Okay. Okay. I think I can remember how to get to your home." Crystal was still groggy and rubbing her eyes. Obviously, she wasn't using her brain as she agreed to drive into the Irish countryside by herself in the evening hours. Maybe she should call Ethan. He was so tired, she reconsidered. She could do this herself!

"Just follow the main road west. Our drive is six point two kilometers from the Aquarium. It should take you about seven and a half minutes if ye follow the limits. Hurry. This is mega-outrageous fer the entire world!" Daria rang off leaving Crystal looking at her cell phone in consternation. As she stumbled into the bathroom, her brain kicked in and she began to run the equations she'd committed to memory. Nothing new came to mind. What could Daria have found that needed her immediate attention?

Soon Crystal was in her rental car passing the Aquarium and holding the wheel with a death grip. "Stay left, Crystal. Just do the opposite of what you think. Actually, don't think!" She made it to the first round-about and couldn't figure out which way to turn. "Oh no! I could be in this thing until Daria graduates from college!" About the time she decided to follow the next car that came along to get out of the roundie, Christian pulled alongside on Brystal's motorbike, a wide cake box bungeed to the passenger seat behind him. He motioned to Crystal to roll the window down, and she did.

"Where ye be headin'?" Christian yelled as they proceeded around and around.

"The Kilkerry home, west of here." Crystal yelled back just avoiding an entering lorry.

"Follow me." He waved and pulled in front of Crystal's car.

"Thank God for teenagers!" Crystal followed Christian out of the round-about.

He pulled over to the side of the road and she followed. As Christian got off his bike, Crystal took a deep breath and tried to relax her fingers. They were stiff and tight.

"Just keep on this road for a few kilometers. Their drive is marked well. Ye can't miss it. No more roundies 'tween here and there." He waved again and returned to his bike, speeding away in the opposite direction.

He'd interrupted his deliveries to get her out of that round-about! What a great kid. Crystal was beginning to feel comfortable in this little village in Ireland, even if they did drive on the wrong side of the road. The thought struck her as a bit funny. She'd never been comfortable anywhere, not even in her own apartment in New York. She simply existed in a safe zone, but comfortable? She was protected at her job, in her small office, in the big city. She had a routine and pattern, but comfortable? Ireland was growing on her like no other place ever had. And Ireland had Ethan, and Colleen, and Christian, and Daria, and...

She looked both ways and decided there was no traffic. It was safe to pull out onto the road, on the wrong side. Just about nine minutes later see saw a sign dangling from a large post box. It announced Kilkerry Farm. She'd made it. Already she could see Daria on the porch, pacing back and forth.

Crystal carefully parked where Ethan had earlier. Before she could even get out of the car, a breathless Daria was already at her window. "What took you so long? Hurry. I have to show you this." She opened the door for Crystal and tugged her out of the car. Holding her by the hand, Daria dragged Crystal right past a surprised Becky and up to her bedroom. Sheets of calculations covered the bed and most of the floor. "Look!" Daria pointed to the last page in an organized string that ended at the foot of her bed.

Crystal knelt and peered at the paper. A series of numbers and letters covered the bottom of the page. "O-kay?"

"See! I figured it out." Daria paused. "I think. Watch." She started at the beginning which was somewhere near her fluffy pillows and worked through each page, explaining how she came to the final answer on the last page.

Becky appeared at the door. "Daria, I'd not be known' ye've invited a visitor."

Daria ignored her mother's comment and continued. "So this! This is the resulting precipitation if you combine these chemicals in a recombinant formula."

"Daria, I spoke to you." Becky was not to be ignored.

"I know, but the world is at stake here, mum." Daria didn't look up from the final page. "This, this one is the evil you felt, Crystal. This guy be the death of millions, if he be let loose."

"Daria, this is chemistry. I'm an accountant." Crystal was following the numbers but not the process.

"Young lady, and I be speakin' quite freely, what are ye talkin' of?" Becky was clearly frustrated with her daughter's behavior as well as an unexpected visitor.

"It's a recipe, mum. Like yer soda bread, only not so good tastin'." She dragged her finger across her throat and hung her tongue out as far as it would go.

"What be ye meanin', gel? Yer da'll be home soon and I need to be getting' dinner on the table."

"I *mean*, chemical/biological weapon, *mum*." Daria dragged out the words for emphasis. She turned to Crystal. "Yer sister's calculations correspond to the drawings, which correspond to this formula. I think it be some new form of neurological toxin."

"How do you even know those words, gel?" Crystal was a bit surprised that Daria's mother did not understand the extent of her daughter's mind. But then no one understood *her* mind either, especially not her parents. They just thought her sorta smart and awkward.

"*Mum*!" Daria shook her head. "I took an online chemistry course when I was nine. Remember?"

Obviously, Becky either didn't remember, or had never known. Crystal thought she might be in the dark about a lot of her daughter's education and activities.

"Somehow, the design yer sis made is the formula." Daria's lips curled and her brows knit. "I just don't know how that part works yet. Do you have one of the pieces she cut?"

"No. Your uncle and I put them in the evidence locker at the police station for safekeeping. There were four and I dropped one. It broke into almost dust." She peered at the calculations spread out across the floor and bed. "Brystal never studied chemistry, as far as I know. I wonder how she–"

"I'm calling Ethan. This may be critical to his investigation. Then I'm going to get dinner on the table before my husband dies of starvation, not some... weapon thing. I guess one more mouth won't matter"

As Becky spoke, Crystal's cell phone buzzed. "No need." She pointed to her phone before answering.

"From my lips to God's ears." Becky crossed herself and left the two alone with their mystery.

"Ethan?" Crystal answered the phone only to have Daria snatch it out of her hand.

"Uncle Ethan, I figured it out! You have to come here and see. It's diabolical. Can you bring a piece of Brystal's work with you?"

"Whoa, Mouse! Why are you on Crystal's phone? Where are you? Where is she?"

"I'm in my bedroom and so is Crystal. Uncle Ethan, focus! It's done, the calculations. You have to see it!" Daria handed the phone back to Crystal. "Make him listen, *please*!"

Crystal took the phone with a laugh. Daria's behavior didn't offend her in the least. She remembered feeling the same exuberance and excitement as a young woman chasing her first forensic accounting case. When she'd finally found the concrete financial evidence, she ran into Chance's office with reams of proof to convict their criminal. He was in the middle of an interview with a new hire and she didn't even notice! "Ethan, Daria called me and I came over to see what she found. I believe I've discovered a motive for my sister's murder. Your niece is amazing. We need a goblet to test her theory though."

"My niece is an anomaly! I'll stop by the station and fetch one. One is all you need?" Ethan sounded tired but interested.

"One will do since they are all the same pattern." She nodded in the affirmative at Daria who bounced up and down with a tiny quiet clap.

"I'll be leavin as soon as I shave." Ethan rang off and Crystal turned to Daria. "He'll bring one. The patterns are all identical so all we need is one."

Daria began picking up the papers in order. "Uncle Ethan won't be understandin' this, but he will definitely want to see the last page. She sat down at her computer. "Look at this." She pulled up a website that detailed the history of biological and chemical weapons. It included everything from historic poisons, more modern mustard gas from WWI and II then moved into research on insect killers that eventually morphed into today's horrendous, and very effective chemical and biological weapons.

"Are you supposed to be on this website?" Crystal watched over Daria's shoulder as the girl pulled up one chemical formula after another, pointing out the similarities and differences between their recipe and the others. All of this information was on the Internet for anyone to find.

"Probably not. The confoundin' part is this molecule." She pointed to one set of letters and numbers that Crystal now recognized as a chemical combination. "I don't know why it is included or what it is supposed to do."

"How is it you know so much about weaponized chemistry?" Crystal was impressed, but also disturbed at Daria's taste in web surfing. At eleven, girls usually giggled about boys and painted each other's fingernails. This girl was deconstructing chemical weapons!

"It be me hobby. 'Tis not as challenging as cross breedin' mongo tomatoes, but interestin' to see what combinations do what to the body. Did ye know Sarin can actually make ye drown in yer own body fluid? Cool!" Daria started gagging as if she were choking. "Makes Quinn sick too, so I can get me more dessert." She giggled.

"You are soooo bad!" Crystal held up her fist for a bump. Not only was she a little genius, she was drama queen for the morbid!

Daria returned the salute to manipulative womanhood. "Did Uncle Ethan say when he'd be here?"

"He said he'd be on his way, as soon as he shaved."

"Oh la, men!" Daria's comment came out like a harried thirty-year-old housewife instead of an almost-twelve-year old.

RUDAIJ ILLIANESCU SAT in his car across from the driveway of the Kilkerry home. He'd followed the Traynor sister from Dingle and now contemplated what she might be doing at the home of Inspector MacEnery's sister. It was a fluke that he'd seen her leave Dingle at all. Luck seemed to be going his way today. The bakery boy had given him the low-down on Crystal's plans to ship her sister's things home. Christian had also added the hope that she might sell him Brystal's motorbike. Brystal's body would remain in the county morgue until the case was officially closed, with or without resolution. That didn't matter. The goblets wouldn't be in the morgue with their creator. Since Hadley hadn't found them at the flat or in the warehouse, and Timmy hadn't found them in the shop before he lost what little temper he possessed, and trashed the place, Crystal must have them. Could she be carrying them around in her car? Maybe she stashed them at this Kilkerry farm. Or possibly the nosey Inspector had them.

Timmy was watching the Inspector's flat. As soon as the man left, he would search the place with strict orders to be clean about it. That left the car and this house. Rudaij made sure Burim Dobrish accompanied his little brother as his appointed driver. Dobrish resented being a babysitter but had been handy when Timmy botched the Traynor hit. Stepping in, Dobrish finished the mess and got Timmy out of there when the boy collapsed at the sight of her blood. Their father had spoiled his younger son to the point Rudaij thought the boy may never grow up. Dobrish wasn't the only one who resented babysitting duty.

In the half hour he'd been parked across the road, observing the house, he'd only seen two women and two kids. Now would be the time to take a look-see in Crystal's car. He pulled out and turned down the drive. Turning off his headlights before he reached the house, Rudaij parked behind a tall tree and snuck over to Crystal's rental. It was not locked and easy to access. He opened the passenger side door and peered into the back, under the seats and in the trunk.

Nothing.

There wasn't even a scrap of paper or a used tissue.

The bitch must have the goblets hidden. Damn! He had to have those pieces. He had buyers and they were waiting. He'd already taken payment from two of the buyers. The family could make good if reimbursement were necessary, but his reputation was on the line. He'd taken a chance, and now it had gone to hell in a hand basket. Hadley should have had the goblets in hand before Timmy got anxious and pulled his stunt with the cutter.

Damn that boy.

Damn their father.

Rudaij snuck across the porch and listened at the open front door. Only a screen separated the woman bustling about the dining room and himself.

It wasn't Crystal Traynor.

A youth watched a soccer game on the television in the living room.

Where was the other kid and Crystal?

He heard a squeal and ducked out of sight.

"Uncle Ethan should be here soon, mum. Can he and Crystal stay for dinner?" The young girl ran through the house. Through a side window, Rudaij could see Crystal on the last step. "Daria, your mom didn't plan on two more people at the table." Crystal stopped talking when she caught sight of the table set for six. Apparently, Daria's mom had anticipated company for dinner.

Rudaij had the perfect vantage point and continued to watch and listen through the open side window. People in Ireland were so trusting. Crystal's car was unsecured. The house was open and inviting. He might just have to invite himself in.

Sneaking around the back of the sprawling house, Rudaij checked the revolver he carried hidden in a special holster in his trousers. It tucked inside behind his hip and showed no profile to the world. Good thing, because handguns were outlawed in Ireland.

Shootings were especially rare, but fistfights were a nightly occurrence thanks to the country's national pastime of beer drinking and boasting.

He tried the back door.

It was open.

Today truly was his lucky day!

The back door led into a mudroom and a kind of pantry with well-organized shelves. Pots and pans were neatly stacked on one side, and cans and jars of various kinds sat, labeled, and shelved. Three loaves of soda bread were cooling on a rack next to a doorway that led to the kitchen. Pressed against the shelves, Rudaij spied on the lady of the house, bustling about the kitchen, preparing the evening's meal. He would take her out if need be, but it would be better to just nab Crystal, take her off somewhere and get the information he needed, then get rid of the evidence. He could go about his deals and no one would connect him to two dead sisters. No one would even miss the woman. Christian told him their family story and he knew Crystal was the only one left.

About the time he was congratulating himself on a job well planned and executed, he heard the woman in the kitchen holler at her daughter.

"Daria, would ye get the soda bread?"

Rudaij withdrew his gun. He could easily intimidate a child into silence.

As Daria came through the door, Rudaij covered her mouth and held her tight against him, the gun pointed at her nose. He whispered. "You want to live? No noise. Hear me?"

Daria nodded. Her eyes were big as saucers.

"Call Crystal in here. Just that, no more or you both die. Got it?"

Again, Daria nodded.

Rudaij removed his hand a few inches, ready to cover her mouth again if she so much as squeaked wrong.

"Crystal, could ye come help me?"

She stood immobile; aware the gunman could see everything. As Crystal approached, Daria tried to get her attention with quick, darting eye movements. As her friend stepped through the pantry door, the gunman spun Daria and held the gun to her head.

Crystal froze. "Don't hurt–"

"Shut it, bitch." He motioned toward the backdoor and dragged Daria with him.

Crystal was terrified. Not for herself, but for Daria. The child was innocent and had her entire life ahead of her. What did this man want? By his accent, he was speaking American.

"Over there. Get in. You drive." He followed Crystal, still holding the gun to Daria's head. "You girly, get in the back. Either of you make a stupid move and you're dead. Both of you."

Crystal saw the black Mercedes with smoked out windows parked near the tree. If she went with him without any trouble, maybe he would let Daria go. Course, if he were after the goblets and the formula for the chemical weapon, the chances were slim either of them would be allowed to live.

"Out to the road. Turn left."

Crystal did as she was told. Just before making the turn, she saw Becky in the rearview mirror. Ethan's sister was waving madly and already had her cell phone out.

~

ETHAN WAS HALFWAY to his sister's when his cell phone showed a call from Becky. He picked it up immediately figuring she needed something from the store, since she wasn't expecting company for dinner. "Aye, sis. What do ye need?"

"Ethan! Daria and Crystal are gone. I saw a black car leaving the drive. I think someone has taken Daria! Ethan, I need help! Rory isn't back. Someone took my daughter!" She added as an afterthought, "And Crystal!"

Ethan stepped on the gas. "Stay calm. What kind of car? Which way did they go?"

"A black car. They went toward Ventry. Oh Ethan, what if…" Ethan knew exactly what his sister was thinking.

"Look, Becky. Stay calm. Try to remember anything you can. Did you see the car drive up? Was there someone at the house? How many people were in the car when it left?

"I don't know, Ethan. I don't know. The windows be all dark, tinted. I couldn't see in. It was one of those boxy cars. It had that propeller on the trunk. In a circle."

"Mercedes. Good! What else can ye remember? Plates?" He was closing in on his childhood home and could see his sister standing near the postbox with her cell.

"That's all. Ethan, what if they kill me girl, like they did 'yers?" The last part came out a whisper.

"Not happening. Now listen. Ring up Rory if ye can. I need to call the station. I'm going after them." He sped on by, leaving Becky looking after his dust cloud.

He dialed the station. "Biffy, Ethan. Get me two squads. Send them out Route 559. Me niece and Miss Traynor have been kidnapped. Black Mercedes. Smoked windows."

"Right-o." Ethan could hear Biffy on the radio calling up the two squad cars and sending them his way. "Inspector, what else do ye need? How can I help?"

"Put out an APB and see what ye can find out about a black Mercedes around town. Get every snitch in and grill 'em, Biff. I can't lose me niece, or Miss Traynor. She found out something about her sister's murder just before she was taken."

"This case keeps gettin' more complicated. I'll be right on it, Inspector. Ring me if ye be needin' anything."

"Biff get O'Haide in Shannon on it. I've a feelin' this is bigger than us and may be blowin' up right soon."

"Aye, sir. Luck be on ye." The line went dead. Biffy wouldn't be getting' his studies done tonight.

Ethan watched all of the side drives as he raced toward Ventry. Whoever took his niece and Crystal couldn't have had more than a few minutes lead on him and he was driving like the devil was on his tail. He turned his police radio on and listened for the squads that should be following him. They were headed toward Ventry with lights and sirens.

"Seven-two-six stop at me sister's and see if ye can find anything useful. Five-three-seven, follow me." He heard their affirmatives and kept his foot on the gas pedal. Ahead he could see the outskirts of Ventry. "Lord help me find them before it's too late." Ethan prayed with all his heart. He already had one Traynor in the morgue. He surely didn't want another. How could he face his sister if something happened to Mouse, because of him? His job had already taken his wife and daughter. He couldn't let it take more.

CRYSTAL PULLED into the parking lot of the Ventry boat launch. "Why here?" She was dying to know where he was taking them.

"Shut up. Not a word. Just do what I tell you and no one will get hurt." He sat in the passenger seat pointing a gun at her beneath the level of the dash, so no one would see. "Now we're going to get out and go to my boat. It's moored out there." He nodded toward a yacht about a quarter of a mile offshore. It was huge and looked to have three decks.

Daria mumbled, "That's not a boat. It's a ship." It was an innocent comment.

Rudaij twisted in his seat and slapped the girl.

"Stop that you brute!" Crystal screamed. "She's just a kid."

"She's gonna be a dead kid if she doesn't obey me."

Daria sniffed in the back seat. Crystal knew she was trying hard not to cry in front of the bad man. As brave as the girl seemed, she was still only an eleven-year old child.

Rudaij looked around before he got out. Standing behind the car, he stuffed his gun in his holster and pulled his shirt over the slight lump. "Gimme the keys. Move."

Crystal and Daria got out. Daria took Crystal's hand and tucked close to her side as they walked down the steep ramp to the dinghy floating off to the side, tied to a big rock. The yacht sat calmly in the bay as if nothing were wrong. As far as Crystal could tell, there was no one aboard and the doors were all closed, shades pulled all the way down. Rudaij ushered them into the dinghy and fired up the engine. Soon they were next to the ship and tying to a swim step at the back.

Rudaij waved them out and up the steps onto the ship without ceremony. As the two stood watching, Rudaij tied the dinghy off and mounted the steps. He pulled a ring of keys from his pocket and opened the salon door. "Inside."

The palatial salon was decorated in typical over-the-top nuevo-rich. Everything was edged in gold and marble. In the center of a long conference table stood a replica of Venus De Milo in glitzy gold. Someone had hung a bikini top on the famous nude. A well-stocked bar filled one half of the forward wall and the other side contained a mammoth television screen. Everything was tan, white, and gold. A polished walnut circular stairway led up to the higher deck and down below. The railing winding up and down was made in the image of two huge pythons, their gaping mouths hissing at each other on the mid-deck they stood on. It was stunning and horrifying at the same time. Daria tucked closer to Crystal.

"Sit. Now." Rudaij moved to the bar and poured himself some form of liquor, downing the entire contents in one gulp.

Crystal moved to the couch and sat, Daria squishing as close as she could, almost hiding behind Crystal. "What do you want from me?" She needed to know how this was going to play out. Somewhere she found the courage to speak.

Rudaij poured himself another shot and gulped the alcohol. "Where's your sister's glasses? She cut them on a contract for me and I want them."

Crystal's mind spun at warp speed. He was the one who provided the specifications for the cut crystal goblets. He was the one who needed the chemical weapon!

"They are a gift for friends. You know where they are. Tell me." He stomped across the floor to tower over Crystal. The glass in his hand had been refilled and now sloshed on Crystal's shoes. "Ah, let me." He grabbed a tissue from a marble holder and threw it down on Crystal's shoes, then stomped as hard as he could on her toes.

"Ahhhh!" She pulled back her feet. Intellectually, she knew he was trying to intimidate her into telling him what he wanted to know. Physically, she didn't want to bring more pain on herself.

"Sorry. I won't hurt you if you tell me what I want to know." He stomped close to her feet with a maniacal grin. "It's up to you."

Behind Crystal, Daria whispered, "Liar!"

Enraged at the young girl's audacity, he grabbed Daria by the arm and flung her across the room.

"No!" Crystal tried to get up and help the girl who had landed on the floor and lay prostrate against an overstuffed rocker. It didn't work. Rudaij slammed her back down leaning in close. "Give me my glasses, or…" He looked at Daria's body. "My brother will be here soon. He likes them young and tender."

Crystal saw Daria's eyelids blink then remain still. She wasn't unconscious, just pretending. Thank God!

"I don't know what you're talking about. My sister is dead, and I have no idea about any glasses she may have made. Why do you want them so bad? You can buy better stuff from the Dingle Crystal shop anyway. Brystal was only an intern. She couldn't have been that good." Crystal wailed like a less-than-smart sister who didn't know anything about her twin.

Rudaij struck Crystal across the face and her head bounced off the leather cushions. She could feel a trickle of blood begin at her lower lip. "The crystal goblets?"

"I don't know–" The next strike was with his fist and this time Crystal's head did not rebound. She heard a sickening crunch and put a hand to her nose as blood spurted everywhere.

"Shit. Don't get blood on my baby ostrich leather couch!" He pulled the marble container off the coffee table and threw it at her.

Crystal caught it, but not before it hit her ribcage. The heavy rock container made quite the impact, and Crystal lost her breath as she grabbed for the box. Pulling several tissues, she held the wad to her bleeding nose.

Rudaij bent over shoving his face close to hers. "The glasses? I can keep this up forever."

As the word forever left his lips, he collapsed into her lap with a grunt. Behind him stood Daria, holding a magnum of champagne, the determined look on her face was almost magical.

Crystal shoved Rudaij to the floor and got up, holding the tissues to her nose. "Good job, Mouse!" Immediately she began looking for something to tie Rudaij, so he couldn't hurt them anymore. But first she removed the gun from his trousers.

"Aye. This mouse be havin' a good swing." She giggled then held her arm. "Can't ye just shoot him?"

"I've never used a handgun. Have you?" Crystal found a roll of duct tape in the fourth drawer she opened. "Ah ha! Daria, help me tape this thug up."

"Aye. He hurt ye pretty bad." She only used one arm to roll Rudaij onto his stomach.

"You too." Crystal knelt next to Rudaij and taped his arms behind his back. Then she taped his feet. Then she put one piece all the way around his head and across his mouth, winding it twice. "That should do it."

Daria laughed. "I'd be thinkin' so. I hope I can be there when they take that wee tape off his head!"

Crystal got up carefully, rubbing her ribs. "He said his brother was coming. We need to get out of here."

"Right-o. Can ye drive that boat?"

Crystal's blank look said it all. "Can you swim?"

"In the bay? I can't even be puttin' me toes in it without losin' me brain."

Crystal moved to the back of the ship and looked at the tied dinghy. "There's oars! We can paddle."

In a heartbeat, they were in the dinghy and untying the rope. Crystal slipped the oars out of their holder and hooked them in the locks on each side of the rubber boat. As Daria released the rope, she began to row.

"Harder, Crystal. We be goin' the wrong direction."

True enough, the outgoing tide was stronger than Crystal's ability to row and they slowly drifted away from Ventry and out into Dingle Bay. Before they realized, they were headed for the open ocean with no control.

"Oh my God, Daria! We're getting farther and farther away!"

Daria opened the front hatch and handed Crystal a life preserver, then took one for herself. "Ye wouldn't happen to have a cell with ye, would ye?"

CHAPTER 18

Trivia...
18 is the only number that is twice the sum of its digits
Americans eat a total of 18 acres of pizza every day.
There are 18 letters in the Scottish Gaelic alphabet.
The 18th Amendment to the Constitution of the US deals with Prohibition.

I think I'd rather be in Scotland eating pizza and drinking twice as much whiskey as I should.

Ethan was frantic! He'd hit the outskirts of Ventry and couldn't find any black Mercedes anywhere. He still had no idea who had taken Crystal and his niece. "Five-three-seven, stay on 559 and I'll check the beach and boat launch."

"Roger that, Inspector," came the response.

Ethan turned off the Dingle Road and drove slowly toward the beach access road toward the boat launch. There were several boats moored in Ventry Bay, but he recognized most of them. One very large yacht had been there for almost three months and belonged to some rich American. He'd not met the fellow, but villagers talked highly of the guy's generosity and friendliness. No one really knew how the owner made his money, but he seemed to be a right straight fellow and there'd been no complaints about parties, loud noise, or suspicious behavior. The sun was low on the horizon promising a fabulous sunset, but all Ethan could think of was his niece and Crystal. The yacht was buttoned down and the small dinghy was gone. He cruised down to the parking lot and his heart skipped a beat. There, parked out of sight of the main road sat a black Mercedes!

"Five-three-seven I've got the Mercedes. Boat launch. Taking a look."

"On our way."

Ethan drove close to the black car as if he were looking for a parking spot away from other cars. Through the front window he could see the car was unoccupied. He parked blocking the front of the car and got out. Peering through the windows, he confirmed his previous assessment.

There was no one in the car.

Ethan tried the door. It was not locked. That was pretty stupid of someone. He opened the passenger side door pulling his shirt over his hands to avoid leaving his prints on the handle. He took the stack of papers from the dash box and thumbed through them. The car was registered to an Albanian import-export company. Insurance papers showed Rudaij Illianescu and Dobrish as the two designated drivers. The import tax had been paid and the luxury tariff was satisfied. Everything was in order. A cold knot formed in the pit of his stomach, feeling like a solid rock of ice chilling his whole body. It had been an Albanian drug lord that ordered the execution of his wife and daughter in revenge for Ethan busting his drug ring on the peninsula. Unfortunately, three of the dealers were killed while resisting arrest when his team took down the entire operation. One of the men had been the drug Lord's son. A month later, Ethan was burying his family while Fedoret Praducheu sat in a limo watching from the road.

"Inspector? Five-three-seven. Garda's Potter and Landeau." Squad five-three-seven had arrived and now the Garda's stood next to the black Mercedes awaiting direction.

"Right." Ethan pulled himself from his memories. "Ask around the lot. See if anybody be knowin' who came in this car and where they went. I'll call the station and see if they can run the plates. Registration is in order, but me sister said the kidnappers used a black Mercedes. Not that many on the peninsula."

"Roger that, Inspector." Both Garda's moved off, talking to people milling about, cleaning boats, and cleaning the day's catch.

Ethan called the station and Biffy ran the plates through their computerized crime base. Nothing outstanding flagged. "Inspector, ye wanted me to get a hold of Stephan O'Haide, sir?"

"Aye, Biffy. Did ye find him?"

"Sure enough, sir. At hospital. The missus delivered a wee baby girl yesterday. Mum and babe be fine. He gave me a number for ye to call. Ready to copy?"

"Aye." Ethan ran to his car and grabbed his notebook and pen. "Go ahead." He copied the number and thanked Biffy. Dialing the number, Ethan had a sinking feeling. Now Stephan would have a daughter to worry over and color everything he did. He would be up nights thinkin' and rethinkin' every word, every move. "Halo Steve?"

"Ethan! To what do I owe this call? Maybe a wee welcome for a me growin' family?" Ethan could hear the joy in his old friend's voice.

"Aye! Would that it be. Give Emma a kiss fer me and congratulations. Unfortunately, 'tis a business call." He paused, waiting for the information to sink in.

"What's the craic, Ethan?" He could hear a doctor being paged in the background. Stephan was still at hospital then.

"Been followin' the Traynor murder case? It be a blowin' gale now. The sister and me niece figured out somethin'. Now they've been kidnapped. I be thinkin' those cursed Albanians be behind this somehow. Ye still with the International and Terrorist Crime Task Force?"

"Aye! Ye think it be the Praducheu bastard?"

"No idea, but I could be usin' a hand. Can ye spare an officer from ye agency?" Ethan would have preferred Stephan himself, but he would be home for a few weeks with his wife and new daughter, as he should be.

"If this is related to Praducheu, be sure the ITCTF will be involved. I'll give ye a call back when I find out what we can send." O'Haide rang off and Ethan realized he didn't really congratulate Stephan on fatherhood. He'd have to remember to make up for that later. Having a child was a life changing event and reason to tip a pint or three.

"Inspector?" Garda Potter stood close. "One fisherman said he saw a man and his family go out to the Breakin' Bad about half an hour ago. Nothin unusual though."

"Heh, Phil, looky here. Me girl wears the same clip."" Garda Landeau held a butterfly barrette up.

"Me Daria was wearing that yesterday. She was in this car!" Ethan came around and took the hair clip. He gazed at the yacht, no glowing orange in the sunset. "So that means she went out to the ship. Obviously, what appeared to be a family was the kidnapper with Crystal and Daria. We have to get out to that boat!"

~

CRYSTAL'S ARMS were aching and still she pulled against the tide. If she could just keep them in the bay, they might have a chance of being rescued. Out in the open ocean it was anyone's guess.

Daria huddled on the floor of the boat watching the water take them farther away from Ventry. She was beginning to get cold as the sun dropped below the horizon and the warmth of the day faded. She wedged herself against the inflated pontoons and the canvas hatch at the front of the boat.

"Daria," Crystal was dripping with sweat and straining at the oars, "you're getting cold. Look in that box and see if there is a blanket or jacket. Something to wrap around yourself to stay warm."

Daria scrambled to her knees and tore the cover Velcro away, peering inside. "There was a silver space blanket in a plastic pouch, a first aid box, and a dry bag with something that felt like a book. On one side was a red plastic box with a picture of a gun on the side.

"Crystal, I think I've found a flare gun!" She withdrew the box and showed it to Crystal. "We can signal for help!"

"Or tell the younger brother where we are." Crystal ground out as she rowed against a wave crest. It was getting harder to row the closer to the ocean they drifted and now the bay looked like a giant river running to the edge of the world.

"Aye. Good point." Daria replaced the box and took the space blanket out of the package and wrapped it around herself. It wasn't very warm but protected her against the wind. She fished around and withdrew the dry bag praying for some kind of snack. They'd both missed dinner and now she was hungry, not really because she'd missed dinner, but because they were lost and had nothing to eat. It seemed to multiply her hunger twenty-fold.

There was no food inside the dry bag, but there was a book on motor maintenance and the initial process for correctly starting the engine! "Stupendousness!" Daria yelled and almost stood up, then crouched down against the floorboards as the boat tipped precariously.

"Daria! Stay down. It's getting rougher!" Crystal could hear the waves breaking against the cliffs.

"Crystal, I found the engine manual. We be saved! Well, once I read the blasted book." She flipped through the thick manual. "How difficult can it be to start and engine on a boat?"

Crystal laughed. "You read. I row."

Daria braced herself against the side of the boat and began to speed read through the book. Halfway in she stated, "Now we be getting' somewhere." And began to read out loud. "Check the tank fer gas. Well, we have gas, or we wouldn't have gotten to the ship, right? Okay. Prime the motor by squeezing the primer bulb. There." Daria pointed to the bulb on the hose between the gas can and the motor. "Pull the starter rope until the engine fires and you control the speed with the twist grip throttle on the handle of the tiller." Daria read through the directions one more time to herself. "Alright. 'Tis easy. I'll have a go at it."

"Just be careful you don't go overboard or the engine won't

matter." Crystal continued to pull against the increasingly rough waves.

"Squeeze the primer bulb three times and pull the rope until it starts." Daria crawled across the floorboards and squeezed the bulb. She then grabbed the t-handle on the rope and gave it a tug. It moved about a foot then stopped. She tried again and got no more than the last time. "It's stuck. Buggers."

"Pull harder. I used to watch my dad and he had to pull really hard."

Daria stood up and heaved at the rope. This time she got about a foot and a half before the rope jerked her back. Studying the rope, she braced her feet and pulled with all her might.

She got about two feet of rope and the engine made a slight noise. "I be too weak. I wish Quinn were here. He'd have this thing a goin' in a second."

In between gasps and straining against the oars, Crystal laughed. "You fight with him every chance you get. You trick him into leaving the table before dessert and then you want him around when it suits!

"And...?" The attempt at a tween attitude was funny and both laughed, between holding on to the rocking boat and watching the shifting direction of the waves. "What are we going to do? I've an irrational fear of the ocean."

"Why's that?" Crystal was on the verge of giving up. Her arms were numb and she held on to the oars through sheer will.

"Have ye not seen the creatures that live there? Two-hundred-meter squid. Whales the size of me da's lorry."

Crystal could row no longer. She pulled the oars and slid to the bottom of the boat holding on as the dinghy rose and fell at the whim of the water and wind. Daria crawled into her lap and pulled the space blanket around them both. "Not even twelve and fish bait." Daria mused.

"ROBERT, CAN I BE USIN' ye skiff? Police business."

"Sure Ethan. No need to be flashin' ye badge. I'll take ye where ye need to go." Robert had just pulled his truck and trailer down the ramp preparing to load his skiff. "Clara, pull 'er up. I be takin' Ethan out. Police business." He hollered at his wife behind the wheel.

Ethan clambered up onto the trailer and jumped to the boat. Robert still had his waders on and simply walked to the ladder and climbed up. The tide was dropping rapidly and soon it would be completely dark. There were tiny red lights on both the bow and stern of the Breaking Bad, but they were tiny targets to search for in the overcast black of night. A light mist was descending lending a foggy nature to the surface of the bay. "I'll be needin' to get to the Breaking Bad as quiet as ye can. It be a case of life and death, Robert."

The fisherman geared the engine down to a soft purr and made a course that would take the skiff well ahead of the bow. "We'll drift back on idle. Me engines don't even wake the fish that way."

As they approached the large yacht, Robert commented. "Don't look to me like there be anyone about. No lights."

"Someone saw the owner and his family go out earlier."

They drifted past the yacht and Robert deftly hooked the swim step pulling his skiff close. "I'll wait fer ye unless there be shots. Then I be off."

Ethan quietly stepped aboard the ship, crouching as he moved up the short steps. The back deck was unoccupied and the back door stood open. Through the doorway, he could see a pair of legs duct taped together. The shoes and trousers did not fit his missing victims. With great care, he approached the legs and peered inside the salon. On the floor lay a man, face down. His hands were taped behind him with about ten wraps of duct tape. His legs were the same. Around his head, his entire head, were two more wraps of tape. It was a very efficient way of restraining someone, if that someone had been conscious. Which that someone wasn't. Ethan checked for a pulse and breathing. The man was alive at least.

The man on the floor wasn't going anywhere and there were no lights on, so Ethan tiptoed around, checking the ship. There seemed to be no one aboard except the unconscious man. Ethan jumped as

Robert appeared in the doorway. "What have ye here?" He peered at the still man on the floor. "Dead?"

"Nah." He rolled the man over and got a weak groan for his effort. "Know this fellow?"

"He's been round. This be his boat. Somebody roust the place?" Robert was curious and soon the entire town would know everything that happened. Robert wasn't a fellow to keep things to himself.

"Not sure, Robert. Would ye be doin' me a favor and bring Garda Potter over to me? I'm thinkin' we may need his medical skills."

"Sure enough." Transporting the police in a medical emergency was tantamount to bein' a hero in Robert's tiny town. "Be right back."

As Robert left, Ethan searched for something to wake the unconscious man. He filled the ice bucket he found on the bar with ice and water. That would wake the bastard! Dumping the container on the man's head, Ethan was rewarded with a groan and a few struggles. Rolling on his side, the man looked at Ethan. Anger burned in the man's eyes. It was past time for Ethan to know what was going on, and where his niece and Crystal were. He got a paring knife off the bar and bent to slice the tape loose.

The man wiggled madly and tried to scream behind the duct tape. The sound came out muffled and weak.

"Ah, hold still man. I'll be cuttin' ye instead of the tape." Ethan approached again and this time the man lay still, his eyes darting between the knife and Ethan's face. One slice and Ethan ripped away.

A wild scream ensued and Ethan noticed clumps of black hair stuck to the tape. "Oh, man up. Tell me what ye did with me niece and Miss Traynor. I know ye brought them out here." Ethan swung the hairy tape back and forth.

"I don't know what you are talking about. I'm going to call the police. Someone attacked me and left me for dead. Get this stuff off me." he demanded.

"I be the police and I'll not be playin' yer game. Who are ye, and what have ye done with me family?" Ethan pulled him to a sitting position and leaned him against the wall. "Me family? Did ye hear that part, laddy?"

"I'm the victim here, you stupid cop. This is my yacht. I'm Rudaij Illianescu and, again, I have no idea what you are talking about."

"Not gonna talk, eh? Fine then." He took a new strip of tape from the roll he just happened to notice on the coffee table and wrapped it around Rudaij shaking head. When it was tightly wound, he patted the tape to make sure it had a good seal.

Rudaij kicked and wiggled, mumbling, and trying to stand. Ethan kicked the man and Rudaij stopped wiggling, pain showing clearly on the parts of his face not covered with duct tape. "Good stuff, eh?" Ethan tossed the roll up and down.

Again, Rudaij wiggled and used his head to point to the champagne magnum on the floor near the foot of the table.

"Ah, someone belt ye with," Ethan picked up the bottle and read the label. "Dom Perignon 1932. Good choice I be thinkin'." He watched Rudaij try to mumble something. "Ah, now ye want to talk?" Before Rudaij could shake his head no, Ethan crossed the room and tore the tape from his thinning hair and reddening face. "What have ye to say? I have a whole roll in case ye be playin' me." Ethan wasn't a mean man, but his family's security brought out the worst in him. Or the best, depending on which side of the tape you sat.

"Someone hit me with it. Then you woke me up. That's all I know." Rudaij had calmed down and now sounded like a wounded man who was the victim of some malicious crime.

Ethan began pulling off another strip of the silver tape.

"No man, wait. They came with me willingly. I was gonna pay the Traynor woman for her sister's work. I commissioned it and I still want it. She came with me to get the money and then she was going to give me the cut crystal."

"That right?" Ethan tore the strip off, swinging it back and forth, stuck to the tip of a finger.

"Then the little chit hit me when my back was turned. I think they wanted to rob me. Where are they?"

"You tell me." Ethan took a step toward the bound man.

"What do you mean? You found me. I was out cold." He rubbed a lump on his head with both hands, still taped together.

"So, where are they? If they were here, where'd they go?" Ethan was losing patience.

"Maybe took the dinghy ashore. I don't know. What I do know is the charges I'm going to file against that little bitch.

No one called his niece or Crystal a bitch in his presence! He swung the magnum and connected. Rudaij was out cold, once again. He crumpled up the tape and shoved it in his jacket pocket, replaced the magnum on the bar's shelf and went out on the back deck. There was no dinghy on the shore. He looked across the bay. Nothing.

His phone chirped.

It was Stephan.

"Aye, Stephan?"

"Ethan, I'm on me way with a couple of me buds."

Ethan could hear the recognizable thwop-thwop of a helicopter rotor in the background. "Stephan, you're supposed to be on leave! What be ye doin', mate?"

"Me job. Just like you. Me ETA be forty-five minutes." By his tone, Ethan knew Stephan was resolute.

"Ye bringin' a chopper?"

"Aye, fastest and most reasonable considering the geography." Stephan was always considering the agency's resources and the need.

"Right-o. I'll be clearin' the parking lot here at Ventry. There be plenty of space to land. Miss Traynor and me niece were on a boat here in the bay. This American fellow, Rudaij Illianescu owns the boat. I found the bloke out cold and secured with duct tape. I can't be findin' Crystal or Daria. The dinghy is gone."

"We'll take a spin around the bay afore we land. See what there be to see."

"Keep me on the right, Stephan."

"Will do." Stephan rang off and Ethan stowed his phone as Robert's skiff eased up to the swim step. Potter jumped aboard. "Medical emergency?" He asked with a grin.

"Aye, inside." He waved Potter through the door as Robert secured the skiff. "This fellow needs your lovin' touch." Ethan joked just loud enough for Robert to overhear.

"No Daria or Miss Traynor?"

"No. I be a bit worried. This bloke won't tell me straight. Says Daria knocked him out." Ethan pointed to the champagne magnum.

"She be a scrapper, that one." Potter chuckled. "Ye shoulda seen the gel at the football finals. She took exception to a ref call and darn near got her brother ejected from the game." Potter shrugged. "Me boy-o plays on Quinn's team. I'd rather see Daria on the team, but she be a tad vicious fer the lads."

That comment had Ethan smiling.

"No doubt she took this bloke out. Shall we wake him?" Potter picked up the handy bucket and filled it from the bar tap. "This be applicable." He dumped the bucket on Rudaij who promptly came to, sputtering and swearing. "Sure enough." Potter chuckled.

"What the fuck is going on? Get this shit off me." Rudaij's demands fell on deaf ears.

"I be thinkin' ye should calm down a tad. There be reinforcements on the way, and I don't give a she's shit about yer comfort. Or ye lies." Ethan stalked toward the man on the floor, his hands balled into fists.

"Let me go. You are on American soil on my boat. You can't do anything."

That got Potter laughing his head off.

Robert joined in. "Who does he think he be? Can't say as I admire this boy's thinkin'. Never quite took to them bastards from the States. All full of themselves, ye know." Robert rubbed the beard on his chin. "Ye must have the healin' touch Potter. I'll be tendin' me skiff. Out back there." Robert was excusing himself in light of the situation, which he had no idea of and didn't want to know, if the police were about to ruff the fellow up.

"Potter will ye radio yer partner and tell him to clear the parking lot. We got a chopper comin' in about thirty minutes."

"Will do." Potter stepped out on the back deck leaving Ethan glaring at Rudaij.

"Stickin' to yer story, lad?" He asked in a menacing tone. Ethan's anger was apparent in every move he made and Rudaij was getting the idea he was screwed.

His brother should be showing up soon and that would only make matters worse, since the boy could not keep his trap shut in the best of times. "I've no other story to tell. Did you find the dinghy?" Rudaij was trying for the confident and innocent victim trying to be helpful. "It has a forty-five horse Merc. They could be back at Dingle by now if they took it."

"What's so important about the goblets Brystal Traynor cut for ye? Why do ye want them so bad?"

Ethan had no idea what Daria had found. He didn't have time to stop at Becky's.

"It's a special design my father drew when we were kids. He had a vase made for my mother and those pieces were a surprise for their fiftieth anniversary. I really need those goblets." Ethan watched Rudaij's eyes as the man crafted his tale. He knew enough about interrogation and neuro-linguistic programming to recognize confabulation when he saw it. And he was seeing it! In spades.

"Enough to kill for them?" Ethan threw out the question. "What does Dharág Hadley have to do with this mess?"

"Dharág who? I don't know the man." Rudaij's eyes slipped to the side denoting another lie.

"Then I be leavin' it up to the ITCTF. A team be on its way. Should be landin' in about," Ethan checked his watch, "fifteen minutes. Me friend, Stephan, be real good at squeezin' information out of a fellow. On American soil or not." Ethan scuffed the rug with the toe of his shoe and snorted. He stepped through the doorway onto the back deck about the time he heard Potter's radio squawk.

"Five-three-seven alpha, I got me two suspicious fellows here. They be looking for their dinghy to go on out to the Breakin' Bad."

Ethan grabbed the radio at the same time he heard shots echo across the water. "Don't… Shit." All three men on the back of the Breakin' Bad turned toward the boat launch. Garda Laundeau lay on the ground as two men got into a dark limo and tore up the road toward Dingle. "Robert, get Potter back there. Go man."

While Robert ushered Potter into the skiff and they took off at high speed for the shore, Ethan stepped back into the salon. "Who was the bastard just shot me Garda?" He kicked Rudaij in the gut.

Rudaij vomited foul smelling alcohol, gasping as pain spread through his gut.

"Tell me, or so help me God, I will beat you to pulp and puke." Ethan spit as he spoke. History was repeating itself and he was helpless to change the path he walked. Now, because of him, a Garda was hurt, possibly dead. Daria and Crystal were missing, possibly dead. His world was spinning down into a tornado of guilt and fear. "Talk ye half-fuck!" Ethan smashed his fist into Rudaij's face. "I swear I'll end yer worthless life if ye don't tell me what I want to know."

Rudaij spit out a bloody lump and snuffed. "I can't tell you what I don't know. I swear."

"Who were those men?" He punched Rudaij again. This time the man's nose spewed blood.

Rudaij shook his head. "Probably my brother and his driver. I don't know. Please believe me. I don't know anything except what I already told you."

Ethan balled up his fist for another strike when his cell chirped. "MacEnery here."

"Ethan, we've spotted the gels!" It was Stephan in the helicopter. "They be off Slea Head goin' out ta sea."

"Jesus, Mary, and Joseph!!! Why out to sea?"

"Don't look to me like the motor's workin.'" Stephan responded. "I'm gonna drop one of me men down to 'em. Maybe get the motor goin'."

"Right-o. I got me a Garda down here. The shooters took off in a limo. Shouldn't be hard to track. Stand by, Potter's on the radio." Ethan answered the radio call as he held the cell phone away from the speaker. "Potter, how's Landeau?"

Potter's voice broke. "Gone, sir. The bastards shot him right through the heart. I'll call it in. Out."

Ethan swore. "Stephan, Garda's dead. We be looking fer a cop killer now."

"Sorry, Ethan. I'll be at ye in about fifteen. Dropping me man now. The gels look to be fine, just wrapped in some tin foil." Ethan knew if the man who dropped into the boat could not get the engine started, he'd bring Daria and Crystal up into the chopper and bring them back.

Robert was pulling up to the back of the Breaking Bad. "Ahoy, the boat." He hollered and tossed the line to Ethan. "How's the Garda be doin'?"

Ethan hung his head. "Gone, Robert."

Robert crossed himself and mumbled a short prayer for the dead. "The blokes be on the lam, but not fer long if they be cop killers. The whole of Ireland will be looking fer them." He stepped aboard the *Breakin Bad*.

"They've found me niece and Miss Traynor. They be in the dinghy out near Slea head." Ethan pointed toward the west. "How in the name of Mother Mary did they get out there is my question."

Robert squinted at the bay. "Tide. It be roarin' this time of year." He pointed to a foam trail moving at a good clip toward the open ocean. "Why didn't they just motor back here?"

"O'Haide said the engine wasn't working."

Robert shook his head. "Probably didn't know how to start it. Yer gel from the states an outdoor type?"

Ethan was coming down off his adrenaline high now that he knew Daria and Crystal were alive and going to be safe. "Not in the least! She be from the city of New York. I've the idea the most she's ever operated is a taxi. Doesn't even own a car."

"Good thing ye man's with 'em, then."

"Aye." Ethan's hands had begun to shake, and his knuckles ached. "Guess we take this trash ashore." He stepped inside the salon and jerked Rudaij to his feet. The front of the bound man's shirt was covered with rivulets of blood and vomit. "Up ye go, ye piece o'shit. Out!"

"No! You can't take me off my boat. This is my sovereign territory. It's the international law of the sea." Rudaij protested.

"Who in the hell put those ideas in 'yer thick head, boy-o?" Ethan handed him over to Robert who promptly threw Rudaij to the bottom of the skiff with no ceremony at all.

"There ye be, King of ye sovereign boat. Now ye be on my sovereign land so shut ye trap, or I just might put ye in a crab pot and throw yer worthless carcass overboard." Robert was so much better at threatening than Ethan. He finished the sentence with a pirate *argg*! It was a good effect.

An ambulance had arrived by the time Ethan, Robert and their prisoner made the shore. A gurney sat near the backdoor of the ambulance, a sheet covering a body as the medics finished their paperwork. There was no hurry now. A large red stain was spreading from the middle of the pure white sheet. Potter stood alone, leaning against the side of the vehicle, his head hung, his hands over his eyes. Ethan recognized the posture of loss. He'd stood the same way just a little more than a year ago, while they took away the bodies of his wife and daughter. He dumped Rudaij on the cement of the wharf and strode over to Garda Potter.

"He be a grand Garda, Phil. I'll get the shooters if it's the last thing I do. He'll have his justice." Ethan patted Potter's shoulder.

"How am I gonna tell his wife?" Tears were streaming down the Garda's face.

"Not yer job, Phil. Let Chaplain Bodrey do his job, then ye can see his wife. Lacey's a strong gel. She'll survive."

"But he was me partner. It should be me." Potter wailed. "He's got a kid!"

"So, do it right. Be there when she need's support. Be there when his wee daughter catches a diploma." Ethan was saying the words, but his heart was breaking just as much as Phil Potter's. County Kerry was a tight county when it came to its law enforcement members. They held close to their friendships, and mourned every loss as if it were their own precinct. "Go with him. I'll take care of this."

Garda Potter got into the ambulance beside the gurney that held his partner. Then the ambulance was off, and the Dingle Station would be missing one Garda. Ethan shook his head.

Behind him, a chopper was approaching from the west. He heard the sound but couldn't bring himself to look up yet. Crossing himself, Ethan recited the prayer he said over the grave of his family, then it was back to the issues at hand, and finding two cop killers.

When the Aerospatiale finally landed and shut down, Stephan hopped out and ran to Ethan. "We dropped our tech down and he got the motor going right off! They're headed back here!"

CHAPTER 19

Number 19 is an auspicious number being associated with success and honor.
It is filled with happiness and joy!
And...
The moon will appear in the exact same position among the stars every 19th year.

Daria heard the helicopter before she could see it. The wind was blowing with the tide and the sound drifted to her on the stiff breeze. "Crystal, do ye hear that?"

Crystal leveraged herself up on sore arms and blistered hands. She'd rowed for less than an hour, but her tender fingers were used to a battling a keyboard, not wooden oars in high seas. "Look!" She pointed to the east at a set of tiny blips of light. She stood and began waving wildly.

The dinghy tipped and dipped, and Crystal grabbed the handholds just before a wave cascaded over the side, drenching them both.

"Sit down before ye go over!" Daria caught Crystal's shirt and pulled her down into the dinghy. "I've an idea!" She crawled to the bow hatch and fished inside, coming up with the flare pistol. "Look. We can signal."

"Oh no, Daria! You're gonna shoot me!" Crystal moved the barrel of the gun away from her face.

"There's nothing in it. Look. I have to put one of these things down the pipe." Daria was pointing to the lid of the box she'd removed the flare gun from.

"The barrel. Don't put your finger on the trigger until you aim the damn thing. Be careful!"

Daria handed the gun over to Crystal. "You do it then."

"Alright. You read the directions to me. Hurry. They're getting closer! They won't see us in the dark." Crystal took the gun in two fingers like it was a dead rat body.

"Push the release button and open the gun." Daria pointed to the picture. "It breaks open in the middle. See?"

Crystal found the button and released the catch. The gun fell open in the middle.

"Take the cartridge and insert it nose first into the chamber. Yellow stripe marks the nose of the flare cartridge." Daria handed Crystal the flare.

Crystal checked for the yellow stripe then inserted the flare into the chamber of the gun.

"Okay. Close the breach and make sure it snaps shut. You should hear the snap. Hurry, they are almost here."

"Got it. It snapped shut. Now what?" The lights on the helicopter were much brighter now and the sound was loud enough to hurt Crystal's ears.

"Point the flare gun up at an angle, away from any person or structure. Pull the trigger until the flare is fired into the air." Daria read.

Crystal pointed the flare gun up and pulled the trigger. Daria watched as the flare shot into the sky with a trailing line of red. At the top, the flare popped, and a huge red glow filled the sky. At the same time, the oncoming helicopter veered out of the way, just in time to avoid being hit by the exploding flare!

"Oh no!" Crystal cringed.

A loud voice came from above. "Hold yer fire. We be the good guys."

Daria screamed with delight. "They found us! We're saved!" She hugged Crystal as they both tipped into the bottom of the dinghy. The rotor wash from above was pelting their heads as Crystal saw someone on a rope being lowered. They sat still as the helicopter maneuvered the man into place. When he was a few feet above them, he released the harness and dropped into the dinghy. He wore a blue uniform and a life jacket.

"I'm Willie. I surrender!" He spoke into a radio mounted on the shoulder of his life jacket. "Down and secure. Testing the engine." Willie knelt, squeezed the bulb three times, and pulled the starter rope. To the amazement of both Crystal and Daria, the engine roared to life. "Engine's fine. Meet ye back at the wharf." Willie threw his crew a thumbs-up as they flew toward Ventry Harbor.

Crystal crawled to the bow with Daria and pulled the space blanket around them both. "Never shot a gun before." She said in way of apology. She was sure that shooting at their rescuers was some kind of serious faux pas.

"Hadn't noticed." Crystal saw his huge white smile in the darkness.

It took about an hour fighting the out-going tide and wind to get back to Ventry Bay. Willie piloted the dinghy close to the shore to avoid the strongest current of the bay's tide. "Spent me young years fishin' these waters. Know 'em like the back of me hand."

It gave Crystal some amount of comfort, knowing the young man knew what he was doing, however, Daria had her doubts. "That's what they all say until ye bash up on a rock. Then, fish bait!" She whispered to Crystal and cuddled closer.

Crystal put her arm around the young girl. Usually she shied away from most forms of physical contact. That was her old life, before Ireland. Before Dingle. Before losing Brystal. Now, she felt a modicum of comfort with Daria tucked close and wrapped up together. At twenty-eight, was her biological clock starting to tick? Or was it this fascinating, wild country that changed her. Something was happening to her, something warm and sweet, like one of Colleen Sweeney's scones with creamy butter and marmalade. She snuggled down as the dinghy skipped a wave and Willie gave a shout of glee. Crystal actually shared the young man's enthusiasm, now that they were safe and almost back to dry land.

~

ETHAN STOOD on the edge of the wharf watching the sea. When he caught sight of the dinghy, his heart lept into his throat. His eyes began to tear up and he swallowed hard.

"Look, here they come. Sergeant Naighler is a local. He volunteered for this duty. Looks to me like he be havin' more fun than workin' a case." Stephan nudged Ethan. "They be safe now, Ethan. Ye can quit yer frettin'."

Ethan wiped a hand across his face. "What makes ye think I be frettin'? I know they're in good hands." He squinted at the fast-moving dinghy. "How old did ye say that Sergeant is?" He could see the young man whooping and hopping the waves in the small rubber boat.

"He's an extremely competent pilot and boat captain. Grew up on the bay, he did." Stephan nodded at the dinghy. "the new generation is so much better than we were at the same age. Makes me feel old and I just made me one."

At that comment, Ethan had to laugh. "And you should be home tendin' the one ye made."

"You need to read this." Stephan handed Ethan an iPad. On the screen was a report detailing specific criminal interests of the Illianescu family over three generations. "If yer prisoner is an Illianescu like he claims, he be a bad, bad man. Ye did good callin' me in. This could be something huge in the international crime world. I've already sent a text to me counterpart in France and Britain."

Ethan took the iPad and read the first two pages. Stephan was right. This, whatever Daria and Crystal had found, was going to be huge. He had the oldest living son of Dacic Illianescu in custody, and the youngest one was most probably on the run after having murdered a Garda of the law. He handed the tablet back to Stephan. "Would ye send that to me?"

"Sure. Now go greet yer niece and that woman ye've taken a shine to." Stephan strolled away leaving a gaping Ethan.

Had he taken a shine to Crystal? Or was he just doing his job? Since she'd appeared on the scene, Ethan had not had a minute to consider anything but protecting the naïve woman from the States. He wanted to make her visit as easy as possible, considering the fact that she'd just lost her twin sister. For heaven's sake, she couldn't even drive on the correct side of the road let alone wander around Dingle, scarin' the livin' daylights outta the locals who knew her sister. During his investigation of Brystal's murder, he'd formed a kind of weird attachment to the gel, and maybe developed an infatuation for the victim, but her sister? He would think about it later. Right now, an eleven-year old was running his way and he was waiting with open arms.

"Uncle Ethan, we got kidnapped and then saved by Willie." Daria's excitement was not dampened in the least after her harrowing kidnapping and drifting out to sea in a ten-foot rubber dinghy. "This is Willie. He came down a rope from the helicopter and saved us, right Crystal?"

"That's right." Crystal lisped through a swollen lip. Both of her eyes were beginning to turn a purplish blue and her nose was crusted with blood and swollen. She looked like she'd been beaten and set in front of a wind tunnel. Her hair was a wild, tangled mess with strips of reddish brown crusted on the sides. Daria held Crystal's arm instead of her hand. Ethan noticed right away how Crystal kept her hands closed.

"Sergeant Naighler, thank ye for fetching me niece and Miss Traynor." Ethan shook hands with the sergeant.

"Me pleasure, sir. Yer niece be a brave little lass." He pointed to Crystal. "And this one had the good grace to miss our chopper with her flare." He patted Crystal's shoulder and took his leave, trotting over to his crew who were sitting on the skids of the Aerospatiale 350.

"Yeah, Crystal shot at the helicopter and missed. I mean, that was a good thing. She wasn't supposed to hit it only...." she threw her arms around her uncle's waist, "Never mind!"

Crystal watched Daria hugging her uncle and wanted to do the same. Instead, she stood a few feet away wrapped in the silver space blanket, watching. Her head ached like she'd run into a brick wall. Several times. The blisters on her fingers burned. One palm was bloody where she'd worn through the skin holding tight to the oars. Granted they'd only been at sea for a couple hours, but Crystal was not accustomed to physical labor, and the skin on her hands was as delicate as a peach.

A medic from the ambulance appeared at her side. "Be ye needin' a bit of treatment, miss?" Crystal winced and opened her hands. " I should think so. Come over to the truck." He led her away before Ethan could see what the medic had.

Perched on a folding chair, Crystal tolerated the man's tender administrations. "I be Adam McKnight, EMT II. And you are?"

"Crystal Traynor," she mumbled.

"Are ye allergic to latex mum? Can ye tell me what happened to ye, lass?"

As Crystal answered his questions quietly, Ethan and Daria strode over to where she sat. A man Crystal didn't know, stood close watching with interest. Daria moved to stand behind Crystal encircling the older woman with her arms and placing a sweet kiss on her cheek.

"Does it hurt much? Ye rowed the skin right off!"

"No. It's fine, Daria. Don't worry, I'll be okay." Crystal winced as the medic carefully wound gauze around the worst of the damage on her palms after applying some kind of smelly salve.

"Ye are most assuredly not fine ma'am. You'll need to be takin' care of these hands for a while. Ye don't want to risk infection. Ye should see a doctor about that nose when ye can. Looks to be broken, but I'm not a doc. I'll not be disturbin the clot and start it to bleedin' again." He daubed some kind of clear gel on her lip after cleaning the wound. "That be about all I can do for ye. From what I hear, ye lucky to be alive." He turned to Daria. "Miss, ye be needin' attention?"

Daria pulled up her sleeve to display the purple badge of honor on her upper arm where Rudaij had grabbed and threw her across the room. To her delight, Adam carefully inspected the bruise. "Jacko, will ye be tossin' me a number three pack?"

From inside the ambulance a three-inch square ice pack came flying. Adam deftly caught it and set to bandaging it onto Daria's bruise. "Now keep this on for about thirty minutes, then unwrap it and put it in the freezer for two hours. Then do the same thing again. You'll need this for at least three applications, lass." He stood and replaced his scissors in his belt and winked at Ethan. "I think they'll both live. Watch 'em for signs of infection or shock. They've had quite the adventure, Inspector. Ye might want to make sure Miss Traynor sees a physician about her nose. Just in case."

Ethan nodded as he took Daria under his arm and kissed her head tenderly. "He be sayin' ye'll make it, Mouse."

"Crystal's the one I be worried about. That man hit her real hard. Did ye kill him, Uncle Ethan?"

Ethan chuckled at his niece's obvious new-found attachment to Crystal. "Nope. Couldn't. He gave up after I picked up this big bottle of champagne. Imagine that?"

Daria buried her face in her uncle's side and giggled.

"Miss Traynor, may I have a word?" Stephan appeared at her elbow speaking quietly.

Crystal jumped. "Who are you and why do you want to talk to me?"

"Crystal, this is my old chum and Inspector with the International and Terrorist Crime Task Force here in Ireland. I called him when ye got kidnapped. He flew in from Shannon." Ethan wound his arms around Daria and held her as he spoke. He wanted to be holding Crystal, but it wouldn't have been appropriate considering his audience. "He brought a team from the task force, and Sergeant Willie there."

Crystal relaxed knowing the man was one of the good guys. "What do you want to know?"

"Well, for starters... everything." He grinned and shrugged.

"I can tell ye that!" Daria broke loose from her uncle's embrace.

"Daria," Ethan chided, "I think the Inspector wants to speak with Crystal."

"No Ethan. She's right. And she can explain it much better than I. She has the chemistry background I don't. And her hobby, I mean, unique interest, in the morbid." Crystal was running out of energy and wavered where she stood. Her arms sat limp on her lap, both palms wrapped in stark white bandages.

"Ethan let's get these gels to the car, then we can talk. Ma'am?" Inspector O'Haide offered his arm to Crystal and escorted her to Ethan's car. "Did ye call yer sister? She probably be out of her mind with worry."

"Holy shit! I haven't." Ethan was devastated.

"Oh, you are in trouble, Uncle Ethan. Big trouble." Daria shook her finger at her uncle. "Mum will be groundin' ye fer a month!" Daria got in the back and slid over. Crystal got in next to her and the Inspector got into the front. Twisting around he asked, "Can you start at the beginning, since I just got called in on this case?"

"I'll try." Between the last few hours thinking she might die, the lack of food and such little sleep over the last few days, Crystal's mind was foggy, and she was shivering. "I'm not sure how all of this came about because my sister wouldn't do what she did, if she knew what she was doing." Crystal rubbed her hands together trying to get warm. "That doesn't make sense. I know."

Ethan stood outside the car, talking on his cell phone. It was clear he was on the receiving end of a good dressing down.

Stephan reached over and turned the key in the ignition starting the car, then turned the heat to high.

She tried to continue. "Anyway, Brystal cut these four goblets as a special project for her teacher, or supervisor, anyway the guy's name is Dharág Hadley. She was an apprentice crystal cutter at Sean MacDougal's warehouse in Dingle." Her teeth began to chatter. "He gave her a design and she cut the pattern. Next thing, she's dead. She was my twin." Crystal couldn't hold the tears back any longer. She was exhausted, hungry, and experiencing a mild form of shock.

Daria recognized what was happening immediately. "We need food and something warm to drink." She opened her door and yelled at her uncle. "Uncle Ethan, Crystal's getting sick. We need to get food and water."

Ethan got in the driver's seat. "Right-o. I'll tell her. No more worries, ye hear. Bye sis." He turned to his niece in the back seat, "Ye mum is fit to be tied and ye'll be answerin' fer this. I know, 'tis not yer fault. I'll have a talk with her when she be a bit calmer. Not to worry," He saw Crystal shiver and was concerned that Daria was right. "Trust me, my place be worse! There be a little café up the road. They've tea and stew. It'll do ye both good."

By the time they'd gotten food and hot tea, Crystal was barely able to hold her head up, so Daria continued the story. "Crystal brought her sister's drawings to me house. She couldn't figure out what all the numbers and letters were. She's an accountant. Deals with concrete numbers and financial algorithms." Daria slurped her stew. "So I took a look. I couldn't figure it out either… until" slurp, slurp, "… until I remembered $C_4H_{10}FO_2P$.

"And just what be $C_4H_{10}FO$ something or other, Mouse?" Ethan knew the list of numbers and letters she recited had something to do with chemicals, but he'd no idea what the combination stood for.

Daria answered with a mouthful of sourdough bread. "Sarin gas."

Both Inspectors asked at the same time, "How do you know about Sarin gas?"

Daria's simple answer shocked the men. "Me hobby."

With a little food in her stomach and her hands clenched around a teacup, Crystal was slowly recovering, and her mind was clearing. "The calculations worked out to a recipe, Ethan. A recipe for mass death. We're talking hundreds of thousands if it were loosed on an unsuspecting population."

"But what have the glasses to do with it? I be a bit confused. Why cut a pattern into crystal? Why not just send the recipe, or formula, in an email? Wouldn't it be easier?"

"I can answer that one, Ethan. " Stephan cut in. "That be part of the ITCTF's job. We've an international monitoring center at Interpol

Headquarters that scans the Internet using the newest search engines. Ye'd be a might astonished at what they pick up."

"We've not yet figured out what the goblets have to do with this." Daria wanted her full fifteen minutes of fame. "Uncle Ethan, did ye bring one for us to see?"

"As a matter of fact, Mouse, I did. In the dash box."

Stephan carefully withdrew the goblet wrapped in newspaper. He unrolled the goblet and held it up. "So, this be what the commotion is all about." He turned it every which way, peering carefully at the cut crystal piece. " It surely be a thing of beauty." He held it up to the overhead light in the car. "Ye say there be four?"

"Was four. I dropped one and it shattered. Not enough of the dust and shards to reconstruct." Crystal finally finished her bowl and wiped it clean with a piece of bread. "Now only three are left. They are identical and cut by the numbers in the drawings. But how would anyone be able to connect the pattern to a string of nebulous numbers. I know there is something horrible there, I just can't figure it out."

"'Tis mind blowin'." Daria finished her meal. "What be fer dessert?" She turned to her uncle. "Except for ye, Uncle Ethan. I get yers!" She poked her uncle in the side, giggling at the fact that he was in more trouble with her mother, than she was.

Ethan handed her a menu and the waitress, who'd been watching the two Inspectors and their motley crew with typical curiosity, came to the table without being called. "What can I get ye?"

Daria scanned the menu, "I'll have me some apple pie with heavy cream and cheddar."

"Cheddar, like cheddar cheese? You eat cheese with pie?" Crystal was intrigued. She usually stuck to a few simple dishes and almost always ate at one or two favorite restaurants where no one bothered her.

"Aye! 'Tis a wonderful combination. Ye should try it."

Crystal shook her head. Maybe a bit of yours, but this stew was very filling." She continued, "Inspector O'Haide, what happened to that man on the boat? How does he fit in to this thing?"

"Well, lass, I be not quite sure yet. He told Ethan he commissioned the goblets for his parents' anniversary based on some design his da made. He'd paid Brystal, or Hadley, or someone already, and wanted his pieces. Then he said ye'd come to get paid and deliver the goblets. Now we all know it to be a line of tarny trash."

Ethan chimed in with a chuckle. "He also said ye'd come to rob him. So that was the plan, Mouse? Rob a rich American... on his boat? I'd not be thinkin so."

Daria's pie and cheese came, and she dug in as if she'd not had dinner at all. The waitress brought three forks and Daria offered Crystal a chunk with a slice of cheddar.

Tentatively Crystal tried the combination. She usually didn't mix different foods on her plate, but when in Rome? "Oh my, that is wonderful!"

"Told ye." Daria snickered around a large bite of pie.

Inspector O'Haide continued. "Ethan called me when ye went missin' and gave me an earful. Then I started pokin' about and grabbed me team. Somethin' is up on the peninsula and I came for a look-see, me self." He casually picked up a fork and skewered a hunk of pie. "Ye be right, little one, 'tis wonderful."

The pie was disappearing rapidly, but Daria was happy to share. The stew had been filling and the dessert helping was huge.

"So, it be a good thing Ethan called. Our Mr. Rudaij Illianescu is a member of the infamous Illianescu Syndicate out of Albania. He be the oldest left of Dacic Illianescu's five boys. Each one has a territory and runs a leg of the family business. That bein' the criminal business; guns, human traffikin', drugs," He took another bite from Daria's plate with a smile, "and apparently weapons of mass destruction, now. If ye be right about this. The youngest of that despicable family is suspected of shootin' Garda Landau on the wharf. Me team's takin' care of the prisoner and leadin' the search."

"Oh, we be right, Inspector." Daria shoved the rest of her plate to the Inspector and began to recite formulas and symptomology for all kinds of weapons. She was a virtual encyclopedia of grisly and gruesome effects of various poisons, both biological and chemical. She continued with life expectancy of the various exposures and possible treatments that could mitigate or resolve the symptoms and end results. At one point, the waitress behind the counter covered her mouth and disappeared into the kitchen.

"Ethan, can I hire yer niece? She knows more about this stuff than the specialist on me team! She be a virtual encyclopedia of morbid statistics!"

Daria waved her fork back and forth. "It just be me hobby, ye know."

"And she needs to finish her grades. She be only eleven, Stephan." Ethan replied.

"Twelve in eighty-five days, Uncle Ethan." She looked up at her uncle with a sigh. "Me last year before teens."

"Aye Mouse. Ye be growin' up too fast fer me." He turned to his friend. "I might be convinced to negotiate a consultation fee for the lass!" He winked at Daria who winked back. "But now, I'd best be getting the gels back to me sister. I'll be stayin' the night, just in case. Daria, would ye mind hostin' Crystal for a night?"

"Oh aye!" The young girl leaped up and enveloped Crystal in a mini bear hug. "Ye can have me bed and I'll bunk with Quinn. He has two singles. He won't mind. He only uses the extra bed for his football gear."

Crystal was beginning to like all of this young girl's hugs and pats and handholding. Something she'd never tolerated well before. What was so different here? Or was it that she was different.

"Careful, Mouse. Crystal's on the injured list. We'd best be takin' care for a bit." Ethan cautioned Daria, who immediately released her hold and patted Crystal's head tenderly.

That set Crystal laughing. "Daria, I'm not that fragile, just sore, as are you." They'd shared a life and death experience and definitely bonded. More than that, they shared so many characteristics. Crystal completely understood Daria's obsession with her *hobby,* and Daria understood Crystal's number thing. They didn't have to pretend to be normal with each other. They didn't have to worry about social niceties or whether something they said or did was awkward or offensive. They were just Daria and Crystal, two humans who completely related.

“So will ye stay the night?”

“Of course.” She opened her arms and returned the mini bear hug, cautious of Daria’s bruise and her own wounds. “We’ll even have our own protection detail. I’m not crazy about going back to the flat tonight anyway. Not until they find the younger brother who shot the Garda.”

“Then it be settled. We should get goin’ before yer mum shows up with her own security detail and shoots me fer getting’ her child involved in this dirty business.” He turned to Stephan, “Drop ye at the helicopter?”

“I’ll walk. It’s only a half click. Keep me in the loop, will ye?”

Before Ethan could answer, Daria spoke up. “Of course, Inspector. Uncle Ethan has yer cell?”

She was acting the true consultant and it set Crystal to laughing again. This girl was eleven going on thirty! Ethan just shook his head. He continued shaking his head as Daria shook hands with Stephan and waved them toward the door. “Shall we go face the dragon?”

“Where does she get that?” Ethan asked Crystal.

“Get what?” Crystal smiled at Ethan who had helped her up and to the door.

“Never mind.” He mumbled as they left the café.

CHAPTER 20

Rockets and Pennies
Twenty pennies in Jenny's pocket,
She bought a red toy rocket!
Jenny spent all the twenty,
Now her pocket is all empty!
Maybe Jenny should have thought twice about purchasing rockets!

As soon as the car had started up the drive, both Becky and Rory were on the porch holding each other tight, deep worry written all over Becky's pretty face. When they caught sight of their daughter, both ran toward the car. Ethan, very aware how upset his sister had been at hearing the sordid tale, stopped short and let Daria out. She sprinted into her parents' arms as Ethan parked the car. He'd called ahead and Becky didn't even hesitate in taking Crystal on for the night. She was glad Ethan would be staying as well she'd said. He wondered about that.

As they all trooped inside, Rory shook Ethan's hand with vigor.

"Thanks, Ethan, fer bringing our gel back, safe and sound. I can't believe the bastard took her right out of our home."

"He's in custody now. Won't be stealin' anything or anybody again. There be much more to this case though."

As they all sat around the dining room table in the old family farmhouse, Ethan went over the details of what had happened and how Stephan O'Haide had come to help, bringing a chopper and Willie. For once Daria was quiet. With all of the excitement and a full dinner, including apple pie and cheddar for dessert, the little one was fading fast. She had taken off her ice pack and displayed her bruise for everyone to see and told them about how brave Crystal had been to stand up to the bad guy trying to protect her. She also recounted Crystal's turn at the oars and how she'd rowed her skin off. Soon the tale was exhausted and so was Daria. Now she slumped in her chair, leaning against Crystal, her eyes half closed.

"Be ye talkin' about the Stephan O'Haide I saw for a time in me grades?" Becky smiled widely.

"The same, sis. He's with the International and Terrorist Crime Task Force over in Shannon."

"Impressive! I always wondered what happened to that bloke." She took her husband's hand. "Not anymore. I got me my man and be happy with me life. Stephan always wanted out of Dingle."

"He gave me some disturbin' intel on this crime syndicate that seems to have settled in our wee town." Ethan hit the high spots and hoped Daria was not listening closely. He didn't need to scare the gel. She had way too much knowledge already.

Becky realized her daughter had reached her limit. "I think this one is ready for bed. I had Quinn clean off his extra bed so off we go." She motioned to Rory and he promptly got up and carried Daria upstairs. "Crystal, I've cleaned Daria's room and set the bed with fresh sheets. Ye look as if ye could use some sleep as well. I want to thank ye for taking care of our daughter. Even on her worst days, we love her to pieces." She looked toward the stairs. "I don't know what Rory would do if he lost his little gel." She kissed Ethan's head. "I'll make up the couch in the solar fer ye, Ethan."

"Thanks, sis." Ethan yawned. "Crystal, can I help with anythin' afore ye go up?"

"No thanks, Ethan. It's enough that your sister will let me stay here for the night. I know where Daria's room is. I'll be fine. See you in the morning."

It was almost midnight when Crystal finally lay, tucked into Daria's bed. Brystal's goblet sat on the bed stand under the reading light. It twinkled as if to say, *I have a secret and you can't have it.* As tired as she was, she couldn't sleep. It annoyed her no end that she couldn't figure out why the goblets were cut and why the Albanian syndicate wanted them so badly. Each square and diamond could be intricately measured and somehow counted and maybe end in the chemical equation that would produce the weaponized chemical, but that was farfetched. Even using a micrometer, any tiny mismeasurement would invalidate the recipe. She was past exhausted, but her brain would not shut off. Every time she looked away, her eyes were drawn back to the mocking twinkle, and she was caught in the trap intricately woven by the numbers.

As her mind spun down into her own numerical prison of cascading calculations, her eyes closed, and she settled into the comfort blanket of numerical synesthesia. The numerals played and sang, dancing through her dreams, acting out their little characteristics just for her. On stage, Two defended the castle as Ten attacked with his double-digit family. Four wore the queen's crown and stood on the parapet commanding the universe from her crystal throne. Clear sweet rain fell from blue and white billowing clouds overhead. As each player looked to the heavens, drinking in the life-giving liquid, each fell dead where they stood. The defender tumbled from his gate. The queen fell from her throne to the soft green grass, now sizzling and bubbling with burning acid. The castle began to dissolve into hideous rivers of bile green and blood red as each character sank beneath the consuming onslaught.

Crystal woke with a start, gasping for breath. The nightmare refused to fade, and she remembered every cry for help, every scream of pain, every gruesome twist and deformation of their bodies, as they fought their own plight. "Oh God!" Crystal held her bandaged hands to her face and dissolved into tears. Alone in Daria's room, no one would see. No one would reprimand her for the silly emotional outburst.

"Nightmare?" Daria sat motionless at her computer, reading the dimmed screen.

"Daria? What are you doing up?" Crystal was very surprised she'd not been aware the girl was even there.

"Nightmare. Several. Every time I be fallin' asleep." She rubbed her eyes. "So, I figured I'd be doin' me some research." She pointed to the computer screen. "I've been deconstructin' both formulas for Sarin and the stuff from yer sister's calculations. They be very similar, with one *huge*," She threw her arms wide for emphasis, "difference. Sarin has a very short shelf-life. It be degradin' in weeks and be very corrosive. The stuff yer sis figured out, doesn't. Sarin breaks down in water or hydroxide. That one," she pointed to the goblet, "doesn't."

"Doesn't what, Mouse?" Ethan leaned against the door. He wore a pair of baggy grey sweatpants and a t-shirt boasting the name of Rory's lorry business. Obviously, he'd borrowed clothing from Daria's father.

"Degrade, Uncle Ethan." She looked at her uncle with a serious frown. "Ever."

Ethan slid down the doorjamb to sit in the doorway. He wiped a hand across his growing beard. "You mean ta tell me, if this chemical be made and released, it won't go away?"

"Never. It can only be deconstructed with hydrolysis to break the P-F bond. There be no way to successfully do that once released freely. At least any way I be known' of."

"So you mean, if this chemical weapon is made and used, where it's used will always be poisoned land, like a dead zone?" Crystal sat up and slipped a robe over the same kind of t-shirt that Ethan wore. Becky had given her the oversized t-shirt and robe before she'd settled in for the evening, explaining Rory had been so proud of finally owning his own transport business, he'd had a hundred shirts printed in Galway. Becky laughed when she told Crystal there were ninety-five left in the shed.

"Aye. Says here sarin gas is eighty-one times more lethal than cyanide and five-hundred and forty-three times more lethal than chlorine gas. This stuff," she motioned again to the goblet on the bedside table, "is worse and... permanent."

"Jesus, Mary, and Joseph!" Crystal was picking up the local sayings. "Who would create something like that and then sell it to who-knows-who, or what?"

Ethan mumbled from his seat on the floor, "Really bad stuff, that be fer sure. I need to tell Stephan."

"I already emailed the Inspector, Uncle Ethan. I didn't know ye were awake. He sent me his addy and cell number." Daria's head hung. For all intents and purposes, her hobby had discovered a world threat, in the form of the most ultimate and permanent chemical weapon.

Crystal picked up the goblet and held it up. "But how does this beautiful creation have anything to do with such a hideous threat to humanity? And why would my sister cut it if she knew?"

Daria jumped up and hugged Crystal. "We be never knowin, unless ye can talk to yer sis in heaven."

Ethan crawled off the floor and grabbed the door for support. He should have been sleeping, instead of considering mass annihilation of the human species and indestructible chemical weapons. "I need a drink. And another piece of yer mum's apple tart. Care to join me?"

"Always!" Daria's smile was back at the mention of apple tarts.

"I think I'll bring this thing." Crystal picked up the goblet. "I don't want to let it out of my sight until I can figure out why it was made and how it will be used."

Ethan didn't want to wake the entire household, so he only turned on the nightlight near the sink. Not only did his sister need her sleep after such a stressful and fearful day, there wasn't enough apple tart to go around, and he was hungry. Stress did that to him, but he often ignored it. However, not when there were his sister's apple tarts available.

"Mum makes the best tarts, Crystal." Daria squirted a pile of whipping cream onto hers. "Have some heavy cream. It makes the tart perfect."

Crystal indulged the girl, and herself, as she liberally added whipped cream. "Don't mind if I do." She set the goblet in the middle of the kitchen's counter. It picked up the light from the intense and directed nightlight, splitting it into a pattern of squares and diamonds on the opposite wall. Crystal gazed at the pattern then moved to turn the goblet. "What a beautiful pattern. Too bad Brystal can't see this." She turned the goblet slowly, projecting the continuing pattern, or at least what she thought to be a continuing pattern.

Daria froze, a heaping spoonful of tart and whipped cream halfway to her mouth. Entranced by the picture on the wall, her lips began to move, and the spoon fell from her hand. "Crystal, you did it!" She hopped down from the stool she'd been sitting on next to the counter. "That's it!"

"That's what? Daria, what are you talking about?" Crystal was confused and looking at the glass.

"That's it." She ran to the wall and traced the squares and diamonds with her fingers. "That's why they want the goblets!"

"What's why, Mouse?" Ethan was tired and even more confused than Crystal.

Daria grabbed a pen from the glass jar that held any number and variety of writing implements, sitting next to the phone near the mudroom door. "Look!" She positioned the goblet in Crystal's hand. "Hold it then rotate it across the wall, like this." She turned the goblet in Crystal's fingers. "Slowly."

"O-kay." Still not following, Crystal did what she was shown.

As Crystal projected the pattern across the wall, Daria scribbled a square or diamond where the light shown through the cuts of the goblet.

"Daria! Ye mum's gonna skin yer hide fer writin' on her kitchen wall!" Ethan was aghast at his niece. She'd been taught better than that. Becky would be furious.

"No, look!" Daria stepped back. Binary–"

"Code!" Crystal and Daria exclaimed at the same time.

"When you project light through the crystal all the way around and draw the squares and diamonds, they are really zeros and ones! Binary code for the–"

"Recipe." Ethan finally got it. Crystal set the goblet down carefully and hugged Daria. Both were giggling and congratulating each other, midnight snack forgotten in light of their revelation.

Crystal sobered as Ethan connected the final part of the mystery. "Brystal must have seen the pattern and connected the dots. I mean the squares and diamonds. She must have figured it out, so they killed her."

"That was why the goblets were in the secret cabinet and the drawings weren't on the walls with the others. She hid them behind the garbage can. When I knocked it over, I found the drawings all folded up." Crystal covered her mouth. "Oh my God! Oh my God!"

Ethan was already dialing his cell. "Stephan, sorry to wake ye, man. We've a breakthrough. Yeah, me niece. Right-o. See ye in the morn." Ethan rang off and turned to Daria. "I be thinkin', Mouse, ye've a career in the service when ye finish yer grades and university." He laughed and tussled his niece's hair.

"Ethan, this is terrible! We have to destroy these goblets, and the drawings. No one can get the formula. Not even the good guys. It's too dangerous!" Crystal began pacing back and forth across the kitchen. "It can never be used."

Always the practical one, Daria commented, "Well, someone created it and gave it to Rudaij Illianescu. So, the knowledge is out there, somewhere. It's no secret anymore."

That made both Ethan and Crystal stop in their tracks. "Guess we have a new topic for discussion with Rudaij," Ethan shook his head. "I be wonderin' if the boy even knows what he's done in the name of his family? Why would they develop such a volatile and dangerous weapon?"

"Inspector O'Haide said the old man, the father, has lost his wits and wants to punish the world for taking two of his sons. Hate be a powerful motivation." Daria weighed in on the subject.

"Yes, but creating a permanent dead zone? That's science fiction nonsense." Crystal still couldn't come to terms with the power and extent of the weapon they'd come across. "Who would be mad enough to create something like that in the first place?"

"Really mad scientist, or da. Maybe it was an accident, like how sarin came about." Daria knew way too much about the deadly gas than any eleven-year-old-soon-to-be twelve, should have. "They be tryin' to make a strong pesticide and they were good at it. Unfortunately, it didn't work on bugs as well as it did on humans. A couple of the scientists died of exposure when they be workin' in the lab. The head guy decided they had a great weapon. Nineteen thirty-eight in Germany. Good thing they could never contain it back then. We'd be speakin' German and all saluting some short bloke with a weird little mustache."

Ethan studied the shapes on the wall. "We figured this thing out, now it's Stephan's job to do the rest. I got me a younger brother to find and cuff in the morn. That family's got two murders to their name and I can't let it be three."

As Ethan made calls to his station and night Garda's, Daria rummaged around in her mother's baking pantry. Soon there was a flat pan filled with a deep purple watery dye. "Watch. I think this may work."

She pulled a long strip of paper towel of the rack and laid it on the counter, then carefully rolled the goblet along the length. "I knew it!"

A string of squares and diamonds printed clearly for everyone to see.

"That be a bit easier than shinin' a light and scribblin' on ye mum's wall." Ethan looked at the length of paper towel. "My God, it could be printed a million times once a buyer has the goblet!"

"There are three left, Crystal! Right?" Daria had already set to scrubbing the kitchen wall and Crystal pitched in.

"Three goblets and your mom's wall. We'd best be getting this recipe erased." Crystal set to scrubbing with vigor.

"Aye," was all Daria could say.

CHAPTER 21

21 grams is the physical weight of a person's soul, according to the physician Duncan MacDougal. He calculated this by measuring the body weight of 6 patients before and after their deaths.
Really?

Daria and Crystal worked furiously, scrubbing, and wiping the kitchen wall until no evidence of scribbling could be found. Ethan had finished his calls and now slept fitfully on the make-shift bed in the solar. The sun was coming up and the bright sunrise of a new day brought a light heart to many on the Dingle Peninsula, used to rain and wind. It did nothing to lift Crystal's heart. She now knew her sister's murder was not a convenient act, but part of a conspiracy to sell the ultimate chemical weapon of mass destruction. She took her sister's handiwork out into the driveway and smashed it with her foot until there was only sparkling powder left amid the gray stones. No one would use it to create mass human suffering and death. That would leave two more goblets in the evidence vault and

Brystal's drawings. Crystal pulled the drawings from her bag and flicked a lighter she'd taken from the kitchen drawer. Touching the flame to the corner, she held the paper away from her until it was engulfed in flames. Dropping it on the gravel, she watched the evil mess burn to cinders, then spread the ash pile with the toe of her shoe. No one else would ever see the drawings to make a connection. The formula would be gone, and her sister's murder solved.

Kind of.

There was still the murderer to be found, and the scientist behind the creation of the chemical weapon to be determined and resolved. Crystal sighed, she was only one person and could only do her part in this macabre tale of woe. She scuffed gravel over the ashes and returned to the house.

Becky was up and fixing breakfast for her brood, humming a merry tune now that her world was in order once again. Completely unaware that one of her walls had contained the binary code for a weapon of mass destruction only hours earlier, she beat eggs and stirred pancake batter. Blood pudding fried in a large skillet. "Good morn to ye, Crystal. Did ye sleep well?"

Apparently, Becky had, since she seemed to have no knowledge of the night's doings. "Yes, thank you." Crystal told Becky what she wanted to hear. "And thanks again for putting me up for the night. It was unexpected and very sweet. I will not forget your kindness."

Becky crossed the kitchen and took Crystal in a warm embrace. "'Tis the least I can do. Ye saved me daughter, and that I'll never be forgettin' either." She turned back to her cooking duties, "I suspect ye'll be family someday anyway. Me brother has taken a shine to ye, gel. Or haven't ye noticed?" She smiled at Crystal.

"I, I... hadn't noticed. Ethan is a very good policeman. He has been very helpful, but..." Crystal was stuttering, and her words would not come. Did Ethan see her the way she was beginning to see him? She knew he'd lost his wife and daughter to the violence of his job. He knew about her peculiarities. How could he come to care for someone like her? Things were changing since she'd come to Ireland, but a relationship? That required so much more. More than Crystal knew how to give. Brystal would have known what to do, how to react, what to say… how to love. But Crystal? She loved numbers and they loved her. She understood them and they understood her. People were so unpredictable and flighty.

The phone on the counter rang with a jingling tone, moving the two apart. It also woke Ethan and Daria.

"Hallo, Kilkerry residence." Becky was crisp and pleasant.

"Aye, Rebekkah, this be Stephan O'Haide. Any chance yer brother be there still?"

"Well, Stephan O'Haide, that be a pleasant *how do ye do* this beautiful morn. And just how be ye? It's been a long time."

"Aye. A very long time. Becky, please, I need to talk to Ethan right straight."

"Of course. Police business it would be then." With that tart comment, she handed the phone to a hovering Ethan.

"Stephan?"

"Aye. Ethan, we found the younger brother and the second man. What a mess it be. Seems Kujtim Illianescu doesn't believe in honor among thieves, as it be. Ratted his brother outright. The second man was an enforcer, made to play babysitter for the kid. Didn't like it much. Doesn't matter, the man be a day stiff and in the bay."

"Kujtim Illianescu killed his father's enforcer? Where'd ye stash Rudaij?" Ethan was counting the bodies as they piled up in his little corner of the big bad world.

"He's being transported to Dublin, then on to the Hague for violation of the Chemical Weapon's Convention of Ninety-three. Possession of, or tryin to possess, a Schedule 1 Substance. There'll be more charges once ye've figured out the goblets, I suspect."

Daria was standing next to her uncle, listening as best she could to the conversation. "Uncle Ethan, let me tell him!" She was so excited at being included in the case and having figured out the mystery, she was almost giggling.

Ethan laughed, "Hang on Stephan. Let me put the little disaster monger on the line."

"Inspector O'Haide we've solved the issue! The crystal goblet was cut in a series of squares and diamonds that produced a binary code print when dipped in ink and rolled out. The goblets are a method for transporting the computer code that provides the recipe for a chemical weapon much worse than Sarin. Ye've got to find the maker. If it be ever produced, it could be the end of the human race." Daria was breathless as she explained. "Brystal figured it out and hid the goblets and drawings, but she knew. That's why they killed her. Whoever made this is a diabolical, maniacal, mega-crazy scientist. Did you really date me mum?"

As serious as the situation was, everyone in the kitchen, and probably everyone in the ITCTF was chuckling and trying to hold their outright laughter. Daria was so animated and excited, she had no idea that she sounded like a typical teenager explaining some new video game strategy, then boom! Right into the personal questions.

Ethan took back the phone so Daria could catch her breath. "That 'bout sums it up, Stephan."

"That's all true?"

"If ye really dated Daria's mum, yep!" The world was at stake and Daria wanted the words from the horse's mouth. "Mouse tells me the stuff is toxic and permanent, never degrades after a while, like Sarin. Can't be reduced to harmless precipitates or anythin' like that."

"Ah, methyl ethyl bad shit, huh?" Stephan's grave tone told Ethan he got the point.

"Yes." Ethan looked around the kitchen for the goblet and the hair rose on the back of his neck. Where was it? "The threat to me family is locked up then?"

"Aye. Rudaij is in the goal in Dublin. Kujtim's in me lockdown here in Shannon. Yer family is safe, Ethan."

Ethan was sure he'd not taken a breath since he took the phone from Becky. Knowing the threat had passed, he let out the oxygen that had been in his lungs too long, then took a ragged second breath. "Good. Great! Thanks, Stephan. I'll be ringing ye up a little later." Ethan needed pancakes and blood pudding, and an IV of straight black coffee. The events of the past few hours had taken their toll.

"Ah, before ye go, there is the matter of the three goblets and the dead gel's drawings. Ethan, they need to be secured, and our task force can fetch them later today." The warning in Stephan's tone was clear as the ringing of the church bell on Sunday. The task force wanted the weapon.

"Sure enough, Stephan." As soon as the words were out, Ethan knew he couldn't allow the goblets to fall into anyone's hands. Not criminal. Not governmental. Not anything, or anyone. "I'll see ye at the station then." He rang off and turned to the two most serious faces in his world.

"Uncle Ethan, ye can't."

"Daria's right, Ethan."

"Does everyone in the world listen in on me conversations?" Ethan was frustrated.

Daria ran to her uncle and threw her arms around his waist. "Ye can't give them up." Looking up at him, she was direct and clear. "'Tis the ultimate weapon, Uncle Ethan. The ultimate power, and ye know what 'tis said about ultimate power."

"I understand, Mouse. Look, I'll be figurin' this mess out. But not on an empty stomach." He eyed the growing stack of pancakes.

Daria moved to stand next to Crystal. She took the older woman's hand as they watched Ethan load a plate full of pancakes and sizzling blood pudding. "I can feel ye both a watchin' me." Ethan turned around. "Have a bit 'o faith." He took his plate into the dining room with a cup of coffee.

Daria looked to Crystal. "Where is the goblet? We need to destroy it. Right now. It can't get into the hands of any government. It's just too powerful."

Her pleading look touched Crystal's heart. "Not to worry, Daria. I've already taken care of that." She pointed to a dark splotch in the driveway. "Goblet and designs, gone. Poof." She tapped Daria on the nose then drew her hand away making an explosion with her fingers. "Now you've got some work to do. Do you know how to *secure wipe* a file so it can never be recovered?" Crystal had a lot of experience recovering deleted files various crooks had tried to erase. There was always a trail to find and eventually a file to recover.

"Please! I'm almost twelve. I certainly know how to secure delete a file. I use Secure Shredder. I can specify how many times the file will be overwritten and where to find the data feed in the Recycle Bin. I catalog all files and their extensions for just that reason. I'll double digital shred the weapon files. Just to make sure they can't be recovered by anyone."

"I can hear you, Mouse." Ethan mumbled from the dining room with his mouth full of pancakes.

"Hear what, Uncle Ethan?" Daria replied as she sped by on her way upstairs to her computer and a mission of complete file destruction.

At Becky's urging, Crystal filled a plate and joined Ethan. "Ethan, I have to confess–"

Ethan cut her off immediately. "Confessions are for the priest and the good Lord." He smiled at her. "I've no idea how the goblet went missing, but I suspect it has been destroyed. As well as the drawings?"

"Crystal kept her eyes on her plate. The eyes being the window to the soul, Crystal didn't want Ethan to see the almost-lie she was about to tell. "Ye'd be suspectin' right straight, Inspector." Crystal attempted an Irish accent.

Ethan heaved a make-believe sigh. "Finally, ye be speakin' me language." Ethan chuckled and Crystal smiled at her pancakes and shoved a huge forkful into her sweet, almost-lying mouth.

Becky joined the two with her own pile of breakfast food and drink. "So, everythin' is about done then fer ye, Crystal. Will ye be stayin' on fer a bit, or crossin' the pond right away?"

Crystal looked at Ethan for a translation. "Crossin' the pond means going back to the States. Across the ocean to New York."

"Ah. I... I don't exactly know. Um–" Crystal shoved more pancakes into her mouth.

"I'd be thinkin' ye have a bit more business to attend. Yer sister's things." Becky paused before saying, "Yer sister." It was a touchy subject but needed to be said.

"I truly believe Brystal loved this place." Crystal thought for a moment as she chewed. "Do you think she can be buried here? Our parents were cremated, and their ashes were spread in Lake Superior. It was where they liked to sail together. Before they were married." She looked at Ethan. "Can she be cremated here?"

Ethan swallowed hard. The topic of conversation wasn't helping his breakfast at all. "Irish people all over the world bring their relatives' ashes home for disposal. I would be believin' it a possibility." He stirred milk into his coffee. "I'll be checkin' into it when we get back to the station. Soon." He licked his spoon and used the utensil to punctuate his statement. "We've a bit of cleaning up to do and best be about it 'afore the hour."

It was almost six-thirty and there were two more goblets that needed to become crystal powder. Ethan also needed to find Dharág Hadley and figure out exactly what he thought he was assigning Brystal to do. In Ethan's mind it was hard to believe Dharág was aware that he was creating a subversive way to sell a chemical weapon. Dharág was a fisherman, a local fellow with only the normal public education. He'd not attended university or worked with chemicals, except to mix glass and blow marketable items. Ethan doubted Dharág even knew how to use a computer, let alone design a complex pattern that would produce the digital formula for a chemical weapon. "I need to be getting' back to the office to wrap this thing up." Ethan used his spoon to draw a circle in the air. "It's been a wild ride and the sooner I get the paperwork done the sooner I can forget those buggers almost killed me niece and Crystal."

Becky recognized the attempt at an apology from her brother and let it go without comment. She'd had the scare of her life, but Ethan had it much worse. He'd lost his family to crime. She'd only lost a few minutes of her daughter's life and added a bunch of gray hairs in the process. Everything was back to normal now and it was time for her brother to realize it. "Leave the dishes and get about yer business then." She rounded the table and kissed her brother on his head. "Will I be seein' ye before ye depart?" She took Crystal's empty plate and headed for the kitchen.

"That would be nice. Your daughter is a very special little gal. I wouldn't leave without saying goodbye."

Carrying the dishes into the kitchen, Becky smiled. She hoped Ethan realized just how special Crystal was before she walked out of all of their lives.

CHAPTER 22

On average, a human takes 11 seconds to count to 22.
That would be two numbers per second times two which equals twenty-two!

Crystal followed Ethan into the Dingle Garda Síochána Offices. "Ethan, what does the sign over the entrance say?"

"Garda Síochána na hÉireann means The Guardians of Peace. Garda Síochána for common speak. 'Tis the name the Republic gave us around the twenties."

Crystal shook her head. "How do you get garda shoe-on out of that?" She laughed. "I don't know why everyone can't speak one language."

Ethan signed the register at the desk. "'T'would take a lifetime fer the world to learn my language." He pointed down the hall. "Let's be about our business before Stephan and his crowd arrive." It was a little after seven o'clock in the morning and Ethan knew what they had to do, just not exactly how they would accomplish it without setting off all kinds of alarms and red flags.

"I was talking about English, Ethan." Crystal followed him down the hall to the vault room.

"I know." He smirked as they entered the room.

The vault door was ajar, and two voices could be heard. Ethan paused and shoved Crystal behind him. Slowly pushing the door open a crack, he peered in at the two men who held the box containing the two remaining crystal goblets. One was Garda Feldig. The other was Stephan O'Haide.

"Inspector, good morn to ye." Garda Feldig motioned for the Inspector and Crystal to come in. "Inspector O'Haide was just tellin' me all about these precious glasses." He held up one goblet and peered at it carefully, then replaced it in the box. "Don't know what all the fuss is, over a couple glasses. Guess they be pretty enough. Inspector O'Haide was just tellin' me they be critical to his case." Feldig took out a Republic Warrant for evidential custody. "Papers are in order, so I'll be releasin' them to him."

Apparently, Garda Feldig could feel the temperature drop in the room because he made a hasty retreat to his desk.

"Stephan, ye be up early." Ethan glowered at his old friend.

"Aye. Can't let this nasty business get wracked up now, could I?" He took a goblet from the box, holding it over the floor with two fingers. "This little beauty is death incarnate, isn't it."

Crystal nodded.

"Such a shame. Real pretty–" Inspector O'Haide released his hold and the goblet crashed to the floor shattering into a million pieces. "Oops. Good thing there is one more." He withdrew the last goblet of death from the box and stared at it for a moment.

"Stephan?" Ethan knew what the Inspector was thinking. A new child. A wife who would be staying home for at least a couple years. Tight to live on an Inspector's salary and raise a family.

"What do ye recon this thing is worth on the black market, Ethan?"

Crystal stepped forward and took the goblet from the Inspector's hand. "More money than God has. And not enough to pay for the lives it would take."

"Well then," The Inspector turned, knocking the goblet out of

Crystal's hand *accidentally*. "Oh, so sorry, lass." He looked into the empty box. "Guess there be no need for this then." He placed the warrant into the empty box, replaced the lid and smiled at his childhood friend. "I'll be on me way. I got me a wee bairn to be seeing. He's probably grown up already and off to college." Stephan doffed his hat. "Be seein' ye, Ethan. Ma'am." He took three small steps through the pile of glass and swiveled his shoes on the powdered crystal. "Probably should clean that up before someone slips and gets hurt."

Ethan smiled at his friend. "Be seein' ye soon, Stephan." He turned to Crystal. "Two great minds with but a single thought. Guess I be fetchin' a whisk broom."

Crystal stood looking at the pile of shards and ground crystal dust. Her sister's legacy was gone. Her sister was gone. The threat to humanity was gone. Soon she would be gone. There was nothing to keep her in Ireland now.

Nothing but her heart, a very special man, and a Mouse.

ETHAN GRABBED the whisk broom and a dustpan from the cleaning closet and headed back to the vault where he'd left Crystal. Stephan had taken his empty evidence box and departed for Shannon. It was time to clean up the mess and the case. But then Crystal would go back to the States and he would be left with the paperwork. Always paperwork. Then what?

Seeing Crystal standing alone in the middle of the vault room, his heart did a little flip in his chest. There she stood, just looking at the pile of sparkly dust and shards. She was biting her lower lip and Ethan thought that was the sexiest thing he'd seen in a long time. Except for the tears. "I'll just get this swept up."

Crystal wiped her eyes and nodded but kept biting her lip. She watched Ethan sweep up the mess and when the floor was clean, she whispered, "So that's it then. Now what?"

Ethan leaned against the vault door, pan and broom in hand. "That'd be dependin' on ye, lass. There's the flat. And yer sister's..." He stopped. It all seemed so final now. In the past few days, he'd grown comfortable with this brave, quirky gal, and her incredible brain. Standing in the vault with only a single bulb lighting the room, she seemed to glow with a soft enticing beauty that had parts other than his brain, working again. Comfortable with her? He grown more than that!

Crystal shifted from one foot to the other, obviously uncomfortable with his silence and empathetic look. "My sister's body. Yes." Crystal leaned against the shelf unit that held evidence boxes, all numbered and labeled on the posts. Her position cast a shadow across her face and Ethan couldn't tell if she was sad or deep in thought. He had gotten to know how her mind worked, but the emotional thing was still a mystery to him. Like his little Mouse, Crystal was complex and highly intelligent. Did that really matter when faced with the loss of your sibling? Your identical twin sibling? He was in no man's land, so he stood there waiting for some sign of what to say. What to do.

Crystal let out a deep sigh and Ethan wanted to cover his ears. The hurt was there, but so was the need to move on. He wasn't sure he wanted her to move on. He wasn't sure of anything anymore.

"Inspector?" Ethan jumped as Garda Feldig spoke from the hallway. He turned to see the officer with paper in hand. "You asked me to be checkin' on..." He thrust the paper into Ethan's hand.

A quick scan showed Ireland's regulations for cremation and burial of a foreigner on Irish soil. With a short note to the correct government agency, Brystal could remain in Ireland forever. He handed the paper to Crystal. "This be the regs fer yer sister's internment. I can make it happen if, that be what ye want."

Crystal took the paper and moved past him into the hall where the light was better to read. As she scanned the document, Ethan watched the expressions on her face. They began with efficient scanning then acceptance, sadness and lastly determination. "Then this is what I want. What Brystal would have wanted, I think." She folded the paper and slipped it into her ever-present bag. "I guess I should get back to the flat and finish what we started, now that there is no one to undo it all."

"There still be one outlier, Crystal. I need to find Dharág Hadley and see what he knows about this nasty business."

"Then I'll go with you. I want to know what part he played in my sister's murder. I'll bet it will be easy to tell if he's smart enough to understand what he had a hand in creating." She pointed over her shoulder into the vault room. "And Ethan, have you thought about where that formula came from? I doubt Rudaij was a scientist."

Ethan frowned. "Aye, I thought long and hard about it. So has Stephan, I'd be bettin'. Shall we go find our Master Hadley?" He put away the broom and pan. "Sean should be back from Galway and in light of everything that's happened, I think we be findin' them both at the shop with their own brooms. Illianescu and company made a real mess."

As they drove the short distance to the Dingle Crystal Corner, rain clouds gathered, and a light mist descended over the peninsula. It made everything look mystical and endless. Ethan loved the bay when all he could see was water and the misty outline of the far away hills all gray-green. As a child, he'd pretended dragons lived in the mist beyond the hills and that someday he'd find the dangerous creatures and slay them. As an adult, he was well aware that there were creatures more dangerous and violent than dragons to find and slay. Like the patriarch of the Illianescu family, the spawn of the Devil himself and his progeny, now incarcerated. "Sean's wife will probably be at the shop, but don't expect to see her workin'. She be doin' chemo every two weeks. It takes a toll."

"Thanks for the warning, but Colleen told me she is fighting a cancer. I had a co-worker going through that. Horrible aftereffects from the chemotherapy, but she made it." Crystal mused, "I never congratulated her. Maybe I should have."

Ethan chuckled. "Nah. It'd be out of character and ye might have given her a heart attack."

Crystal actually laughed at his statement. "Exactly! Why can I be so free here and when I think of going back to my apartment and job, I feel–" She stopped.

She felt? Ethan had not seen Crystal at her job, or her life in New

York. He had no idea what that person was like. He only knew this Crystal, emotional, smart, funny, stubborn, and brave. Very brave. "Here we be." He pulled into a tight little parking spot across the street and shut the engine off.

They could see two men through the broken-out window. The men worked quickly and efficiently. Near the counter, a woman sat wrapped in a fluffy quilt, drinking a cup of some hot beverage. The steam from the cup rose adding to the misty picture. "The shorter fellow be Sean. Maggie should be at home, resting, but she's a goer, that gel. She and Sean be married some thirty-five years now. Can't imagine Sean without Maggie. She's run the store fer some twenty years, ever since Sean came back from Waterford. Loves Sean's art. Loves Sean. Ye can see it in her eyes when they be together." Ethan's comment was wistful and soft.

"Let's go see what Hadley has to say for himself." Crystal was in her investigative mode and ready to move.

As they entered the shop, Sean MacDougal stood with some difficulty and rubbed the middle of his back. "Inspector, welcome to me shop. Havin' a fire sale we be." His chubby cheeks broke into a grin. Until he saw Crystal! "Faith and begorrah!"

"Sorry about the damage. This is Crystal Traynor, Brystal's twin sister." He moved to catch the older man, caught off balance by seeing the image of his dead assistant, alive and walking into his shop.

"Aye, I thought me be seein' a Gollum, fer a second." His smile was back and he stepped forward, hand extended. "Ye sis was an excellent student. Pleased to be meetin' ye." He kept moving his head back and forth, staring at Crystal's face. "Identical fer sure. Whoo-ee. I can be bettin' folks round here get a bit of a shock when they see ye, lass."

Crystal took his hand with a healthy shake. "That would be true. I came when they told me Brystal was dead." The matter-of-fact statement slid hastily off her lips. "Sorry. I meant–"

"Nah lass, I be the one sorry, fer ye. Brystal was a wonderful gel. A right good cutter and a simply happy person. She added light to our shop." Sean shook his head. "Right bad thing that happened to her." He turned to the Inspector, "Any ideas what happened?"

"That's what we be here for Sean. I need a word with Dharág Hadley."

At the mention of his name, Dharág dropped his pan and took a step to run.

"Don't be doin' that, boy-o. I just want a word." Ethan warned.

Sean was puzzled. "Dharág, what be ye doin' lad? Come talk to the Inspector like a right proper fella."

Dharág had nowhere to run anyway. Dingle was his home. Everyone knew him. Sean had given him a straight job after he lost his boat and fishing career. He stepped forward. "What be ye needin', Inspector. I don't know nothin' about Brystal's death." He turned to Crystal, "Beggin' yer pardon, ma'am."

"Dharág, ye gave Brystal a design to cut. She completed four goblets." Ethan peered at the man as he slowly spoke the next few words. "Those goblets were why she was killed."

Dharág kept his eyes down and simply shook his head. "I'll not be understandin' that."

"Where did ye get the design, Dharág?" Ethan prodded.

"Nowhere. I designed it myself." Dharág was shifting from one foot to the other. "Brystal said she wanted to cut it. I let her."

Crystal stepped forward. "I had your design schematics, Mr. Hadley. The measurements. If you drew the design, tell me what numbers they were based on."

Dharág's anger was barely concealed as he spoke. "Ye wouldn't understand, missy. It be very complicated."

"Unfortunately for you, Mr. Hadley, I do understand. And ye be a spoofin'." Crystal was taller than Hadley and leaned in for intimidation, a trick she'd learned from one particularly brutal attorney she'd had the displeasure of working with.

Ethan stuck his hands in his pockets and proudly announced to Sean. "She thinks she's learning Irish."

Crystal poked at Dharág with her index finger. "You Mister, are a bold-faced liar."

Dharág knew he was in trouble and looked to Ethan for help.

"Inspector, what be the targe's problem? I wouldn't put me arm into ye. Me head was turned, and I needed Brystal to get me up."

Ethan knew Crystal wouldn't understand the local lingo and offered a translation without request. "Means ye be a tough woman and he wouldn't con us. He got behind in his work and needed yer sister's help."

"Me project needed some handlin'." He turned to Crystal apologetically. "Yer sis be real good. Better than me if I be tellin' the God's truth." He hung his head, mostly for effect. "So, I put her to the task. But I never got the goblets. She got knocked off afore she delivered. I think me client did this." He motioned to the store floor.

Sean stood silently watching his apprentice. Ethan was aware there would be a serious discussion when he and Crystal were out of earshot. "Why do ye think that? Who is yer client?"

Dharág was in over his head. He looked around for a plausible story but just couldn't wrap his head around anything that would make sense. Finally he said, "A foreigner. Albanian guy from up the coast. Said it was fer a special gift. Paid me on the dock."

"The Albanian guy from out Ventry Bay way. Paid before he got the goblets." Ethan translated for Crystal.

The anger came from some place deep and Ethan watched it surface in Crystal's every move. "So, you got paid and my sister got dead." She spun in a circle. "Your boss got this!" She put her head against Ethan's shoulder. "And I've got nothing."

At the emotional explosion, Maggie leveraged herself off the chair and took Crystal into her arms. "No, sweetin', ye've got us. Always. Brystal was like a daughter to me. I'll not let her sister be takin' the trake all by yeself." Maggie pulled Crystal to the bench next to her chair. "Let me wet a tea fer ye."

As Maggie made tea from her little hot pot on the counter, Crystal waited and listened.

"Dharág, this client of yers, what else did he say about the goblets? Be straight with me, man. Rudaij and Kujtim Illianescu be both in custody."

With Ethan's statement, Dharág looked up again. "They be in the lock-up?"

"That's what I said. The rouster's na be with 'em, he went in the bay."

Dharág held a hand to his heart. "I be safe? I be safe!" He hugged Sean and went to hug Ethan who held up a hand to stop the fellow. "Rudaij brought me a series of squares and diamonds he wanted cut to exact measures. Said it was some kind of a gift fer his parents. Something about a message in code." Dharág shook his head. "Crazy Albanians. So, I took a see. I be midlin 'bout it, but Brystal, the lass was all over it. She liked a challenge. So, I gave her the project." He looked to Sean in a manner of apology. "I kept if off log. The blasted bane shifted me cash on the head, so I told Brystal I'd split it with her when she cut the job." He wiped a hand across his face. "She rang me up and said it was done. The next minute, she be dead as dung and cold stiff on the back steps of the An Droichead Beag. Didn't make the parse till that bloody bastard shows up at me flat sayin' all kind of naff." He wiped his face again. "Then this. Shows up in the door all straight and pretty-boy. Gives me a tonguin'. That be all I know, Ethan. I swear on me mum's grave."

"Buck eejit." Sean mumbled and went back to cleaning the floor.

Sitting next to Crystal, Maggie whispered, "Means he did some really stupid things."

Crystal nodded and sipped her tea.

"Did ye ever wonder what the message was in the squares and diamonds?" Ethan kept his questions light and simple. He was now fairly sure Dharág had been a pawn in the whole scheme of things.

"Nah. I made me grade eight and not much more. I'm not good with numbers and such. Do ye know? Do ye have the goblets? Maybe I can sell them out."

"No. They were destroyed. You could ask Rudaij Illianescu about the message. He'd be in the Shannon lock-up."

Ethan laughed at Dharág's shudder at the thought of approaching the man who had paid for a set of goblets and never got the delivery. He was pretty sure Dharág knew there was something fishy about the goblets, but as the fellow told, he wasn't good with numbers. He never would have figured out the digital code and the chemical formula for a weapon of mass destruction. "Maybe ye should consider a refund fer yer customer."

At that, Dharág stepped back and held up his hands. "To the devil with ye, Ethan. I'll be banjaxed afore I be settlin' with that jackeen. To the goal with them all. Albanians be the death of Ireland yet."

Now that Dharág knew the Illianescu brothers were in custody and their thug was crab bait, he felt whole enough to keep the money. "Or maybe reimburse Sean here, for the damages ye caused while he was away helpin' out his wife with her therapy." Ethan laid the guilt on thick. Dharág was the reason Sean's inventory was gone. He was behind Brystal's death, even if he didn't do the deed himself. He needed to repent. Money was the Catholic way.

At Ethan's suggestion, Sean stopped sweeping and stretched his back with a deep groan.

Crystal bit her tongue to keep from laughing.

CHAPTER 23

Psalm 23 is the most quoted passage in the Christian Bible:
"The Lord is my shepherd..."

They all stood on the deck of the Lady of the Mist. The sun was shining, and the day was entirely Irish-beautiful. The green hills were the color of green only seen in Ireland and the bay was calm and flat. Crystal had been in Dingle now for almost four weeks and she still found things that needed her attention. Or at least that is what she told herself daily.

Brystal's household goods were packed and shipped. Her motorbike was now in the capable hands of Christian, who had proposed a payment plan before his mother could stop him. Crystal bartered, knowing the young man was headed for university in a year. He would need to save up, but most of his tuition would be offset by his father's teaching job. So, she agreed to a twenty-five dollar a month payment but left an envelope containing his first year's room and board with Colleen. Crystal was a very wealthy woman and lived a frugal life. Christian was a straight young man with a great future ahead of him. Why not help the family out that had taken care of her sister and treated Brystal like family. In fact, Crystal felt like she was now part of the family as well. She'd been supping with Colleen and Christian all week when Ethan didn't collect her for dinner at Becky's. She'd met Oisin, Christian's father, and they talked long into the night about archeology and the legends of Ireland.

Sergeant Willie Naighler piloted the Lady of the Mist, an Irish Republic Coast Guard vessel on lend for the burial of Garda Matthew Landau, and, of course, Brystal Traynor. Daria sat at his right, carefully studying the controls as Willie explained everything at length. Daria had informed Crystal that she would be learning everything and anything she could about running engines and navigating. She was committed to never being adrift again. She promptly informed Crystal that she would make it through life without becoming fish bait for the monstrous creatures of the deep! When she unabashedly informed Sergeant Willie, he sat her at the helm and proceeded to tell her everything. Everything! Bless his heart, he even let her guide the vessel in the open water. Crystal smiled. Now if she would just grow up with some muscles, she'd be able to pull the damn rope!

Father Selguire stood at the bow. Before him, on a stout table sat two small boxes in the center of wreaths. The circle of flowers surrounding the remains of Garda Landau bore the colors of the An Garda Síochána. Brystal's wreath was a mass of colorful wildflowers of Ireland. When the prayers were done and the Father had blessed each container, Garda Landau's wife and young daughter committed his ashes and wreath to the waters of the bay. Ethan helped Crystal with her last duty to her sister, and it was done. She stood at the railing watching as the wreath drifted off, slowly submerging as the bay took its own, forever.

"I be thinkin' Brystal would have loved this." Ethan put an arm around Crystal and pulled her to him. "I never had the pleasure of meetin' the lass, but knowin' ye, she must have been somethin'."

"Aye, she was." Crystal lay her head on Ethan's chest, feeling the comfort from this man she'd only known for a few weeks. She could hear his heartbeat. She could smell his aftershave. She could feel his strong arms. Crystal heard the rumble in his chest and felt him bump against her cheek. She looked up, "What?"

"I love to hear you speak Irish." He grinned down at her.

"Yer such a…," she couldn't think of a word for funny in the local slang. "Goofball."

"If that be a drink, I'll take one." He nodded toward his niece and her newest best friend. "I do believe Sergeant Naighler has a fan. Poor fellow."

At that comment, Crystal did laugh, appropriate or not! "Did she tell you she was going to learn everything about boating so we'll never be adrift again? Like we'll be off sailing the seas together? Something about creatures eating us?" Crystal sobered at the thought. Not of being eaten, but of leaving this amazing land and the people she'd grown so close to in such a short time. How could one person want to be in two different places at the same time and be so torn? Was that how her sister felt about Ireland and Dingle? This place had changed her, and she loved the way she felt here in this magical land. But she had a job, a career. She had an apartment on the seventh floor in New York. People needed her and depended on her. Chance needed the money she made him. Sandra needed her job. She was one of the top employees at Larson, Davidson, and Evans. How could she abandon all of that?

How could she leave Ethan and Ireland? And Daria? And Colleen with her scrumptious bakery right downstairs? What about Becky? How would she keep up with her daughter's shenanigans without someone who understood what Daria was capable of?

She leaned into Ethan as the ship swayed with the current and plowed through the waves on its way back to the main dock in Dingle. Crystal sighed and let everything drift away on the breeze. For right now, she was just a woman in a man's arms. Not thinking. Not planning. Not saying goodbye.

Ethan's arms encircled Crystal and held her close. She was such a brave woman. So smart and so good. So incredibly warm and… so not his. She had concluded her business in his little town, and now she would be leaving to resume her fast paced and demanding life in the

States. In New York City, of all places. After everything they'd been through, how could he let her go? His heart had taken the plunge without asking his permission. Now he held her, but not forever. His heart wanted forever. His brain knew better. He'd lost love before and it had almost done him in. Now he looked to a bleak future of missing the quirky woman and their silly banter.

So completely immersed in clinging to each other, neither Ethan nor Crystal heard Daria's approach. "Well, it be 'bout time." She stood with her hands on her hips on the stairs to the pilothouse. "I was beginnin' ta think ye'd never figure it out, the both of ye."

Ethan was the first to respond. "And what be ye thinkin' we've figured out, Mouse?"

"Ye know, Uncle Ethan!" She made a kissy face and smacking sounds. "The adult stuff me mum thinks I don't know." More kissy faces and she walked past the couple to the bow. "We be makin' the wharf in five. Willie asked me to tell ye all to get into the cabin. We've got to tie up."

Crystal looked back up at Ethan. "We? Did she enlist?"

Ethan shrugged with a smile and drew Crystal toward the cabin without letting go of the physical contact he craved. He had to get everything he could before she flew away and he would never see her again. His heart was pounding, and his mouth was dry. He'd found something he did not want to let go of, but the choice was out of his hands. He knew Crystal was devoted to her boss and her job. He couldn't change that. This amazing woman should have everything she wanted. He would live with the loss. He was used to that now.

Inside the cabin of the Lady of the Mist, Crystal huddled close to Ethan on the bench seat. It was a beautiful, warm day, but all Crystal could feel was the icy cold hands of separation. Brystal was gone. At least she'd be with their parents now. Crystal was the one who remained, alone, in uncharted waters.

"Will ye be headin' back to the States now?" Ethan had to know.

"I guess. This," She waved a hand across her lap, "was the last thing I had to do."

"Ye could stay a bit and rest up. I can't imagine going back to yer job will be easy."

Crystal sighed heavily. "I've been gone for four weeks. I talk to Chance about every other day and there are no difficult cases pending but having one employee out for such a long time must be a burden on the others." She watched the wharf drawing closer through one of the round portholes. "He says my admin assistant is bored to death."

"Hmmm." Ethan didn't trust his mouth to not say what his heart wanted it to. In four short weeks his world had been turned upside down and inside out. They'd stopped a notorious crime syndicate from setting up camp in Dingle, and solved an unsolvable murder. And he'd fallen in love.

"I guess I should make a flight reservation and get on with it." Her head felt so good on his chest.

"I can deliver ye to the airport in Shannon if ye book it that way. We can stop by the ITCTF headquarters and check on Stephan's investigation. He's gone back part time, even though he should be home tendin' his wee babe and wife. Said 'twas dire circumstances." Ethan chuckled and watched Crystal's head bump with his chest. "Me thinks he be a bit constrained at home. 'Tis hard with a new one."

Ethan's last sentence made Crystal's heart flip. She knew he'd had a wife and daughter. She also knew how that had ended. She'd never considered children of her own, until she met Daria and fell into the crafty little mouse's web of intrigue and giggles. Would she ever have a child? Would her child be like Daria, all elbows, haunting creatures, and such enthusiasm for life? Or possibly a boy, like Christian, crazy riding a motorcycle, hell bent for election? Before she came to Ireland, her life was scheduled, organized, complacent. Complacent? Why did that sound so unsatisfying now?

The ship bumped against the dock with a slight lurch and she could hear Daria's excited shouts to Willie. One of the Garda's that had been present at the burial was tying up the lines as Daria supervised a few feet away. The Garda had a huge grin and asked for directions at every step. Did everyone fall into that young gal's trap so easily?

"I'll have to wait to call Chase for a few hours. It's," She looked at her watch, " four AM there. He'd be still in bed right now."

"We've time for a leisurely lunch then. If ye be up to it."

"Everyone's got to eat, right? Will Becky mind if we take Daria?"

Ethan laughed as they both stood up to leave. "Becky'd be beholden. We may not be able to pry her away from her duties here though."

As they walked to the gangplank, they watched Daria scrambling over the ship's ropes and equipment. She was like an uncaged monkey, checking everything out before racing to the next. Willie stood outside the bridge talking into his comm. Ethan could see Daria pause, and talk back through a handheld radio. She had a radio? Oh Lord!

"Daria, would ye be havin' lunch with us?" Ethan yelled loud enough for Willie to hear above them.

Daria came running and tackled her uncle around the waste. Out of breath and wild with excitement, she sputtered, "Can Willie come, too?"

"He's probably got duties to tend to, Mouse."

Crystal took the radio from her and handed it to the closest seaman available. "And I've got questions for you. Classified stuff." The last few words were whispered as Crystal put a finger to her lips.

Daria considered the request seriously for a moment. "Then I'll be leavin' me crew." She waved up at Willie, who shot her a thumbs up. "Willie told me about the Youth Garda. I can join next year and be a copper too!"

At that, Ethan shot Willie a thumbs up. Did the young officer know what he was in for? "Alright, let's be off." Ethan herded Daria and Crystal to his car with a shout of thanks to Willie and the crew. Across the parking lot, Garda Potter was helping Mrs. Landau and her daughter into his car. As he looked up, Ethan could see the streaks on his face where tears made his emotional goodbye to his partner apparent. Ethan nodded and Potter nodded back. It was a simple acknowledgement between two professionals who'd unfortunately, done this before.

Inside the car, Daria asked, "Uncle Ethan, can we go to the Treehouse? I've a need for carrot cake and Mallory is baking today. She makes the best cake in the whole world." Still out of breath a little after her exciting day, Daria reconsidered her statement. "After me mum, that is."

Both Ethan and Crystal laughed at the girl's exuberance. "To be sure. Ye'll have to get a sandwich as well, or ye mum will box me ears." Ethan saw Daria bounce up and down in the rearview mirror. Oh, to be young and so excited about... everything!

"I'm not sure if sugar is what your niece needs." Crystal murmured to Ethan.

As they were seated outside the little café and the waitress took their orders, Crystal spoke quietly to Daria. There were no other customers near and she was sure no one was in earshot. "Daria, have you deleted the things we discovered on your computer? All of the traces? Search engine history, and all?"

"Of course. I even searched me cookies listing and deleted all reference. I know how to cover me tracks, Crystal. Believe me!" She'd calmed a bit and was considering Crystal's question carefully. "What will Inspector O'Haide do to that ugly man who hit you?"

"Rudaij? He's been arrested and will be transported to the Hague after his interrogation." Ethan sipped his cup of tea. "I'll thank ye not to talk about that man to anyone but meself. He be a member of a huge crime family and this may not be the end of things here." Ethan sat his cup down and leaned in close. "I'll not be scaring ye, Mouse, but this dirty business may not be done yet, so ye must be vigilant." Ethan hoped his warning would keep her in check, if only for a while.

"Your uncle's correct, Daria. The Illianescu family syndicate is like a spider's web, lines everywhere. The head of the family has just lost two sons and he won't be happy. You need to keep an eye out and let Ethan know if there is anything suspicious at your home or school. Your name is not in the records, and Rudaij thinks you are some silly little girl. Let's keep it that way." Crystal was trying to impress Daria with the seriousness of their situation. "And absolutely no surfing the names or people involved, no matter how tempting it may be. You know what happened to your aunt and cousin." She nodded Ethan's way. "I'll not be coming back here to send your ashes overboard. Do you understand?"

Daria nodded gravely then held up her pinky finger. "I promise, Crystal."

The pinky shake was as good as gold in Daria's book and Crystal took the girl's finger in hers. "I'll hold you to that, Mouse."

It was such a heartwarming display between the two, that Ethan swallowed hard. Crystal was going back to New York, but knew Daria would only be a keyboard away. He was sure Crystal would be significant in helping Daria keep her promise. There would always be a small string to keep Crystal in their lives, if only in Daria's life.

Daria talked incessantly over lunch, relating everything she'd learned with Willie and *her* crew. It gave Ethan and Crystal a little breathing space after the emotional events of the day. Ethan was glad. With everything they'd been through and the thought of Crystal flying off, he could put things out of his mind for a few minutes and simply enjoy a family lunch.

"Next year I can become a Youth cadet in the Garda. Willie promised to sponsor me. Each cadet needs a sponsor who be responsible for the training and testing of the cadet. Willie said he'd be very hard on me. He said I had to be rememberin' everything he'd be teachin' me."

"That's a lot for a young girl." Ethan commented.

"Uncle Ethan," Daria pulled a face and looked incredulously at her uncle. "I don't forget. Ye know that." She pointed to him with a fork full of cake. "How long have ye be knownin' me? Since I be born and all that time ye not be known' I can't forget?" She stuffed the cake in her mouth and mumbled around the dessert, "It be a loathsome burden at times."

"I know exactly what you mean." Crystal picked at her cake. "You know, I never thought there'd be another like me in the world, but you are about the closest, Daria."

Daria smiled at her friend; carrot cake stuck to her teeth.

Crystal shoved a piece of cake into her mouth and smiled back.

Ethan cleared his throat and looked away.

CHAPTER 24

It takes twenty-four hours for the earth to rotate once.
Sunset, sunrise. Sunset, sunrise.
Swiftly flow the days.
One number following another,
Laden with viciousness and fear.

Ethan had kept his promise and delivered Crystal to the airport. Christian had returned the rental car for her, and now she sat in the first-class cabin halfway between two destinations that both called her back. She should have been happy to get back to her *normal* life, but now normal had a different meaning.

"Ma'am, can I get you anything else?" The flight attendant handed her a hot towel with tongs.

Lunch was on its way and smelled delicious. Some kind of chicken with oriental salad, a bun and cheesecake for dessert. Wine was included, but Crystal thought the better of drinking when her boss would be picking her up from the airport. "No, thank you." She stared at the towel before rubbing it across her hands.

What was she doing?

Four and a half weeks ago she was sobbing on the floor of her kitchen, having just learned of her sister's death. Now she sat in a fat-boy seat, crossing the Atlantic for the second time, like it was an everyday occurrence. She sipped her third cup of tea and thought about the last few weeks. Brystal. Ethan. Daria. Colleen and the Sweeney Bakery. Christian. Becky. Stephan O'Haide.

On their way to the Shannon Airport, she and Ethan had stopped at the International and Terrorist Crime Task Force Headquarters. Stephan was hard at it and loving every moment, but missing his wife and child. Talk about one person torn between two places! He interspersed their briefing with quips about his new son. It went like; *Turns out Kujtim is a scoundrel like his brother, but not privy to the family business yet. Did ye know me son can smile like nobody's business? Rudaij lawyered up as soon as the cuffs hit his wrists. I've got to remember to get nappies on me way home.* Crystal bit her tongue to keep from laughing so many times there was a raw place on the end. They looked at so many pictures of the new baby they were almost late for her flight. Ethan had laughed all the way to the airport comparing new daddy events. There was pain in the telling but a healing as well. Stephan asked Ethan to be his son's godfather and Crystal thought he would collapse right then and there.

All of these people who had entered her life in a very short time were dear to her. And she left them behind. In a foreign country she might never return to. A piece of her was still there. A big piece of her heart.

As the plane landed, Crystal gathered herself for the culture shock that awaited. She'd gotten used to driving on the wrong side of the road. Good thing she could walk to work! She'd fallen in love with soda bread and apricot scones and would need to find a recipe or an Irish restaurant where she could buy some. Her hair flowed loose and wild, not in a tight professional bun, and she'd decided she liked it that way. Even when the Dingle Bay wind turned it into a mass of tangles and kinky curls. The New York air pollution would probably damp it down, but Crystal was determined to live on the edge now.

As she deplaned and strolled toward the baggage area, she spotted Chance, and Alana. They held hands smiling at each other like new lovers. Apparently more than just her life had changed in the last month.

Alana waved. "Crystal, welcome home. Chance thought we should both meet you here in case you needed–" Alana stopped mid-sentence. "Wow! You're different."

Crystal grinned. Was it that obvious?

"Welcome home, Crystal." Chance stood his ground, not exactly knowing what to do. His Crystal looked... different was not a strong enough word to describe how his forensic accountant had changed in such a short time. "Looks like Ireland had some kind of effect on you."

Crystal hugged Chance, then Alana. "It's good to be home." Her enthusiasm wasn't quite what it should have been, but more than that, she'd hugged her boss and his wife!

Chance stood stock still while Alana laughed and returned Crystal's hug. "I can tell you've been to the Adare Manor. It changes a person. Despite the emotional toll you must have endured, you look wonderful."

Alana thought she looked wonderful? The most beautifully crafted woman in the world thought she looked wonderful? "Thanks. I've got three green bags and a large blue one. They shouldn't be hard to spot. A young friend bought them for me." Crystal pointed to the moving baggage carousel. "They're green so I wouldn't forget Ireland." Crystal grinned at Chance who still hadn't moved an inch. She waved a hand in front of his face. "Chance, are you all right?"

"Who are you and what did you do with my Miss Traynor? Hum, um–" Her boss took a breath and cleared his throat. "Of course. Green bags. I'll get them." He walked to the carousel looking back at his wife and Crystal who had begun to exchange memories of the Adare Manor House and the people they'd met. Alana gasped, then laughed outright as three huge lime green suitcases came through the baggage curtains. One had an enormous smiley face glued to the front. The second had a gnome with hot pink hat and fuchsia trousers, and the third was covered in yellow and red polka dots.

"Daria didn't want me to lose my baggage. She's just about twelve and quite the jokester." Crystal whispered watching Chance lug the outrageous suitcases to the side and stack them in a rolling cart.

"I guess so." Alana peered at Crystal. "This tale I have to hear. I know you're probably tired, but how would you like to stop for a bite to eat. I'm thinking there is more to the story than Chance has been telling me.

The grin on Crystal's face just kept getting bigger.

Once the blue one and her greenies, as Alana named Crystal's suitcases, were stowed in the back of their Suburban, Chance drove Crystal and his wife to a quiet restaurant in New Jersey. He continued to study his protégé with an almost rude curiosity, and finally Alana commented on her husband's behavior. "Honey, Crystal has been through a lot in the last few weeks, but you don't have to stare like she's grown another head."

"It's alright, Alana. I know I must seem a little different. I am a little different. Actually, I think a lot different." Crystal launched into her story starting at the very beginning. When it came to being headed for the ocean with a child in a dinghy, Chance had to stop her.

"You read that in a book, didn't you? The Crystal I put on a plane four weeks ago wouldn't even step outside the crosswalk lines on her way to work. On foot, mind you! You expect me to believe you and a little girl rowed out to sea with some crazed Albanian syndicate thug after you?" Chance shook his head.

Crystal smirked. "I told Inspector MacEnery no one would believe me. We were rescued by the Irish Coast Guard and a Sergeant named Willie." Crystal had amended her story to exclude the hideous chemical weapon discovery and her sister's part in the event that was set to become a world disaster of the worst kind. She glossed over a few facts and managed to only mention Ethan's name a few hundred times.

Alana was catching on rapidly, but Chance was still in the dark and wandering in his own head. Alana nudged her husband under the table. "Honey, I think Crystal is trying to tell us she has found a friend. Of the boy kind."

Chance came out of his daze and said the first thing that came to his mouth, without his mind. "Crystal doesn't like men. She likes work."

"It's okay, Alana. I know I've changed, and it may be hard for some people to accept that, but I like the new me. In Ireland I saw things that made an impression on me. I know I have some quirks and not everyone can understand. Chance did in the very beginning. He got me out of that rat hole and doing boring taxes. I will always be grateful for that. He has helped me along the way and now I feel like I'm grown up, standing on my own two feet. It just happened." She sipped her tea watching her boss. "You two have been great and I want to thank you for everything. And getting me at the airport!"

Chance mumbled under his breath. "And she doesn't say thank you."

Alana kicked him.

"Ow."

"Let's get this one home so she can rest up and unpack." Alana motioned to the waiter for the check and soon they were headed for New York City and an apartment that held little interest for Crystal.

CHAPTER 25

25 is the average percentage DNA overlap of an individual with their half-sibling, grandparent, grandchild, aunt, uncle, niece, nephew, identical twin cousin (offspring of identical twins), or double cousin. Family is mathematical, but family by choice is magical!

Crystal had been back to work for a whole two weeks and still she was the topic of intense gossip. To still some of the chatter, she actually tied her hair up in a chignon one day, but all it got her was compliments. She had to admit to herself now, she didn't really mind the nice comments and smiles that came her way. Chance stayed on the top floor and only spared her a passing glance in the lobby. It was like he'd lost his rag doll and it had been replaced with Moviestar Barbie. It seemed like he was a bit afraid to go near her.

She'd not gotten around to unpacking her sister's belongings, now hers. The greenies still sat in the hallway of her apartment, tripping her every once in a while, to remind her they were still there. She'd gotten about fifty emails from Daria, but only one from her uncle. He wanted to know if she'd made it home and was all right. Not exactly the warm snuggly hug on a Coast Guard vessel, but it would have to do.

There were no big cases at work and she quickly dispatched each investigation with her previous speed and efficiency, only to find another less challenging case on her desk. LDE was opening a new division out in California, the real den of financial iniquity. There was talk of employees relocating. There was talk of promotions and financial incentives, but Crystal was comfortable where she was, if a tad less enthusiastic than she been before her visit to Ireland.

"As I live and breathe, Boss." Sandra stood at her doorway. "You look like you're pining away. That frown will give you wrinkles, you know." She slapped a stack of manila folders on the side of Crystal's desk. "More less-than-imaginative fraudulent activity to clean up." Sandra huffed. "Where have all the smart, sneaky criminals gone?" She spun to return to her desk.

"Sandra, do you have a minute?" Crystal swung in her chair and motioned to the seat near the door.

"Sure. What's up? I'm dying of boredom with these."

"Have you ever heard of the Illianescu Crime Syndicate?"

"No. Are they laundering money? Printing it themselves? Illegal investments? What?" Crystal had Sandra's attention.

"Probably all of the above and more. Human trafficking, drugs, weapons. They've got some kind of division here in the states. They're Albanian. Could you do a little digging around? When you're bored, of course." Crystal tried to maintain a casual tone, which Sandra saw through immediately.

"This has to do with Ireland, doesn't it?" She sat up a little straighter. "You came back so different. I mean, everyone has noticed, not just me."

"Yes and no. I'm actually not sure but I can give you a name to start with." Crystal scribbled Svetskaine Alexi Illianescu on a post-it note. "Be careful and keep this between you and me, please."

"Of course. As always. And thanks, Crystal. I was going nuts out there doing normal stuff. That's not me, or you." Sandra threw Crystal a thumbs-up and returned to her desk and computer terminal with a big smile and a determined look in her eye.

By lunch Sandra was still glued to her screen and Crystal was curious what she'd found that kept her so seriously engaged. She decided to ask. As she headed out her door, Chance caught her and waved her back into the office and closed the door behind him. He'd never closed her door before.

"There's a call for you. From the Director of some task force in Europe. Line six." He took a seat in the chair next to the door and pointed to her desk phone.

"For me?" She squeaked.

"He asked for you by name." Chance wasn't moving out of the chair.

Crystal picked up the phone. "Larson, Davidson and Evans. This is Crystal Traynor." She didn't recognize his voice right off, but by the time he's said his third ye, she was fairly sure it was Stephan.

"Miss Traynor, how be ye doin' across the pond?"

"Inspector, it's good to hear your voice." She turned her back on Chance to hide her enjoyment at hearing a sweet Irish lilt again.

"I'd be thankin' ye, lass but this is not a social call."

"I see. How can I help you, Inspector?" She sat down in her office chair and pulled out a yellow pad and a pen.

"Do ye be wantin' the bad news first, or the good?"

She could hear a familiar voice in the background saying, "Just tell her."

There was a rustling noise, and that familiar voice came over the line. "Crystal, Ethan here. Kujtim Illianescu's been busted out. He's disappeared right out the back wall, the right bastard."

"So, what is the good news?" Crystal looked at Chance for a second and scribbled a note, handing him the yellow tablet. The note read; *we need to talk. Give me a minute.*

Chance rose and left the room, closing the door quietly. Crystal could see him pacing back and forth outside her office.

"Rudaij is in solitary confinement in a maximum-security facility in Belgium. He'll not be givin' us the slip. If Kujtim gets back to his da, there'll be hell to pay and ye be knowin' who he'll come after. Ye'll not be safe, lass." Ethan's voice almost broke at the last statement and Crystal remembered how he'd lost his wife and daughter. "Stephan's got an idea. I'll let him tell ye."

More rustling was heard and then Stephan came back on the line. "Crystal, I'd like to be having ye here on furlough 'fer a bit. I could be usin' ye brain and have ye under our protection at the same time. The ITCTF be leadin' the charge on this one. What say ye, lass?"

"I'll have to get back to you. Can I have a good number? My boss is pacing outside as we speak." Crystal peeked through the blinds. Chance peeked back and she almost tripped over her chair.

"Would it be of help if I got me Director to pen a letter?" Stephan must really be in trouble if he was willing to go to the Director to procure her services.

"Let me see what I can do first. I'll get right back to you." Crystal wrote the number on a post-it note. "Daria's okay, right? And Ethan's sister?"

"They've round-the-clock protection. Our best. I got Ethan here with me, but we still haven't found the chemist, only his bank account. We need yer help." Stephan was almost pleading. "Ethan, ye tell her, boy-oh."

The next voice she heard made her heart flip cartwheels again. "Ethan, are you okay? How is Becky and the family?"

"They be fine. Moved the lot to a safe house in Shannon. We need ye." His voice lowered. "I need ye, gel. I won't be losin' me heart again. I've missed ye more than soda bread." His attempt at humor in the seriousness of the moment told Crystal just how critical the situation was.

"Let me talk to my boss. I'll call you right back. I've got the number. Stay there." She hung up the phone and opened her door. "Chance, Sandra, in my office, please."

The entire floor went silent. Crystal had never ordered her boss and her admin into her office. She closed the door behind Sandra and waved to the chairs. Chance took her office chair and Sandra sat next to the door. In Sandra's hands were several printed sheets of paper.

"I haven't been exactly honest with both of you, and now I've got to come clean. What I am going to tell you cannot leave this office. Ever. Understand?"

Both her boss and her admin nodded in the affirmative. To say they looked surprised would have been an understatement.

"I need to go back to Ireland. Now. That was Inspector Stephan O'Haide of the International and Terrorist Crime Task Force for the European Union." Crystal clasped her hands as she paced and spoke. "My sister's death involved a conspiracy to sell a chemical weapon that is ten times worse than anything man has ever seen. We, Ethan, Daria, Stephan and the Dingle Garda, the Irish police, foiled the plot and the major players were arrested. Long story short, and it has to be short because there is not time, one of the guys was broken out of prison. He's gone and that's a really bad thing. The ITCTF thinks they will come after me, here in the states." As Crystal paused to take a breath, Sandra slowly handed the papers she held, out to her boss. Crystal could read the title of the biography in block letters at the top. It said, Svetskaine Alexi Illianescu. "Oh my God! Sandra, go back to your desk and delete all the files you've been looking at that are connected to this man. Hurry. Then come back in here. Don't forget to delete the cookies too!"

Crystal leaned against her white board shaking her head. "If they have a reverse bot watching for any searches, LDE could be in trouble. Sandra could be in trouble. Chance, I need to go. Can you officially release me on furlough at the request of the ITCTF?"

Chance stood and hugged Crystal. He peered down at her. "Why would I send you back to a place where your life is in danger?"

"Ethan will protect me. He did before. They need my skills to trace the chemist's account and find the bastard. The man who created the formula for this weapon of massive mass destruction needs to be stopped. We destroyed all of the copies of the formula. We need to destroy the man who made it."

"That's the job of the police and this task force you talk about." He didn't want his number one forensic accountant alone in a foreign country playing Nancy Drew.

"No, you don't understand! I have to go. They need me!" She was backed against the wall and Chance blocked any avenue of escape. The old Crystal would have gone into meltdown, being trapped in close proximity to another human being, especially a man. The new Crystal stood her ground and said the only thing she could. "*He* needs me."

Chance backed up and sat down with a grin. "And you need him. Alana explained it to me. How she figured it all out is beyond me, but there you have it. I think I hate Ireland. I think I hate him, whoever he is."

Sandra came through the door like a whirlwind out of the desert. "I did it. I deleted everything and shredded what I printed. I hope it's enough."

"I hope so too. Chance, you'll have to keep a watch on Sandra while I'm gone. These guys are bad. They actually passed bad two generations ago and moved on to worse bad."

"Wait. Where are you going, Boss?" Sandra sat with a plop. "This is not going to be good. I can tell already. I just got you back all new and sweet, and now you're off again? Crap."

Crystal dialed the phone number Stephan had given her. She hit the speaker button.

"Crystal?" It was Stephan O'Haide.

"Yes Inspector O'Haide. You are on speakerphone with my supervisor. We've discussed the situation and he's agreed to a furlough." She could hear a whoop in the background, all the way from Ireland.

Chance mouthed, "Is that him?"

Crystal's mile-wide grin was all the answer he needed.

She was going back to Ireland and Ethan! The circumstances could have been better, but at least they would be together, and on the trail of the chemist. She might find the chemist, but she'd already found what she truly needed; love, family, a home, and the greenest green she'd ever seen.

CONNECT WITH MIRIAM MATTHEWS

Many people ask me where I get the ideas for my books. This particular story was born in a country far away. I spent a couple weeks touring Ireland with a friend and ended up meeting Sean Daly, a Waterford trained crystal artist, in the small town of Dingle. He invited me to his shop to see how he created stunning crystal pieces. Intrigued by the intricate cuts that produce so much beauty, I saw a story in the light patterns cast by Sean's amazing work. My crazy techi-brain saw binary code. My creative side saw a conspiracy. I wrote the outline on the plane home, but had no time to actually create the entire story... until now. I hope you enjoy it!

And the adventures continue...

Check out the pictures of me making refrigerator art! I actually got to try my hand at cutting crystal under the wise supervision of Sean Daly. ☞

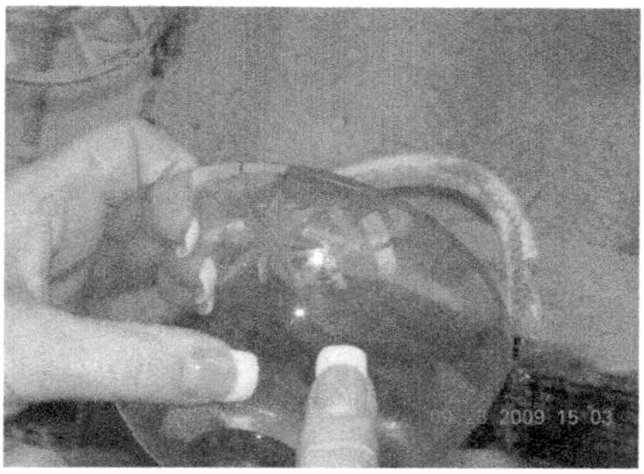

MORE BOOKS BY MIRIAM MATTHEWS

The Vamp Squad Series

Book 1: Strange Beginnings

Book 2: The Death of Innocence

Book 3: The Secrets of San Leyre

The Good, the Bad, and the Bet

The Ghost of Port Chicago

On the Side of Angels (Wild Rose Press)

You can always catch up with Miriam or send your comments to:
miriamthewriter@gmail.com

See what's new in Miriam's life on her website at:

www.miriammatthews.com

You can also follow Miriam on FaceBook and keep up with her news, new books and trivia notes at:

www.facebook.com/miriam.matthews.773

Made in the USA
Middletown, DE
06 February 2021

32199680R00176